DWARF STORY

D1189843

DWARF STORY

W.W. MARPLOT

WAXING
GIBBOUS

Soon to be Published by
Waxing Gibbous Books
Manuscripts from the piles of
W.W. Marplot
Edited by Gertrude G.D. Marplot

Dwarf Story (published Summer, 2020)

Space Story (Summer, 2021)

Friends Story (editing)

The World, End of Story (aka TWEO) (compiling)

Time Story (curating)

Circles Story (collecting)

Original Research by
W.W. Marplot

*Fairy Migrations and Myths from Prehistoric Caves,
to Ancient Egypt, and After That*, compiled by W.W. Marplot

Stories from Out in the Universe, collected by W.W. Marplot

How The World Will End, According to Wise Old Tales,
curated by W.W. Marplot

Travels in Space And Time And Minds, edited by W.W. Marplot

The Legends of J

From the Library and Bookshelves of W.W. Marplot

Poetic Diction, Owen Barfield

The Yellow Dwarf, Madame d'Aulnoy

Histories or Tales from Past Times, with Morals, Charles Perrault

The Castle of Otranto, Horace Walpole

Orlando Furioso, Gustave Doré

Vathek, William Beckford

The Princess and The Goblin, George MacDonald

The King of the Golden River, John Ruskin

The Hobbit, J.R.R. Tolkien

Dwarf Story

Copyright © 2020 by W. W. Marplot

All rights reserved. This book or any portion thereof may not be reproduced
or used in any manner whatsoever without the express written permission
of the publisher, except for the use of brief quotations in a book review.

Printed in the United States of America

Cover Design and Interior Layout by Claire Flint Last

Waxing Gibbous Books
DWARFSTORY.COM

LCCN: 2020905762
ISBN: 978-1-7347583-0-6

For all the mythmakers great and small,
whom time has joined.

CHAPTER 1

Arty

I found a Dwarf, and there is something funny growing in my yard.

That's what I was thinking as the Dwarf—short, rectangular, and grunting—and I ran through the woods, early in the morning, trotting away from the bus stop, his breath like fog, his beard like a flapping flag, and his axe like a swarm of wasps—which was making me very nervous, even though he hadn't stung anyone with it.

Yet.

He made me miss the bus.

I kept running. He followed me, and I followed him.

I didn't have a beard to sway or an axe to swing, but in comparison, my overstuffed backpack bounced back and forth behind me and released loose school notes and to-do lists to the wind and to the ground.

A Dwarf and a funny thing in my yard, I thought, again.

I didn't want to worry about that funny thing yet, and since it wasn't following me and my new, strange, dangerous, and impossible friend, it was easy to forget.

But the Dwarf—a wide, muscular, fantasy-warrior Dwarf—was easy to remember and hard to ignore. When he followed me, I led him: from the corner bus stop and away into the wet morning trees. As we ran, I grasped for breaths and for reasons why: why I found a Dwarf this Wednesday, why he followed me, and why I followed him. And what: what should I do with him? And whether: was I still asleep? And another why: why were my dreams now about fantasy characters? I hate that stuff and am more of a scientist who likes math and logic and making lists of things to do before doing them—and keeping them on color-coded sticky notes like the ones flying from my bag and leaving a pretty trail behind us.

This was like those games other kids play, rolling dice shaped like extra-credit geometry, pretending to have swords and sorcery, imagining Elves and Orcs fighting, arguing over treasure and whether charisma is better than a catapult and how many dragons fit in a dungeon. There aren't even any rules to that nonsense.

But there I was, a human running wildly with a fantasy character whose axe had already killed a tree, scared my dogs, and made me make at least two bad decisions already. He kept yelling things in some strange language that sounded like how cement mixers might communicate. And I couldn't even stop to keep track of it, or take notes or pictures, or anything.

CHAPTER 2

Emma

his is Emma, friend of Arty, the kid who found the Dwarf, the kid who didn't start from the beginning.

A lot more happened, before and after his trot through the woods. I was there for most it, though that Wednesday morning I was on the school bus, the one Arty missed.

Arty is never absent, so that is a strange story even without the Dwarf, though not a good one without the Dwarf. And if Arty didn't let me into the story it would have turned into a science project; while he was measuring the Dwarf's foot or something, all the good stuff would have happened.

So yes: Arty is smart and organized—lists everywhere—but that is not a good way to tell a story, so I told him I would help. He needs it; he can barely get started.

And: Wouldn't a logical scientist start from the beginning anyway? Not in the middle of a run through the woods?

CHAPTER 3

Arty

guess I should tell you a little about me.

- My name is Arty.

- I was born on April 9th. So, my birthday was twenty-two days ago.

- I am now thirteen.

- The bus comes at 7:32 AM.

- I am 58.3 inches tall.

- I don't like surprises.

CHAPTER 4

Emma

All that is true, I guess.

I should have mentioned: being Arty's friend, sometimes I need to kick him to get him to do anything fun, like when he tries to read his lists of facts and figures when there is a KILLER WILD AMAZING STORY TO TELL, and while FANTASY CREATURES' worlds are crashing into our world, which is all more important than making your own yeast in Biology Club after school.

So, I knew it would not be easy for Arty, to deal with fast-moving, unplanned action, unscientific magic, and unreliable characters: friends, non-friends, enemies, powerful enemies, mysterious others, AND a Dwarf who won't tell you what he wants, AND other folktale creatures who either seemed as confused as we were, or seemed to be the complete opposite of us—powerful, purposeful, legendary.

So, I understand, and I kick.

CHAPTER 5

Arty

People told me to start at the beginning, which sounds logical, so I will.

It began when I woke up that unscientific Wednesday, early in the morning—a normal day until it wasn't.

Yawning and stretching, I tapped off the alarm bells coming from my phone, listened with eyes closed as it explained a chance of rain, then dragged myself to a pyramid of notebooks I'd built yesterday to block the awful glare of the morning sun. The window above my bookshelf faces directly east, and yesterday the sunbeams did a perfect Stonehenge right into my eyes. Today there was only a dull, grey glow. I rotated the perfectly aligned spiral wires of the notebooks to take a look.

It was foggy; it had rained all night. I half-remembered the slaps of rain on the roof, which is also the ceiling of my bedroom, the attic loft of our house. My parents and brothers and sisters and our nanny were still asleep on lower floors; as usual, I was up first.

The early bird gets the Dwarf.

Between streaks of rain on the window, I watched wet treetops droop and misty air swirl—then something moving, and moving strangely and moving fast, caught my eye. It crossed the side yard into shadows of the woods beyond. The large trees there had wide leaves that prolonged the morning dark, and the figure slipped from sight.

I yawned.

But I kept looking: What I had seen was too big to be a squirrel, or a raccoon, which are numerous among the old oak trees that canopy my entire neighborhood. It might have been one of the whole families of deer that sometimes jump our property fence. But if what I saw was a deer, it was a talented one. Walking on two legs and sideways, and carrying various items that dangled at its hip, and all that.

I watched and removed the last sleep from my eyes. Nothing else moved in the thick, wild woods between houses, or on the walking paths that lead through crisscrossing valleys to the cliffs overlooking the beach and bay. I dressed, jumped down two flights of stairs, then ran to the back door to investigate more. I turned the knob, then considered that a smarter move would be to let my dogs out, just in case it was not a crooked deer but a prowler, a burglar, or worse. I've never encountered any of those people, but I watch a lot of TV and Internet videos and therefore know that anything can happen—especially if it has never happened before. And when it does, it is worth a video post. I grabbed my cell phone.

I have three dogs—two small, one large, all useless. They trap and yelp at any curious or dangerous creature they find, so I sent them out first. Their stampede broke the quiet, dark fog of the morning, upsetting the silence. My own slow footsteps were spooky. The squeak of sneakers was dangerously out of place. Everything else was softly dropping dew or rain or lightly crackling with spring. The mist was thick and lay just above the grass like a lazy cloud.

The dogs had picked up a scent immediately. They thundered right to the spot where I had seen something move. All three galloped right past the funny thing growing in the yard without a pause or sniff. I don't want to talk about that yet.

Soon they were away into deep mist and barely visible. I followed. A bit. I waited. I followed. I listened for more movement, but all had now gone quiet. My heart beat into my skin. I waited.

A thrash of wild barking speared the silence. I moved in and looked ahead at both the phone camera screen and the actual background of fog and leaves. And then I heard: *"Ugla karn tach marcha indu!"* It was a grumbling, tumbling, rough voice. My ears bent, my breath stopped, and the view panned outward as my forward steps turned backward somehow on their own. Which was fine with me.

The dogs remained quiet—in surprise, I suppose. Then it repeated: that harsh sound and those words—if they *were* words—split the air again.

"Ugla karn tach marcha indu!"

Or whatever.

I was only watching through the phone screen now, which made it feel less real. Our old dog backed off and lay down, quiet, but the small dogs barked wildly, pointing their snouts into the woods. The yelling voice came again; maybe this time the words were different, but it was the same voice, deep and gravelly, as if it came out of the ground. The sound came on strong like an avalanche of large stones.

I called to my dogs, but they didn't come. I took two steps forward, then three steps backward again. I called, "Who's there?" but my voice quivered and died in the fog. I sounded like a wimpy little thing. I deepened my voice, steadied my legs, took another step, forward this time, re-pointed my camera phone, and yelled louder, "Who are you? What do you want?" I tried to rumble the earth like the voice I had heard but only managed to shake a few leaves.

The answer came: *"Vagga Indu! Bashka! Bashka…"* which sounded like a threat and definitely not like a *hello,* which I'd hoped for, or a name, my second choice. It quieted the little dogs—the elder, bigger one was still lying in the grass, almost, it seemed, at attention and awaiting orders—but not from me.

I took another step forward. The two little dogs were circling a tree thick enough to hide what they were sniffing after. I saw colors, too, red and green, low to the ground. Clothes maybe? Was someone lying there, their back to the tree?

I took another step, and six things happened quickly:

1. The little dogs barked.

2. The voice rumbled, this time saying, "*Altak!*"

3. My stomach flopped upside down and back.

4. I saw a bright flash from behind the tree. Something whipped and whooshed through the air, reflecting the red and green of the…what? Boots?

5. The tree creaked and cracked, and bark and wood flew out like chunky sparks. The tree began to tilt, from roots to topmost twigs, and then, after only a heartbeat thump or two, bent and split and fell back toward the woods. It crashed through other trees, thin ones with light spring leaves, and hit the ground with a loud boom.

6. My stomach flopped around again.

A few seconds passed as trees and hearts settled to quiet. All three dogs—the oldest had risen when the tree smashed—backed up toward me, scowling and scared, and I realized that I had moved almost all the way toward them as I viewed things through the camera screen. I could see something small and stout, a body shape, run up the log of the fallen tree. And it was swinging an axe.

I had found a Dwarf.

CHAPTER 6

Arty

And he was not happy. I think the death of the tree was a warning, meant to scare the dogs away. The Dwarf could have chopped my pets into two or three pieces each. Maybe he was as confused as we were.

Or maybe not. The dogs ran back and hid behind me, as the Dwarf tucked his axe into his belt with one hand in a single, smooth motion. He straightened his beard with the other hand, folded both his thick arms to his thick chest, stood with his feet apart and steady on the tree, and let out a snort. *Sort of bragging,* I thought.

As the morning mist burned away under rising sunlight, I could see him clearly. He was not pretty to look at. Picture a Dwarf in your head. Short and cute, right? NO—those are silly, plastic things for the garden. They make cookies and help Santa, yes? NO, those are TV elves.

In cartoons, Dwarves wear vests with large buttons, have adjectives for names, and help people lost in the woods. In real life, in the twenty-first century, in a backyard and around family dogs and houses, they look like rocks, have bad tempers, and don't care if they appear to you as axe-wielding maniacs. And they don't sing or whistle while they work; they grunt. And spit.

As I was observing the fellow, he looked at me and did spit in my direction, adjusting for the wind. The leftover dribble stuck in his beard. This and the thick, dark hair on his arms glistened like dewy grass, and the skin of his face and hands also shone, but with a dark, nasty sweat.

Yuck.

My fear shrunk, which let curiosity grow in its place. I was a very interested scientist only concerned with how much of him might fit under my new microscope. I continued to record him.

Another minute, or three, passed. The dogs stared and yawned; I stared and studied. The Dwarf did not move. He seemed as though he was perfectly happy standing on a log in my yard, that this was exactly where he meant to be, as if every Wednesday morning should be like this. As if it were perfectly natural to wear red and green boots and a funny hood, have a two-foot-long beard covering a three-foot-long body, and to keep it all perfectly still.

Eventually, my wonder grew tired, and my confusion woke up. I began to edge around him. The dogs followed me and sniffed the air. Things stayed still—the fresh clear air, the trees, the grass, the Dwarf's boots, his axe—as I paced a large semicircle around where his log lay, my phone focused. I stopped after a half-circle lap. My phone started buzzing with reminders and calendar events popping up, each with their own theme music. I had to get on with my day.

Some people may think that finding a Dwarf was at least an excuse to take a sick day, if not an all-out emergency. They might call the police and the fire department, maybe the army, maybe Disney or the comic bookstore president. Or put up signs to see if anyone had lost a bedtime story creature. I admit that maybe all this was beyond my morning brainpower, because I could think of nothing else to do but walk away and see what happened. The only useful experience I had was helping a few lost animals find their way home or getting a spider out of the tub. Dogs and cats have collars and ID tags. An armed Dwarf is different.

And anyway, somehow, I didn't think calling the fire department would accomplish anything. I pictured my Dwarf standing on top of a pile of firemen in yellow and black jackets, snorting a deep laugh from his chest and throat, their fire hose chopped into two-foot sections.

I made sure that the Dwarf saw my goodbye wave.

"*Ga!*" he yelled to me.

I walked a few steps, then ran a few more, to the house. I tripped on something bulging from the grass that was not a root and was not there yesterday, a funny thing, but I don't want to talk about that yet. Then, once re-balanced, I made it to my back door.

He did not move.

CHAPTER 7

Arty

A healthy serving of confusion helped me ignore the fact that I had just seen a Dwarf. I gathered my things for school—backpack, lists, tablets, electronic accessories. The angle of light from the window, the sun beginning to pierce the mist, told me to rush back downstairs. I was late; my bus comes first before my brothers' and sisters'. They were just waking up.

I ran upstairs for final bathroom duties, making two yellow and one blue notes in my head—things necessary to get me back on track today. My new plan was to make a new plan after school. I slung on my backpack, and I went to the same bedroom window where I first saw the impossible. The glow had turned from misty grey to sun-yellow, and there was no sign of any Dwarves.

I chugged down the stairs, past the smell of toast and maple syrup, yelled a general goodbye to the waking house, grabbed a light coat, and rushed out the front door...

...crashing onto my face on the cement of the front stoop.

"Tana doe! Faza..."

I had tripped over my Dwarf. He was not happy, but I lived to tell this tale.

Worried about the noise, and thinking without thinking that this was a matter that I should keep secret, I sprung back to my feet and motioned for him to follow as I ran toward the stretch of woods that connects my backyard to the deep forest trails.

He followed! The Dwarf bounded alongside me, grunting as if he was impatient with how slow I moved. He was light on his feet, surprising since he looked like he weighed 580 pounds. Picture a small boulder but on springs.

When I stopped and looked around to see if anyone had noticed our sprint, he stood with his feet apart like before, arms folded, and would not talk to me. I tried talking in my language, then in a sort of sign-language that I made up on the spot, pointing to him and me and the trees. He hardly moved. Let's face it: he didn't move at all—not a hair, not a muscle. His eyes did not blink in the sun, and his beard did not move in the wind.

I tried speaking the words I remembered of his language, saying, "*Ga*" and then "*Faza*," to which he crinkled his eyebrows at me, big furry eyebrows that came together in a down arrow, and he let out a small moan. I pictured his body made of stone, partly because that's what some of the legends say about Dwarves, and partly because that's exactly how it appeared. He was so still and hard. His murmurs echoed in internal caves deep within his body. He gave me a *sternmore* look.

I made up that word: sternmore. Because this guy was always stern, and his gaze was just more so. It was becoming clear that my language was not good enough to communicate with this rocklike fellow. Maybe I wasn't good enough either; even his beard looked stronger than me.

He wore a long hood that arched over the top of his wide head and curved back and down to end in a pointy cone that hung stiff and dirty. All his clothes were in different stages of unclean, spotted, and worn, a sad, dull brown and grey patchwork in the shade of the trees. Everything he wore looked like it had been through a war that only ended last night, but the fabric winked here and there in gleams of gold and of silver. His getup must have been beautiful when it was new and polished—the emblems and stitched lines formed wondrous patterns. Maybe these were symbols of a Dwarf language; maybe they told an important story about this Dwarf, if someone were brave or stupid enough to get close enough to read it.

His axe hung low and heavy in his hand, just as his black beard did from an unseen chin. His face—dark red cheeks, long and forceful nose, eyes like smoldering fire, and a dark brow as furrowed and lined as a farmer's field—was framed by the hood. His boots were green and red and stretched up his tree-trunk legs to the knees. Below it all were sledgehammer feet that, like everything else, were short in size but wide with strength.

Geez.

I tried to think of other things I had read about Dwarves from old legends and kids' stories and movies. They lived in the mountains. They liked to work with hammers and make things out of iron and gold. They were good with axes.

We didn't have much in common. I lived near the beach, I wasn't good with a hammer, I couldn't make things that weren't electronic, and I knew which side of an axe to grip, but not much more. And I was mostly thin and hairless.

Imaginary characters are fun to read about and to see on a big screen in the movies. What is much better is when there is one a few feet away, who is not imaginary and, if you want, you can smell him. Or, better, you can look into his eyes.

They were dark like a winter pond and ran just as deep; their gaze seemed able to look through the trees that surrounded us, through any fog on any Wednesday, past thunder-clapping clouds and straight to the sun. Yet his eyes also looked inward, deep inside his thick, motionless body, to remember and consider things that were far away. In his mind, was he wandering around the stone caves of his home? Was he wondering, like I was, how he got *here*?

I sat on a wet tree stump, worrying that my day was running further ahead and leaving me further behind.

Time was running out if I was going to catch the school bus. My butt got wet, and my brain got dry thinking of my next move. I needed more information, or I needed help, or both. I wanted to take scientific notes of the facts and my observations. I could not talk to him, and I didn't even know which of his grunts might be his name. I certainly didn't want to call him "dude" or anything.

Eventually we called him Thryst the Magnificent. I would learn the "Thryst" part soon, but the "the" part I changed a lot. At first I thought he was Magnificent. Actually, at first I thought he was Thryst The Dream, then The Dangerous, then The Badly Distracting, then The Confusing, then just Very Cool—all before Wednesday lunchtime. Eventually he became The Magnificent.

How could I figure out what he wanted? It must have something to do with me. He came to *my* house and was now following *me*— and making *me* feel very nervous. I looked at him, but he didn't look back. Instead, he stared into the woods and all around us, his eyes burning intensely as if he had lasers attached to them. Now and then he would look at the sky, but he made no more sounds.

In a few more minutes, the entire neighborhood would be awake. This is not Middle-Earth or Never Wonderland or whatever—people here drive cars to work or ride school buses and sit at desks and use computers and come home to their families and eat dinner and take turns going around the table telling how their days were. And very, *very* rarely is there a Dwarf involved in any of this.

Did the Dwarf know about this stuff? About the real world—my world? How do Dwarves make money? Do they make toys or just cut things in half all day and eat rocks and dirt? He looked more like the rugged type—maybe even a warrior. Give his people laptops and cell phones, and they would probably throw them at each other. Their backpacks would be filled with gold and silver, not sticky notes and books.

Whatever he did all day, it was definitely something grittier and *earthmore* than what people around here do. Yes, earthmore—another word I had to invent right there on the spot as I tried to understand why a Dwarf had appeared in my yard. I had questions that needed answering. The scientific world would need to know.

The bus must be close, I thought.

I tapped my foot.

I am not good at this.

Then it came—the moment when I had to decide what to do. I heard the bus engine grinding along a few streets away, coming closer and toward the last bend of the road to my house. I looked hopefully at Thryst for a clue about what to do. I started to say, "Yeah…"

But before the whole "Y" sound came out, and as the bus creaked, stopped, and rocked, and its doors split open, Thryst pulled out his axe. It rang a hollow sound like a faraway church bell and shone in a spear of sunshine that appeared from above. He looked ready to use it. I jumped up and screamed, "No!" raising my arms in front of him, and I moved closer until my hands were over him, his axe pointed at my stomach. The Dwarf's eyes smoked with barely controlled fire, but as I moved around him and streaked into the woods, he followed and lowered his axe.

Obviously—as we both seemed to agree—he wasn't ready to enter modern American society yet. We were soon deep in the woods and even deeper in thought. My butt was wet. There was something funny growing in the yard. I had missed my bus and found a Dwarf—neither thing had ever happened before. My day was completely off schedule and off list.

CHAPTER 8

Emma

OK, wait. This is Emma again, and here is when I got involved; so, first, a short introduction to me.

I am a human, a girl, Arty's friend—and not his girl-friend, so don't even try that. We are thirteen years old, though Arty acts older and like a boring, dusty old science professor. He's not the ready-for-action type, unless it says "Action, Wednesday, 8 am," on a sticky note of the right color.

Back to that action: I was sitting on the bus, the one that takes us to seventh grade at Fontaine Middle School where Arty is a science geek. Whether that type of kid is with friends or alone depends on the latest viral app game everyone is playing. I am not one of those. I'm a writer, and a good one: two of my poems won school awards and were read to the whole grade. This counts as a public performance. I am also beginning to draw—sunsets over the beaches, the deer running through the woods. Nothing worth hanging yet.

Arty and I are friends because we pretty much grew up together—his yard and my yard are connected by paths in the woods that go between the houses of Belle Terre, which means "Beautiful Land" in French. The part of town that lies out into the water and ends with the cliffs that surround the bay is our neighborhood. It seems like the two of us have wandered around here together since we were babies, in the forest and to the edges that overlook the valley of the beach and docks and million boats of Belle Terre Harbor. There's a lot of history here, a lot of oldness, so there's a lot for both a scientist and an artist to see. But since my mom got her job, Arty and I only hang out now and then. Mostly then.

I live alone—well, with my mother, but it's just the two of us—and this morning, like every morning, she was already at work when my phone alarm played violin music to wake me. So, I was pretty tired and not trusting my eyes when I saw Arty and the Dwarf that he found that he calls *Thryst the SomethingThatChangesEveryHour* running away from his bus stop.

The bus was only one third full before it stopped at Arty's. The middle schoolers on board were as loud as usual, all yelling immaturely about something immature, the cracking voices cancelling each other out. No one else was looking out the sun-drenched, morning-wet windows. I had my forehead against the glass to warm my eyelids, but when the bus stopped at Arty's driveway, my eyes opened in sync with the bus doors. I saw a strange, short shape darting back, forth, and along one of the trails that Arty and I know like the backs of our hands. I saw Arty vanish through the trees. The bus driver gave up on him and drove off.

Half asleep, I didn't know what I was looking at, of course, and I sure wasn't thinking, *Dwarf chasing Arty*. If you asked me to list all the things on Earth or in movies or in dusty old books that might have been running along with Arty through the woods in the early morning, that list would have *ended* with:

- A dinosaur with atomic bomb earrings
- The President and a giant mouse tied together with a cell phone charger
- A small robot named FricklePickle
- A Dwarf
- A girl

I assumed it was a dog. Maybe his oldest dog, the big one, had new hips installed, or maybe Arty's brothers finally talked their parents into getting a fourth dog. Nothing makes that kid miss school, or even be late, so if he was running through the woods with a huge dog in a red and green sweater hopping behind him, you can bet that either it was on a list somewhere and part of a careful plan—or his day had gone disastrously wrong.

I had a feeling I should make sure to find him right after school.

CHAPTER 9

Arty

There we were, my Dwarf and I, running through the woods on a Wednesday, looking for somewhere the two of us could hide and one of us could think. I'd dropped my backpack and was worried about missing school, thinking about everything I'd have to do tonight and tomorrow to make it up. Thursday would spill into Friday, and Saturday's plans were unchangeable, so that would mess up the whole week. I could, ok, *maybe,* use Sunday from 1:30 to 4:30 to do some of the Thursday and Friday work that I couldn't do Saturday. Among all this mental clutter, the piles of colored to-do lists in my mind, this Dwarf had landed, crushing my calendar under his feet and using my sticky pads for axe practice.

He followed behind as I cut among the forest paths that my feet know by heart and my heart knows by feet. We ducked under low branches and sprays of sunshine through the thick woods that border neighboring houses until reaching a crossroads, where I knew another decision awaited: whether to continue down to the valley woods and from there to the beach, or turn off the path and go back to the houses and streets, or stop and re-plan my next steps.

I kept running. It was better than thinking.

I heard the Dwarf behind me sometimes as I led. If our path was blocked, even slightly, with fallen branches or with new, green, thorny vines that were livening up for spring, there would then be a small grunt, the ringing of what I assumed was his axe rising, or some other blade or knife or who knows what, and the Dwarf would leap ahead of me, almost magically, and cause something to bite the dust. With serious skill.

But mostly his footsteps and breathing were even and quiet—for a guy as gentle-looking as a fire hydrant, he was light on his stony *blockfeet*. Which I added to my Dwarf dictionary. Dwarves' own language must have lots of ways to describe rocks, square hard things, small squat things, dirt colors, etc.

We eventually made it down, along, and through the valley, past the thicker trees and prickly bushes—leaving impressive damage in our wake—and crossed the valley that cut diagonally toward the shore. The valley's paths lead down to the shoreline, but first they wind up and along grassy ridges and back and forth among rocky bluffs: steep, windy cliffs that are 300 feet above the water of the bay to the west and of the larger, louder water and broader beaches of Long Island Sound to the north.

This is where Emma and I live: Belle Terre, on the North Shore of Long Island, New York, United States, North America, Western Hemisphere, Earth, Awake. A real place, not a dreamland. A Land of Humans. You could see a lot of our town from where my real imaginary Dwarf and I were headed—a secluded and secret spot up high on a cliff where I wanted to stop and rest and, at last, think about things. My life. My Dwarf.

Soon we were at the edge of a steep cliff that suddenly exposed its long drop from between the low tree branches. Just off this intersection was the spot where I wanted to continue my Dwarf language lessons.

The Dwarf disagreed. He planted himself just like he did back in my yard, and he twisted his head around wildly again, laser-pointing his eyes about, putting his nose to the air. I think he could smell the water below us and felt the open air straight ahead where there was nothing but a beautiful view of the lightening blue sky. He went perfectly quiet; his eyelids closed and smothered the fire behind them.

Trying to convince him to continue ahead only made him grunt—for some reason, he did not want to go down to the beach. He stamped a heavy foot down, then opened his eyes, and they burned through me. I thought about all my options and decided to sit.

It was time to talk again.

I raised my arms, hands high, palms toward him to say, "Ok. Fine," then twisted and waved my arms toward the water to say, "No beach, we stay away." He grunted his stony satisfaction and sat, cross-legged just as I was. Progress! We were communicating. A little at a time. His bulging body, a knotted pretzel of muscle, contorted into an even more compact space than usual and looked more like a small boulder than ever.

I spent a few minutes in study—courteously and respectfully, without staring and ogling. I really wanted to take more video or at least write down notes, but I didn't dare. He looked like he'd come a long way—he was dusty and dirty, and his medieval Dwarf clothes were definitely ready for the Dwarf hamper. *He's travelled a long way,* I thought. *From where?*

He seemed ready for battle. Every part of him looked like a weapon, especially the weapons. I always thought how fake it was in fantasy video games and movies that the hero always pulled out whatever he needed at any time: a sword, a battle axe, a bow and arrow, a slingshot, a knife of the perfect size, a shield—just in time. But you never see them carrying all this stuff—plus maps, crystal balls, magic food, and all the rest of the things that adventures call for. I got caught once sneaking homemade cookies into the movies. But this Dwarf had an array of armaments packed very neatly. I saw short swords like knives at each side and a belt with a hammer and various smaller metal items sticking in and out and all around. His short cloak looked to have some deep pockets that swelled in spots, and yet it wrapped around him smoothly.

I figured that I should first ask where he was from. I also wanted to know why he was here, why he was following me, why a Dwarf would be in my backyard, why he was so angry with everyone but me, why he was alone, why everything-else-about-this-day that was getting way, way, way off schedule. "Why" questions would be really hard to ask with my arms, or by drawing in the dirt with a stick, which is what I had to do to ask "where," which I tried next.

I pointed to him, and then back to me, and waved my arms at everything around, then drew a spot in the dirt. I then scraped a line that showed the path back to my house and driveway and street. He nodded—without grunting or slicing anything.

So far, so good. Nodding was something we had in common.

Then I drew a square for my house and pointed at my chest again. I noticed that I was speaking out loud the whole time—English, of course, mostly to myself, and emphasizing the words "Me/Arty" and "house" and "path" and "you." Maybe he could learn English better than I could learn Dwarfspeak. Maybe he could add in all the necessary words I needed to express *Dwarfthings*.

Maybe. But for now, the important question still had to be drawn in the dirt and spoken with hand and arm and facial maneuvers: *Where are you from?* I drew a circle where I first saw him, then pointed to him again. I added three dots around the circle, then put my hands on the ground and said, "Ruff ruff. Ruff ruff ruff. Arooooo," with my neck arched up, my throat barking to the sky. He nodded.

He then took the stick from me and changed the circle to a triangle. He pointed to himself and handed the stick back. *Yes,* I thought, *a triangle seems to suit him, with his pointy hood-hat and all,* and so it was my turn to nod. Then the Dwarf sat up straight, stared two smoky eyes at me, and cleared his throat roughly.

No—he didn't—wait—he was saying something: "*Thryst.*" That sound was a word, a name, it was definite from the look in his eye; somehow his look made me understand. "Thryst" was what he called himself. It rhymed with *list, fist, wrist*—but to pronounce it correctly, have a friend strangle you as you say it. That's a Dwarf name for you....

Magnificent, I thought.

Now I was ready to ask the big question. I pointed to him, waved my stick around my little dirt map, pointed to my house symbol, pointed to him again, then at the Thryst triangle, made the usual questioning motion with my arms, and put the usual confusion on my face. "From Where? Where Do You Live?" I asked with my best charades moves.

Thryst just looked at the map and grunted. I waved all around, pointing at him, made an imaginary drawing of a house in the air, pointed to him, mimed *Where?* again with my face and arms.

He looked at me, pointed at the map, touched the triangle, and left his finger there. I wasn't sure if he misunderstood my question… or maybe—wow, maybe he didn't *know* the answer. That thought hit me hard and made my temples squish with pain—the possibility that maybe he did not know. And maybe I didn't know enough about Dwarves. Most of what I knew came from video games. And I knew from a friend who tried to drive a car once without permission that video games are not real.

To communicate with Thryst better, I wanted to do some research on the Internet on Dwarves and also on any mental sicknesses that cause people to imagine they're seeing Dwarves, just to be scientific about it and cover all the possibilities. I thought I should show him some real maps, some aerial photos of the community. And, yes—speaking of reality—was I supposed to feed him or something? I was getting hungry. I'd skipped breakfast, and my morning work, and my whole routine.

The aerial photo thought gave me an idea: If he would walk to the edge of the bluff with me, he could see a very nice view around and below of everything to the west, north, and south, almost as if from a plane. He could point, maybe, or give me some clue.

I flappy-waved my arms to tell Thryst to follow me. I took a few steps. He stood up. I took a few more steps along the path that led to the open air of the seaside bluff. He planted his feet apart in his usual *Thryst the Monument* fashion and rooted his boots there. I ran the last few steps to the edge of the wood, sideways to keep an eye on him, and made it to the edge. I pretended to look all around, animatedly putting my hand to my forehead, shielding my eyes from the sun, although it was hidden in clouds, all to act out what I wanted *him* to do: have a look around and tell me where he came from, how he got to my yard, where he got his boots, where he lived before he had a beard…or even where he wanted to go. Anything.

I gave up: he didn't move. He didn't move *until* I gave up, I should say, because as soon as I started to walk back, kind of dejected I have to admit, he turned, pulled out his axe, and used it to clamber up a nearby tree—a big one, a fifty-foot oak. What moves! The strength it showed was impressive and super fearless—but he did lose some style points when his pointy hat came off and floated down to me. A tough, leathery hood, grey-colored and sturdy but light. I held it for him.

At the top he looked around toward all the blue horizon. Obviously, he wasn't afraid of heights. He looked down, appearing small and odd so far above. I waved to him with his hat. I felt the tree and ground vibrate as he exclaimed something loudly in his language. It sounded as if he didn't like what he saw. He came down in an acrobatic way, clutching branches with his hands, not using the axe, and landed with a pounding thud. I handed him his hat, and he bowed.

I felt a little strange, but I bowed back. He pointed up at the tree, looked at me—directly into my eyes so I would understand—and he shook his head. This we had in common also: head-shaking means *no*.

So that was the answer: *No, Thryst did not know where he was.*

He took a quick two-handed axe-swing at the tree he'd climbed. Its curvy blade rang like a bell in a tower; this was starting to be a familiar sound. The axe stroke had left a notch in the trunk of the oak so big I could have stuck my arm in it, if I were stupid. One more swipe, and it might come down. I'd hate to be this guy's enemy: that swing would've killed a small crowd and all their pets.

I let a minute pass and thought, but I knew that I had to head home and start learning what I could. I accepted that I was in an adventure fit for a thirteen-year-old, but I needed to proceed as scientifically as possible—I needed a plan, steps, and lists. As we walked, I started the first list in my head—things that I had learned already, from personal experience:

Dwarves:

1. Stubborn.

2. Hate trees. And the beach.

3. Dangerous.

4. Strong.

5. Surprisingly nimble (can 5.A run fast and 5.B climb fast).

6. Polite if you return their hat.

7. Not big talkers.

8. Adventure follows them.

9. They are ready.

CHAPTER 10

Emma

I can't be sure about everything Arty just told you. I wasn't there. Our stories will join soon, and it'll be fun to see Professor Arty try to use black-and-white, Courier-font science facts to make sense of a fantasy realm character landscaping his backyard. He'll have to admit that he's just a kid and was awfully afraid during that whole Dwarf-in-the-woods episode, even though fear is not part of the "scientific method" that he brags about all the time. I'm much more normal than he is and much more unique at the same time. And more popular. So, my version will be different, more colorful, more alive, and more imaginative—which is the way fantastic things deserve to be treated. They need to be drawn, believed, written about in long poems.

Especially with what happened next…

CHAPTER 11

Arty

Thryst and I began walking back to my house. He stopped trying to gash things and followed, which I figured meant he expected me to do something, to help him somehow. Of course, I had no idea what he wanted, and I had no idea what any thirteen-year-old American suburbs-kid could ever have that a warrior fantasy Dwarf would need. I was missing something…

And so was Thryst, or that's what it seemed like. As we walked, he seeked—sought?—and I watched. The source of every noise had to be found out, and all hidden spaces—between bushes, in small hollows in trees or in the ground, under stones—had to be searched. Yet he always returned to follow me. I made a mental note to check the video on my phone—the one starring three dogs and a Dwarf—for clues. Then I made a mental note to make fewer mental notes and make more paper ones instead.

I stopped to do just that as we reached a small, bright clearing. I took out my notepad, removed and rested my pack against a tree, patted it and my pants and raincoat pockets for my phone, and felt my stomach rise each time it did not appear. "Don't tell me I lost my phone!" I said to the sun, and it obeyed; it said nothing, hid its face in a cloud, and avoided the lie. Like most people my age, if I had to choose between (A) losing my phone and (B)…I would choose (B).

Thryst the Dwarf came close, where I was scratching pen to pad furiously. He looked down at my backpack. He looked at me as I looked back at him. He looked at my pad. He looked at me.

He looked INTO me. And then I saw. When his fireball eyes met mine, they beamed directly inward, our sights connected, and *I saw*.

There: scenes, stories, pictures, movies, feelings. Action, lots of it. 3D. I couldn't tell what was in his eyes versus what was in my own head, or if maybe all these scenes were my deepest and most wishful thinking and he'd made them come to life. In my head it went like this:

I was with him in another place, we were walking, I was tired, but he kept moving, and I knew I had to keep up. I could see what he saw: a road ahead, heading between a pass of very large spires of pine trees, beyond which the land spread open. The way widened to a landscape of larger and larger hills, dark and moody, like a stormy sea of dark swells. Still farther on—wow—there were white peaked and miraculous mountains that stood ever higher and higher, and the path wound forward and right up to the black slopes of their feet. I felt I could see the whole road ahead, through every hill and turn and up into the stone of the mountains, even though it was all still miles away, as if there were a map in my head. I somehow knew all the land, every destination and route. Large things were small, distant things were close, near and far met in my head.

And small things were large…and blazing: every leaf, every lump of grass, every sound from the blowing wind was as clear as if the world were cased in crystal and sat in my hand. Every movement sent its vibrations directly to my ears and eyes. Even the earth, even the stones— large and small, round or flat, rocks and boulders—everything had marks that told a story and moaned deeply, humming songs of the past.

I was nowhere near my home. This was a strange, other world. Thryst's home. I saw it, and I knew it.

I began to understand and control the visions, but I got tired and closed my eyes, which returned me to my world. My balance lost, I swayed against a tree, and Thryst caught me and held me straight.

"Abra sa zaxa," Thryst said quietly. His eyes stared up at mine, red like twin sunsets…

Ok, I thought, *let's go…*

And we returned to his world.

We walked up and down hills, nearing the mountains, where the stones came even more alive—almost singing, and rocking and rolling. Many of them stood at the openings of tunnels, which led down into caves, the caves into caverns, the caverns to underground canyons and cities. Here the earth itself was under the command of their lords and leaders, the Dwarves.

A small Dwarf—smaller than Thryst, definitely younger, his beard short and thin, his hood clean—came to him, whispered up to him, then quickly left. Before Thryst could follow, the holes opened, and Dwarves came from underground carrying weapons and calling to each other. They followed Thryst, forcing him to lead.

More Dwarves came to join us. They were alike; they had the same focused purpose. They walked behind, and our army formed. Yes—this was an army. We were not lost, we knew what to do, there was an adventure ahead, and a battle—every step moved us toward a clear and definite point.

Looming larger, in the mountain passes, dark clouds formed in bubbling rings that hid everything except the snowy peaks that stood out, above all, white and sharp. This vision had meaning, was trying to tell me something—a black tale, bad and evil—but, here, my senses softened, and my foresight blurred. I could only feel an uncertain dread, as if life was asking questions I could not answer. Though there was something I now knew beyond any doubt: Thryst was on the side of good, and up ahead were the enemies of his world.

My eyes closed again. Back in the Belle Terre woods. Thryst held me up despite my wobbling knees, shaking me and grunting. I had not seen everything he needed me to see. He wanted me to go back with him. I nodded. This time his glance was misty, glazed over, the fires doused.

This time:

I sensed a black, empty hole, somewhere in the tallest mountain, now rising directly ahead, swallowing the end of our road, which had come past seven lines of growing hills, each darker and darker with twisting, depressing trees. And now smoke. Farther ahead was the peak, below it a wide plain where there were brief flashes of flame like sunbursts, far in the distance, shooting though a creeping, black smoke. A battle plain.

Past the hills, at the mountain pass, the last of the Dwarves joined us, and I knew from the map in my thoughts that we were now to head underground. I felt the excitement and fear of the army, their pride and determination, and their magic and history. The Dwarves all around spoke in their language, harsh and growling. Their leaders waved maps and began to agree on a plan—the pages glowed and shone as the great Dwarf leaders spoke and chanted, fire leapt from the pages, it seemed, and from their long beards. Soon a few of their generals—with grim, old faces that looked battle-hardened and battle-hungry—gathered around Thryst and me. It seemed that the time and place were ready.

They were. But Thryst was not. The march started again, but he stayed. Shouts came from the leaders, pointing at their fiery maps, showing the urgency. But then the small Dwarf with the thin, black beard returned and held his own map, as I saw when he unrolled it for Thryst.

Thryst gripped his axe and swung wildly at nothing, and he suddenly left the ranks of the army, running wildly and screaming to the sky. He stopped and pulled at his beard, then howled his own name, with other fire-forged words of his language. As if he were answering some other voice that I couldn't hear, he continued to shout, his voice clanging like iron against some foe that fought with words fiercer than any weapon. The other Dwarves stood amazed and called to Thryst, but he suddenly ran back to the hills as if he had been called, pulled by a force he could not resist. With a raise of his closed fist, and one final word—a shout from his gut that rattled the dirt beneath me—a stone slab arose from the grass near his feet, the ground split open, and he disappeared down into the earth.

I felt torn in two.

The clouds burst, a shock shook the world: there was a flash of light, there was a crash of sounds, I could feel some spell over me that made me afraid and sick, a nightmare was closing in. I tried to wake up, to leave this dream-vision. I wriggled physically within my own brain and skin. I felt cold cave walls near me, and I fell to the ground.

And things got fuzzy.

Panting, I opened my eyes—not knowing what world would be in front of me. Thryst's eyes, their glassy discs now cloudy, told me I was back home. He then turned away. He had said enough for now: who he was, where he was from, and that I had a lot to learn.

CHAPTER 12

Emma

finally come back into the story after school and near to dinnertime. I found Arty where I expected I would find him: at the local library. My friend spends so much time at the library that they let him use a private conference room, which makes him feel like he's cool. What I didn't expect is that he'd be with a Dwarf—*Thryst the Impatient*. Which I could understand: a sleepy village public library is no place for a battle-ready Dwarf.

Arty was surrounded by books and some scraps of paper when I snuck up on him. "What are you up to?" I accused him suddenly. I startled him. Ha.

"Oh, man, Emma, don't scare me like that…"

"Why weren't you on the bus? Or in school, or after?"

"I'm…sick," he said, looking all around. "Don't move!" he instructed and paced around the room, looking in corners and under desks in a nervous, panicky way. He hustled back to me quickly, said, "Don't move" again, and left the room. He rushed back in, said, "Keep don't moving," and left again. As a friend, and as an "A" student in English, I can tell you his grammar was usually a little better than this. He soon poked his head back in and said, breathless but thoughtfully, "Don't move, please. Don't move unless a fireman tells you to." He left. He came back. He came near, put one arm around me, and said, "Pal! Friend!" Loudly, as if we were on a stage.

I took in the weirdness but challenged him on his lame excuse: "Sick, huh? Arty—get off me—you don't get sick unless it's scheduled in advance, and you don't miss school or anything without a backup plan and without telling me." I removed his arm from my shoulder, but he hurriedly put it back.

"'Cause we're friends! That's right!" he practically yelled. "I have some stuff to do here," he continued in a normal tone. "Can I just explain later?" He turned me around toward the door and tried to walk me out.

Ok, I thought, and I let him.

"Sure—fine—that's what tomorrows are for, I guess…" I played along. I left the room, counted to eight and a half, and burst back in.

"Who's *that*?!" I said, knowing I was using both a question mark and an exclamation point. I pointed to the corner, where I'd noticed—even before Arty's panicky search—a pair of dirty, dark red and green boots, though the body they belonged to was blocked by a small bookshelf that was on wheels and definitely out of place. Someone was hiding. Someone with no sense of fashion. And the same someone I saw running through the woods with Arty that morning.

Arty looked confused, also staring at the boots. He spoke, but more to himself, and began writing on a pad, saying, "Why doesn't he disappear? Why doesn't he try to kill her, or at least pull out his axe? That's strange…"

What was he talking about? He was serious, apparently.

"Ok, fine." He stopped writing. "Emma, meet Thryst. *Thryst the…*" Arty rolled the small bookcase away.

"…Dwarf," I finished. Because there he was, a Dwarf, as anyone could see. Though only Arty and I had, so far.

"Yes, *Thryst the Dwarf,* very good. But I'm confused…" Arty said.

Thryst bowed to me but then stood still as stone. I copied him.

"Really confused," Arty went on. "Everything else that moves he either threatens to slice in half, or slices in half." Arty bent over to make another note, this time using his laptop, which was on the desk among two piles of books and a yellow pad. And sticky notes everywhere, but that goes without writing.

"*You're* confused?" I asked, shocked and still pointing my finger at the boulder of a man—at his hood, actually, since he wasn't very tall—although challenging him to basketball was out of the question. The artist in me was excited at this unique meeting. The teen in me knew from overheard nerd-talk about video games and sci-fi movies that this character was a classic, fantasy Dwarf—or at least he was dressed like one. The skeptic in me was starting to assume it was a joke—but Arty did not set up complicated, punky pranks like this, and my coming here was definitely not expected. Maybe someone was playing a joke on *him*?

"Arty, what…?" I tried to ask something, anything, and left it at that.

"I don't know." Arty summarized, pushing my finger down, since Thryst was starting to bristle his eyebrows at it, "Thryst and I have sort of a communication problem, in this world at least. I know his name is Thryst, and even that took a while."

"But you said he threatens everyone…"

"With his actions. See that axe?"

I did see that axe.

"He knows how to use it. In lots of ways."

"You think he's, um, real?" I had to ask.

"You think we are both imagining him? There are a few trees in the Belle Terre woods who wish we were."

"No, I meant…" I wanted to explain that maybe Arty was the victim of a very impractical joke. But, now that I thought about it, the idea that someone hired a small actor to pretend to be a Dwarf from a role-playing game to fool Arty, who didn't even play those games, seemed exactly equally silly as the theory that there was a real Dwarf named Thryst who had come to cut down some trees and follow Arty to the library.

Arty was acting very jittery, and he had a scratch on his arm, I noticed, and a Band-Aid around a finger. It wasn't like Arty to be banged up, he wasn't the physical type. Arty wanted to help me put aside my doubt, my confusion, and my instincts, and so he calmed himself enough to tell me all the events of his Wednesday (so far).

I listened.

Arty began. Then he finished. Then he said, "Look into his eyes," and pointed toward *Thryst the Silent.*

I did—and Thryst looked into mine. I felt as if I were suddenly deep underground, miles under, in a cave lit with candles, and there was the sound of dripping water. I thought I could smell dirt, a strong scent of earth, and I wanted to grab Arty's yellow pad and draw what I felt, to help me capture it and remember it. I couldn't. The Dwarf's fantastic eyes and magical gaze seemed beyond description, for the moment.

There was more: The caves and candles turned into something more familiar, a scene at my own house, maybe. It felt like a memory, but was confused and fuzzy, as if my memory was being shared with this Dwarf. It seemed he was there, and he wanted me to know he was remembering something, too. Something personal.

Arty stood between us and interrupted. "I call it *deepdownded*, that feeling you're feeling right now. I've had to make up some new words." That answered my half-smile, half-squint. "What did you see?" he asked.

"Caves and lights and water, but then it turned into my house, I think, like dreams do—but he was there," I pointed at Thryst, "and something happened to my...to both of our..." I stopped before sharing a personal feeling that I was already starting to doubt.

Arty quickly typed a note into his laptop but did not look away from me, though I looked away from him.

The library conference room had a row of half-open windows that let in some late afternoon light as various springtime smells rode in on the breeze. Three sudden and short beeps of a car horn brought me out of my brief trance and deep thoughts.

This Dwarf is no actor, I thought. Definitely not.

Arty spoke again. "And there's something funny growing in my yard. Remind me to tell you about that—later, not now."

But I forgot.

CHAPTER 13

Emma

I recovered from the surprise of seeing Arty with an unscheduled Dwarf and started to pepper him with some obvious questions. "Where did he come from?" "Why is he here?" "Why is he following you?" "What kind of Dwarf is he?" "What kind of Dwarfs are there?" "Is it 'Dwarfs' or 'Dwarves'?"

"I don't know." "I don't know." "I don't know." "I don't know." "I don't know." And "It's *Dwarrows,* actually," were his *mostly* obvious answers. He explained further. "I've tried to talk to him, to use his language, to ask him all that, but I don't think he knows where he came from. He might be lost. I came here to hide and find out more."

"Not hide from me, right?" I folded my arms like a mom. "You were going to tell me, right?"

"Of course. I found him in my yard, and it is your neighborhood, too. But anyway, I've started reading about them. It's thrown off my whole day, but…"

"Oh, give me a break, Arty, this is HUGE. Well, you know, *short* and huge. But you can go off your schedule for one day."

Arty laughed, and I was glad he did. "I did get him to tell me his name. '*Thryst.*' I call him *Thryst the Magnificent,* which seems to fit, but so does *Thryst the Stern, Thryst the Dangerous, Thryst the Athlete.*"

My turn to laugh.

"Seriously," he said. "That's why I was surprised when you burst in—not for me, but surprised that he didn't split you down the middle. So, I wanted to make sure he knew we were friends."

"Thanks!" I said.

"Watch this," Arty replied. He moved back to my side, put his arm on my shoulder, looked at *Thryst the Very Still, Still,* and said, "Thryst, this is EMMA. Em-ma." To this, Thryst bowed low, same as before. When he came back up, I bowed, and on my way up, I felt something, a humming vibration, in the room. It wasn't a phone, or a truck motoring by, and it wasn't an earthquake. It came from Thryst. He was gargling with battery acid. No, he wasn't: He was saying something.

"Thryst."

Quite a rumble it made. The word started in his hairy barrel of a throat and came out to push against the room and everything in it. Hard to believe this counted as only one syllable.

There was a gleam in the Dwarf's eye, which made Arty say, "Wow. I've never seen that expression before. A boulder in a good mood? He must like you."

I returned to my questions: "How did you get him here? How do you sneak a Dwarf into a public library? And does he just follow you everywhere?"

"So far, yes. But I don't have to hide him, he hides himself, or he completely disappears, I have no idea. So far you're the only person he's let see him besides me."

"I wonder *why us.*"

"I don't know. There's a long list of things I don't know. But I've read about Dwarves most of the day."

"Find anything useful? Beyond the stuff in movies?"

"Well," he answered, "I didn't get too far, because it was hard to focus and keep an eye on Thryst at the same time. But it seems like most of the fairy tales I read about have certain Dwarfy things in common."

"Like what?"

"Like they were made of stone, or that they return to stone when they die." *Thryst the Inconspicuous* stirred a little when Arty said this.

Arty went on, "And they're good at making things out of stone, or out of gold, silver, jewels. They live deep in the earth. They can do magic." Another snort came from *Thryst the Not Exactly Wordy*. Arty went on, "And they use runes, which are like symbols of their language. Dwarrows are small—of course, and hairy—but they're also tough, strong, and fearless." Another grunt. "And they don't like Elves, who are usually sort of the opposite of them: Elves like the light, the outdoors, are more into light magic than dark…"

Another grunt shimmied the room, and then Thryst actually moved, shooting his eyes up toward the open windows above us. Arty and I stiffened in concentration, listening and looking for whatever was bothering his Dwarf. We heard nothing, and there was no movement inside or out; no shadows had passed by the windows that overlooked the library street and busy sidewalk. The panes were dotted and dripping with a light rain—which was unexpected after such a bright day—but that was it. After a moment, Thryst stared back at us with concern in his eyes and a grip on his axe handle.

"Something he doesn't like?" I asked.

"He doesn't like much," my human friend answered. "I started listing them in my notes. He seems to hate trees, and the beach, or maybe the water."

I decided to draw, my usual response to any strange experience. I dug into my bag for my journal and put the date at the top of a page, then thought, *Would Thryst be good to sketch?* Or make a good sculpture? Animation? Scenery for a Broadway musical? Design for wallpaper? My pencil doodled various hood shapes.

I was interrupted—Thryst moved so quickly, he startled me. He thrust his shoulders and head around and upward to stare at the high, short windows. I heard his Dwarf axe ringing as it moved in his huge arms, a tone that floated and fluttered and never quite disappeared. The ghost of its song stayed in my ears.

W.W. Marplot

Keeping my journal ready, I stared at the axe as Thryst twisted it back and forth in a massive hand. The muscles of his wrist and forearm pulsed with strength and readiness.

"There must be something coming, or someone, I guess," Arty said. "We should go." And we did.

But two people had been watching us.

CHAPTER 14

Ted

Ha! Yes, one of those people watching was ME. I am Ted. You know what's great about me? I can get involved in any story whenever I want. I am good at it.

Also, Emma likes me, like as a boyfriend, but won't admit it, so I used to follow her around sometimes. It is none of your business.

Today I watched Arty and Emma go into that room at the library, and saw them leave, but first I noticed what they were doing…They weren't nearly careful enough when putting back the books and returning the printouts: their stuff was a mess. They were in a hurry. Emma is hard to catch up to sometimes.

I saw that she brought her journal with her—her grey one, which means she wanted to do some new writing, which means something interesting was going on.

They left in a hurry. Just out the front doors of the library, they ran down the hill toward Main St. It was raining hard all of a sudden, so maybe that is why I slipped and fell. And I lost them.

I could not chase them, because that is when I saw the man again, the same dude I saw after school, and he reminded me of the guy in my dream. Emma and Arty didn't see him, but it was ok, I knew I could protect her. *I will lose him. I think he is following me. I think, I can tell, that I should run from him.*

They were all up to something, but so was I.

So, what was I saying? I lost Emma and Arty. For now. I knew I would catch them sooner or later. It was for their own good. I know how to keep an eye on those two, either at school or at their houses, and anywhere they might go. They won't mind, we are all friends. Not that I would tell you any of that. They probably wouldn't either.

It's not like it's spying.

CHAPTER 15

Arty

That spying jerk. That's exactly what Ted is, so now you know, too. Emma and I are the good guys. Ted is questionable. *Thryst* is *Magnificent*, mostly—but dangerous, as Ted almost found out.

Looking over my shoulder as Emma and I ran, I saw Ted slip and fall on the rain-soaked sidewalk outside the library. At the same time, we heard the cart-rattling "*Tarn!*" grunt—as Thryst had done in the library. But: I could not see my Dwarf. He had a way of not being seen in public or by anyone he didn't want to see him—which is why I was happy when he bowed to Emma before.

Nobody bows to Ted.

When the kid hit the wet pavement, he made his own grunting noise, thin and wimpy. I almost went back to him. But another noise stung me just then: Thryst's axe was tolling, though we still could not see him. It was a warning, I guess, or a practice swing, since nothing nearby was notched or had fallen down.

We had to get Thryst away. From the sound, he seemed to be heading back toward Ted—and that would have been bad news for Ted and whoever cleans the sidewalks of Belle Terre. So, I yelled, "No!" in the direction of the axe song and in as deep a voice as I could. I flailed my arms wildly to signal the Dwarf to follow us, and not chop Ted into firewood, or whatever fantasy warriors do to spying nuisances. Clouds conquered the sky, the rain came harder, and Arty and I ran. I didn't hear any screams or ambulances, so I assumed Thryst followed us.

We sprinted from store to store, side-street to side-street, until we reached a tree-covered path up the big hill that leads away from downtown and toward our homes.

We lost Ted, but I still felt we were being watched.

CHAPTER 16

Emma

I'm used to Ted following me. He's not exactly nice, as you can see, but this time his jerkiness could have been dangerous. He's part weasel, part snake, and part fox. Plus: he's spoiled, from what Arty's mom says. Actually, most moms have said this.

We were glad to lose him, but our long walk home was dark, dreary, and rainy, and I was not dressed for any of it. Since Thryst's axe bonged outside the library, we hadn't seen or heard our warrior friend. Arty assumed he was with us, just staying out of sight. "That's how we got to the library," he said.

The downtown part of Belle Terre is called its "village," and it had never seemed like such a scary, dismal place as it did during our walk home. The feeling that we were being watched grew. The avenues seemed haunted and strange, with more alleys than we remembered; the older historic buildings became mysterious enemies that stared with windows and tried to catch us with doors. An early night was on us by the time we reached the deeper woods at the top of the big hill. Arty was nervous: he knew from his adventure today that anything might happen, and if it did, of course it would happen in the dark.

We talked to keep our brains busy. Arty told me how he imagined Thryst must feel, that it must be hard for a Dwarf nowadays. "I would be a good Dwarf," he said, as if he'd been asked what he wanted to be when he grew up.

"Once you can shave," I added.

We reached the top of the hill that marks the beginning of our neighborhood, a small part. A large gatehouse, with always-open iron doors held by thick castle-like walls, always meant *almost home* to Arty and me since we were kids. *Gates into the unknown darkness* it seemed now. The woods were almost black, one big shadow with frayed edges that moved in the wind. We still had over a mile to walk. There was no sign of *Thryst the Very Good at Not Being Seen*.

With our shoulders bowed under eerie suspicions, we walked familiar streets that had turned into a world of shadows. The random road noises—rain on treetops, branches bumping in the wind, small animals tramping through dead leaves—did not help our battered nerves. Nothing did. We listened hard for signs of Thryst—a grunt, a falling tree—but heard none.

Where a field opened on our right, we stopped short and gasped. Ahead, low in the sky, coming between dark and distant trees, we saw a strange light, dull and ghostly grey. We didn't pause to wonder; we ran out of fear. Arty and I ran until the threatening grey-lit enemy showed its face—the smirking face of the moon. We all made friends again, and I was thankful for some light.

Finally, we arrived at Arty's house with our heads downcast and wet. Our Dwarf was ahead in the driveway. Thryst followed from the driveway to the front door but vanished when he sensed the others in the house.

In Arty's dry and warm living room, with the lights on us and a nice—though late—dinner in us, things seemed almost normal again after a unique day. Arty's mom made us feel as snug as chubby kittens until the rest of his family left for a brother's basketball game. She's a very nice mom.

Arty has a large family, and a large house. There are three brothers, two sisters, Arty in the middle somewhere, and parents who are very nice and who are always in motion. There's a nanny, or an *au pair* as they call her—her name is Gretel, just like in the fairy tale. She's from Europe, she's tough, and she's definitely the boss. Arty is her favorite, since he gives the least trouble: he never talks back, he does what he is told. Or—I have to admit—he does not *need* to be told because, *man, is that kid organized.*

So, when he misses school, people aren't mad or suspicious, they're worried. Gretel handled all that and covered for him. She's a good ally in times of emergency. Gretel knew something was up when Arty whispered to her, "Have you seen my phone anywhere?" She had not. Arty was bummed about this; as middle-schoolers, our phones are part of who we are and how we live. I lost my phone once for five hours, and I wanted to move to Africa to cry.

Arty soon returned to being Arty and was in a planning panic, trying to figure out how his usual Thursday (tomorrow) could make up for his lost Wednesday (today), and yet still take into account the needs of our new warrior friend. He and I went to his attic bedroom with cookies and iced tea to regroup. "I still have a lot to tell you!" he began as we went up the two flights of stairs. He yelled down to Gretel, "If Ted comes over, we aren't here." She laughed in German.

"Where do you think he is?" I asked as we entered Arty's perfectly ordered room. By "he" I meant *Thryst the Quiet Lately.*

"No idea." Arty walked toward his bathroom window and exclaimed, "Oh! Here he is!" Thryst was in front of the toilet, facing us, in the familiar pose: feet apart, arms folded, not matching the wallpaper. I laughed. Thryst bowed. I said, "Hi." He stared at the wall.

"He obviously likes you," said Arty.

"Great—between him and Ted, I'll never be lonely. Do you think he saw anything?" I meant Ted.

"I don't know, maybe. The sneak. But we can handle him." Arty walked over to his desk. "I want to show you something that I read about." He started to tap and type into his laptop, and I watched him zoom around the Web, back and forth between Google and Wikipedia, through some weird medieval-looking websites. He left the web pages and opened one of the books he'd borrowed from the library.

"Let's see—yes—this is the right version. *The Denham Tracts...*" Arty started to say, but then a bunch of things happened.

First, Thryst grunted, which I felt as much as heard. It gave me goosebumps—or maybe the goosebumps were from the something that touched me, brushing past my arm. That was the second thing. The third thing was I felt a shiver of breath on my ear, as if someone was whispering. It was very faint, and I couldn't make out any words—but it was NOT my imagination. A haunted feeling, cold as ice, crept down my body to my knees and toes. I froze. At the same time—a fourth thing!—there was a noise from the closet next to Arty's bed, a mysterious thump, as if something had fallen off a shelf to the floor.

"Arty," I said, my voice and legs quivering, my hair standing up. "There is something in the room with us." I could feel it and sense it. I shook. I gripped my own elbows to make it stop.

Arty then did a brave thing, I have to admit. He opened the closet door. He bent to pick something up and said, "What the...?" He showed me what was in his hand: his phone.

I jumped with fright—not because of the phone, but because Thryst had shouted, "*Tarn!*" He was standing right behind me, his hot breath on my back, replacing the cold. Dead winter passed directly to high summer. *What is going on?* I said to Arty, but without words, just with my eyes, the way Thryst taught me. I felt meek and pulled my arms closer to my body, to protect myself.

Arty answered my eyes with his shoulders, shrugging that he didn't know. We looked at Thryst: he was gripping his axe handle. *Thryst the Ready.*

"Arty—I felt something on me before. Something else is here."

"And Thryst doesn't like it," Arty added. "Same as at the library. We were definitely followed. And I don't mean Ted..."

"*Tarn,*" Thryst said. That's what it sounded like anyway. If you can get someone's cigar-champing grandfather to cough for you, it would make a good impersonation. Then Thryst snorted and shot a sharp glance around the room. I was afraid. I felt the icy touch again, and the cold breath again, the ghostly whisper again, and I almost screamed.

THEN, as if blown by a strong wind, the pages of the big book on Arty's desk started to turn, rapidly, flopping over in a mad haste. Then they stopped. I did not feel any wind, and the bedroom windows and door were closed.

"Arty…" I said, meaning: *What the heck was that? Books don't read themselves.*

Arty dropped his phone to his bed and stepped to the desk.

"Arty!" I said, meaning: *Don't. Aren't you scared?*

He answered while inspecting the large book as if it were a magician's hat. "It's ok, Thryst is here." He now picked up the book with both hands. "Wow! Hey—what did Thryst just say?"

"I don't know," I said, somehow using real words.

"It sounded like *tarn* or something, right? T-A-R-N?" He spelled as he flipped through the books' pages.

I relaxed enough to stutter, "It s-s-s-sounded like there w-w-were more *R*'sssss and *N-N-N-N*'ssss."

"This is an old book I found, a dictionary of fairytale words, and it has all the creatures and legends. It opened to the T's…Someone wants us to read certain pages from it—pretty clever," Arty said.

"And that someone is still here." I trembled. I could feel it. Something was watching us—and had been since the library.

"*Tarn*," said *Thryst the Protector.*

I was still standing, trying to remain still but quivering like newly served Jell-O because of the thing that kept touching me and whispering in my ear, the thing that had turned the pages of the book. I tried to speak, but on my ear landed another whisper, so I jumped and shrieked. Thryst's axe sang out, alert and ready to strike. But whoever and whatever was near me was quicker—I felt a whoosh of wind through my hair, just after which the book jumped from Arty's hands to the floor. Thryst moved and swung his axe, two-handed, all around and as swift as a small bird making short flights. After three or four misses, the Dwarf commando stopped and hurrumphed.

Arty asked for quiet—the book's pages were turning again as it sat on the floor. Arty sucked his own breath sharply when the pages stopped, picked up the book as if it might be hot, and then read through the names listed on the selected page.

"It's on the S's. It's trying to tell us something again. Spunkies? Spunky?"

"NO!" I screamed, and I had a good reason. "*No*" had just been whispered to me—a slight but clear voice said the word in my right ear, and then it laughed. Obviously, I was startled, and the goosebumps traveled over my body like a hundred wormy monsters, but I was able to remain calm—almost as calm as Arty, and definitely calmer than *Thryst the Strikeout King*.

"No?" Arty asked me.

"No," I said again, shaking, gripping myself in a bear-hug. I was actually just as afraid of Thryst taking another swing as I was of the chilly breath on my neck: the Dwarf's eyes were blazing with orange fire.

Arty read the next entry from the book, asking, "*Sprite?*"

"No," we answered—the whisperer and I.

Arty tried again. "The only other entry on these pages is *Spriggan...*"

"*Me,*" said the whisper, and I felt the bodiless voice move away. "That's the one," I said and fell over onto the bed.

Arty then read to us what a Spriggan is, according to his fairy encyclopedia. Spriggans are the ghosts of Giants, sent to be guardians of all fairies and any other magical, mythical creatures. Spriggans are small but can grow to giant-size when necessary. They are prone to mischief, or worse things, when protecting others. They are vengeful, sometimes in creative ways, and dangerous. Although they are ancient, some people believe that they do fade away eventually—but others think that, like ghosts, they can hang around forever. And you won't find any of their faces on the covers of magazines, if you know what I mean.

Soon after, we saw it clearly for the first time, a small thing that zipped and zooped magically to wherever he wanted to appear next, partly by flying, partly by jumping, and sometimes skittering like a very worried hamster out of his cage—but we only saw him when he wanted us to. Once Thryst gave up trying to chop him, the Spriggan slowed down—though never quite stayed still—and we got a good look.

It—which I guessed had to be a *he*—was EXTREMELY ugly, which is probably why he kept moving. Small and ugly. He had lumpy orange skin, a not-quite-round-but-a-little-squashed shape to his head, and the same for his body and parts. His strange, wing-like things stuck out at uncomfortable angles. His face was out of order, with eyes, nose, mouth, other holes, and antennae all looking crooked and lopsided.

Our excitement became hope that we could now learn what was going on—finding a Dwarf and a Spriggan on the same Wednesday deserves explaining—since this icky little fella could speak English. Though he did not speak much. Was he not talkative, or was English not his native language? Sometimes he'd say things we couldn't understand at all, and then some English words would follow that were just as puzzling.

The first thing we learned was that Spriggans could be a pain in the axe—and both Arty and I added that to our notes. He was clumsy, for one thing. When we lost track of him, we just needed to wait a few seconds and eventually something would tip over, or fall off a shelf, or we would hear a bump on the ceiling or wall.

I called the Spriggan "Sprugly." The name just popped into my head after he broke Arty's soccer trophy, the one sports award of my friend's whole life. Sprugly didn't seem to mind this name even after I apologized. Soon Arty and I both believed this new fairy creature was here specifically for me. The Spriggan was *mine* somehow, just as *Thryst the Pissed* was *Arty's* somehow. Not *mine* as in "*my cell phone I bought with my own money*" but as in "*my bodyguard.*"

CHAPTER 17

Arty

mma and I were not afraid anymore. Now, we wanted to learn.

By pointing at maps and doing a lot of waving, using beginner sign language, playing charades, and watching book pages flop around, Emma and I asked my "*where*" questions: *Where are they from? Where are they going? Where do they think they are?*

We didn't get much. "We're here," Sprugly whispered, in English, and flew around, until we were sick of it.

"New Island," he said next, and he repeated it until Emma and I were sure of the words. Each time he spoke, he would *zing* away from Emma's ear, then *zoing* back. Next, he said, "They were there," slowly, until we repeated it correctly.

"Where? Where?" Emma and I pleaded.

"*Here and everywhere,*" was a typically useless answer.

The globe on my desk then spun, and the maps we had laid out on the bed flopped around, folding and unfolding, piling then un-piling. When they stopped, my glass of iced tea spilled over.

Emma and I did not understand. We asked again and again— where, where?—and the globe would spin, and maps would flop, and something would break or fall. Thryst was not getting used to our new friend. His usually fiery eyes had squinted into an icy glare.

What did this mean?

There was more. Maybe. "All. Here. One and one. And one!" Sprugly puffed into Emma's right ear. As if blown by the cold fairy breath, the old book pages turned, stopped, and turned again with each word from Sprugly. On those pages were stories of fantastic creatures. Fairies from folktales and myths, magical beings like the ones we still have in modern stories and movies—though we don't usually run into them on our front steps. Our science tells us that they don't really exist.

"No offense," I said to Thryst.

Fairies are not human but close, not dreams but almost, not ghosts but sort of, not imaginary but not *not* imaginary—they exist in some world in between and around and inside and outside and before and after our "real" one. There are thousands of stories, of course, of fairies and more, with Dwarves being in a few, Elves in more, and then there are Trolls, Pixies, dragons, Giants, and Leprechauns.

There was nothing in my books about a *New Island*, however, and Sprug did not want to tell us much more. Either that, or he was learning English one word at a time and had just started last weekend.

What could this mean? Could all these legends be true, be real? Be here? Were there more of these, um, *fairies* living around Belle Terre? Was this serious? Were we making scientific history? Or was Sprugly just a silly trickster with a face like a kindergarten finger-painting?

We wondered about my phone, thinking maybe the little Spriggan found it in the woods and brought it to my house. How he carried it was a mystery; perhaps he did the *grow-to-enormo-size* thing that the book talked about. I would hate to see that. He also hinted, with a "No, no," in Emma's ear, that videoing was useless—which I proved after trying to get a shot of him dancing in the puddle of iced tea and only getting a picture of a dark room. Interesting. And, sure enough, the video of Thryst that I thought I'd expertly directed this morning showed only a very blurry scene of a boy playing Dungeons and Dragons or something with his dogs.

Lastly, exhaustedly, we learned how much we still needed to learn. Once my notes were updated, I had four full pages of questions, starting with, *What is New Island?* It was too much for a camera-shy Dwarf and a Spriggan who spoke only one syllable at a time between acrobatic mishaps. I needed to look into this myself and proceed scientifically.

CHAPTER 18

Emma

I was very tired, though I was spraying excitement outward and upward like a shopping mall fountain. I had found a Spriggan, and Sprugly was sort of "mine" since he stayed on my shoulder as I bounced down two flights of stairs from Arty's room while his other eight hundred family members were huddled in the den, watching cat videos. I timed it that way. I figured their presence would make our fairy friends disappear, and I wanted to keep mine.

It was fair that Arty and I each had a new "friend." This would be fun. Though Arty seemed to think there were more, somewhere.

"Really?" I was swaying from foot to foot at Arty's front door as Sprugly tried to decide which of my shoulders he preferred. "There can't be more of these 'here and there and somewhere.'" I tried to imitate Sprugly, after which the little monster yanked my hair. Then I pointed at the book in Arty's hands. "Aren't they just legends, old folktales, fairy tales?"

"Say that again," Arty replied, "but this time without a Spriggan on your shoulder."

I laughed. "Good point. But if there were lots of these—look at that list: Elves, Trolls, dragons—if they were all around, we would know about it."

"Why?"

But as he asked, Sprugly fell off my neck and flew too close to *Thryst the Very Ready*, and the Dwarf could not help himself. He had put up with Sprugly for two hours, but instincts are instincts. It was like Arty's cats and dogs—they get along indoors, but outside they become enemies again. So, Thryst took a swing with his axe—we heard a whoosh, the first note of an axe-song, a grumble, a grunt, and lastly the dogs joined in with whining and barking for the fun of it. Sprugly knocked over an empty umbrella stand and then perched on my shoulder again. Thryst replaced his axe into his belt and bowed to me unhappily.

Arty rushed us outside since his parents were shouting for the dogs to shut up. "And put that Dwarf and Spriggan away. You can play with them tomorrow," they added.

Just kidding.

Lights came on inside the house, so we moved along the driveway. My house was only a short walk through the woods, or a little longer on the street, which seemed like a better idea. The rain had stopped, but collected clumps still fell on me from the large oak trees. Dull moonlight came weakly through a cloud in a fuzzy blotch. The road was wet, looking clean and polished.

The two-legged thing standing there was very tall.

CHAPTER 19

Emma

Yep, there was a two-legged tall thing standing in the road. Arty saw him at the same time as me and pulled me behind a giant oak tree.

"Are you expecting company?" I asked.

"No."

"What kind of fairy is that?"

"The same kind that Ted is. Not."

"A human?"

"Yep."

"What do we do?"

"I guess it depends what our new friends do..." Arty answered and turned to watch our Dwarf and Spriggan.

But they didn't do anything, nothing we could see, because we couldn't see them even if they were doing anything. I felt very nervous; I didn't like the looks of this man. I couldn't make out a face or anything; his arms were long, his legs were long, the normal human shape just stretched a bit. He was wearing a hat.

But he wasn't a normal human. I knew it with every cell in my body.

He walked back and forth along the road, always stopping at the driveway, not coming onto the property—onto Arty's front yard. And here and there we caught a gleam of some sort—yes, he was holding something in his hands that would give off some kind of glow, a dull blue, and it lit his face as he stared down into it. It was too big to be a phone.

It did reveal that he had a beard.

"This guy is obviously here because of what we found today," Arty whispered, almost speaking to himself.

"So, he knows also?"

"I guess."

"Does he have any?"

"Any what?"

"You know, Dwarves or Spriggans or Giants or anything."

"I don't see any Giants," Arty said.

The man then—very excitedly—ran from one end of Arty's property line to the other but was careful not to come any closer to the house. His long strides were creepy to watch, and we had to circle the tree to stay out of his view. He stopped, then popped up onto his toes, holding the blue-shining object up. Then he rose into the air! Actually, Arty said there was a large tree stump there that the man—just a man—could stand on.

"Emma," Arty said.

"What?"

"I have a lot to learn still. But we aren't alone. Let's meet tomorrow at—"

"The library," I interrupted. For Arty, books only lead to more books.

Arty peeked back at the man, then decided to move closer. I offered to help by staying behind the big oak tree and closing my eyes for a while. But before Arty took a step, the man vanished, the glow disappeared, and there was nothing more to see.

I could not be convinced to move until our new friends reappeared. I soon heard Sprugly at my ear and saw Thryst standing nearby, like a forgotten statue, grey beneath the weak moonlight. They and Arty walked with me until we could see my house. We didn't see or hear or even imagine anyone the whole way.

I thanked them all as Arty said, "We can figure out more after school."

School. The word landed between us like an elephant dropped from a blimp. Arty wanted us to act normal until he figured out what to do, to keep it secret. But: *school*? How would we do that? Bring the fairies? How? What if they didn't come? Say goodbye?

The moon peeked out at us, our short shadows appearing for a second, until a cloud stepped in front rudely. "I guess we can't control it either way," Arty said in and around a yawn. "Whatever happens will happen."

After a few minutes waiting for a hand to reach out from a mountain-top in the sky to guide us—which did not happen, sadly—Arty spoke.

"I need to make a list...have to clean my room..."

I rolled my eyes, but he went on, sleepily, "Need more info, books, and maps..." Arty trailed off, yawned some more, and twisted his fists in his eyes like a giant baby.

"Get some sleep. See you on the bus," I said.

Bus. A gorilla dropped from a treehouse. Arty opened his mouth, but a yawn tackled the words before they escaped.

Arty and Thryst walked slowly away, the boy lumbering like an early morning zombie. I hoped he would sleep.

CHAPTER 20

Emma

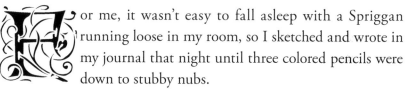or me, it wasn't easy to fall asleep with a Spriggan running loose in my room, so I sketched and wrote in my journal that night until three colored pencils were down to stubby nubs.

Arty doesn't have a "journal," just lists and plans. And old lists and old plans that are used to make new lists and new plans. My writing, on the other hand, is where I let the real world become a dream, and vice versa. I draw and then write about what I create, and then do it again. Arty's lists do not have pictures.

As Sprugly investigated my room—and the whole house, which was black and silent when I came home—I drew: ugly fairy creatures and Giants, rainbows leading into caves, Dwarves and wolves, walls and walls of books, orange castles and princesses with grey beards. More than once, my head clunked to the sketchbook, my mind exhausted.

I wrote:

> *I remember I used to like to watch the trains go by. Mom and Dad would stop and make sure I saw them when we drove over the railroad crossing. I thought there would be some adventure waiting for whoever followed the tracks, through the woods, past cities, under mountains. I was little, and the world was*

full of magic—in my garden at home, in the lights at holidays, in the colored picture of rhyming storybooks. When I turned nine, then ten, it was harder to find, and Mom didn't stop at the tracks anymore…but I would watch planes in the sky. I wanted to be on every one of them, to disappear and start my own fairy tale. Now I'm a teenager, and I understand the world, and people and their lives, the reality on TV and the fake effects in movies. But every morning, early, when everything is paused and quiet, and the sun is still sharing heaven with the stars like a big family sharing a large house, I feel hope that there's some small magic somewhere. And late at night, on grey and white winter days when the skies are wide and black, I feel there will be a springtime for spirits, and something amazing will come to me to grow and live again. And now I have a Spriggan, a new magical friend.

And then my little fairy flew up to the top of the dresser, looked at me, and, with his small hand, knocked over a perfume bottle and watched it crash to the floor. He looked back with a big, crooked smile.

"Yes, thanks," I said.

That's what my new life was like. Annoying. Magical but Annoying. I couldn't control Sprugly, so he'd fly in and out of my hair, sneak up to me and whisper nonsense in my ear, bounce along the ground around my feet—I tripped over him a hundred times, easy. He was so clumsy. He trashed my room and my bathroom; I had no idea why. It was all new to me.

So, I added to Arty's made-up words: *jumpfly* was what Sprugly did, for example. He leapt, bounced, and wafted his wings to get around—but all as quick as hummingbird blinks.

Sprugly was supposed to be a protector, so I asked him why he was such a pain in the butt, and he said:

"Not a fairy. Not one. Not one of the ones."

I'm not a fairy, so he wouldn't protect me, I guess. Cute. So, I said:

"But Thryst wasn't exactly thrilled with you either. Aren't you here to protect him?"

"Not one," he said, then splashed water out of my fishbowl. The fish stared at him. I stared at him. You can see it all in my new sketches, which are of Spriggans cleaning up and repairing things.

After getting tired of this, I gave in and simply asked, "Can I look into your eyes, please?"

"Yes," he whispered, then he stopped his flight in midair in front of me and floated there.

And then we were in a crowd.

I saw lush grass, tremendous flowers, and wild, exotic trees of every size and shape, all looking freshly popped from a children's book. All around—in trees, in the air, and marching on the ground— were very happy, very odd creatures, all singing. Their motion and their song were directed, orchestrated, to a single purpose—some ancient tradition had them gathering, the symphony rising as they did. It was a scene of musical, magical make-believe that was both too grand and too good to be true.

I felt very glad.

Their parade continued, synchronized movements in the sunshine, in the leaves, and through the green and blossoming field. Creatures as varied as the trees and flowers—some had wings; some walked on two legs, some four; some were human, some animals; many had wings; some were ghostly and seemed to float; some seemed so much a part of the earth or trees where they gathered that it seemed that the land itself was breathing out music—seemed to send me their thoughts, and that sense was the highest and sweetest feeling of life that I had ever experienced.

I felt young, and on my own. There were no problems in this world, not for me. I used to think I had a good life back in my room, I had friends, and a nice neighborhood, and school was a pain but also fun. Here, now, I realized how much lighter my life could be. There was an unspoken promise of better things, and there was no loneliness, or anything that ever could remove the enchantment. This world was a new and better poem, a work of art that could never be created back home.

The next thing I saw was a wide, flat sky of dingy white—and I realized I was on my back in bed and staring at the ceiling. I was alone in my house and alone in my shadowy room.

I squished my ragged hair—a Spriggan's nest—into a ponytail and began to face reality. I had a fairy to mind, school in the morning, plans with Arty and his Dwarf, and Ted to deal with, and all on a Thursday that would follow the first Wednesday I would ever remember by name.

I finally, calmly closed my eyes, snuggling under a blanket of sleep that the night threw over me, trusting that Sprugly would remain out of the sight of others—namely, my mother, who was now home but had, luckily, gone straight to bed.

CHAPTER 21

Ted

Yeah, she got to bed late that night. She was at Arty's until past 10:30! And her bedroom light didn't go out until after midnight.

The man didn't show up at her house. I saved her. And he can't find me.

Just like in my dream, which was almost a nightmare, but I won.

It's none of your business.

From,

Ted.

CHAPTER 22

Emma

ood morning, and welcome to Thursday. This is Emma, waking to my alarm clock and to a big mess; ahead is my first full day with my new roommate Sprugly the Spriggan.

It was a beautiful second day of May that followed the nasty rain of the first, and all that dark excitement under the moon, the nighttime of mysterious frenzy learning about—and learning from!—fairy tale creatures. There were new worlds in their eyes.

And there were others, like the man in the woods…What was he up to? Did he know?

My Spriggan was doing his thing all night, so the morning sun was eavesdropping into a very messy room. Luckily, my mother slept through it all and the rest of the house wasn't disturbed.

The odd little fellow really liked my clothes. He didn't leave many clean ones for me to wear to school, and as I was getting ready, he would jumpfly around while trying on one article after another. He covered himself in a sock, rose beneath a hat, ran through a pant leg, eventually settled on a scarf. I thought this might at least help keep him hidden during the day—a day that I was dreading.

With the air already bright and warm, I sweated at the bus stop in jeans, a turtleneck, a coat, and Sprugly's scarf, none of them matched in color or style. I'm no expert, but I thought the extra layers would help in case my Spriggan needed places to hide.

I felt Sprugly around me, but he stayed quiet, and no one suspected anything, not even when I tripped going through the bus doors. Waiting for Arty's stop, the next one, I stared anxiously out the window, wondering if I'd see *Thryst the Definitely Stands Out in a Crowd.* Would anyone else see him? Would *every*one? I had no idea how he'd hide. Already I wished Sprugly had taken a sick day: he was nestled in the scarf on my shoulders, and I was already stressed out and paranoid and overheating. I hadn't heard from Arty, but I assumed he was sticking to our plan to try to have a normal day. It takes a lot for Arty to change plans, but I'd forgive him: he has a good—and strong, broad, bearded, and axe-wielding—excuse.

Along came Arty's driveway and mailbox, and there was Arty, a notepad in his arm, pen in his hand, writing furiously and without concern for the Dwarf standing behind him! As plain as a rock with a hood!

!, I thought.

I caught Thryst's eye, under scrub-brush eyebrows, and he caught mine. Immediately, I experienced again that feeling that Thryst had knowledge of deep, dark, cavernous things and that his heart was hard and solid. He bowed, I smiled, and then he was gone. He had stepped behind Arty, and now I couldn't see him at all. *Some sort of magic,* I thought, since Thryst was four times as wide as Arty. My friend was no Giant and couldn't hide even a regular-sized seventh grader behind him, let alone a muscular warrior Dwarf in full gear.

Arty sat with me, of course, and I gave him the warmer window seat. No other kids were near enough to stop us from talking and swapping notes. Ted—a definite concern—is always driven to school.

As Arty sat, Sprug came out to my shoulder, whispered something incomprehensible, and before I could react to save a disaster, he sped off, leaving us alone. I worried but stiffened still for eight full seconds in anticipation of loud and many middle-school girl screams. An ugly Spriggan hopping loose around the bus would be worse for them than a team of spiders riding millipedes up shirtsleeves. But apparently

Sprugly went unnoticed. Good boy. I don't remember exactly, but I think I then exhaled.

"Ok," Arty said nine seconds later, "here's my plan." He handed me a folder marked "TTM Plan. May, 2015," and within was a stapled report, with a cover sheet and everything, of ten pages, typed, two-sided, and with headings and footnotes. Arty was good at word processing. The last page had a summary table of the plan that listed tasks, due dates, times, and the person assigned—him and me on each one. "So far," he said. A pencil fell out of it and into my lap.

"What is TTM?" I asked.

"Thryst the Magnificent," he said.

"Ah," I said.

"Yeah, well…" He looked tired.

"Where is he now?" I asked, meaning Thryst.

"I don't know, probably here somewhere."

"Did you sleep?" I asked.

"I had to get things done. I missed extra credit science lab yesterday, and Research Club. And, of course, all the schoolwork."

I tried not to laugh at the mention of Research Club and its oily members and failed.

"Don't you think," I said, recovering nicely, "that running through the woods with a Dwarf, and studying fairies in the wild, make up for it? Don't be so hard on yourself. Was it tough to sleep? Sprug made a mess of my room, and he was up most of the night. He likes to play dress up."

"The sister you never had, that's nice," Arty answered through a capital Yawn. "No, Thryst didn't bother me. I think he slept in the crawlspace in my basement; I found him down there. But I left him alone. Obviously, it's a place a Dwarf would like."

"Makes sense. What about Ted?" I asked.

"I don't think he saw anything. We would know by now. He fell. That's it." Arty tossed out his words as quickly as he wanted to toss Ted's name out of his notes and plans.

Skimming Arty's papers, I returned his contagious yawns with my own as the bus bumped along the road. Awash in boring facts and figures, the report was like reading an AM Radio talk show about the history of AM Radio.

Until: I got to a loose single sheet of paper in the folder, separate and with a description, in Arty's blocky, print handwriting, of his mind trip through Thryst's eyes—the army, the path, the mountains, Thryst's tunnel escape. Amazing.

"You didn't tell me all of this," I said, pointing the pencil at him. "Why is it separate from the report?"

"It isn't scientific," Arty said.

I asked him to please give me a break. "I looked into Sprug's eyes, too," I then said.

"He sat still for that?"

"I had to ask him nicely."

"Well? What happened? Was it cool?"

"It looks like a great world in there."

Arty nodded.

I then read Arty's "Plan Summary," which listed what he and I were supposed to do next. Many steps.

I put the pencil behind my left ear, so I wouldn't stab Sprugly, who was perched behind my right. I asked, "For number 5—what are we supposed to look for? If other people had fairies following them around, it would be all over the news and the Web and completely viral."

"Really?" Arty replied. "'Boy Says He Sees Elf in Tree' would be big news, you think?" The combination of the sarcasm and the rudeness—he wasn't even looking at me!—made me mad, which made me sweat, which made me mad, and so on.

"Listen, little man, Thryst can't protect you from me, so don't get snotty. So, are you saying that you think it's only kids finding them?"

"Just like I say on page six."

I yawned for what seemed like a long time and skimmed more of Arty's report. "Boring..."

"What?" He was offended. "How could this be boring to you?"

"I only care about the unusual things. 'Thryst's approximate boot size' and 'Dog bark count' aren't important. Thryst's eyes and the sound from his axe and Sprugly's secrets and mischief—that's the good stuff."

"Well, mine is proper science. It's the only way to get answers."

"All wrong answers," I said back, "because this can't be explained with logic and formulas—so you'll be wrong."

"Well, don't you want to know why they're here? Or are you just following along?"

"What's wrong with trying to just watch and enjoy it? I would like to know why, yeah, but the wind direction isn't going to tell you 'why' anyway. '*Why*' is harder than math." Arty turned his head away, but I went on. "But I tell you what: I'll make you a bet. I don't know *what* will happen, but I bet I know why they're here."

"Why?" Arty puffed into the bus window.

"We have to bet. Write down your guess. Your advanced NASA report doesn't say '*why*' you found a Dwarf."

"How do you know? You only skimmed it."

"I know you're sick, nerdy, scientist mind."

"Fine. What are we betting?"

"Winner gets to write the book," I declared.

Arty saw what I meant. If I got to tell people what happened, it would be worth reading, with masterful artwork; if he did, it would be all charts and theories and Greek letters, the stuff *he* likes.

"Fine," he agreed.

We wrote our why-guesses, folded them, then I took a small white envelope from Arty's portable desk of a backpack, put our guesses in, and sealed it. I shook my head at the assortment of geek toys he carried around with him—two flash drives, two old tablets with their insides sticking out, chargers of every shape and length, pads in different colors, red and black ink pens.

Compare that to what Thryst carried!

We arrived at the school, the bus squeaking into its place in the long line, the other kids rising in volume and energy. "Good luck! Text me as often as you can, ok?" I said. Arty nodded and looked out the bus window nervously. At the school, among the swarm of a hundred kids emptying out of buses, worrying about where your Dwarf is was a new experience for him. And it reminded me of my own problem: How would I get through this while bumbling around with clumsy, clumsy, unapologetic Sprugly the Spriggan?

Our thoughts were deep. Silently, we got off the bus, joined the crowds, and went our different ways to class.

"Arty!" I called, before he disappeared down a hallway, "what about the thing in your yard?"

"I don't want to talk about that yet," he yelled back. Nobody looked at us.

Except Ted, who was right behind me.

CHAPTER 23

Arty

I didn't want to talk about the funny thing growing in my yard, or anything else, with Emma, or anyone else. Going to school on a Thursday morning in a world that was completely different than it had been on Wednesday morning was a challenge that needed my full attention. I had to be on guard every second. I had only slept a few hours, and my dreams weren't exactly peaceful.

Axes. Smoke. Beards. Giant piles of firewood.

I tried to act normal in class, to focus on my schoolwork like normal. That was the plan, and I needed to stick to the plan. I dreaded having to talk to anyone. Entering school, I avoided friends by ditching into bathrooms or offices.

Could I get through a whole day like this?

Meeting back up with Emma was eight hours away. Thryst was still with me, and Sprugly was still with Emma, and this problem—I mean "adventure"—wasn't going away on its own, it seemed.

Because: yes, Thryst was still with me as I walked the hall before classes. I could sense him, I could smell him. I saw his reflection in my locker, but when I turned, he was gone. I felt his beard brush my face as I was bent over at a water fountain. Walking to my first class, I knew at any moment I might hear a snort, or the ringing of Thryst's axe, or see tall Principal Edmondson teeter and fall like a chopped tree, and I was a nervous wreck. And how could a thick

Dwarf possibly hide among all these skinny kids? What kind of magic was this?

I tried to focus, to be cool, to act natural. Maybe no one would notice.

I walked to my first class. Then:

"Hey! What's that? A Dwarf!" someone yelled. I closed my eyes; the shout came from behind me.

Great, I thought. I almost survived a whole fifteen minutes. I braced myself, prepared for Armageddon. This was it. All I had left to do was write "The End" in my report. Thryst was going to kill all these children, and I'd have to explain why I didn't call the police, the fire department, the Dwarf squad, or anyone.

I turned, and the owner of the voice was coming toward me, his large body weaving around the crowd like a stream down a hill. It was Cry. Yes, that's his name, "Cry." I don't know his real first name. Every kid, every teacher, even on the first day of school, called him Cry. I wish it were otherwise.

I leaned on him and pushed him with two hands into the closest classroom and asked, "What?" I wasn't sure whether to sound surprised, or mad, or how to act. I wasn't ready for any kind of act. I hoped—in my plan—that Thryst would stay out of sight to everyone. It would've been better if he hadn't come to school at all.

We were alone in the room, Cry and I. With Thryst, who'd leapt onto a desk and was looking down with eyes like a Texas barbecue.

Luckily, we were in the art room and nobody had art class this early.

Cry was staring at Thryst, caught by the Dwarf's steady gaze. The boy was now speechless. Obviously, I couldn't pretend like nothing was happening. I counted Cry's arms and legs and head: since Thryst hadn't chopped anything, the Dwarf must be ok with this human boy. Thryst must have *allowed* himself to be seen. There was no other explanation. There must be something special about Cry—though, of course, there definitely isn't. Again, I found myself stuck on a "*why?*"

For now, there was nothing else to do but introduce them.

"Thryst the Magnificent, this is Cry Chesterton. Cry, this is Thryst."

"The magnificent..." Cry said, and I saw a teardrop in his eye. I wish it were otherwise.

CHAPTER 24

Emma

mma here. Things went just as badly just as quickly for me at school. Sprugly was out of sight but not out of mind. Though maybe he was out of *his* mind. When I publish my book, you can read all the details, so let's just say for now that, within the first hour at school, I was accused of pushing someone's books out of their hands, of talking to myself, of saying the 'K-word'—whatever that is—and of stealing a baseball hat. And that was *after* I lost Ted.

I quickly decided to go with a Plan B that I made up on the spot: act sick and go to the nurse.

Even this was not easy. At the nurse's office, I was constantly adjusting my scarf—which is code for *I was constantly adjusting my Spriggan*. There are a lot of things that can be knocked over in a nurse's office. I wish I could find Sprug a fairy to protect so he'd have something to keep him busy.

"What's the matter, Emma?" Nurse Loretta asked. "You look like you're burning up."

I was, since I was wearing many layers of Spriggan hiding places. "I don't know—I just don't feel well," I answered.

"Stomach, headache…?" She was hinting for specifics. "You look a little twitchy…Skin rash?"

"Yeah, all of it. You know?"

She looked at me, her eyes narrowing…until something crashed at the back of the room. I was getting used to the suddenness of random noises; this time it was a glass breaking, and now its contents were dropping to the floor. Classic Sprug.

But it startled the nurse, and she looked toward the noise.

"How did that happen?" she wondered aloud. At the moment, there was no one else in the room, a normally clean and shiny place of glass and tile and metal. "That's strange." Nurse Loretta walked away to investigate but continued talking to me. "Well, you don't look good." This was also true. I was dressed funny, my hair was a *Sprugmess*, I was very tired, and it showed. "So, do you want to be sent home; is it that bad? Or do you want to stay here for a while and see if you feel better?"

"I want to go home," I answered.

And then I said, "Hi, Ted," because he was now standing in the doorway of the nurse's office.

CHAPTER 25

Arty

I explained to Cry as quickly as I could why there was a Dwarf nearby. The boy sneezed a few times while I spoke. Meanwhile, *Thryst the New Kid* was investigating, with serious focus and attention, each painted rock in the art room where we stood. Every now and then, he would tap one with his axe blade, exclaim something, then stroke his beard.

"Awesome," was Cry's reply to nearly everything I said.

After a pause, Cry did ask, "But why is he here?" I explained that he could get in on the "*why*" bet Emma and I had going if he wanted.

"But please keep it a secret," I said.

"The bet?" Cry asked.

"All of it," I answered and invited him to come to the library with us after school. He thought this would be awesome and sniffled his enthusiasm into a tissue.

"Have you seen his eyes? Up close?" Cry asked me. I nodded and smiled as Cry went on: "Amazing. I thought I was…there." Cry's own eyes were wet and glassy. "There, in Dwarf land, or wherever he's from. It's like it's all still in his head, or in his mind, or kept in his eyes like that. Like his world is always with him. He must be looking for something."

"Funny you should say that…" I said, but I didn't get to finish my thoughts, since Cry went on.

"And he's probably wondering why you brought him to school."

Another good point, I thought, but we were out of time. "We'd better get to class," I said as we left the art room. I sent Cry off to gym class after the big boy begged to come with me to math. "We can talk more about it at lunch," I offered, whispering. "Keep an eye out for anything weird. There's a lot you still don't know. So far, only you and Emma have seen him."

"Ok," he sniffed as he stared at me.

"Don't stare at me. And don't tell anyone."

"Who would believe me?" Cry said and took out a small tissue holder—like a leather wallet, a trifold, and it even had his initials on it: "CC." He wiped his eyes.

My first class—math—went smoothly. No one else noticed the red and green boots that sometimes appeared in the room, in a corner, by the door, under a desk. *Dwarf magic,* I thought. It must be.

Afterward, Cry, with a smile as big as the moon, found me and was ready to break out into something—a laugh, a scream, a story, a song and dance about Dwarves. One thing I knew about Cry was that he was a big fantasy book, mobile app game, and sword-and-sorcery fan. He was loving this; I was happy for him. He was also envious. His smile glowed with it. I felt strange—so far, I'd only looked at things logically, without much emotion other than to be worried and nervous. Now I was starting to like it. That wasn't in the plan.

We saw Emma in the hall, and Cry pointed to her, and his smile grew even brighter and wider in a curve like a cartoonish crescent moon. I thought he would burst. He tried to speak and blubbered instead. "Ok, ok," I whispered, "calm down!" But his spirit was contagious, and we both laughed. He sniffed.

"But I have something to tell you…" Cry said, just as my smile was torn from my face: I saw that Ted was walking right behind Emma.

Whatever this means is bad, I thought.

Emma stopped, her eyes shifting all around like a Spriggan in a fishbowl. "I don't feel good, I'm going home," she said. "I texted

W.W. Marplot

you—your nanny Gretel is going to pick me up. My mom didn't pick up her phone."

Ted spoke, the creep. "I'm walking her to get her things." He seemed proud. I wondered about all this, and it showed.

Ted stared at Cry's giggly face for six of my heartbeats, and then he looked at me suspiciously for another four. I wondered if Thryst would strike. He didn't.

"It's ok," Emma indicated and slipped me a small note while Ted was suddenly called by Mr. Blake, the vice principal.

"Mr. Ted. I need to talk to you about what happened earlier," came stern words of authority, and Ted was whisked away, which is always nice.

Emma turned and left suddenly and without explanation.

CHAPTER 26

Arty

"Tell me," I ordered Cry as we walked to science class, "what you said you had to tell me."

Emma had ditched us without explaining. All her note said, in curly script, was

It's ok, read ur texts tho soon tho

After her sudden appearance with Ted and her sudden disappearance home.

Cry told me that while I sat in math class, he could "not concentrate" in gym, so he left it early to meet me. We saw, down the hall, Emma walking with Ted just before first period ended.

"But there was a guy, a tall guy, really thin, I thought it was a deliveryman or something, walking with Mrs. What's-her-name, the guidance counselor."

"So?" I asked.

"When the guy, he had a beard, saw Ted and Emma, he went right over to them, so I got closer because I knew Emma's secret, but I didn't think Ted knew, and who was this guy? And you told me to look for anything weird."

"This qualifies—keep going…What happened?"

Cry was panting with words; they came out with no tears and no grammar. "The guy said 'What is your name? That was you, out late last night, huh? What is your name?' Or something like that."

My face panicked into various colors, I could feel it, and Cry saw it. "What did he do?" I pressed. "Was there anything flying around? Did anyone see?"

Cry answered me, then claimed, "That was it."

Of course, that was not it. "Did Emma say anything? Was she ok?"

"He wasn't talking to her, he was talking to Ted."

I stopped walking. Cry's answer sunk into my head as my body sunk against a locker. "Are you sure? How do you know?"

"Because Ted stood still, and Emma took a few steps backwards like this." Cry did so, backing into three kids who swerved around him. "And then the man, he was all in brown, went over to them. He went up to Ted. That was it."

These words sunk in; they were heavy enough to slide me down the locker, my back scraping on its lock.

Cry stepped back and bent over me and went on because that was still not "it." "What's-her-name, the guidance counselor, she pulled the man away from Ted and said that he can't talk to the students, it's a rule, there's security, and all that, and she said he would appreciate that when his own children were here. Or something like that. That was it. And then he asked what Ted's name was, and she said the security thing again. That was it. The man said, 'Sorry,' and walked away with her, but he kept looking at Ted. It was weird. Then the bell rang, and everyone came. That was it."

That was it.

"I hope Ted is ok," Cry said.

That was definitely it.

I needed to look at my text messages, but we are not allowed during class, and class was starting.

CHAPTER 27

Arty

There I was, with Cry, in science—biology—class. Emma's note said, "It's ok," so I tried to calm down. She'd be spending her Thursday alone, with a fairy tale creature at home, alone. I had to last in crowded classrooms with crazy children, questioning teachers, and curious Ted-types all day. So, yeah, she was ok, for sure. I had the hard job.

Sitting in biology, one of two classes that Cry and I have together, focusing on normal things, was impossible. In my head were lists of things all trying to be listed first. Emma and Ted. This man in brown that Cry saw. Where *Thryst the Sometimes Magically Invisible* was, what he was doing, and how many small victims were piling like fallen trees.

And Cry kept whispering to me every time he thought of another "awesome" thing we could do with our very own Dwarf, especially a "Battle Lord Dwarf," which Thryst must be, according to Cry.

When I was then called on to answer a question that I didn't hear, it was explained to me that I wouldn't learn anything by staring out the window. I could only listen politely and nod instead of saying, "*I thought I heard a Dwarf growling*" and "*I'm trying to save lives here.*"

After science, Cry asked if he could look in Thryst's eyes again. He seemed to think it was a video game. It wasn't. He suggested we could both look at the same time, and play "online." I was getting tired of him and his strange ideas coming at me while I only had a few minutes to plan: *Should I cut class? How do you do that? Is there a permission slip?*

I hurried us through the hallway. Thryst was with us. I could see him and wondered if anyone else could. When the Dwarf suddenly jerked toward our school librarian—like maybe he was going to speak to her!—I had to jump in front of him, posed like a praying mantis, and tell him with my eyes that I wasn't ready to make introductions.

Then, after passing three teachers in a row and their three double-takes, I detoured us into the auditorium to regroup and to pretend, if I had to, that Thryst was part of some play we were rehearsing.

This gave me an idea: I could dress him up. Put a costume on him, to hide his muscles, his weapons, some of his dirty, leathery, animal-skinned outfit. And maybe a wig over his head, or a clean hoodie to replace the one he mined with.

With a quick look at Thryst, his eyes told me: *That Is Probably Not Going to Happen.*

I collapsed into a seat near the auditorium stage, and Cry followed, crying; tears of excitement, I guess. I wanted to cry, too—tears of giving up. Thryst studied my shifting emotions as I told Cry again to get to his own class and keep his eyes open and keep the secret and I would see him at lunch, the period after next. Cry offered me a high five, then a fist-bump, before heading up the aisle. He was having fun. I couldn't.

As Cry left through one set of doors, high above at the back of the auditorium, another set opened at the other aisle and someone came in suddenly, a long body bending forward and its head searching purposefully. The man in brown.

Thryst moved quickly, slicing the ropes that held the stage curtains open, and the Dwarf hid himself that way. The best my human brain could come up with so quickly was to throw myself on the sticky floor, which was bad since my seat then squeaked noisily while rocking upright and back for a few seconds.

I held my breath as the auditorium doors closed. The man didn't try to find me. So, I reversed the action: I decided to find the man.

Which didn't take long. He was in the hallway, talking to any kids who happened to walk by, and I was able to listen from around a corner and peek with enough skill to make a few notes.

The man:

1. Dressed all in brown. Cry was right.

2. Not holding anything in his hands, and nothing glowed from his bag, a brown satchel, overflowing with papers and books.

3. Wore a brown, short, round cap.

4. Had long legs and long arms.

5. Bent over to talk to the much smaller schoolkids, and was obnoxious about it, and asked about Ted.

6. Had a short, clipped, neat, reddish-brown beard, just as Emma and I had seen on his shining face last night. It was wimpy, like a professor's. Thryst probably had a better beard when he was a baby.

Thryst went unseen as I listened, but I knew he was there. That smell.

"Do any of you unnecessary little loinfruits know that other little boy, in grey shorts and red t-shirt with a green monster emblazoned? He was walking with a young lady before?" The man's voice was deep and flowing like a river of chocolate milk.

"No. Who do you mean?" came answers from below him.

"I am trying to find him. It is imperative."

Silence.

"He is a sneak, and he *spies*." The man hissed these words. Turning his voice back to honey, he went on. "Not a nice boy, not like you proper children."

"Probably Ted," a girl's voice said.

"Don't tell him anything," another girl whispered loudly.

"Who are you?" a third girl asked upward.

"Yes, of course," the honey voice flowed, "you should be careful, correct, and conscious. Very good. But, of course, it is right here on my name tag. So please tell me—"

The man was interrupted as a boy spoke. "A-B-C-D—what is that? You made that up. It's supposed to say your name on your nametag."

"Ah, my good, little, observant, pedantic boy. Do you know Ted?"

"Don't tell him," said a girl's voice, joined now by others who were curious of the scene, of the man.

"I have candy. You should tell me," the man said.

What a weirdo, I thought. *Is he from another century or something?*

I realized I shouldn't rule this out.

"Does he live in the town?" The deep voice rose a little, annoyed, calling after the children, who were dispersing and bored with the stranger. "I saw him late last night, where he should not have been! In Belle Terre village. Hmmmm? If you help me, I will show you something fantastical!"

Pathetic, I thought.

"This is why no one likes children," he finished as part threat, part opinion, as Barry, our front door security guard, arrived.

"Sir, you have to come with me. Let's go," Barry said, then scoffed. "Clever nametag. Can I ask your real name, Mr. Alphabet?"

The bell rang, and I headed to English class.

CHAPTER 28

Arty

ne more period, and I can check my phone, I thought. And, while I was supposed to be learning some useless thing about grammar and copular verbs, I was also thinking:

I wonder if Emma has run into the man in brown? I wonder where Thryst is? I wonder why Emma was with Ted? I wonder why the man is asking for Ted? I wonder if Cry has told anyone, or everyone? I wonder who that man is? I wonder what to do next? I wonder why Thryst let Cry see him? I wonder what Emma's texts will say. I wonder what her Spriggan did in school.

And I wonder what a copular verb is.

Otherwise, unless you count everyone asking me if I was sick and telling me that I didn't look good, third period English class was fine. *Wonderful*, in fact.

The bell rang, and I disobeyed school rules by running to the cafeteria so I could obey school rules and use my phone only there. Cry met me, and we sat apart and alone as I read Emma's texts.

Leaving out the symbols and emojis and emoticons and finger drawings, they said what Cry had already told me, that the man in brown, the same from last night in front of my house, tried to talk to Ted. She decided to go home sick because Sprugly was "*hyperpestering*" and she was afraid Ted would follow her, but luckily, he didn't.

"Ted had to go the office and explain what happened with that man," Cry informed me.

"Good," we both said together.

There were more texts from Emma.

> Im afraid of this othr guy, tho
> he ws after Ted, nt me—ignrd me

> Ted sd he didn't no wht it ws abt. but sounded
> afraid, then he said 'y don't YOU tell ME?"

> I h8 Ted, followed me all day, sai I
> wuz in his dream (creepopotomous)

> Oh and I got this->

She had sent a picture, then more texts.

> don't know what it is but it is NOT paper. when the
> man went to Ted it fell out of his bag. Sprug told me.
> i picked it up and have not stopped shaking since
> hurry home.

I zoomed in on the picture.

"Is that all she said?" Cry asked.

"Just a few more new ones that she's home alone and drawing and waiting for me."

"She's a good drawer," Cry said. It's sentences like this that I didn't have time for today.

I zoomed in on the picture. It looked familiar. I knew what to do—but not why.

CHAPTER 29

Arty

I let it all sink in and was happy to rest for a minute, a new plan formulating in my brain.

To keep the big boy busy, I handed Cry my folder of notes. "Here," I said. "You might as well see all of it. I'll keep a lookout while you read."

I kept a lookout, my second one in two days, my second one ever. Although now that I trusted *Thryst the Crafty* would not cause a fairy Armageddon, there were new mysteries: Ted and the man in brown.

Cry read, and now and then he took a bite of a large sandwich that looked disgusting. I ate one of my two apples.

Again, my thoughts ran as wild as a Dwarf up a tree. *Will there be more fairies popping up "here and now" like Sprugly said? Maybe some have already. Maybe this man in brown is selling them, or buying them. Those kids over there: maybe they each have a fairy they're keeping from us, thinking they're the only ones. Maybe those jerks over by the garbage pails have Orcs they play with, or maybe those giggling girls have wizards doing their homework. Maybe every kid in here has a Sprite, or a Brownie, or a Bugga-boo, or a Pixie, or a Wight...*

The list of creatures from the old legends was long.

Maybe everyone here was keeping a secret, and fairies only show themselves to special friends or walk in disguise. Or never come out and are never seen; they only whisper while kids sleep or protect them without them knowing. Maybe all the little accidents in our lives, the bad unlucky things, or small lucky chances, are actually being controlled in secret and from another world. Each event is matched to a folktale being, and it is all real.

I started my second apple. Next to me Cry said, "Ewwww."

"What?" I asked.

"Is the Spriggan really that ugly?"

"Yep, from what I saw."

"Do his eyes really open from the top down?"

"I didn't get that close. But that's what Emma says…"

"This is awesome," Cry said, finished with the notes but not his sandwich. "We can have Dwarf wars, or battle the Dwarves against the Elves."

"We have a Dwarf and a Spriggan. It won't be much of a battle. I have seen them try to fight."

"Are they magic?"

I gave Cry a look he must be used to. His disemboweled sandwich was lopped to one side in his hand; some of its guts lay between his fingers and shined on his bowly cheeks. Just a regular, nice, ordinary kid. Big and pink.

"We can have Thryst build us cave mansions, protected by magic runes," he said as he chewed. His imagination was unstoppable; it almost made me envious. "We can mine for silver, and gold, too. He can build us sorcery rings, jeweled crowns and necklaces, crystal balls…"

"Where are you getting this from?" I laughed.

"Don't you know anything about Dwarves?" the expert replied, while trying to fit a large angle of bread into his mouth.

"I have a ton of stuff about *fairies*," I replied. "That's what they call all these things from fairy tales, folktales, old stories, riddles, nursery rhymes, whatever. I have lists of books, and I'm going to find the oldest ones and keep digging."

"Like a Dwarf in a mine. Awesome." Cry had dropped the rest of his sandwich, but a grey ooze still coated his face.

"Yeah," I said and handed Cry a napkin. Then another. "Do you know what 'New Island' is?"

"No. What?"

"I don't know. The Spriggan said it."

"Cool," he said, wiping his large, smeared lips and cheeks. "We need to see what kind of magic spells they have that we can use. We should bring Thryst with us over to that group of jerks and see what…"

Cry was eyeing the pack of large teens that we daily avoid. I interrupted him. "Noooo, he's not for that. I want to find out why he is here and how to help him."

"Help him what?" Cry asked.

"Exactly," I answered.

Cry packed his garbage in his hands like a trash snowball and finished a water bottle. I was down to my second apple's core. He said, "All you need is a map."

"What do you mean?" I asked him, smiling with curiosity and apple juice. You will see why soon.

"All great fantasy genre stuff starts with a good map."

"This is not a genre," I said. "But it's weird that you say that…" I then showed him on my phone the picture Emma sent me, shading it like a periscope's eyepiece for only Cry to see.

"Where did you get that!" he shrieked.

"Emma. She said that man in brown dropped it." I pulled it away as a crowd went by.

"It's a map!"

"It has runes," I added with a nod, "and they look like ones in some books I found. We have to be careful. But…"

Cry's face was a globe on which the oceans were smiles. As I spoke, he put his head down into his arms on the table. I couldn't tell if he was laughing or crying, but he finished my sentence for me: "…this is awesome." The words were muffled downward into his own chest.

I caught myself smiling also. His enthusiasm was contagious.

Then I told him something I'd just decided to put on my list. After school, Emma and I would go to the university, a few miles out of town, to use their huge library. It had a whole room of old maps, so we could figure this out, to try to find New Island. He could meet us there—if he wanted to see map runes, that is.

Without lifting his head, he happily swore secrecy, again. He didn't ask about what was growing in my yard. That was good, since I don't want to talk about that yet.

CHAPTER 30

Emma

rty keeps saying that, and I didn't want to talk about that yet either.

Nor about anything else—not with Ted around. This is Emma. As you saw, Ted just *happened* to be at the nurse's office when I was. To give you an idea of how weird and spoiled he is, here is the conversation he had with our school nurse.

Nurse Loretta: "Hello again, Ted. Bad dreams today, just in time for a math test? Like yesterday?

Ted: "I'm fine. Can I go home with Emma? Make sure she is ok?"

Nurse Loretta: "Of course not."

Ted: "Why?"

Nurse Loretta: "Obviously, no one is allowed to just go home with their friends whenever they want."

Ted: "Well, I thought you would make an exception in my case."

Nurse Loretta: "Why?"

Ted: "Excuse me?"

Nurse; "Why would we make an exception for you?"

Ted: "What do you mean?"

Back to me. I had my own problems, and they were bigger than Ted's: Arty's German nanny, Gretel, picked me up from school. My mom usually can't get off work, and Gretel used to watch me a lot when Arty and I were small, so she and I go *way back*. And *way back* is where I sat in her big SUV truck, hoping to keep Spruggie

Baby as far from Gretel as possible, explaining my distance with, "I don't want to get you sick."

The drive home was a long and challenging five minutes during which Gretel made some direct, thick, German-ish small talk.

"How iss your mom?" she asked.

"Fine," I said. "Busy."

"You are lookink fery varm." Gretel's foreign, stern, but loving accent was still so cute to me, it reminded me of a strong, upright tulip.

"I know, I am chilly though. I must have a cold."

"Strong voman should nefer get sick. You are schtill ein baby!" she teased.

"I'm thirteen..." I answered.

"You vorget German speakink?"

"Ummmm.... thirteen is..." I counted to twelve in German in my head, my limit, "zwolf, plus one!"

"Zat's cheating." She smiled. "I liken your scarf."

"Thanks. It was a gift, I forget from who," I said.

"Did you hear about deer?" she asked.

"No—huh? Vut deer? I mean, what deer?" I don't hang around Gretel as much as I used to, and her words are sometimes a challenge, especially with her willingness to throw some in where they don't belong. Sometimes I think she does it on purpose, but eventually I worked out that she was talking about an incident with the many deer that live in the woods and by the beach around our neighborhood. Most people think the animals are a pain, and a danger, but I think it's pretty cool that they live with us. There's a lot of open forest and space between houses, and not too many yards are fenced in completely, so the deer are able to get around and survive.

Gretel told me that people saw a group of thirty or more—big bucks with their pointy antlers, but also females and young ones—running around together, like a stampede. They went through the roads then headed to the beach, the whole group.

"Vow," I said, pretending to remember my German but realizing I sounded like someone on a forced vacation. "That's strange, you never see more than a few of them together."

"Ja, zees vere schtikink togezer. Zey are at zee beach now, vant to go unt see?"

"Sure," I said. This was very *eeenteresting*, as Gretel would say— but then I felt Sprugly near my ear as a reminder of what was *really* interesting. "Uh, no, you know, I should just get home, I don't feel good. I'll check it out later, that's what tomorrows are for." I tried not to try too hard. "If I feel better."

"Ok. *Sehr gut*," Gretel said, which means *very good*. She pulled into our woodsy neighborhood, passed the gates and bright walls into Belle Terre—the same entrance that seemed so different last night in the dark. Gretel went on to tell me that the police were down at the beach, keeping an eye on things, with people that worked for the town, perhaps the environmental conservation people also, she thought, seeing all the green trucks.

"Oh, well that's good," I said. Then silence. I had other things on my mind. And on my shoulder. She didn't mention a man in brown, and neither did I.

Finally, we were at my house. Gretel asked if I needed anything, reminded me that I could call her, and said goodbye—all with a funny look. She knew I knew that look.

At last I was home where I knew I could be alone. It was a beautiful day, and spring was springing everywhere, a perfect distraction from my worries. The wet of the morning, the slick shine on the trees and paths, all had dried, sending last night's rain back to the sky.

I sat outside and listened to the leaves wave in answer to the small voice of the breeze. I watched the birds fly from tree to tree, from yard to yard, and hop happily in the grass. I did not see any deer. It was quiet enough to hear the beach gulls when the wind blew from the bay, a horn blast of the large passenger ferry, the whistle of the train from the village station, and the Spriggan whispering in my ear.

"She's coming," he said.

"Who?" I asked.

"Tonight," he said, his eyes blinking up, then down. Gross.

"That's not a name. Who is coming?" I asked.

"They all know," he said.

"Who? My mom?" I guessed, though I doubted it was that simple.

"Tonight," he said.

"Ouch!" I said.

Sprugly flapped himself into and out of my hair and in that one millisecond tangled it all. Again. *So annoying, finding an untrained Spriggan,* I thought. I went inside for a hairbrush and my journal. The ugly fairy followed but didn't say anything more, and didn't hint either—no books fell off shelves, no pages turned, no globes spun. I don't think I have a globe. I didn't want any new information anyway, I decided. Leaving my bag and the man-in-brown's strange not-paper behind, I avoided the flailing Spriggan-wings and left my room.

As I did, I heard two sounds: my phone buzzing and moaning from my mother's room down the hall. The phone showed a text from Arty, saying only that he had a new plan and wanted to go to the university after school, and a promise of "more later." Strange, but not strange enough to interest me. I then recognized the sounds from my mom's room—it was her voice.

"Mom," I called out, going to her room. "Why are you home?" My voice dropped as I thought that *she* should be asking *me* this. She didn't.

"Headache," she moaned.

"Where's your car?"

"My friend borrowed it."

"Oh. I tried to text you, I—" I began.

"Honey, did you hear any noises outside, or voices?"

She might have heard Sprugly, so I said that I didn't.

"Ok, honey." With that, I think she went back to sleep. She didn't come out, but I wasn't relieved that I wasn't relieved.

Sitting on the lawn near my garden, I daydreamed and watched a blooming, bright, happy world.

In between moments, I sketched. My pages lit by the overhead sun, I observed my Spriggan jumpfly easily through blades of grass, and those seemed to bend with him and watch him and wave. He went up and down trees with a light grace and unimaginably soft steps. He danced around the flowers—and they danced back. He was at home in nature, with an understanding that seemed mystical. Maybe I could draw it. *Let's see Arty explain all this with his science and his accurate factual footnotes*, I thought.

In a thick patch of thorny brush where our backyard lawn ends, I noticed a small hare. She stuck out her head, nose and whiskers twitching, her ears at attention. Another emerged, forelegs on the grass. I didn't see Sprug, though where he last sat was a hole exposing a dark brown bowl of earth, and a matching clump of grass nearby. *Is he hiding? Tunneling?* I looked back to the two hares, but there were now four, no, five of them, and they were closer, fully onto the grass, out from their shelter. Six.

This would make a cute sketch also, if it wasn't for that bright white sneaker in the background.

That I thought I saw.

My heart jumped, a breeze blew, the sun blazed my face for a moment, and with a second look, the sneaker was gone. I guessed that a foot was in it, and the person attached to the foot had run off.

I breathed and wondered what to do as a small red robin landed among the hares, then a group of birds came, a mini-flock—but of all different sizes and colors. They milled around nervously, as if in as much shock as I was. The bunnies didn't move, despite the flurry of wings and anxious squawks. The morning stillness was further broken by noise from the farther woods: the rustling of animals in the trees, small paws scurrying on the ground, the recognizable clicking of squirrel-talk, a ticking woodpecker, raccoons scratching in the garbage pails, deer jumping, foxes crouching.

They were gathering together. And all looking in the same direction at something they were not used to…

…as was Ted…

…at Sprugly.

Ted's white sneakers had returned. My Spriggan had come back also and sat just a few feet from me, covered in dirt, his orange lumpiness settled at the foot of a large tree. I stared along with the animals.

Ted did not move but seemed confused and simply glared, stiff. He was away behind some trees; maybe he thought I couldn't see him.

I was annoyed and slammed my pad down, ready to chase Ted away, when Sprugly sprang and climbed to the top of the large tree, partly with his weird hands and partly in short winged flights. I watched, but again the sun streamed through a gap in the new leaves, straight to my eyes and to the back of my brain so that I lost sight of both my Spriggan and my admirer. I wanted to climb the tree and escape with Sprugly. I started to draw again.

After a minute, and with frantic noise, the animals all departed at once—hares to the bushes, birds to the air, squirrels to the hollows of trees, deer scattering over fences like Russian dancers. As cold tingles traveled up each of my vertebrae, I saw why: A large deer had come from across my front yard in a loud fury and was now chasing Ted. And this deer was not a deer; it was a man, all in brown, and swinging long arms that held a brown hat, running and jumping over rough bramble where the bushes grew thick. Ted had escaped, though, his messy black hair was a blur, and he made it past the gate at the back of my yard and through the neighbor's.

I ran also, to my house. I heard the man yelling as I did—but again, as in school, he was interested in me but was yelling at Ted.

"You have what's mine!" I thought I heard, though Sprugly had perched on my shoulder, loudly, and he seemed heavy. More shouts came but faded. "You don't understand! Why were you there? For 1752? For 1752?"

Huh? The man's voice was deep, and his accusation was strong, but both died in the wind and distance. I paused at my back door for just a second to hear more clearly.

"It is mine! I need that page! You stole it!" Then the voice was gone.

The map page. I was stung with the fact that the man in brown *should have* been after me.

I was torn as to whether to help Ted—!—and tell the tall, scary stranger that I had what he wanted, or just wait for Arty. I decided that I was mad at both Ted and the man in brown and went to my room, where Sprugly was three times his normal size, his facial ugliness alone enough to protect a family of fairies, and he clumsily banged from window to window for the view.

I lay on my bed to think.

I heard, outside, the man's voice again, distant but clear, smooth and threatening. "Don't look into their eyes."

This was making me mad. Sprug did not move at this or react in any way. He was in my closet looking for something to wear, in fact. I considered going to the window to yell back at the man but heard, through my own shut door, my mother's door opening down the hall and her footsteps.

She called, "Hon?"

"Yeah?"

"Oh, ok. We should get a dog. A big one," she yawned. And I heard her door close again.

I went to the window and saw and heard nothing. Soon there were Spriggan-whisperings in my ear. "She's coming."

Again.

"She's coming. Tonight."

Great, I thought, *maybe "she" can explain.*

I waited for Gretel and Arty to pick me up for our trip to the university.

CHAPTER 31

Emma

I hadn't moved. I was too tired to draw or write or think anymore—in fact, I napped under the lunchtime sun while Sprugly climbed trees.

I awoke, warmed by the sun. And since Arty was taking his time finishing school, I started to think about our childhood and also about Cry, who I met a few years ago...

CHAPTER 32

Ted

t is better if I tell about Cry. He was my friend first.

CHAPTER 33

Emma

ince Ted won't be fair, or nice, Arty and I decided that it is better that I should tell about Cry.

CHAPTER 34

Ted

ut they realized what is best, and they gave in, of course, so I get to tell it.

Emma

es, but he promised to be nice.

Ted

Whatever. Ok—Ted here. Emma couldn't keep me out of the story. Which is lucky for her. And for you. Because soon you'll see how I was one step ahead of them.

And it wasn't easy—I'd been having bad dreams, and weird dreams, and daydreams, too, sometimes. The teachers picked on me sometimes, but all the kids loved me: I had a lot of friends.

And maybe a few enemies. This alphabet guy, in brown all the time, talking funny to everyone and asking about me. Something in my brain told me to stay away from him, and something in my dreams, too. I didn't know why. I'd been pretty smart about staying ahead of Arty and Emma. It'd been worth a little trouble, but that guy scared me. But I had friends to protect me, too. Emma and Arty didn't even know that I knew what I knew.

Cry did. But he didn't. I was helping them, though, right?

Cry was my friend, too, but what a crybaby. Don't tell him I said that, he is pretty big and pretty strong. His hands fit around my whole head, and his head is like a bowling ball. I watched him pick up this kid Jason once. And I don't mean *grab-him-in-a-bear-hug-and-lean-back*. I mean, Cry held his arms out straight, grabbed Jason by the elbows, and lifted him off the ground like he was a kitten. I saw him *throw* a kid once when they were playing around, wrestling. They want him bad for the football team, and his family are total athletes and always working out or playing every sport in the world at their house. But he isn't that into it. He reads a lot and is pretty emotional. The sport-kids love him, and the bad-kids give him a hard time, but only when they're in a group. I've watched all this. But Cry is not that interesting otherwise. He's boring.

Emma is much more interesting and way cooler.

And for the first time back then, even Arty was doing something besides reading—so you never know, people can change. We made a good team...someone said that...

I decided to help them whether they wanted it or not. I was good for them, right?

Arty had to get out of the books and see what was really going on. There was a lot.

So, Arty and Emma and Cry ditched me after school and made it to the big college library, but I caught up with them later. Like I said, one step ahead...

CHAPTER 37

Arty

Sorry about Ted's chapter. But, yes, we could not keep him out of it completely—though we still wondered how he was already in so deep. He's a troublemaker, but was he actually involved with strange men who knew about fairies? Or did he just break the brown guy's window or ride his bike across his lawn or something?

After the cafeteria, nothing much happened in school, and I made it home with Thryst popping in and out as usual, looking around, then hanging out, then looking around, then hanging out.

Emma's story scared me, the map excited me, and since she couldn't get a ride to my house, Gretel and I picked up my co-adventurer right after school.

I explained to Emma the new plan: The image she had sent me—the one she now regretted "stealing" from the man in brown—though, as I told her, Sprugly was an accomplice—was only a piece of a map, since the edges didn't end cleanly.

She handed it to me.

Like Emma said, it wasn't paper but some flimsy, almost-glass and almost-metal and see-through material. I recognized parts of the area where we live—the lines and borders and coast of Belle Terre, its village in the middle, our neighborhood to the north, and the bordering towns and coasts on each side. The shapes were all there, and it had an old style that reminded me of the ancient maps

I'd seen at the historical society and museum in town. Ha, joining their Youthful Historians Club was NOT a waste of time—and the university had a whole room dedicated to old maps.

"Only you would know this," Emma said.

"See? Joining the Youthful Historians Club was NOT a waste of time," I countered.

Gretel drove us to the university with the usual talk about pickup plans, not being late for dinner this time, and all that. I was tempted to tell Gretel about Thryst. Her stern face had lines of suspicion—it's hard to fool someone who helped you learn how to walk—but I decided not to tell her anything. Yet.

Emma sat in the SUV's back row of seats, since Sprugly was digging and rummaging within her clothes and being his usual energetic *hypernuisance*. My dangerous Dwarf hadn't decided to show up yet.

On the university campus, the main library sits somewhere in the middle among the many other buildings that have classrooms, meeting rooms, offices, other libraries, and the dorms where students live and sleep and eat and have parties that you can watch on social media.

The late afternoon was still bright. Emma told me about the beautiful day I had missed, even though she knew I didn't care. Yes, I wish I had more daylight to get things done, but clouds, rain, snow, mist, hail—they're all ok with me because I'm usually inside. If this were her chapter, Emma would describe the university campus architecture, give the colors of the trees and flowers in bloom, a cute version of the thoughts of the bees and birds, a frustratingly unscientific description of the scent on the air, and a summary of the buzzing talk and loud laughter among the college students whose classes were ending.

None of this data matters, except that it was sunny and warm, and the weather was supposed to stay that way for the next five days.

The university's Main Library is called that because it's huge and because there are many other libraries, one for almost every subject taught here: math, physics, engineering, computers, English, and the rest. I love it here. I come almost every week to study and do my projects; it's a cool place to wander around and explore and meet adventurous-looking things.

For example: Emma and I were in the "catacombs"—what my dad calls the underground passages that tunnel from building to building all across the campus. They can be a real time-sucking maze because at certain points you have to know which door to use to continue the path. Which is part of the fun. In each building there are also rooftop passages and floors in-between floors.

There's usually no one down here, in the Main Library's lower levels, which is also at the center of the catacombed hallways. If we lost electricity for a week, then this would be a great place to play a war game or a fantasy, role-playing, nerdo Dungeons-and-Drag-ons-magic-imagination game, the ones that Cry likes. You can get from every building to every other one without going outside. You could lose yourself, and your friends, and your enemies, for hours down here.

Emma and I entered the library's deepest floor—two below the nearest other people—and found a row of desks in a dusty, drab corner surrounded by old books on tall metal shelves. We were also close to a door that I knew was a shortcut exit. For emergencies only...

As we sat and tested the lonesome silence by being quiet ourselves, Thryst appeared, behind Emma, standing as if guarding the row of desks. I thought Emma would scream, but as she told me later, Sprugly had warned her with a whisper.

The four of us waited for Cry.

"Did he get lost?" Emma asked, attempting a text message but thwarted by our underground location.

"I think he knows how to get here," I said. "Let's get started without him."

For me, this was simple, though I was glad to have Emma as my laboratory assistant: there are books here that are much older and have more about fairies than the books from the village library, and there are hundreds of old maps in wide, flat drawers and filing cabinets that I needed to search to see if they might help me understand the map page that came from the man in brown.

"Here," I said to Emma, taking out a long, pre-prepared list. "These are books to look for, the titles and numbers." I ripped the paper in half, handed her the bottom. "I'll do the rest; the map research room is just over there. Meet me back here when you've got all the books."

"Can we switch?" she asked, explaining, "because you know your way around these five thousand aisles of bookshelves with fifty shelves each, and Thryst is easier to travel with." She twitched with Sprugly active in her long hair.

We switched and agreed to watch out for the man in brown. Or Ted.

After a half hour, I returned with my arms—and the large arms of my steady Dwarf—filled with books that were mostly large and old so that my heavy breath puffed dry and dusty, chugging like an old, tired choo-choo train. *Thryst the Happy*—he definitely liked being underground with us—hardened himself in another lookout pose as I sat at a large wooden desk, emptied my backpack, and spread the materials in front of me like they were magic crystals and potions that held all the coolest secrets of the earth.

This was fun.

Emma returned, and she looked sad.

"Where are the maps?" I asked. "Did you go to the map room?"

"We got kicked out."

I laughed. "I'll do it. Wait here."

She and Thryst waited. In ten minutes, I was back with pain-in-the-neck tubes of all sizes. Inside were maps of Belle Terre from past and present and every decade years in between. The long, white, cardboard containers were under my arms and chin, and I looked like a walking set of bagpipes but made it back to the big desk by kicking one of them along over the last twenty feet or so.

I had what I needed, and this was now even more fun.

Except: Just as Emma opened her mouth to speak, we heard music, like from someone's cell phone, and that someone was coming.

Thryst was stiff, alert, and still visible, so I wondered if we were in for a battle. But as I watched, my guardian Dwarf did a curious thing: he bowed and stepped aside. It was Cry approaching, lumbering noisily from the opposite end of the long row of bookshelves that *Thryst the Watchman* watched.

"Awesome," Cry said.

He came to the desk, struggling with his backpack as if it were a heavy thing that didn't *want* to be carried.

Without a word, my large, round friend sat next to me, and without a word and without delay, he opened his bag—and a *something* came out. Something *ran* out. Something ran out *holding a small branch and leaves from an oak tree*. Something ran out holding a small branch and leaves from an oak tree *and ran up the nearest bookshelf to the top*. And there, the *something* spun around a few times.

I could describe the *something*, and try to identify it, but—as if to save me this step—at that moment, the thick leaves of a *History of Fairy Kingdoms* book flapped loudly, settled on a page, and, well, the thing that was spinning around on the bookshelves was, I quote:

> *…dressed in green, was redheaded, had pointy ears, a turned-up nose, a short face, and tiny wings. It would help brownies, and mislead travelers, unless they were given gifts regularly, such as clothes….*

"Oh no!" Emma said, laughing as she looked at the open book's pictures. "Cry, she will raid your closets and make a mess. Good luck!"

"I don't think she is 'ugly,' why does it say that?" Cry mumbled sadly.

Cry had found a *Pixie*. A strange one. It looked like a girl.

CHAPTER 38

Arty

The Pixie had a cold, or something. She couldn't stop sneezing: a funny, squeaky sound, with a kind of whistle at the end. Cry said he had found her that way. Sneezing. She was in his driveway, hopping toward his house, when he got off the bus after school. No one else saw.

It was the familiar *kid finds a fairy* pattern. I took two pages of notes.

The poor little thing looked afraid as it sat high on the bookshelf. "Oh!" Emma suddenly exclaimed, with a twitch of her head, which meant that Sprugly had spoken, and sure enough her Spriggan then darted off away from us.

"She seems friendly. Harmless, right?" I asked Cry, pointing at the Pixie.

"So far. She's like a baby, acts like a tiny bird or a puppy mouse or something," Cry answered and rubbed his eyes, wiping them with his arm. I saw no tears, and he sounded fine.

He went on. "She didn't like the trip in the bag, and I had to cover the noise with some music. What a pain." He sniffed. "I'd rather have a Dwarf, or a dragon. Want to trade?" he asked me.

We all looked at Thryst, who was staring up at the bookshelf, fingering the blade of his axe. With the Pixie was Sprug, who seemed to be in a protective stance, strangely still and quiet, and looking a little thicker in the face and legs.

"This could get interesting," Cry said.

"Makes sense…" Emma began. When we looked toward her, she explained, "Before he flew up there, Sprugly whispered, '*One of the ones*' to me. That means he will protect this fairy. Last night, he said that to me, too, that me and Thryst were '*not ones.*'"

"Now we're learning…" I said, scribbling.

"Awesome," said Cry, "but what's next? I can't take care of this Pixie thing, no way."

"How did you get this far?" Emma asked.

"It was easy, except for the noise, and that she does not like the backpack, and that everything went wrong. She likes trees. She went up in one after she found me. And whenever I looked for her, she was still there." Cry grabbed his nose, then wiped his eyes, then went on, "I figured it was mine, and some kind of fairy, after what I saw at school with you guys, so before I got in the car with my mom, I filled my backpack with some branches, and she hopped in."

"Your mom jumped in?" I asked, joking, of course.

We laughed. Thryst mumbled, "*Tarrrnnnn,*" low and slow.

The three fairy creatures seemed content to stay as they were as we three human creatures, Emma, Cry, and I, read the books and looked at the maps. I gave Cry a bunch to read about Pixies.

"Awesome," he said after a few minutes.

Emma and I looked at him. She asked him, "Say more, please."

"Dragons," he said. He should not have, though, because it caused a medium-sized event: *Thryst the Natural Dragon Enemy* began to gurgle. Then he started moving his feet, like he was pacing in place, but it soon grew in force until he was stamping the floor and our pens and pencils jumped. The Pixie squeaked, and Sprugly sprung, coming down to fly in circles above the Dwarf's head. This did not help Thryst's mood. His eyes glowed, and the gurgling formed into strong, loud words that were indecipherable because he was so excited and pulling at his beard. This was a Dwarf rant, a mountain of a hissy fit.

Watching this, Emma spoke. "I have a theory," she said, sounding scientific. "Note that once Arty found Thryst, I saw Arty and

found Spruggie. Then after Cry met the four of us, *he* then found…"
Emma pointed toward the upper shelves but paused, since the little
Pixie wound up for a sneeze (*eee eee eee*), then sneezed (*schooooeeeee*).
"…her," Emma finished. "What's her name, Cry?"

We looked at our fellow fairy-finding friend. He started to talk,
lost his voice, cleared his throat, started again, choked up, stuttered,
and finally went ahead with these risky words: "Um…Uh…Peanut?"

"Cute." Emma went on directly, "Fine. Peanut. So, maybe that's
the pattern."

"What is?" Cry asked.

"Once you see one, you find one," Emma answered with two
swings of her arms.

"Maybe," I said, but secretly I liked the idea a lot since it meant
I was first.

"Probably," Emma said. "But why?"

"Same old question," I said, shaking my head.

"Can I make my guess?" Cry asked. "Can I get in on the bet?"

"No," I said, chewing on the delay like fatty steak.

"Sure," Emma said, handing a rip of paper to a red-eyed Cry, who
eagerly, furiously scribbled while I tapped my own pen on the desk
as hard as I could. Emma sealed his guess into a new white envelope
that she scooped from deep in my backpack. She combined those into
a third white envelope. I made a note to buy more white envelopes.

"Can we now," I asked through clenched teeth without wanting
an answer, "figure out what we can do and leave the *why's* out of it?"

CHAPTER 39

Cry

This is Cry. I'm not a good storyteller, and I don't like taking notes, but I do read a lot, and I wanted to have my own chapter.

All I can tell you is that I found Peanut the Pixie, but I would have liked a Dwarf better, or a dragon. My Pixie—Peanut—seemed like a baby. She wasn't very strong or useful or exciting. There was so much I would've done with Thryst and Sprugly, and I would've made them do things for us, like go on adventures and have wars. But Arty and Emma would have told me, *No, it isn't scientific*, or *No, it isn't right*, or *No, people would find out, and it would be ruined*, or *No, there are laws against everything you want to do.*

What would have been ruined? I didn't get it. These creatures were ours—we should be able to have fun with them. I think an underground Dwarf mansion filled with jewels and weapons and a secret path to it guarded by Pixies and Spriggans would be a good way to start things. We could be famous, get rich, and control all the legends from now on. People would write new fairy tales, starring the three of us, or even better make a global, viral, Japanese mobile app game with me as the Game Master and with real fantasy creatures. That would make me *very* happy. It's *very* sad that Emma and Arty are so boring.

Peanut was on top of the bookshelves, sneezing and cuddling up to Sprugly. She was quiet now, but when she freaks out she starts *scringing*—like when I first found her.

I made that word up—get it? Screaming and singing at the same time.

What an ugly couple they were. Sprug, wearing a scarf, had placed Peanut in a glove—one of Emma's—but how that all happened I didn't see. Peanut felt safer up high, in trees, or near the ceiling. I didn't know what Spriggans liked. They seemed pretty *pesty*—a word I also made up—but I wouldn't want to see one get mad. Whenever Sprug stared at *Thryst the Awesome,* the Spriggan looked a bit bigger, and more muscular, like he was pumping up for a fight. But it wasn't just an act; Sprugly really did grow. I wondered how big Sprug would get if he really had to fight. The fairy book said that Spriggans were ghosts of Giants. Maybe that's why they were so clumsy: they're not used to being small. Does that make sense?

Most of the time, when we could see him, Thryst stood still and stared at the little fairies up high or gazed at the floor and walls. He was mostly grey, looked like stone, and acted like stone. I thought he looked sad sometimes. But he didn't talk to me.

Arty all of a sudden had something to say. He'd been staring at the glassy map thing and one of the books for a long time.

I will let Emma tell the story of what else happened there in the library, two floors underground.

CHAPTER 40

Emma

I was happy. For now, Sprugly was out of my hair while we talked in the gigantic library. He stayed up high with Peanut. So cute.

Arty explained to us what he knew. The fairy tales we all know, and the lists that he talked about, the encyclopedia, *The Denham Tracts*, and some even older lists—they all came from stories out of Europe. Mostly England and Ireland, some also from the north like Norway and Sweden, some even from Iceland, and some further east—France and Germany. There were fewer and fewer stories that survived as you moved eastward across Europe, he said, or south into Africa. We could, if we wanted, see how the legends changed over the centuries, going back a thousand years or more, and how the creatures acted differently as time went on.

We did not want to do that.

So Arty had another idea. "The other thing I noticed," he said, "was that from 1820 to 1840 or so, the lists stop growing: there are no new creatures. Then from 1860 to 1880, the stories start to die out, too. One book says that once machines were invented, and the world became modern, people were embarrassed by the old fairy stories and stopped telling them. They either didn't believe in them anymore or stopped *admitting* what they believed. Science kind of took over in the 1800s, all over the world. Logic took over. Magic was out."

"Makes sense," Cry said, now staring up at Peanut and Sprug, who were nestled together in my clothes. Weirdly, Sprug had a glove. I don't wear gloves. *Where did he get that glove?* I wondered.

"I guess," Arty went on, "people grew up and stopped believing in these things."

"Or all the *fairies* died," Cry said, upsetting the fairies that were alive and well and a few feet away. Thryst grumbled a few words that all must have begun with a capital G and ended with another g or two. It made the desks rumble. Cry was sorry.

"Or maybe," I joined in, "the fairies went into hiding because they don't like machines, or to get away from magic-less humans." We heard happy, squeaky noises from the bookshelf, like squirrels laughing, yet only sweet silence from the Dwarf. I think they liked my explanation better; no one wants to hear that they are extinct.

Arty frowned but nodded and went on. "But why are they here? Why America? How did they get here? And why now? The only hint we have from Sprugly is 'New Island.' Which I finally found—New Island is Long Island, here, where we live."

"Cool," Cry said.

But I said louder, "What book says that?"

"This one." He pointed to a thin, hardcover book that had a fading blue cover. It was a cracked and tattered old thing, with yellowing pages like dried November leaves. There were very faint markings on the cover that I couldn't read from even a few feet away.

BUT...

When Arty held the glassy map page next to it, a part of the map glistened. It was so weird. There was a mark in shiny blue ink, like a letter from a foreign alphabet, with three lines connected by loops and dots. The blue light spread through the map and out the clear sides, and sparkles reflected off Thryst's axe blade, which was right next to my head. (He'd come over for a closer look.)

"A rune!" Cry said and sneezed, and Peanut sneezed, and the Dwarf huffed, and the sounds all rhymed.

Arty was smiling. "And look!" he said and showed us that the blue rune on the map page was also on the book's cover, a large one and also shiny, in gold, once we cleaned it up a little.

"That map is magic! You knew this would happen?" I asked.

Cry's mouth was open in a big O.

"I don't know how it works. But, no, I just noticed it when I took your map out in the map room—a different rune glowed, in red, and it marks this spot, right here, the university's Main Library."

"Where?" Cry asked and returned his mouth to open O position.

Arty pointed on the magic map the where he thought were. "The rune is small now and not lighting up. Weird, right?"

Cry nodded, a very happy mute.

"And even weirder," Arty went on, looking at me, "do you see anything different about the map? It is not the same picture, it doesn't show downtown Belle Terre anymore, it changed, it shows here, the university."

"So, the map is…what?" My mind flipped through a lot of ideas at once. "It's telling us where we've been, or what's happening, or where to go, or—"

Arty cut me off and I thanked him for that. "No idea," he said. "But I have a few experiments in mind…"

"I want to try it," Cry said, but I had a different, darker thought.

"The man in brown had this," I stated. "What's he using it for? He must know a lot more than we do. Why is he after us?"

"I don't know…" Arty trailed off, his smile gone. Fantasy turns to fear quickly, and it filled the air and made us feel trapped, below ground, with enemies and strange creatures coming for us.

Sprug whispered to me, breaking the silence and changing the subject. "New Island," he said, and I thanked him for that.

"New Island," I reminded Arty.

"Oh yeah—thanks," he regrouped, "the blue book has it."

W.W. Marplot

Arty picked it up, turned carefully through crackling pages, and read from it, putting on a teacher's voice.

"New Island is afterlife haven-place whereupon living things will to die or be to die, viz, where corporeal ancient fairie progeny may for incorporeal demiurgus-similitude purgatorial metem-psychosis; or ineffable supernal regeneration. Opposing forces oppose, a refuge by choice. The world too light of dark, a place of reflective adytum banishment. Respite from unbelief."

Arty stopped reading, thankfully.

"What?" Cry asked, for both of us.

"I don't know—but that's what it says. Want me to read it again?"

"No," Cry and I answered together.

Arty handed me the blue book, saying that, as a writer, I was now in charge of all those big words.

"The only ones I know," I said, "make New Island sound either like jail, heaven, or Disney World."

"And we live here!" Cry said.

This excited Sprug. He jumpflew down to my ear and whispered, "Yes," and flew back to Peanut, who had fallen over, unable to stand properly in two fingers of a glove. She sneezed, a big wet one.

"Sprug says, 'Yes,'" I reported to the boys.

"Ok then!" Arty said. "We're onto something. This blue book is over two hundred years old but says it was actually translated from Old English, whatever that is."

"I know," Cry offered happily, his hand raised. "That's a language. An old...English..." he ended unhappily and put his hand down.

"Thanks, Cry," Arty continued. "The blue book has a bunch of underlined parts. Someone marked it up in grey pencil, and three of them reference other books I want to find. I looked up one already, it's here," he meant the university, "but at a different library, the Old English Library, actually. What a coincidence..."

"What's the other book called?" I asked, handing the crumbling blue granddaddy back to Arty.

He mumbled something using many syllables and changing volumes, then gave up and pointed me to his note pad. *"Ahreddenne Gelyfed Heofenum Carcern"* was circled. He put me in charge of that.

Something suddenly made Sprug spring to Arty's shoulder, and since that shoulder does not have the experience that my shoulder has, Arty jumped back and dropped the book—but faster than gravity, the Spriggan saved the ancient text from a fall, grasping its tattered spine, saving its life.

Sprug returned it to the desk and perched on it.

Arty walked to the opposite end of the long table, to his computer, and to the white cardboard map tubes that rolled and scattered as if they were afraid of Arty opening them.

"Shouldn't we just go wherever the map lights up?" Cry asked him and then reconsidered. "Or DON'T go where it lights up?"

"Neither. We need to do this step by step," Arty lectured. "We can get to the Old English Library using the underground passageways and tunnels, so we don't make a scene."

I knew Cry would love that, and sure enough, he was soon blubbering with excitement and refilling his small leather tissue-holder from a larger one.

Arty left the conversation so he could investigate some more, find the other things that the blue book wanted us to. He rolled out some of the old, non-magical maps and pecked away at his keyboard as Cry and I shrugged our shoulders at each other.

I now noticed that *Thryst the Uninvolved* had been pacing to and from the large desk where Arty fumbled to flatten the large, normal maps that desperately wanted to curl. *Thryst the Newly Interested* now took a permanent place at the desk and stared as if mesmerized at the curious, magical, not-paper map that Mr. Alphabet must want back.

I watched the Dwarf's glowing eyes and watched the twinkling map, and I wasn't sure who was transporting who...but suddenly

Thryst's powerful shape turned and he looked at each of us, his face wearing a question he didn't have to speak. He wanted help.

Cry wiped his nose with his sleeve.

Thryst seemed to change. He didn't just seem like an impressive and polite rock; he looked, for the first time, human. Until then, he could have been an expertly dressed, expertly programmed robot for use in the background of a movie. One with two modes—*violently active* or *still as stone*. But now I saw an *in-between*, and a weakness. Thryst was unsure and had questions and wanted help.

Arty was face down in his computer, but I remained in the Dwarf's burning eyes, where I saw new things, different from when I shared Sprug's world for that little while in the sunshine today. Awaiting me were not caves or trees or legends or distances in time and space—instead the feeling was closer, recognizable, something the Dwarf and I had in common, as strange as that seemed. His eyes became more like a mirror than a window. It was as if Thryst and I *shared* something—in that moment, and within our happening adventure. *What?* My mind tried to grab onto a feeling that parted before me like I was walking into smoke. I closed my own eyes after the silent, sternmore Dwarf closed his. I searched inside myself, testing my own feelings for the one that might fit.

When I opened my eyes again, all I saw were Thryst's, as unbeatable as a noon summer sun. Looking there, I knew: that Thryst was looking for something, that he felt alone, and that the caverns of his eyes were home to a deep love that was gone now, leaving his heart empty. It seemed replaced by a fire to...*do what?* Was something taken from him? Did he need to complete a quest? What was Thryst missing? What was it, so deep inside him, deep enough even to reach me?

I'd keep these thoughts personal, telling them to my journal only.

The Dwarf continued to look at the map, searching.

CHAPTER 41

Thryst

Aga, arga. Tarn, na, Teg achtra thryst tomadma zak tigil ro finnadar. Arda, mordail-arga.

(Thryst bows.)

CHAPTER 42

Arty

I have to admit that I—Arty—didn't notice any change in Thryst until later. As a scientist, I was concerned only with the new data and the new plan, not whether the stiff old guy had feelings and what they were. What do Dwarrowian mood-swings have to do with anything?

I was at work. I looked up the other two books that were underlined—but first, since so much had happened, I was craving a new list:

1. The underlines in the blue book point to other books we need.

2. The 1st one is here also, but a few buildings over at the OELib.

3. Why are it & the blue book here?

4. What is the red mark on the magical map?

5. NI is LI.

6. Also—the M is a m of here (I was right), but it changes.

7. The mm belonged to man in brown who for all we know could be a (snotty, weird) wizard.

8. Ted is involved somehow, the pain.

After that unorganized but necessary brain spew, I went back at it and found some information about the third grey pencil-underlined part, which was actually a cookbook! *Huh?* I squinted at Emma and Cry out of habit, but they were busy playing with Peanut, who was scringing and running between Thryst's beat-up boots.

Recipes from Queene Faerie Habundia, and Other Youthful Cooking Legends, by Willimina Bakely, was out of print. I put this on a pink sticky note; the color means "do soon."

The second thing that was underlined in the blue book was the most puzzling puzzle yet; I saved it for last. There was no name, just hints: "*The Book that Should Not be Used, The Book That Can't Be named, the Book of Unspeakable Words and Unabiding Acts.*" Why would a book like that even exist? But it was underlined, with the other two, so I needed to find it. I needed to try. I needed more time to hack away at the Internet like an explorer's machete through a savage jungle. Later, at my desk, it went on the pink sticky.

Of course, those three books might point to nine other, older books, and those nine might point to twenty-seven, then eighty-one, then to 243 decomposing, decaying books that not even Thryst could carry. I hoped not. At least we were getting closer to the mystery of the folkies—three of them now, here, on their "New Island." Did they need our help? Did we need theirs? Did Thryst and Sprug and Peanut arrive for an epic adventure quest?

Or were our fairies just lost?

That's probably it, I thought. If my house was on the way to fairy jail, I'd know it already.

I added to my list:

9. Someone with a grey pencil, a long time ago, left clues. They knew what would happen. And it is happening now.

CHAPTER 43

Emma

rty says he doesn't care for fairy mood swings, but he couldn't ignore this one: They decided to leave us.

Yes—one minute I was playing peekaboo with a stuffy-nosed Pixie, and the next we were all running or flying, depending on what world you were from.

I had noticed Sprugly acting strangely as we all waited for Arty. When the Spriggan finally launched off the old blue book, he stayed in the air, circling and darting—directionless, as if gathering information from our underground space itself. Peanut sneezed and sniffed, sneezed and sniffed, until she got Thryst's attention also. He moved his bulky hand to his axe handle and closed his eyes.

Then, without a sound, without a message or a song, they bolted, the three fairies, off through an aisle of books, running and flying.

Just as Arty said, "Wait!" on behalf of we three humans, and struggled to pack all the books and map rolls and his notes and computer and the rest of his travelling Professor Nerd office, my breath was taken away by the clang of a door and the bang of footsteps—the echoes of shoes clacking on the cold tile of the library floor. They were the first we had heard since coming to this isolated bowel of the university.

Followed again? Man in brown? Ted? Ted in brown? Someone new?

Arty was panicking and trying to decide whether to cover our tracks—books, trashed notes, maps, Spriggan feathers, Pixie germs—or keep up with the folkies. My vote was definite: These weren't clues anyone could follow anyway, we needed to run. I voted loudly to Arty and Cry.

Sprug came back to us and helped—by carrying the blue book in his red hands. Arty froze for a second. The map was lighting from the middle outward in waves of shiny rainbows, its flimsy width curving in his hands like a thin sheet of metal. Sprugly jumpflew back and crashed into Arty's ear to get him to move. I loaded Cry like a mule, packing the rest of all our things in our backpacks and plopping the backpacks on his broad back and shoulders. He didn't budge from the weight, but he looked pale.

We ran, Arty leading, and soon we saw that the fairies hadn't gone very far; Thryst was standing on a high desk in a corner, hood bent at the ceiling, and Peanut was scringing loudly and pathetically on the floor nearby. The poor thing. Cry scooped her up and put her back into her glove-nest. We all—folkies, too—then followed Arty, who mentioned knowing "another way out" to avoid the nearing footstepper.

He led us all out a nearby, quick-getaway door. We made a sharp right through another, which looked tightly locked and had a big red alarm sign on it—but Arty knew better and pushed it open so that we passed silently through and into a short hallway that ended at an intersection. This pattern continued—many short hallways, many doors, many decisions, but my old friend knew them all. Only silence followed us. I was relieved…

But that didn't matter to Sprugly and Thryst; they hurried us to keep moving.

As we ran and as Sprug flapped wildly, so did the cover of the poor old blue book he had in his weird hands. Pages were tearing, and some were loosed and tumbled out, through the air, past Arty's swiveling eyes and through Cry's big fingers.

"Grab them!" Arty yelled to me.

"I tried!" cried Cry.

"I am trying!" cried I, clutching only at air until the browning pages hit the floor, three of them. I hustled to catch up to Arty.

Sprugly then flew close and showed us, by flipping blue book pages, that the pages falling out all had the same symbol as the underlined pages in the book, the ones Arty had noticed and read. The ones that fell out weren't part of the book but notes left by someone, that same someone who did the underlining.

So, they all went together, somehow: the green on the map and the underlined books and the words on the loose pages, but it was too much to figure out while dodging underground with two wild fairies, a nerd, his Dwarf, a magic map, and a weepy human (?) mule. We had to keep running.

"Read them to me!" Arty yelled over his shoulder.

"I'll try!" I yelled back, my eyeballs ping-ponging in my head to stay on the words.

The first one started with "EL 9110.04J"—it took me a while to read each digit correctly as I bounced. The handwriting was old and spidery, in grey pencil like dull silver. The rest was easier and made just as much sense—none: "When the time comes, as the Elf lord foretold…" and there was more, but I stopped because of the green glow. The map shone and showed a bright spot, a symbol, a rune, I guess, that matched a scribble on the page I held.

Arty looked amazed and did the best he could to read the open blue book with Sprug's jumpflying and flapping and his own legs aching and all our heads avoiding walls and concussions.

The map still showed light from the blue rune, too, same as before. But no red, as Arty pointed out.

"Wow! Makes sense!" Arty yelled. "We're the *blue*. The *green* must be where the cookbook is."

Maybe that made sense to Arty, and maybe it would rhyme in a fairy tale, but I had no idea what he was talking about, and Cry was starting to sweat directly from his brain.

"So, we should follow the map?" he whimpered. "Are you sure?"

"Nope."

"Here's another one," I said, readying to read the next fallen page as we rounded a stairway turn at a high speed. I used Cry to bounce off like a runaway bumper car so I could keep steady. "'She is coming. New Island. And she is coming,' it says."

"Twice?"

"Yes. And then: 'Eastward Manor. Map this and more…'" and more, but the lights went out, so I stopped.

The lights went out, so I stopped—stopped reading, stopped walking, stopped breathing, stopped beating my heart. We were instantly in the dark. Cry's loud galloping stopped with a screech of large sneakers. I crashed into Arty, and when I did, the note I held passed over the magical map, and they both glowed in white.

"Wow," Arty said again, and we could hear Cry blubbering as he squeezed in tight between Arty and the tiled wall. "But the map changed—did you see that? It is not the university anymore, it shows a totally different place! And look—there's no more blue spot. And no red symbol either."

Arty seemed calm and happy, since having a logic puzzle to solve kept him from the gloom of the blackout. Instead, he enjoyed the nice, clean, white luminescence of Mr. Alphabet's map as if he were snug in bed with a good mystery novel and a book light—safe inside, while a storm raged outside.

But if he had looked around, he would have seen that the storm was raging *inside.*

With the darkness came strange sounds—calls and squeaks as if from animals big and small, and patter as if those animals were in a hurry to get to class and out of the library—and not necessarily by using the tiled floor. The scratch and scrape of claws and paws—and maybe teeth and tails—were coming from the ceiling, the air vents, the large pipes that ran above in these long hallways that seemed to run through the bowels of the buildings. We hadn't passed many windows, and any off in the distance were small, though they let in a merry sunlight.

But now I was glad we were in the dark; it saved me from not having to look at the creeping things, whatever they were. I accidentally saw a small human-shaped creature, dressed like a cartoon Leprechaun, run alongside me, almost up to my knee. His shiny belt and britches reflected the map glow for a few seconds when soon he grabbed hold of a water pipe and clambered up it and through the roof somehow. That was enough; I kept my eyes focused on Arty's back.

I heard Peanut scringing at something that flew near to him and made Cry swat with one free hand as his other tried to hold all the luggage. Sprug came and seemed to chase it away. I also noticed Thryst moving about in a protective stance, searching corners and clearing the way forward.

We couldn't hide or stay, we had to move no matter what fairy creatures were there and what they had planned for us—because now we heard the footsteps again, and they were below, but too close. Arty made some swift maneuvers, guiding through the almost-dark. He held up the map for light—it was back to normal, he said, and showed the blue rune, and also the red symbol again.

Using that glow, he took us down half a staircase—and through a bolted door in between floors. In here were endless, brightly-colored pipes—red, yellow, green, white—some of which were four or five feet around, looking like giant, bandaged limbs and barely fitting under a short ceiling. Cry and I had to duck as we ran. From what I could tell, this was the mechanical guts of the whole building, if not the whole university.

After that squashed maze, we dashed through another quickly-unbolted door and up a half-stair, whipped around a quick left, right, and left again, shoved through huge double doors, and zipped up a full flight of stairs into a closet then up a ladder—yes, a straight-up ladder like a fire escape—where we stopped solid.

The problem? At the bottom of the straight-up ladder, Cry hesitated, gazing upward as if it were a thousand feet downward. "Geez," he mumbled, "this place is bigger inside than it is outside." He wiped his eyes with a sleeve, all true to his name, and wound up for a sneeze.

Then and there the lights came back on. Cry gasped, which shorted his sneeze into a snort. His large legs stepped upward. I didn't see any other creatures or hear any footsteps of any kind or number of feet.

"Do you know where we are going?" Cry asked Arty's butt—directly above Cry's big head as they ascended.

"Yes," Arty said.

"Are we following the map?" Cry asked Arty's sneakers. "I don't think we should."

"No," Arty answered.

Then at the top of the ladder, he told us there wasn't much farther to go.

"For a kid with so many maps, you seem lost," Cry said, and I nodded.

"We're not lost," Arty protested. "We're close by the main stairwell that'll lead us back down and to the Old English Library."

With that and the Dwarf's gentle urging—a snort of syllables that would've quieted our school cafeteria, strong enough to blow one corner of the map from Arty's fingers—we continued at a slow jog. Cry, our faithful burro, was wheezing a bit, but he didn't complain or honk or anything.

Arty asked, "Emma—show me the last page."

"From the blue book?"

"Yeah—bring it to the map."

I did, and the magic, strange not-paper glowed in purple around the edges, but otherwise showed just a rough rectangle made up of tiny dots like little violets. It wasn't much of a map anymore, it was more like the Etch-a-Sketch my dad gave me when I was four. After a few crappy, choppy diagonals, I had put it in my closet, and it is still there.

The page read: "Dead legend and should not be unburied." *Great,* I thought.

"Oh well," Arty sighed and shook his head. "Do the first one again."

"Can you say please?" I prodded but did what he asked. With the first note near the map again, I could see that where we were was marked in blue, and where Arty said we were going was marked in green. "No red," I said.

"Nope."

"Which means?"

"No idea." Arty spoke honestly.

CHAPTER 44

Arty

 e stopped jogging, and I took attendance: there were only we three humans and our three found fairies. No other beings had come along, and I couldn't hear any footsteps tracking us.

We went through one last door, leaving the maze of back passages and finding ourselves in a main stairwell. That told us to go up five floors to reach the Old English library.

The steps were cement, dull and grey, with a drab yellow railing attached to the grey walls, and it all rose outside the library building itself, a sort of bunker or castle keep enclosing these stairs and nothing else. It was cold with very narrow, deep windows that appeared once we were back above ground. Not much light came through.

Once we were at ground level, I said to Emma and Cry, "We're back on a main road. There might be people all over. It could be dangerous."

"You're worried about college students? We are being chased by fairies and stalked by a magic man," Emma pointed out.

She was right. Sprug and Thryst were very anxious, and Peanut was hiding in Cry's clothes somewhere. It looked like Cry would've liked to hide in someone's clothes also. But so far, no Giants, ha-ha.

We went up three levels, took a rest, then zigzagged up the remaining flights. Though there was no sign of anyone, I knew that through the nearby stairwell exit was a short hallway leading to the Old English library.

Cry and Emma had questions, but as I began to answer them, both Sprug and Thryst left us again. We were too tired to follow, and I wasn't going anywhere without the next book, its symbol shining in green at me from the magical map page. We were so near to it.

"What if we aren't safe here?" Emma asked.

"They wouldn't ditch us," I answered.

"What if the alphabet man comes? What if they went after him, and he defeats them, and then he comes after us?" Cry asked.

"I don't think they're worried about him. It seems like they're scared of something else." I was guessing, of course.

"How do you know we lost him?" Emma said, pointing at the map that never left my hand the through whole chase.

"There's no red rune…"

"Why wouldn't it be brown?" Cry asked, very logically.

I couldn't answer that, but I explained everything else I could. The piece of map we had from the man in brown was pointing to the Old English library, the green spot, so that backed up my plan. It was also reacting to—probably pointing to—all the other books we needed, which was good because I might have trouble finding them.

Emma gave me the pages that had fallen out of the blue book— but only after taking pictures of them "for my journal," she said.

"Pretty lucky," I said to her, "that all these papers keep coming out of thin air to you."

Sprug and Thryst appeared, mysteriously, and they looked tired but did not grunt or whisper anything.

I showed my friends something else I had noticed: a small, orange symbol on the map shaped like a loopy, upper-case G, lit in a reddish-orange like a tiny, evil, twisted eye.

It blinked and went out as we watched. When it did, Dwarf and Spriggan left us again.

So strange.

CHAPTER 45

Emma

I was staring at the little orangey G and the rest of the swirls on the map, and I was hypnotized by Arty's explanations. I felt tired from the escape across the university, and my mind was quivering from the craziness as bad as my ankles were from the steps. I could have fallen asleep there, leaning on the cold grey cinderblock wall, gripping the yellow handrail—and almost did.

I felt as if my mom was calling me, and as if my ears were suddenly blind and all my senses mixed up....

When the G blinked and flickered out, and the fairies left us, I awoke. I guess.

They came back soon, as Arty was looking at his notes one more time before going to the Old English library for his book. Sprug told me, "It is well," but he also whispered, "It is coming."

"She?" I asked.

"She came. It is coming," he said. "Tooshees."

Tooshies?

Tissues?

Tushies? I thought.

Sprug's tiresome hints were making me even tireder. Then I had this thought:

Does anyone want to swap fairies?

Until it hit me.

Oh: *Two shes.* I get it.

"Who is the other one?" I asked him.

"Don't know," Sprug whispered.

"Well, who is the first one?"

"She. She came."

So strange...

CHAPTER 46

Arty

I was ready for the next step of the plan. I put the map page and blue book pages into my bag and left everyone—which I hoped was only two fairies, two humans, and one Dwarf—behind in the stairwell. As I entered the Old English Library, I passed the person at the front desk—a student with quick thumbs and a pink phone—without being noticed.

I followed the signs and made four rights and three lefts along perfectly sectioned rows of book stacks until finding the right shelf. I love libraries.

I found the book. It was slim and a dark, battered orange with a rough old cover that had no signs of green and no markings on it anywhere—except for a taped piece of paper with its library index number, *EL 9110.04J.*

Breathing heavily with anticipation and quivering with leg pains, I opened it. The pages smelled like antique excitement.

The book was also written in Old English, the *language*—all the words inside looked like the four long ones in the title. *Funny*, I thought, *I'm in Old English* the building.

But then my own thought repeated: The book was in Old English, the language. Which meant I couldn't read it! I should've known. But you'd think Old English would be just a wrinkled version of English, with maybe some *thou*'s and *o'er*'s and an *alas* or two. It isn't. I could only guess a few of the words. This was a dead end.

Except…for the note. As I tried to put the book back in its place, somehow that book fell out of my hands and, with Sprug-ly-clumsiness, landed flat and open, face down on the floor. When I picked it up, a small, brown slip of paper remained behind on the white tile.

Another paper falling fatefully to guide me. And yes: this was another brown-edged, ripped-out page from the blue book. *Thank you, whoever*! In neat, small handwriting it said, "Pointing. Do not bury. Discard This." There was a code after it: "EL 5674.3453."

Whoever wrote all these notes was pointing to another book right here somewhere, in this same library. *Thanks again.*

By now, my heart was pounding, jumping around like a lumpy Spriggan under my clothes. I needed to hurry. The others were waiting on the stairs with their fairies and my Dwarf, and they had no easy escape if someone came.

I hurriedly left-ed and right-ed in search for this other book and soon saw it—high above me. It was very thick, its dark brown—which maybe used to be green when it was younger—and wide back looked like a tree trunk compared to its neighbors. Being oversized, it didn't fit on the normal shelves so was stored at the top. *That big, big brown one way up there*, I said to myself as if I were picking a prize at a carnival.

I had to climb on the lower metal shelves to get at it, kicking in books on each level as I went. I needed three steps—but on the third, as I stretched from toes to fingertips to reach the topmost ledge, my foot slipped, and I lost my balance backwards and tumbled down. And so did the whole top shelf, with twenty or so large, heavy, old books, and it seemed that they all fell corners-first. The shelf itself just missed me. Another Sprugly-esque move, lacking grace but full of dust and noise.

As the books settled, a sneeze snuck up on me, and rushed past and through me like a runaway train. So, I was part Peanut also now, sitting there.

My head ached, and I had something funny growing in my back-yard. But I couldn't think about that right now.

"Bless you," said a female voice, the student who was working the checkout desk. She also asked if I was ok and helped to uncover me, placing the books on an empty shelf behind us one at a time and with both hands; the books were that large, that heavy. I helped, while trying to pick out the one I was looking for. I showed the student the number, and we found it, *EL 5674.3453*. Its title was in a foreign language. German, I think, since the letters looked like Gretel, my nanny. They reminded me of her. The book itself had many, many chapters of the same, odd-looking, long Germanic words. It had pictures inside—of tree roots, and only tree roots.

Tree roots. Many pages of them, in between lots of big words that meant nothing to me.

Why?

Another dead end, I thought.

I thanked my helper and handed her the giant German book as she started to replace the other gigantic, heavy, dangerous things back in their age-old home on that Mt. Everest of shelves. I walked away, rubbing the top of my head.

"Wait," she called back to me. "Is this yours?" She was almost done re-shelving, only the beastly brown German tree-root book remained in her arms, and she pointed downward.

Near where I had landed and where the books avalanched, half-hidden atop the lowest row of books, was something that the student librarian now picked up and brought to me. I could see that it had the same shape and aging color as the blue book orphan page in my hand.

This note said, "Do Not Bury, Discard. Eastward Manor. Code: EL 5674.3468."

Sounds familiar…

Tedious, but familiar. I squeezed past the girl, right back to the same spot where my earlier climb had failed: Everest Base Camp.

W.W. Marplot

"Sorry!" I said to her and hopped on the tall stool, reached up to the topmost shelf, pulled out the green (!) book that someone wanted me to have, and jumped down. No other books jumped down with me.

The college student looked confused, shook her head, muttered about kids and libraries, took out her pink phone, and walked away.

I wasn't confused. I looked at the title, and my heart was jumping again. Maybe even jumpflying. This book was newer and smaller than the dead-end root one but also in German, and again made up of many short chapters.

But this was no dead end.

On the cover, among the foreign words were at least two I could read, and these two leaped out at me like an excited heart out of a boy's chest: *Queene Faerie Habundia*. This was the middle part of the title.

I remembered the name of the cookbook, *Recipes from the Queen Fairy, and Other* whatever legends, etc., etc.

Could the book in my hands be the same as the cookbook but in German—the one that was waiting for us at the white spot on Mr. Alphabet's map, which I could figure out using the real maps I had in those annoying tubes?

Or I could follow the magical map, maybe—but I wanted to do this myself. I guess.

I opened its dilapidated cover and fanned though some pages. Yes, of course: the short chapters were not chapters at all, they were *recipes*. Now that I had the hint from the title, it was obvious, and it made sense. A little. I needed to find the white spot next.

A good plan.

I was stung with a panic to get back to the others; I had taken too long. I borrowed the book using my special research card that allows me to use any library on Long Island. At the checkout counter was the pink phone, the girl attached to it, and also the thick brown German tree root picture book. I took that one also, just in case.

I ran back to the others, ready to apologize for taking so long but with a great story to tell.

I opened the stairwell door and opened my mouth, but no words came out. The stairs were empty.

No sight, no sound of my friends or their creatures. But, wow: how the weather had changed.

CHAPTER 47

Arty

rty here, still. I'd rather have Emma handle this chapter, but I couldn't find her.

I went up and down the echoing stairs until my legs and lungs hated each other, and then I needed to sit and think. Something bad must have happened, but there was no sign of damage from Thryst's axe, no Spriggan-halves or Pixie body parts, and no crime scene investigators, so that was good.

My best guess was that Emma and Cry had to run from someone again. But why not stay nearby and wait for me?

The weather was just as surprising—and worrying. The small windows that had earlier let in enough bright sunshine to light the whole stairwell were almost completely dark and reflected the wimpy overhead bulbs that were now on. I looked outside to the overcast sky; dark storm clouds had rolled in, the sun was gone, the day was over—the bright spring day was done. It was now a rainy night, all of a sudden. Thunder struck, bouncing off the buildings and up and down my spine. There was no lightning.

It was getting late, and I had to meet Gretel back where she'd dropped Emma and me off a few hours earlier. Gretel would kill me if I were late, and no matter how many German books I was carrying, she would kill me worse if I didn't have Emma.

I was a worried, miserable Dwarf-owner. A tired, confused Dwarf-owner looking for a fairy cookbook translation, and who now had to run

Dwarf Story 141

across the whole university campus in a thunderstorm. But that was the best thing to do, since Emma would head that way also to meet Gretel. Hopefully, Peanut the Pixie would stay out of sight with the others. Hopefully, she *wanted* to stay hidden, like the others. Emma could manage it.

The sky was pouring rain. Large raindrops smacked my back hard, like some jerk who thinks you're his friend, and the two extra, ancient books I now carried weighed my pack down as heavily as if they were tombstones.

Whichever way I ran, the wind hit my face; it was like running while attached to an open parachute.

My gear banged against my shoulder and side as I ran. I tried to move from tree to tree to stay a little drier, but I also considered the lightning and so kept moving. My eyes bounced with the paces of my slow jog and searched between buildings for signs of Emma and Thryst. There were none.

Ahead was Gretel in our truck. I hopped in, drenched with rain and sweat and very nervous.

"No Emma?" Gretel said instead of a hello.

I panicked. "Well, I can explain…" then realized my mistake: there was something funny in Gretel's voice. She wasn't asking a question, she was stating a fact. *No Emma.* "I mean, what?" I asked, blowing wet hair away from my wet face.

"She just texted me. She is sayink she did not needen zee ride."

"Oh…OK." I slumped. I couldn't hide the fact that I was as confused as I was tired. I panted because of both.

"Vut iss it goink on, Art?" Gretel asked me in her adapted English. "Vy you runnink so kvickly?" I had a hundred thoughts going at once, droopy, dripping thoughts. One wondered whether Emma had told Gretel anything. Another searched for a good excuse for having a German cookbook, so that I could ask Gretel to translate it.

I checked my phone for messages—Emma had sent me four pictures with no explanation. They were pictures of pages of notes, and definitely not her handwriting. With no explanation.

She was always finding cool stuff. I texted her that.

I waited four seconds.

No reply.

"Did Emma say anything else?"

"No." Gretel answered and did not make any moves to drive away yet. I felt her stare. "Iss somesink vrong?" she asked.

What could I answer? I was worried about Emma, what was happening, and how she would get home. I was afraid of all of them getting caught, Peanut the Pixie being taken to the doctor, Sprugly arrested for trying to protect her, and *Thryst the Always Up for a Fight* cutting off policemen's arms and legs. But if I told Gretel these fears, she'd think I had lost my American mind. And I had no Dwarf to show her as proof.

Emma must be ok if she sent us texts, I hoped.

Emma will be ok if she sent us texts, I figured.

Emma should be ok if she sent us texts, I decided.

"Everything is fine," I said to Gretel. She made a mental note of something, while looking at me—I could almost hear a pencil etching into some small yellow sticky-note area of her brain. Then she looked away.

"Ok," she said in perfect English.

And on the way home, she told me stories about her day.

CHAPTER 48

Arty

Arty here. AGAIN. I *really* don't mean to hog all the chapters, and I wish Emma had been in touch so she could be telling us all about where she was instead. Other than the pictures, there had been no sign or word from her as I lay in my bed. Those pictures—four pages of notes or something in a fancy, swirling handwriting—were coming out of my printer, slowly, grinding out one line at a time. I lay looking at pictures of German tree roots in a very distracted way as rain beat hard on the roof, my attic-room's ceiling.

I was worried, and tired, and I missed my Dwarf.

My latest, perfect plan had gone well at the university libraries except for the chase scene. But this new part was a disaster. I gave up on doing homework; I started to feel sick. I kept my phone close to me, but there was no word from anyone. I put my TV on, waiting for interruptions of earth-shattering news—an invasion of dragons, the university taken hostage by goblins, mountains appearing out of the water, pots of gold at the ends of rainbows—but apparently nothing in Belle Terre was newsworthy except the sudden downpour of rain and a police standoff with some deer—both I already knew.

I kept repeating in my head, and sometimes out loud: *Emma texted Gretel. They must be Ok. Emma texted me. They must be ok.*

I tired.

I need to get out of here, I thought.

I snuck past many family members and out the front door with Thryst-ian skill so that I didn't have to explain why I was going for a walk in a violent storm. There in the rain, my mind lost its grip on logic, and the possibilities—where my friends were, who the man in brown was, what was in the three books, why Emma sent me pictures that were taking so long to print, what was up with the Ted mystery—became endless. For example, I considered that maybe it wasn't even Emma who had texted Gretel; someone could have been using her phone. Someone bad. Someone that crept out of a cave or a drain or somewhere worse.

That is what sneaks into the unlocked windows of my mind, at night, sometimes, when I feel helpless.

I decided to look around a little longer. Drenched and chilly as I was, the air felt good. I was curious: while driving home from the university, Gretel told me about the deer—the same strange tale she'd told Emma as they drove home from school. Yet there was more: Gretel said she saw, all around Belle Terre, all that day, police and fire ambulances and "environmental safety" people. They were busy with the animals and the trees.

The animals were going berserk.

The trees were falling.

Two of our neighbors had reported raccoons trying to get into their houses. Others reported squirrels trying to get in through upstairs windows. Our neighbors in back, old Mr. and Mrs. Kenning—who are big-time animal lovers—even told Gretel they found their four large pet rabbits huddled together with three small foxes they'd never met before.

Gretel didn't believe them. She says old man Kenning is a bit of a *schpinna*—which is very funny when she says it and means that the reason he's popular with the squirrels is because he's nuts. So, Gretel shrugged it off—until she saw for herself: A large rabbit and a small fox ran by as she left our neighbors' yard. Side by side, sniffing the air, and running across the lawn.

And the birds: thousands of them, circling, and flying from tree to tree.

And the trees again: Gretel said she saw five or so down across the roads to the beach.

And the beach: The water was at high tide all day.

And the day: Our dogs wouldn't stop howling all through it, and neither could any of the other dogs in the neighborhood.

All I saw now were dark clouds, all I heard was wind, all I felt was rain.

I thought I should go back and at least do whatever reading I could, check the map, check the new books, read what was slowly printing, when something caught my eye.

A light—whose color and flash looked like the glow that came from the map page sitting in my room. But there were many lights, and they floated in the air, down at the road where last night Emma and I had spotted the mysterious, meddling, menacing man in brown.

And there he was.

Again. And again, I jumped behind a tree. Its leafy umbrella helped me see more clearly, but from there the way back to the front door meant being seen by my mysterious enemy—he had moved along toward my driveway.

Crouching, sliding one eye around the oak bark, I watched the man in brown's long arms wind and flap, up and down and forward and back, and his hands juggle something that caused streaks of sharp light like small fireworks, and then twist them in the air, as the rain came down hard upon his head and splashed all around the twinkling scene.

The glow might be more pages of the map, like the one Emma had taken from him.

And there's something here that he wants, I thought. Did he think Ted was here?

Is Ted here, somewhere?

There is something funny growing in my yard....

I could not connect any thoughts together, their ends did not fit, their shapes were all different. And without Thryst, without Sprugly, and without Emma or Cry, I wasn't tempted to do anything but go inside. The man didn't come onto my property; he moved back to where I first spotted him, then the lights went out, and he was gone.

Good. If he wasn't looking for me, I wasn't looking for him.

Although, upstairs, I did have a piece of his map. And something was printing.

CHAPTER 49

Emma

Still in the third-floor stairwell outside the Old English Library, Cry said to me, "Emma, it's ok, I'll go."

And I said, "No. I can't let you. I will."

This was an ongoing argument, but it had nothing to do with selflessness or bravery. Neither of us wanted to babysit our little fairy tale friends alone while the other went to hurry Arty along.

Because they were acting alarmingly odd—coming and going, leaving for no reason, staying for less reason. They'd been nervous since the Main Library, since seeing Arty's magic map tricks, I think. And I think Arty was right: They weren't afraid of footsteps or Alphabet Men in Brown; it was something else. They were running *to* something, not away.

Oh boy.

Our debate ended when Sprugly, who had just returned to perch atop Cry's backpack guarding Peanut, quickly flew to my ear and whispered something I didn't hear, because my other ear heard the return of echoing footsteps. From a few flights above, someone was coming down, their shoes sounding determined and brown. Cry rose to run; I decided it made the most sense to run toward our ride home, Gretel, who was expecting us soon. Arty would think the same. He might even catch up to us since he was traveling lighter than we were, or so I thought.

Cry followed as I bounded down the first flight of steps, turned the corner at a high speed, then heard a crashing thud of bone against dull cement, with the skidding and grunting sounds that go with it. It echoed against the ugly walls.

"Are you ok?" I turned.

"Yes, you?" Cry said as he bumped into me.

Then I realized: the crash had come from above—the pursuing footsteps had stopped, and the grunts were now a deep, dark-honey voice speaking words of…well…bad curse words. Large, interesting ones.

Magic Mr. Alphabet was above us, and he had fallen.

And down came Peanut, flapping wildly and flying handicapped because her head was skirted with a piece of paper that her pointy ears had punctured, and she looked as if it had been forced over her tiny body, or as if she had flown through it as part of a comedy routine.

Down came Sprugly, too—they had been above.

I removed the paper for Peanut. It wasn't a blue book sheet this time. She sneezed as down floated other pages, back and forth, rocking on the still air of the stairwell in the slice of vertical space between the handrails. I caught these in the air—better with practice—while looking upward, where the view ran six or seven more flights up to the tower ceiling high above. Between the rising walls was a bearded face that looked down at me with a brown scowl.

Aaagh! I was startled but pushed into action by my Spriggan, who helped me lightly jumpfly down the remaining zigzagging steps to catch up with Cry and, I was happy to see, *Thryst the I Was Happy to See.*

"Keep going! Hurry!" I yelled.

Just as the footsteps began echoing again, we made it to the ground floor—then, since I didn't know the underground tunnel catacomb route, I peeked outside. Sun and wind hit my face, as did a view of hundreds of college students.

Cry and I stuffed a loudly peeping Pixie into his bag, and Sprug jumpflew into it as well. I put the four pieces of paper—which I saw now were filled with fancy, beautiful handwriting—into my own bag. *Thryst the Spry* was now unseen. This was my first time on my own with him, so I just trusted in his ability to stay out of sight.

We walked quickly among the buildings, avoiding crowds, from the Old English library to the parking lot. Here and there I saw a bright boot or a flapping hood—sometimes ahead, sometimes behind. I wished to the sky for a peaceful trip to Gretel and the truck.

I soon saw that the weather was turning its back on us—charcoal clouds were moving in from all directions, the wind gushed and whipped and rushed noisily with an evil laughter, the fairies grew restless, and Cry struggled with his load. Then even Thryst stayed closer to us. College people ran for cover, ducking into doorways.

The multiplying clouds rolled onward and inward and covered the last bit of sky in a black blanket. The world darkened, and the rain came.

Maybe the change in weather explained the fairies' change in behavior. When we could see the parking lot ahead, and just as we started our last run for it, Sprugly popped from Cry's bag and pulled at my hair, and then at my shoulders and neck, to force me to turn around. I'd never felt strength like this in him before. Still in the bag, Peanut was whining loudly.

"Follow!" Sprugly whispered, and I was directed away from the parking lot and toward a path that ran closely along a low building, with dense woods on its other side.

"No! Ow! Why!" were my responses. Peanut sneezed and sniffed; Cry tried to hush her as he followed me in this new direction. Ahead I saw Thryst, already at the woods, with his axe held out in both hands and his wet beard swinging in the wind. His eyes blazed as he looked every way, even up trees.

"Follow!" Sprugly whispered again. "She is coming."

I froze. The words sent a chill through my neck, down my spine, and out my toes, like an electric shock. Until now, Sprugly's hourly warnings of the mysterious "*She*" seemed cute, like maybe his hairdresser was coming to town. That was back in the bright sun and light green leaves of morning. Now, on the run in a dark storm with even *Thryst the Brave* acting nervously, I pictured "*She*" as the queen of everything that can bite your face off in the dark.

Peanut was crying wildly, shrieking, and Cry's backpack jumped. He opened it, and his Pixie came flopping out. Sprug grabbed her in his almost-human hands, and they flew off toward Thryst and along the path near the woods.

Then into the woods.

Cry ran after. He stopped before entering the trees and looked back at me, the rain streaming down his large face.

What should I do? I was scared. There was a thunderclap that came with no warning lightning, and that made me jump and shiver again. I couldn't see the fairies—they weren't going to wait, they headed away, and at this distance, I couldn't even call to them. The wind was howling an evil siren, and the large trees added their own terrible noises of whipping leaves and the cracks of violently crashing branches.

I had to either leave the fairies or go after them and miss my ride home, which meant losing Arty and any guarantee of safety from… who knew what?

Where were they going? If "*She*" was "coming," shouldn't *we* be *going*? Was it smart to run into the stormy woods and not home? The weather seemed like something conjured by another fairy, like some bad magic we'd found to go with three good-magic creatures. I had no answers to my questions, but I was learning that *anything is possible.* It occurred to me that I might now be in great danger.

But I was afraid that I'd never see our fairies again if I went home now.

"Emma! What do we do?" Cry yelled, blowing water from his face like a spouting white whale. He shrugged his wide shoulders and pointed to the woods to indicate that our fairies were now out of sight.

And then I knew what to do.

"Follow them!" I hollered, running to catch up. "Keep an eye on them! Tell Sprugly to wait!"

CHAPTER 50

Arty

My life was exciting, too—if you count reading and researching, which I do. And I was locked in my room, with the storm trying to break the windows and my dogs hiding under the bed. Every ninety seconds or so, I checked my phone, but I never heard a word from Emma or Cry. I was friendless and fairyless and alone for the night, unless you count Mr. Alphabet in Brown and whatever else might be crawling around outside.

But I wasn't bored, at least. In fact, I had a new list:

1. Read the books from the University Main Library, especially the Blue Book, especially about "New Island."

2. (Try to) read the German cookbook from the Old English Library.

3. Study the map page (with other maps from lib) (symbols and runes).

4. Stare at the extra Blue Book pages left by some strange stranger from the past (since I can't figure them out).

5. Read the letter pages that Emma texted (once it is done printing).

6. Make a new plan for Thryst and me (and the funny thing in the yard—not yet).

The blue book taught me about New Island. That I was living on it. New Island was Long Island. It also had tons of strange symbols— what Cry liked to call runes, though lately he calls everything a rune—that matched symbols on the German cookbook. Not such a big surprise since the two books referred to each other, and someone else—whoever left the notes for me—had already made the connection. But I was proud to notice it; it gave me an adventurous thrill, just like chasing three fairy creatures through the woods during a storm.

The symbols in the books and map pointed to other symbols in other places. It was all like a big, multi-book index. I would've loved to see what else Mr. Alphabet had.

So, I gave the German cookbook to our German cook, Gretel, asking her to translate the entries that had New Island symbols.

I moved on to the map page, thinking about the mystery of the man in brown, Mr. Alphabet. I watched the glowing symbols, knowing they all meant something, just as the blue and white ones pointed to the books in their homes at the university, and in their new homes here in my room. And the red one was the man in brown. I guessed that. It always showed up right before we had to run.

The books and the clues were somehow telling us what to do, and the magic map reported what we were doing. But there was more of the map—and Mr. Alphabet had it. He must know a lot more. And he was against us.

I used the curly old-fashioned maps to figure out that the white spot on the magical map—with the symbol of the third book, the weird cookbook—pointed to the Historical Society Library at the Historical Society building of the Historical Society of Belle Terre. I looked online and, yep, they had a copy of it, a nice, plain-old readable English version.

I added to my plan: We would go there tomorrow.

There was no sign of the second book, the one that was all symbols...all runes....

I wondered what else the magic markings could tell me. The map and the blue book both had a lot of information, a lot of symbols, a lot of mystery. My head swam with thoughts playing tag in my head, one to the next.

Outside moaned the noise of forceful rain and battered tree branches.

I laid the magic map on my bed. Its soft, thin glass rolled and curled easily, and even folded, but I still worried it might break. I watched, and it changed—its single flimsy page seemed to ripple and move, an illusion it gave because the lines and lights on it would shift and shimmy, lighting and dimming with motion. It seemed somehow to be linked to the storm—in fact, in some weird way it looked like a weather map. I compared it to the radar image on local weather web pages. Where our storm was centering—in the woods somewhere between here and the university—the map was alive with swirling circles and flashing lights. This seemed to be centered around a familiar symbol, that orange rune that looked like a twisted and tortured upper case "G." Now it was bigger and oranger.

There were no more hints from the grey-pencil-wielding, mysterious underliner, but I knew I could figure this out myself. I just had to think it through.

Hmm, could I use the books to translate all these symbols?

Yes, I could! I started with the most obvious symbol. In the upper right-hand corner of the flimsy map page was a symbol that looked like the map itself—a small box with a small box in its upper right-hand corner, with another in *its* corner, and so on, more and more—fascinating! By some serious drawing skill, they looked like they went on forever.

Sure enough—that symbol was in the German cookbook and in the blue book.

It meant "map."

There was more to learn. On the map, there was a gaggle of these same little-box map-symbols—moving back and forth outside my front yard.

In red.

That must mean more maps—and that must be what the man in brown had in his hand out there where I just saw him. A red box symbol meant the map itself, and not the man in brown.

Oh. So, he probably knew I had a map, too. His. I would have felt safer if the dogs weren't under the bed whining, though I was actually energized by these scientific, deductive discoveries—backed up by magic. So, I kept digging.

I wondered what that wacky G symbol was, in the middle of the storm? *Orange....*

I found its meaning in the blue book, and my hands shook with excitement.

Another G symbol was looking up at me—it was on the letter that had just finished printing; its last page of long, flowing handwriting had fallen off the printer desk and to the floor and looked up at me. My hands shook with fear.

G stood for "Gwyllion." That was the name in all these books, the name they all used for the dangerous evil being in their stories. She was also known as The Old Woman of the Mountains, a hideous, dangerous creature that all pages of all books warned about.

And as Sprugly tried to tell Emma, "*She is coming.*"

The printer stopped printing.

CHAPTER 51

Emma

ry and I luckily caught sight of Thryst's bright boots—up in the air. He was climbing a tree. This allowed us to catch up and catch our breath in a dry spot under drooping oak leaves.

We hastily implemented the classic teenager plan, advanced thirteen-year-olds that we are: I called my mom and left a message that I was going to Cry's house for dinner, and he used my phone to tell his parents that he was coming to mine. They say you get to do this—lie, that is—once you have earned enough of their trust. But ours was only a little white lie, really—they *had to* trust us: these were extraordinary circumstances! And I knew that my mom was not the type to call Cry's parents to check our stories; she would take it as an opportunity to work late.

I then remembered the four pieces of paper from the stairs—one of them delivered by Same Day Pixie—and took pictures of them, pressing and smoothing the one that had two Peanut-ear-sized holes and one standard Pixie head hole. They looked like personal letters, ones that I had no time to read, so I texted them to Arty and followed them with many abbreviated words in a very large message bubble about how we were ok and all that was happening and what I thought he should do and what I thought I should do—and I regretted it all as soon as I lifted my thumb to send. Before my finger came down, my phone turned black. Then and there my battery died.

I threw the phone in my bag after considering in a painful flash how many chances I'd had to charge it earlier. Then I moved on; there was nothing more I could do. Thryst had come down from the tree. Arty had described this in his notes, but the Dwarf's climbing skills were a thousand times cooler than the little scientist described. I made a mental note to remember to draw this next in my sketchbook, if I lived.

Cry and I now needed to move fast. Although there was no path, the fairies were zooming betwixt the trees with some ancient, legendary skill. Sprug carried Peanut as she sneezed out the rain, and he jumpflew through it.

At our next rest, I had many questions for Sprug—but first Cry had many questions for me.

"How are we going to get home?" he wanted to know. It was a good question.

"I don't know yet. But we have a few hours to figure it out."

"Can we walk home from here? How far is it?" he also wanted to know. Two more good questions.

"If we have to. It's about five miles back to Belle Terre. It would take a couple of hours. Your house is a little closer."

"But this is bad," he said. I'm not sure if that qualifies as a question, but it was a good one anyway.

"We can make it, unless it changes to snow," I joked. Cry didn't laugh. It was dark and cold, and snow seemed as possible as anything. Today, as a matter of fact, a full blizzard under the sun with talking daffodils eating the snowflakes and frogs making snow angels seemed more possible than walking home from the university with a Dwarf, a baby Pixie with a fever in a glove, and a Spriggan wearing my scarf.

"And that's if we go straight home," Cry said. "Who says that's where they're going? What's the chance of that?" The boy was on a roll, a good-question machine.

"Maybe they are. Who knows?" I said but obviously did not believe my own words. I can't fool me.

Cry looked sick. He turned his face away and dug in his coat, I assumed for tissues. I went on, "Well, where else would they be going?"

"I don't know," Cry answered with his back to me. "Back home? I mean, to their home? Should we really follow them there?"

I turned Cry around and said, "Yes!" as loud as I could without shouting. And I smiled, a big, wet smile, my eyelashes dropping into my face, rain running down my cheeks. It looked like I was crying with joy, I bet.

Cry laughed, finally, and said, "Awesome."

"Let's just see what happens," I said more calmly. "This is the way home, anyway." I sounded confident of the direction because, so far, I was. I knew the area well enough, though I knew that Cry didn't. "Once we come out of these woods, we'll probably be near the open fields by the golf course. We just have to cut across and then get to the main road that goes straight back to Belle Terre."

"What about Arty?" Cry asked.

"Good question!" I said and reached into my coat for my phone for just the one second that it took to remember that it was dead. "Oh man, he must be going nuts. Hopefully, Gretel at least got my text." Then to the fairies, a short way up on a large tree bough, I yelled, "Sprug! Where are we going?" But Sprug wasn't talking. *Thryst the Guard Again* at least gave me a look that said it was ok. He also growled something that sounded like it began with an "X" and ended with "*ZZZZ…*" He bowed on the bough, then flipped off forward in a tumble that landed him in his usual feet-planted-apart position and with his axe extended out fully from his arm.

"Awesome," Cry thought. I could sense it.

Our party moved ahead once more, with Thryst keeping watch from side to side.

Cry and I followed, jogging with heavy, wet exhaustion but needing to keep up. I kept my eyes shielded from the rain and strained as best as I could to keep our leaders in view. I didn't notice what was going on in the woods around us. I also barely paid attention to Cry as he said, "I meant to tell you and Arty that my dad told me he saw some strange stuff going on at home. In the fields."

He stopped at that, since thunder struck again and we had just climbed a small, cluttered hill that ended with an open view of fields and roads—we were at the end of the wood.

A few things now caught my attention.

The first was Gretel's truck as it passed through the university exit that was just visible to our right. It joined a side road and passed closer, and I was sure I could see Arty in the back. I let that sink in…

…as I watched Thryst climb another tree. In the open wind and driving rain of the hilltop, it was even more impressive. I caught his hood as it blew off, out, and down after a devilish gust. I could hardly see what he was doing; he was very high up in a camouflage of leaves, and staring upward, my eyes were battered with water balls from the ends of soaked branches and my face was smashed sideways with wet, cold wind. Sprugly followed Thryst. About halfway, he placed Peanut, now wrapped in my scarf, carefully in a high but thick angle of trunk. The boughs swayed, but Peanut was quiet.

We were all quiet.

The wind even stopped for a moment. The trees calmed, the storm paused. Everything was still.

Then—*plunk!* Thryst landed at my feet, Sprug flew down past my ear, there was a shocking blast of lightning, and the trees started swaying together as if hit by a single, massive blow, and on the return their branches whiplashed with horrible sounds. Thryst bowed as I gave him his hat back. Sprug was carrying Peanut and put her in Cry's backpack. Cry was wiping his face. The lightning gave no thunder. Sprug hopped to my shoulder, and he seemed bigger and heavier, maybe because he was soaked with rain.

Thryst hurrumphed and cleared his face with his bulging upper arm sleeve, then started to jog down the hill and along the edge of the trees. Sprug followed, and Cry and I also—at least they were still heading in the direction of home.

Once the trees were less thick, the rain hit hard again, first in cold, downpouring waves, then in sideswiping slaps. I told Cry we were nearing the train station: the railroad tracks that ran through stops on the university grounds toward its last stop at Eastward, the station in Belle Terre. A train had just left—there were people running to their cars, covering their heads. I can only assume no one noticed us as we zigzagged through its parking lot to a fence that ran along the tracks. There was a hole where we came to it, and we all went through and ducked under a small cement trestle supporting the tracks. This three-foot-high roof was just enough for a Dwarf to stand in if he removed his rain-soaked hood, so there we hid for a moment. The ground was dry, and Cry and I plopped down, breathing heavily, Cry's backpack landing with a thud and a *peep-peep*. Large, grey concrete cylinders held up the roof where the train had just passed.

I asked everyone, "What are we doing? Where are we going?"

Sprug answered me in a loud whisper, landing hard and heavy on my shoulder. "She's here."

Cry heard this also, and he looked around wildly. "Who's s-s-she?" he stammered.

"The Old Woman," Sprug hissed. "The Old Woman of the Mountains."

I had to repeat it for Cry, though I didn't want to.

"Oh man," Cry said and put his head into his chest as he sat on the floor, wet, scared, large, and miserable. "That doesn't sound good," he said softly. We heard a few peeps and a sneeze from his bag. "God bless you," Cry said, his voice muffled and sad.

"Well," I said to my uglier-than-ever Spriggan as I felt Arty's Dwarf standing next to me with his axe blade near my shoulder, "who is this old mountain lady, and what do we do?" There were no mountains around here, not for hundreds of miles. Lots of hills, but nothing to brag about if someone was writing a new fairy tale.

I had a few other questions and wished I had Arty's books, and I wished I had Arty himself, with me.

Sprug answered by jumpflying off, with Thryst following. We were on the run again.

I wondered more about Arty and how he must be wondering about us.

CHAPTER 52

Arty and Mary

ere is the letter, warm and smudgy off the printer, as it trembled in my hands. Just the words, not the music. Dearest long lost cousin, my estranged and missed Trudy:

I am deeply sorry for my previous letter, if it caused you confusion or concern. I hear the voice of your reply, the surprise that I exist. But I do! And your life, and our families, are important, and I will come to New Island, I will come to your Eastward Manor.

Soon!

I wonder if you know enough—please keep up the work until I arrive. The hints are everywhere—and all you said was correct. Though incomplete. Keep going. Take care to be safe, but with care you will be safe.

Your guesses are correct; she is there. She is strengthening, her allies are now numerous and bold. There are many stories with many characters, but she is there, the Old Woman of the Mountains, who you rightly named a Gwyllion. She took fairies, of many kinds, of all kinds, a rainbow of lives and beings. She wants New Island, as she tried before, generations ago, as you know, and further, to "1752" and all that. So, there are kidnappees. My heart tells me there are already escapees! So be ready. And fighters will come, rescuers. And fighters, armies.

(There will be battles, cousin, small and large, seen as storms, small and large.)

And others, there are others. In a growing tale like this, there will be others. Getting close. Look for unexpected bravery, cleverness, foolishness, rashness—humanness…But be careful, she works through many in magical, devious ways. Some may get too close and be either with us or against us. Who can tell? Remember, cousin: *It is not their war…*

She has such spells—I know our part and am ready, the long years make us ready. Yet I am unsure; I don't have all the anti-power. I wonder what will come, my dreams are dark storms, my line of sight is blocked and bent.

Keep with the map!

Do not look in their eyes!

I hope you understand.

Yours in belief, yours as always, yours as supposed,

Mary

There were symbols, and those around New Island matched the books and map. And so did the "G," for Gwyllion as I'd guessed, the Old Woman of the Mountains.

I kept reading, listening to the storm, the battle outside my window. Hoping it would end, and hoping it would not be "The End."

CHAPTER 53

Emma

We were still in the storm, Cry and I, and not in our cozy beds like Arty. We weren't wondering about the storm; we were running through it and under it and around slick and swaying trees along the railroad tracks. We weren't dreaming of animals acting funny and giving us strange looks—we were *watching* animals acting strange and giving us funny looks.

None of it was ha-ha funny.

Some creatures tried to follow us. Behind us as we jogged, I saw a few little forest friends running along, or hopping, or flying, or scurrying, or slithering, or bouncing the way deer do. When we stopped—which happened twice for Thryst and Sprug to zip up a tree—the animals stared at Cry and me with a blankness as large as all of nature. Wet squirrels and shiny birds sat next to each other on tree branches and looked down at us. A miserable cat and a fat raccoon peeked out from behind a round stump.

"Our cat is always getting into fights with raccoons," Cry noted.

"Yes," I said. It was the oddest part of the whole night—so far— watching such new friendships being made.

During the second tree-climb break, Cry and I wheezed while trying to catch our breath and many little eyes watched us. I had an idea. Out of Cry's bag I took little Peanut, still in my glove and scarf, and held her up so that our animal audience could see. It didn't go over well—a hundred birds flew off like arrows shot from an army of bows; a small bunny nosed the air and darted off quickly; a frog followed it.

We heard a dog howl from downwind to the north. A tortoise crawled near our feet; a crow swooped and tried to pick it up. A tree fell into thickening mud.

I have to say, we were getting used to trees falling. The wind gusted with frightening, forceful strength at times, there seemed to be an additional spooky and dark magic at work, and I suspected that Thryst every now and then took out his frustrations, or made his path easier, by felling trees that bothered him.

Here and there when the woods weren't so thick, I could see where we were: still heading east, between the train tracks and the open fields to the north that bordered the coast, and toward our homes.

That is where we were in this world. It seemed that Sprugly and *Thryst the Lumberjack* were navigating their world at the same time. After the latest tree bit the dust, Thryst in frustration came up to me and said, "*Panachchhhchh.*" Or maybe it was, "*Pownruaachccc.*" I remembered Arty's notes on trying to communicate in Dwarrow-ish, but this was going in the other direction, and also nowhere.

He reached into his pack for something, which he now held tight and hidden in his dangerous right hand. He looked into my eyes for a brief second, and a word came into my mind: *Map.* He wanted the map. Wow. *Do that again*, I thought, trying to be telepathic. But he wouldn't. Instead, Sprug came over and smacked the back of my head.

"Oh!" I said. "The map! I don't have it, Arty has it."

Thryst looked at me again.

"Oh, right!" I said. "Yes, I have a picture of it! But—it's on my phone, and my phone is dead."

Thryst looked at me again.

My phone buzzed. I brought it out for them, and they watched it glow for a second. They handed it back, dark and powerless again.

Wow. "Do that again," I said. I wanted to text Arty, for one thing. Sprug whapped me again, and the trek resumed. They never let me play with their magic.

The rain came down. I wondered who the "Old Woman of the Mountains" was, about this crazy storm, what the animals knew that I didn't, where in the world the fairies were taking us, and which world. Cry asked all the same questions.

I knew that if we followed the tracks all the way, it would start to take us too far north and we'd have an even longer walk home. I was tired just thinking about it.

As Thryst landed next to me again, holding his hood in his own hands this time, lightning struck, and I could see that we were half-way home. I looked at *Thryst the Wet*. A sweaty Dwarf, who had just climbed a tree with his axe and bare hands, his muscles bulging and his beard glistening in the rain, the clean blade reflecting in blue the bolts of lightning, is really impressive to see—especially if he looks directly into your eyes, and you see that he can read your mind, the way sometimes we can live in his.

He now knew that Cry and I wanted to turn for home.

Thryst grunted some words to Sprug, as the Spriggan flew to my shoulder. I don't remember these words and had no way to take notes—but sure enough, the fairies then led us off the railroad path and more to the north.

"Thank God," Cry said as he blubbered with happiness and rain-water, relieved we were heading home.

There was a whisper in my ear: "She is busy, with one and many. Many Wights, many more." I had no idea what that meant, and by this time I didn't want to know. The Old Woman of the Mountains was busy; good for her. The animals in the forest were busy and scared. The fairies and Dwarves I knew were busy and liked to keep secrets. Cry was busy trying to calm down his Pixie.

"Peanut's cold is going to get worse," he said quietly to himself.

But I was not busy—I was wet and tired and getting hungry. I took a last look at the railroad tracks we were now leaving. Ahead, just where the tracks bent around out of sight, I thought I saw two red dots, like bright eyes far away, and then they vanished. I turned away and did not mention it to anyone, even though the sight stayed in my stomach.

Sprug and Thryst cut across paths that went north, and through big fields, and groups of trees that were thick with vines. The way wound back and forth—but heading north and east meant that soon we would hit the main road home.

When we did, it was at a point where there were no stores or houses, just woods on either side. We popped out and looked east and west along the slick, glistening pavement.

It was empty.

How was that possible, at rush hour?

It was less than two more miles to Belle Terre. We ran across the road, in the dark, the only light a dim yellow streetlamp atop a pole away to our left, to the west, high and lost among tree branches.

And there I saw the two red spots again, far away eyes, far away and dim, and I rubbed the rain away from my own brown eyes, and the red ones vanished. I ran ahead to join the group in another stretch of woods just off the road. Thunder struck. But there was no lightning. Tonight, the two didn't seem to care about playing together.

We found a narrow path northeast. I knew where we were now; home was along the road we had left. Dark woods lay in this direction and open fields, and the wide, muddy avenues of power lines that were bordered with tall chain link fences and were thick with thorny undergrowth. Within were the large towers of electric wires that ran from the power plant by the water outward in all directions to deliver electricity to Belle Terre homes and beyond. I remembered seeing these from up in a plane once, when my mother and I went to Florida on vacation. The clearings cut through the woods in straight lines, looking like a big spider web across the Long Island, centered at the water and our small town.

We were coming up to one such lane now. We stepped out of the woods into a wide space dark enough to seem like the night sky had fallen into it.

This seemed to make Cry nervous, and he stopped short. He said, "I never got to tell you what my father told me, what he saw in the field behind our house…"

But he didn't get to tell me then either. Ahead of us, in the field, was a Giant.

CHAPTER 54

Arty

I considered the letter, wondering whether a real fairy "battle," large or small, was going on here on New Island. And with my friends in it. While I read.

The handwriting was girly and looked like one long decoration, with looping, connecting curves and script letters that seemed to come from hundreds of years ago—though the language was our modern English. With a fairytale accent.

Mary must be one of the good guys, I thought, then I wrote it down.

The letter was addressed to a Trudy, so who was the man in brown? Had he stolen it from Trudy? Who was Trudy? Who was Mary? Where was she? When was she coming? There was no date on the letter. There were many other "runes" but too many to attack without a new, serious plan.

I wondered who *we* were in the letter—Emma, Cry, and I. Some of the "others"? Did "Mary" know about us? Ted was involved somehow, the leech, the spider that he was. Were we in the plan? Would the Old Lady use bad magic on my friends? *She has such spells…*

I made some notes, with a new theory that Peanut was a kidnappee. And Sprugly was a rescuer.

What was Thryst? Must be a warrior, army leader, from what I saw, from what he let me see.

And yet he also acted like there was something else on his mind.

I worried about the magic map. We had one page—which also belonged to Trudy. And this letter. We should give them back. Maybe the good guys needed the map; maybe we should find the rest of it, take it from the man in brown.

Maybe I should stay out of it.

I kept reading. I needed to get to the historical society. There was a lot I didn't know.

Though I knew more than Emma and Cry.

CHAPTER 55

Emma

The Giant was at the top of a hill. Its monstrous shape stood as tall as the trees against the farther glow of the lights from the Belle Terre village. The hill formed a long ridge and was rutted with deeply cut bike paths. These fields were a favorite place for older teen bikers; the trails zigzagged, jumped large hills, and went on for miles. They were now all mud. The rain still pounded us from a dark sky.

You don't need much light to see a Giant, however. The thing stood for a moment, its head swiveling back and forth. Then it walked, slowly, just as I always pictured giants doing, and away from us.

I tried to remember Arty's fairy books and any fairy tales I had ever heard with Giants and could only think of one—*Jack and the Beanstalk.* Silly me.

The Giant's back was toward Cry and me, so I couldn't see many definite features. I'm not sure if that makes it better or worse when you see your first Giant. I saw a head shape, shoulders where they should be, arms of human proportions, and a soft and lumpy, hard-to-grasp ugliness all around its outline. Large shadows moved and shifted over the field.

In those first few seconds, as the thing moved, I wasn't afraid. Instead I was distracted—trying to think of something that I was trying to think of, if you know what I mean. *Other Giants? My journal? Cry's comments?*—one of these, or a combination of them, pulled at me and bothered me. I knew I was forgetting something.

But it was hard to concentrate in the shadow of a Giant who was now climbing a power line tower.

Now—what did *that* remind me of? I was frustrated with my own brain. *King Kong?* Well, yes and no. That wasn't it. I watched the Giant take another step up. The power line towers were tall, pyramid-shaped metal frames, their lower rungs a good ten feet apart, and the Giant had walked up as easily as a man going up a ladder. The Giant's head was almost to the wires. That made him thirty or forty feet tall. I looked over to Cry. He was standing back, behind some trees. Frozen, he seemed, staring ahead with his mouth open dumbly.

I could barely hear him mumble weakly, "Is this the Woman of the Mountains? I pictured a witch..."

It hit me then that I should be afraid. So, I started to be afraid. I dashed behind Cry's tree trunk. I could hear Peanut now, shrieking loudly in Cry's soaking wet backpack. I wanted to calm her down, so I went to open the zipper, and Cry yelled, "Don't!"

Too late. With one-inch unzipped, Peanut ran out, up my arm, and off to the tree next to us, a large oak that went way, way up into the dark wetness. She was gone. Cry tried calling to her, but we were both thinking the same thing.

He said it first. "Let's get out of here. We have to run away, too. Forget the adventure, it's over, I want to go home." He looked around for a direction to run.

I couldn't argue. This was a disaster. That thing in the field was no cute little fairy. The weird storm, this witch-talk, a giant monster—it was all too intense. I looked back to the field; it was now awash with a grey fog. Some dimly lit, evil mist had rolled in with the winds from the water and formed swirls where the Giant had stood. It—the Giant—was still there, stepping back to the ground. It was all like some mystical vision from a dream, a bad dream: a tremendous glowing ghost in the fog. My eyes were half-closed, shielding the rain, squinting in the darkness.

I forgot to stay afraid because something was still bugging me. *Giant. No little fairy. Ghost.* My heartbeats pounded my head to a bad ache. And: *Where is Thryst? Where is Sprug?*

Then *I'd better get out of here.* I turned to follow Cry but suddenly heard a sound I'd never heard before. I stopped, and so did Cry, a few steps ahead. He heard it, too. But he *had* heard it before.

"Did you hear that?" he said. "That's her! That's Peanut!"

"That's not like the other scringing," I said. It was a low, soft hum that I had to remain still to hear, given the racket of the wind in the branches. Its sound was so different from the nasty cracking and wheezing of the storm that it stood apart, faint but clear.

Peanut was crooning from high up somewhere. There's no other way to describe it.

It sounded as if she was laughing, too. No other way to describe that, either. Not then and there, anyway, while I was having trouble describing things. My brain was a few steps behind. "Peanut Serenades During Storm"—*I should draw that,* I thought, after sketching "Thryst Climbing Tree" but before painting "Giant Tramples Me to Bits." That's what tomorrows are for.

Through the fog, I saw that the thing was now looking our way. The dim but ghoulish glow in the distance seemed to seep straight through it. Cry let out a cry.

"What's going on?" I mumbled.

Lightning struck, the foggy air in the field lit up, and the Giant did also. It appeared like a ghost, almost see-through. I was not scared. The lightning burst once more, and there I also saw Thryst, *Thryst the Way Too Brave,* small but solid compared to the ghost near him and moving wildly. His axe was at work, swinging like crazy.

But not at the Giant.

"What's going on?" I wondered aloud. Peanut scrang and laughed, both. There was no thunder. *Welcome to the world of fairies,* I thought. This was more like it—all magical and strange and weird and wonderful, and it's a good thing my brain was not working correctly, or I would've curled up in a ball on the ground.

Cry looked at me, his wide eyebrows scrunched. The many animals that had lined up two-by-two behind him in the woods looked at me similarly. My body refused to be scared.

"Come on!" I yelled and ran into the field. As I did, the world went completely black. The lights from Belle Terre had gone out. Though they were pretty dim, I wished for them back since now all was one big shadow, even though it was barely past dinnertime. The clouds above were threatening and thick. The mist disappeared, and so did everything else, even the hands in front of my face. I stopped dead in my tracks and turned back to feel for Cry in the empty, black air. As I did, I saw the red eyes again—far off in the direction of the road. I saw four this time, slanted fiery eyes of creatures moving along together.

My brain bumped into me, catching up: *Now*, I was scared. "Cry!" I yelled, just as we collided, making us both jump. "Come on!"

But strangely, my legs ran into the field, instead of away; toward the Giant, instead of away; toward Thryst, and toward the metal power line towers that I could not see anymore.

I wanted lightning to strike again, and it did. I used the two seconds of whiteness to look ahead. We were heading straight for Giant Hill. We kept running. I could hear Cry's backpack banging around just behind.

After the flash of lightning and the bright moment of stillness it brought, the world seemed suddenly to change. The sounds of wind and rain, of my feet sloshing and of Cry's backpack banging, were, in an instant, replaced with loud shrieking and crying, and with voices yelling in strange languages. I heard thuds of contact between living things, and rocks and trees thrashing and bashing and moving unnaturally. There was the bang and ring of metal against metal, hard items battling and colliding with force. All around me, I felt whips and whooshes of air as things flew past.

Then the feeling changed again. I was blind, but I felt like I was in a different hemisphere, in a different season, and in a different age of the world. This was like looking into Thryst's eyes but more real, and somehow more personal. Inside me somewhere was more bedlam: a fight for control of what I *did know* and what I *should know*. And I felt like I was on the losing side.

I stopped. To run any farther and blindly was madness. Though *everything* was madness: around me the whirlwinds of battle still raged. There were a lot more creatures than just the three fairies who found Arty, Cry, and me—and more even than the others that Sprugly had us read about. Many more had joined our world; Arty was too late figuring things out. Weather and creatures and land and sea and plants and animals—and I—were all here, now, and all was embattled.

I stopped. Cry wasn't with me. He hadn't followed, or maybe he'd turned back. I dropped to my knees with plain old human exhaustion.

I watched. Creatures were drawn to various sides—I saw when the lightning struck, or fires flared, yet also felt it within me. The battle was waged with magic, and with living souls, on the ground and in the air, with wings and weapons. There was a force coming from up the hill—the hill where I first saw the Giant. That seemed like a long time ago already.

Fires blasted upwards more regularly, grey plumes of smoke all around as I sat and hid myself under my coat and tried to disappear into the earth. Were these from the spells of Dwarfs or Spriggans or Pixies, or their enemies? Groups of living and breathing things fought and flew and ran—and clashed and tumbled and yelled. And all the time, from up the hill, I felt a dark power that pulled at me from inside my body. I could not move. I did not want to move. I felt safe somehow, almost as if I wasn't really there.

That's when the eyes came.

Were they the eyes of the hill itself? Was it the Giant? They were large, but I couldn't tell whether it was because I was close to them, or because they were the size of the world—but it didn't matter, since they were all I could see. They glowed, like a low, comfortable fire, dull red, almost orange. Looking, once again I felt that I was in a different world, the fairy world that I knew from Thryst's eyes and from Sprugly's eyes. But these were neither. These eyes spoke to me, and in a mother's voice. But not my mother's, or at least not in any way I've ever heard. I felt like a swaddled baby, warm and protected from the storm, resting in the large arms of some new world. The eyes spoke to me, cooing with loving reassurance.

The words tempted me. To stay. To be safe. To be loved, to be happy among the creatures that were singing—the same ones I'd seen in Sprugly's eyes yesterday, in my room, a world away from here.

I smiled. I think.

Then mountains seemed to move. The ground rose in new hills, and they came at me, at us—myself and the owner of the eyes, the great Mom of the Earth. I was being pulled, but I did not want to move. I wanted to stay. Strong arms pulled at me and now lifted me over a hard shoulder, and my hair hung down around me, upside down. I knew I couldn't resist the arms, so I made a promise to the eyes that I would come back.

As I did, there were angry words spoken—by who I could not be sure, but they were harsh compared to the singsong of the woman's voice. Though I heard them, clearly, and I felt them, and I knew what they meant, I could not remember them. They passed through me like a spell. Then everything changed again, and I was back in the rain among the wildly flaring flames.

I came out of my swoon, out from the world of the eyes.

The hill now appeared like a mountain—it grew with each crash of firelight. Or was it getting closer? The ground shook, and I smelled new earth as holes sprung up around me. I heard axes then; they rang and mixed with the grunts of Dwarves. I didn't see Cry or hear his cries.

W.W. Marplot

I curled into a tight ball like a baby as all around grew closer and louder. My heavy eyelids blinked with every flash, so slowly that each time I blinked, I almost nodded into a dream.

A breeze touched my face and roused me. It was a warm breeze that felt familiar, but then changed shape and formed words. I felt a push, which forced me up and moved me to a gargantuan tree with a nest of tangled and knotty roots where I hid again. I saw Thryst as he walked away; he had moved me again, leaving the battle to lead me here.

But he did not go back to the fray. Instead, I watched as his creeping shadow moved about in a new, orange light that lingered from the spreading flames and made everything appear like an old movie—rough, dark, and staggering jerkily onward. Thryst went back and forth, not fighting, not escaping, not helping Dwarves, not joining them, and not pursuing enemies. He seemed to be looking for something. He went up trees, and down holes, and back and forth.

He went among the many other creatures—large and small, many-legged or many-winged, breathing fire or slinging ropes, some screeching, some silent, some dressed in human clothes, some naked as animals.

It was bewildering, but all ran from Thryst when he came near; a spirit like smoke followed him around, and a clean light shone from under his brows.

I swooned again—perhaps setting a new swooning record for my age group—and a new vision came to me, that of lamps, two glowing fireballs bouncing at the horizon in the direction of Giant Ghost Hill, as if they were torches carried at the head of an army. The lights approached and grew bigger—they turned into eyes. I shut mine—but still saw a huge hideous face, a monstrous expression gazing directly at me, coming near enough to eat me alive within a gigantic smile. I cowered down low and hugged my tree.

That was the end.

The next thing I remembered was being awakened by another breeze, this one carrying the smells of familiar land, air, and water. I shivered with cold; the rain still poured and had soaked my clothes completely. It was still night. As I opened my eyes, the mist lifted, as did the fog of uncertainty in my waking head—as I looked around, a much clearer scene slowly emerged.

It was quiet, and a soft light lay on the leaves of my tree and the land around. The field behind and hill ahead were empty. I felt the cold mud on my knees and rose to my feet to walk toward the slope. Cry was then at my side, which didn't surprise me, though there was no reason to expect this. We ran together.

Sore, our legs burning, we pushed up the hill. I heard again the low humming of Peanut the Pixie singing a strange song. At the top opened a wide view, but with my next step I plunged knee-deep into a muddy pit.

"*Uk*," I said loudly.

"*Kaza, togla tanna noo*," I heard, and was lifted up and carried and placed onto a large rock.

"Thanks, Thryst," I said, and he probably bowed, but I was wiping rain and mud from my face and legs. Cry was whimpering next to me, leaning on the rock, I could feel his big shoulder against my little one. I heard the humming stop. You can hear something when it stops only when everything stops, which it did. I did not feel any rain and looked up. The metal power line tower was above and next to us. A maze of fallen trees lay on the ground, and soon the stillness was broken by chirping and scratching and squeaking and sniffling and the hustling and bustling of many small animals of the field and trees. Their home was a mess.

We moved, too—Cry and I followed Thryst without a word, descending the hill and meeting a bike path at the bottom. The Dwarf was no longer searching for anything; maybe he found it, maybe the battle was over. Our path led to the backs of houses, then followed a large fence that ran along their backyard borders, the boundary of the power lines and of the homes of Belle Terre.

After the last of the houses was an opening in the fencing—a large section had been knocked down. We walked through this space, and as we did, I said, "Oh!" Sprug was on my shoulder and in my ear. His breath surprised me, and just as in Arty's room, I felt a small shiver down into my knees and toes. This time I almost fell, since he seemed heavier and larger than ever: He was covered and weighted with clothes! He jumpflew around and gave us a fairy fashion show that also featured Peanut, who was peeping on the ground ahead of us, wrapped in a different scarf and wearing a small, matching hat. Where a Spriggan would find dry Pixie clothes at a time like this was beyond me and my non-magical human brain.

Welcome to fairy land, I thought once more. It kept getting weirder and dangerous-er, but I began to understand. I thought of the other world, those supreme eyes, and now remembered my promise to go back there.

Cry yanked me back to his weepy world, asking, "Where's the Giant?"

I smiled, took a moment, then said, "Ever see how dogs and cats puff up and try to look big when they fight? Well, this was ridiculous."

Sprugly, small again, said to me, "She's away. For now."

"Who?" I asked, though I now understood. "The Old Mountain Woman…right?"

"Yes. One's escaping, many fighting," he answered.

We walked back to Belle Terre, and our homes, under strange-colored moonlight.

CHAPTER 56

Ted

Ted here, I saw some of the battle, too, and if Cry and Emma were scared and in trouble, it serves them right for sneaking away from me. And all this is nothing compared to my adventures, and my dreams.

And even in awake life, I'm ahead of them, as everyone will see soon—AGAIN.

CHAPTER 57

Cry

This is Cry. I didn't feel good. Peanut slept with me after that long walk home in the storm-battle, my parents were worried sick and mad, and I heard animal noises all night coming from the field in back of my house. I thought I knew why—but maybe Ted was right, and I shouldn't believe any of this.

CHAPTER 58

Emma

This is Emma. I feel tired and torn. I was split between worlds, my heart was split, and my mind was splitting also with a headache. I heard words during the storm, in the battle, and then a spell that released me—but not completely, since those words went around and around my brain as if stuck on a roller coaster. When the storm ended and the rain stopped, the world was warm and clean, like it had just had a bubble bath, but there was no one to wrap me in a big towel like my father used to—so instead, I felt like I was just shivering naked after a cold shower.

I twisted in my bed for hours until falling into a blank, empty, dreamless sleep. I woke when Sprug whispered into my ear, "You did good." But I didn't think I did anything.

CHAPTER 59

Arty

rty here. Still here, though it's finally Friday morning.

Last night's storm went on for hours before stopping suddenly, like a door slam. The roof went ominously quiet, the map curiously dim. The clouds evaporated within minutes, and a bright, orange full moon appeared and glowed like a plastic Halloween pumpkin. Animals howled at it. People gawked at it.

Orange. It reminded me of the G rune on the map, and I tried not to look at either one.

Still typing up my notes, but still with nothing from Emma, I eventually fell asleep…

…and into a sunny and bright-orange springtime day filled with golden flowers and baby bunny rabbits and rainbow butterflies—something Emma would draw. Everyone in the world was enjoying it, except we fairy-finders. Cry was crying and dressed like a troll. Emma was chasing Sprugly, who was flying around with her sketch pad. Thryst sat knocking over little plastic army men with his hammer.

I was trying to read a to-do list that was ten feet long, a train of yellow and green sticky notes that grew longer as it moved away from me, humping and stretching like a flimsy caterpillar. I felt like a summertime fat kid trying to keep up with an ice cream cone.

Then Peanut squeaked, "They are all coming."

I turned, cold and sweaty at once, and I shook. A wind blew hundreds of tiny scraps of paper around like a bathtub emptying. Thryst jumped up and started digging, into hard rock.

The sound of it, the clacking scrape of metal against stone, survived the dream and awoke with me. I saw three faces. My dogs'.

Though I shook the sleep from my head, I could still hear the tapping and scraping of Thryst's two-headed hammer. It was either from deep inside my brain, or deep inside my house.

I looked around my room with one eye, the other buried in the pillow. It was early, sunrise, and there was pale yellow light shining onto my desk and its pile of books. The tapping continued as, like a searchlight, my one eye scanned the room for what was real. Between dreams and fairies and daydreams and large orange moons and storms and sunrises, it took a minute to remember what the plan was.

My eye found my phone, on the end of my bed. I jumped up to check it.

Texts from Emma! They had come late last night, at 1:35. The first one read, "We hd to flw thm, more soon, nd to chrge, Mom's room." The second said, "Nd to sleep, battle was rough, more ltr, ttyl." The third: "Hope u r ok, we are home, more tomm, ttyl." And the last: "It's ok, I have Sprug & Cry & 'Nut, ttyl."

I texted her back, then called. No answer. *Still sleeping*, I thought.

What does this do to my plan?

Battle?

I still heard the tapping—and felt it through the floor. It was real! I followed the sound to my basement, and through the playroom to the entrance of our crawlspace—long home to storage containers, holiday decorations, and mildew. The space was four feet high, with cinder block walls—a definite Dwarf hangout.

I lifted myself in—the entrance was four feet off the basement floor. The crawlspace runs under the main floor living room and entrance foyer and bends around in an L-shape. I flicked the chain to a bare, single light bulb and crawled along.

Ahead of me was reality: A Dwarf, sitting cross-legged. My Dwarf, *Thryst the Depressed*, as so he looked. There were woodchips in his beard. He didn't look at me, only downward, tapping the cinder block walls with his small hammer for no reason. It looked like he had been digging a bit also.

"What's wrong?" I asked. "Were you with Emma? What happened?"

He simply slowly sighed. He was sad, it was obvious. He was slumped over, mindlessly banging the hammer into the wall, dragging it around, his axe lying at his side, his hood back, his eyes cloudy and dull. This was the most shocking sign; there was no light in his eyes, just a deep, old sadness.

I reviewed my plan and decided that I would stay home from school until I figured this out.

CHAPTER 60

Arty

as it real, or not?" I asked Emma. We were finally talking on the phone after a long night and depressing morning, and her hints about their adventure, their bunch of adventures, in the woods were maddening.

"It's complicated. I'll tell you when I get there." She was gone again…for now.

Emma also decided to stay home from school. She was up and out early and gathered what news she could—and then at long last came to my house. We went downstairs to the basement playroom, where Thryst awaited but only nodded to Emma before returning into the crawlspace. We heard his tapping and a low, moaning sigh every now and then—deep and sad, like the sound I once forced out of a school-orchestra tuba before being asked to switch to cello. The dogs would join in with a howl from outside, off in the yard somewhere, like a next-door choir.

"What's with him?" Emma asked as we climbed the stairs to my room. "He sounds like an underground cow."

"He's mopey. Is Sprug with you?" I answered and asked.

"Why is he mopey? No, Sprug isn't with me," she asked and answered. Emma's body language, completely opposite to my Dwarf's, was peppy.

"I don't know why Thryst is so mopey," I said. "You tell me! What happened last night?" I heard again *Thryst the Stringed Instrument* humming another long note of depression. It reminded me: "I made up a word for that: *Dwarrow-sorrow*. Add it to your list, Emma."

"Uh, yeah, well that's actually two words just jammed together, so maybe we can leave that one off."

I ignored this. "Where's Cry?" I asked. "I haven't heard from him at all."

"He can't get out, he stayed home sick, too. I told him we would call and see if he can meet us at the historical society. We're still going, right?"

"Yes," I answered and asked, "Then it was real? The battle?"

We'd reached my room, where Emma looked at me until our eyes locked. She held us there until I was about to speak and then answered, "Yes, it was. It was real."

"Wow," I said and meant it. "Tell me everything!" I hoped she'd written it all down properly, but, no, instead she excavated from her bag crumpled loose notes and a notepad filled with late-night sketches—and that was all. I scrambled for my own pen and pad.

She told me everything. I took notes, adding to her story with what I knew from the letter, the books, and from watching it all on the magic map.

The Old Woman of the Mountains. The Gwyllion. She was at the center of it all, whatever she was.

"Yes," Emma said again. "It was dreamy but physical, I could feel it all going on around me. It was like I'd walked through a door and—even though I was still on the same land, in the same field with the hill and the power lines—there was more to it, like there was more land, and more sky, and more…history, or a another dimension, or something…And many other creatures, all over the place."

Noticing that I'd stopped writing, she stopped talking and, noticing that I had one hand raised in the air, Emma let me ask my question. It was an important one.

"Can you slow down?"

"Sorry!" she said, taking out her own notepad and phone and plunking on the floor next to me. She called Cry and put him on speaker, welcoming him to join in between sniffles.

"Peanut says hello," he said.

Emma couldn't sit for long and bounced around the room while remembering the battle of the hill and paused as I rubbed my handwriting muscles and tried to catch up. I didn't comment on any of it, except to say one thing, "Sprug the Giant!"

"Cool," Cry said.

"Yep," she said proudly and continued her tale.

I asked if Emma had read the "Mary" letter; she said she had. So, we both knew: The Old Woman of the Mountains had kidnapped fairies, and there was now trouble here on New Island.

"Peanut was kidnapped, I think," I said. I heard a squeak on the phone.

"And Sprug is here to rescue her, I think," Emma added. Sprug whispered something. "No, I know for sure…" Emma corrected.

"And there are armies, warriors, also. Wights…" I said as Emma shuddered, "and the Dwarf gang I saw, with Thryst."

"Oh yes, there definitely are, trust me." Emma grinned with the memory. "But, Arty, I don't I think Thryst is here to fight. He's looking for something. Desperately."

"What?"

"I don't know. I don't think Sprug knows either."

We agreed on that. Thryst's actions, his interest in the map and climbing trees, and avoiding even his own Dwarf army…*why?*

"So, we are the 'others' in the letter?" Emma asked.

"I think so," I said. "Which kind?"

Emma read from the letter. "Are we 'unexpected bravery, cleverness, foolishness, rashness' or 'humanness'?" she asked. I laughed, though she looked serious. Cry admitted he was lost.

We heard my dogs echo a deep howl from underneath the house. I dropped my pen, looked to my friend, and sent her a smile that died when reaching her face.

"There's more, Arty," she said, as serious as if someone had died. No one had, but the look in her eyes made the air in the room stop, and I almost gasped.

"What?" I inhaled.

"The 'Old Woman' spoke to me. I think I saw in her eyes, the way we do with Thryst, and I did with Sprugly." Emma slowed to a stop. She stood, took three steps from the desk, then sat on my bed.

I was concerned, and she knew it. This did not sound like a good thing.

"I'm ok," she mumbled, her hair drooping over her downcast face. I could barely hear her voice. Then she explained.

"It was like a dream, at first, but the Old Woman of the Mountains wanted me to come with her. To join her. In her world, and here also. She said us females should stick together, and that she needed me. She said some personal things…"

Not knowing what to say, I tried, "You are a young woman…" and then "There are no mountains around here…" to try to distinguish my childhood friend from this other thing, this fairytale character that, according to most stories, was pesky at best and evilly dangerous at worst.

Emma looked like she was going to cry. I sat next to her, not daring to say any more.

She went on softly, "She knew what to say to me. She knew how to make me feel. And she said I was supposed to have brothers and sisters, and…" No more words came for a while.

I watched her, her long hair hanging like the dark leaves of a sad tree, one turning away from wind and weather.

"It's my mother's fault…" I thought I heard her say. I didn't write any of this down.

"Do you remember what she said exactly? Maybe we can figure out…something." My voice cracked on the empty words.

It took another minute until Emma raised her face just enough to tell me that she didn't remember. I didn't say anything, although I didn't believe her. She needed more time with this secret, and my investigations could wait.

Soon, however, the leaves of her hair parted, and a warm smile blossomed. "I'm ok. I do remember the other words, not the Old

Woman's but the ones that rescued me. It was like a spell was broken—I heard the Giant speak, and I was then pulled away from the gaze of the old witch." To my surprise, Emma was suddenly excited and bouncing again, making my bed a raft out on a choppy sea. I fumbled with my pad and dropped my pen. "Thryst carried me back to the field."

"Wow," I said, not quite like a genius, and I felt not quite like an idiot while reaching for a pen that had apparently rolled to England. I went to the desk for another, saying, "Ok, what did the Giant—Sprugly—say?"

"It was *'Anail chuid focal ar na fir na gluine a thabhairt do dhuine a mbainfear anail.'* And then I was back. I'll never forget it; it sticks in my head like a catchy song mixed with a car crash."

"Awesome," Cry said through the phone speaker.

I wrote it all down, shaking my amazed head. *A fairy spell? Magic? A curse? Kidnapping Emma? How can I ever figure this out?* I wondered at the challenge. I hoped the trail of books I was following would answer the questions…but *magic spells?* I wasn't a wizard.

A new thought nagged at my brain, an uncomfortable connection that I had to ask. "You said it was like a dream, in the spell…like what Ted said?"

"Yes, I thought of that, too. Maybe Ted was under a spell. He asks for trouble—"

"I feel bad for him," Cry interrupted.

"—and maybe she found him," Emma finished.

"I don't think I feel bad for him," I said.

Emma smiled. "And he is being chased by Mr. Alphabet."

"So, we should help him?" I didn't smile. "We have enough trouble. But I think we need to get the map and the letter back to whoever they belong to."

Emma read from the letter again. "'She has such spells' it says."

"Yes," I recalled and remembered to shiver. "And Mary might have the 'anti-power,' whatever that means."

"What are you guys talking about?" Cry asked loudly. I offered to catch him up.

"The Old Woman of the Mountains is a female fairy, one of the Gwyllion who—"

"Whoa, a gwillion! That's a lot!" Cry interrupted. "That would explain—"

"No!" I smiled. "*Gwyllion* is not a number, they are girl fairies who waylay travelers, it says." I was stuck on the word. "What's that mean? Make them lost, or…"

"No. *Waylay* means to attack them, or hide somewhere and jump them," Emma answered.

"Like you guys in the field," I observed.

"Yep," she said. "Good word for it. We were waylaid. I think." Emma paced.

I went on, partly jealous. "Also, they're afraid of iron, or something, powerful iron weapons, and they come in stormy weather…"

"Interesting," Emma said.

I heard some more sounds of Dwarrow-sorrow from the crawl-space, then the dogs howling outside.

I went on, "…and they like goats, they sometimes appear as goats. Freaky."

"Ghosts?" Cry asked.

"No. Goats," I repeated.

"Goats?" Emma asked.

"G-O-T-E-S?" Cry asked.

"Definitely. Goats," I repeated.

Emma smiled. "That's it?"

I nodded. "From what Sprugly said, this one Old Woman must be a pretty powerful Gwyllion."

"Ok," Emma said, spinning (?) in place, "read the Wight stuff next. What's a Wight?"

Cry answered for me. "They're pretty bad," he said as I flipped through pictures in two of my books. "Like wicked fairies, evil, supernatural—just bad news. They haunt people, and they haunt places. They can even kill sometimes …"

Cry faded out, and the same memory, of the battle, seemed to be passing over Emma's face; she wore an odd look, pale, ghostly.

To change the subject, I told them about the map, and the G—for Gwyllion—and about the notes, and about how much we still didn't know. Who was Trudy? Who wrote these notes? What was Eastward Manor? It all connected somehow.

Our next step was to go to the historical society and get that cookbook.

Cry spoke quietly, almost a whisper. "I wish I could come. Peanut is scared. Why did they find us?"

"I have a theory," Emma said, back to normal, with a finger in the air, trying to act scientific. "I think they come to us because they trust us. Maybe it's instinct or something, not to go to adults. Anyway: a Dwarf finds you. You tell me, and then a Spriggan finds me. You talk to Cry, and a Pixie finds him…" Emma looked at me to finish.

I did. "I get it—whoever we trust, they will trust and come to them. I like that, good thinking, Emma. But Cry was able to see Thryst; that's why I talked to Cry in the first place."

"Maybe they can sense it," she answered, "who we trust, who they can trust. They never let anyone else see them."

"Maybe," I said, thinking hard, trying to remember—then I smiled and nodded. "But there are only Thryst and two fairies. That's not enough scientific evidence."

"True, but we can test it!" Emma said triumphantly and with a fist pump. "You'll like this, Professor Arty: We just need to list everyone you and I have talked to, and see if anything, you know, has found them. Maybe when the kidnapped fairies escape, they try to find kids they can trust."

"And all the other ones? At the university? In the storm?" I asked.

"Are bad, or good, but not escapees."

I heard another sneeze, a small one.

"Bless you, Peanut," Emma said.

"We are pretty sick," Cry said and blew his nose. For a while. Either that or he decided to start learning the trombone right away. It was gross no matter which. The phone's small speaker rattled in pain.

"I don't want to find a Wight," Cry said, his brain handling our conversation in a random order.

"Obviously—but those weren't kidnapped. I want to test this—let's call whoever we spoke to yesterday and ask them…"

She stopped mid-sentence.

I realized why: we had a problem, as I pointed out. "Ask them what? Have you found any Elves? We can't. We have to spy on them."

"Oh no!" Emma exclaimed, visibly upset. "That reminds me! Oh no…"

"What?" Cry and I both asked.

"We all spoke to Ted!"

Another problem; a worse problem.

We let this sink in. Did we send the kidnapped fairies the wrong message—would they trust Ted? The last kid we'd want taking care of a legendary creature, and taking care of the *secret* of taking care of a legendary creature, was Ted.

Cry was silent on the phone. Then I heard one sniffle—large—and one sneeze—small—and he said, "I think everyone would know, if Ted knew, especially if he wanted us to know, and he knew, right?"

He had a good point—I think—but not good enough.

Emma came out from behind her thoughts. "Yeah, I'm sure we'd have heard from him if something happened, or everyone in town would have heard, or there would be a reality TV show by now, so let's not worry about it yet."

Cry started to say something, then sniffled instead and said nothing. Literally. "Nothing…"

Emma set to work, and we compiled the list of kids each of us had spoken to in our short time at school yesterday, or after, and the list was:

Isabella J., Olivia P., Jacob M., Ethan S., Sophia H., and Alex Z. Ok. Good.

We let Cry and his baby Pixie off the phone after reassuring and God-bless-you-ing them a few more times.

But then: *all heck broke loose.*

Our cell phones both blew up—our ringtones don't go well together, and they blared a blended, awful noise, each buzzing across the desk and toward each other.

Who called? Well, it was:

Alex Z., and Sophia H., and then Ethan S, then Jacob M., Olivia P., and Isabella J.

They had some interesting stories to tell.

They had all stayed home sick from school and heard that Emma was sick also, and that there was a stranger at school, and that Ted was in trouble.

And, besides that: had some interesting stories to tell.

Emma and I looked at each other, dazed. And there was something funny growing in my yard, but Emma does not want to talk about that yet.

CHAPTER 61

Emma

mma here, and I was excited. After the six phone calls, one each from Alex Z., Sophia H., Ethan S, Jacob M., Olivia P., and Isabella J., I was able to say proudly, "Looks like I was right." The "Trust Network" was real, and the fairies used it.

Arty nodded. I asked him what we do next.

"We have to get to the historical society museum quick and get that book!" he said. "Hopefully, it explains things. We have to have answers for everyone."

I knew that "everyone" meant all the friends that just called because, although we had sworn each to secrecy, we figured this barely-teen secrecy would expire in a day at most.

Lastly, Arty said, "We have to move fast."

Stuck at the back of my mind like a burr was a prickly thought: "Hopefully, Ted didn't find anything, because that would be another thing to worry about. Who knows what side he's on, and when?"

"I don't see what harm Ted can do at this point, but the less we see him the better. Just like always. But if Alex, Sophia, and the others all found fairies, then maybe Ted did, too."

I realized that the last twenty minutes of phone calls had come and gone so quickly that not even Arty had taken decent notes. "I think we need to tell the whole story about the other six," I said, looking ahead to the day when one of us—whoever won the bet—would have the right to write the book, if they wanted to. "We can't just leave their parts out."

"Sure we can. We have the important data; we don't need to confuse readers by making it complicated with useless info," Arty said. "More importantly, there isn't time now to stop and take notes."

I ignored that. "We can write an *interlude.* It's not a real chapter, just a quick middle part, to tell all the new stories together at once."

"Fine," Arty agreed, after I promised to hurry with the notes.

"Interlude"

Ted: Oh, come on, what is an "interlude"? We were finally getting to the part where I am the hero…

Emma: Be quiet, Ted. Cry and I think this is one of the best parts of our adventure, everyone's stories with the fairies that found them.

Ted: Oh yeah? Well, Arty doesn't.

Arty: That's true. Sorry, Emma, but it is also because kids don't stick to the important facts. And most of them didn't even know any facts. I had to look it all up for them.

Emma: Yes—but do you realize that you agree with Ted?

Arty: Well…I guess.

Ted: Ha.

Emma: Be quiet Ted. Ok, here goes.

Hi, this is Alex Z. I found a Hobgoblin, and it tried to rub some cream on me or something.

Arty: Yes, I had to explain that a Hobgoblin is a typical fairytale creature, not really like what people today call a goblin (which are larger and scarier). These use something called "fairy ointment," which lets you see them better if it's put on your eyes. Next.

Hi, my name is Ethan…uh…Ethan S. When I was at the bus stop, someone asked me if he could come into my backyard. But I couldn't see anybody. It sounded like a man. But then I saw in the tree a small person laughing at me. And it sounded like a different tree was growling, and then another tree was crying. So, I ran inside and hid under my bed and played with my 3DS, but the Elf followed me.

Arty: It was a *Tree Elf* that found Ethan. There are lots of tree spirits that sound like they're living near him, too. The books say that elms are sad, and oaks are mad, and that willows will follow you. The legends say that oak trees have a powerful magic and attract powerful spirits, and Ethan's yard is full of large ones. There are also the *"Oakmen"*—spirits that will ask permission to enter oak woods and then spread their power and mischief. So, this all makes sense. By the way, the worst are the elder trees—there are a lot of weird stories about them. They can either offer shelter from witches—or they can *be* witches! So, that's no help.

Cry: Awesome. I thought a willow followed me once. Next.

Jacob M. Jacob…M! Yeah, baby. Ok—I found a teeny tiny Elf, all in green, friendly little guy, but he doesn't speak English. I knew I would find something like this eventually for my whole life. The only time he got upset was when he saw my room, but then we played football outside and he stinks. Oh yeah, I named him Elfy. Oh yeah, one more thing, and when he turns around, he has no back. Just a front.

Arty: Okaaaaaaaay, Jacob. It looks like a typical *Light Elf* found him. They are small—like elves on TV commercials, or Santa's helpers. There are Tree Elves like Ethan's, and Light Elves like Jacob's. There are *Dark Elves*, too. These are like Dwarves, almost. (And there are *Water Elves* also, as Isabella will tell us.) The reason "Elfy" didn't like Jacob's room, I think, is that Elves don't like certain human faults, untidiness especially, according to the books. They also hate eavesdropping and selfishness. And, yes, it is possible that this Elf really had no back! Fairy creatures have certain "defects" that we should not stare at, and having no back is one of them. Nasty: it is just empty.

Cry: Awesome. Next please.

Hi, this is Isabella J. In our fake pond there was a thing.

Arty: Eventually, we got Isabella to tell us about this thing, and it sounds like it was a *Shellycoat*, a type of Water Elf. Isabella is lucky, it could have been worse: Shellycoats are a type of *Bogie*, as in *boogie-man*, which can be truly awful and evil. (They're also called *buggaboos* and a bunch of other names.) Shellycoats, however, live in the water and are not so bad, though they do like to play tricks and create some general mayhem. They're like *Ted-elves*, I guess. Bad bogies can really torment people. They used to be considered almost gods but grew less powerful and became plain old *Hobgoblins*, though definitely more evil. They terrorize children and steal the ones who don't shut up or who cry.

Cry: That stinks. Who's next?

Should I go? Now? Ok. This is Olivia P. I found a Silky right in my house, cleaning my room, a small thing that was wearing one of my old antique dolls' dresses, a long silk one with lots of layers. I helped, and we get along great. She is not as pretty as me.

Arty: A type of *Brownie* is what you found, Olivia. These are usually little men, but when they're women, they are called *Silkies*. They do chores and don't like lazy people. They are also related to things called *Phynnodderees*, which are huge and strong and ugly.

This is Sophia H. There was something weird in my garden. I thought I heard singing, early in the morning, it was just barely getting light, and it woke me up. I got closer, and it was a tiny fairy, flying around the garden, landing, and jumping and dancing. It told me stories. One was about some magical beings who fixed someone's hump, a guy named Lusmore. Then a kid named Jack Madden asked to have his hump removed, but he was rude, and they gave him Lusmore's hump as punishment, so then he had two. The other story I did not understand, and I was falling asleep, but it was something about the Land of the Ever Young.

Arty: This is my favorite. Both those stories are part of ancient folktale legend. Imagine: a fairy tale creature telling stories to you! But that fairy is not the funny thing growing in my yard.

CHAPTER 62

Emma

Arty was able to explain a lot about the new Belle Terre citizens—all fairy creatures who would not be attending school. And although it seemed to follow the trusty-friend-of-a-trusty-friend pattern, there was still the question of who the others were in the storm battle, and what the Gwyllion—the old mountain woman—was up to.

"We have to get to the historical society for that," he said, and we began to walk. It was noon on Friday.

I was very tired from my long, late adventure, but since we were ditching school like teenagers, we couldn't ask for a ride. Arty had told Gretel he was sick again, but she had been gone all morning shopping for his large family. My mom always worked from early in the morning until after dinner.

It was a beautiful day with a niceness that I appreciated more coming after that wicked storm. There was no sign of any unfamiliar beings in the sky or on the ground. The local news talked about the strange weather and sometimes of small and odd animal mischief—and there were many videos going viral of scenes that were all too familiar to Cry, Arty, and me, like of enemies walking paw-in-claw—but there was nothing about magic or monsters. Or war.

About halfway to the village, Sprug appeared. He popped from nowhere onto my shoulder and whispered, "Hello." I hadn't seen him all day; of course, by then I knew he wasn't here to keep me company. I had a new respect for him, as did Thryst, who bowed when he saw the Spriggan. This was easy since *Thryst the Mopey* was already slumped over and halfway bowed as he walked.

We talked, Arty and I, about how the fairies—the less wicked ones, anyway—were finding our friends. Most kids our age were already half in some fantasy world with all the games and movies, and now some of them thought that Arty was some kind of fairy wizard. Whether he really was or not didn't make much difference; I guessed they would obey him no matter what.

We were encouraged that we were on the right track. The notes Arty had found pointed to one another, and also toward the historical society museum, and the books talked about fairy queens and New Island, and it couldn't be a coincidence. Arty felt special having found them.

"I've read a *lot*," he said as we walked down the large hill into the village. "A lot. And there's always more. Folktales and old legends—there are millions of them. The fairy tales you heard when you were a baby are nothing compared to what's out there. There are hundreds of old books filled with stories of other creatures that people don't believe in anymore. And now we know better!"

"So, what do you think was going on last night?"

"I don't know."

"Did it seem like anything in the stories you've read?" I asked.

"Maybe. I don't know," he answered.

"Are the new ones—Ethan's, Jacob's, Olivia's—all good?" I meant *good* as in *nice, cuddly, calm, not murderers*: like that.

"I don't know," he said.

"Where are the bad ones from the battle?" I asked.

"I don't know," he said.

"Why us?" I asked while making a big W with my arms.

"I know!" he brightly yelled and stopped short for added drama, I guessed.

Surprised, I said, "You do?"

And he said, "No."

"Me neither!"

Our laughing brought us to the bottom of the hill, where we took care to stay out of sight of the village buildings and so had to sneak across narrow streets. Two kids at midday tended to stick out, not to mention their stocky, droopy, armed warrior Dwarf with a two-foot beard that was shining with daylight. The sun showed its full beaming face directly above; Friday had opened its arms wide.

As we made our way, Arty continued. "Depending on what you want to believe, fairies are either the dead or an old, forgotten people. Or they are small, minor gods."

"They don't seem like gods in real life," I observed. "Are gods klutzy? And into clothes?"

Thryst and Sprug had been silent as we walked, almost forgotten. They were out of sight of course, hiding as they did, while we approached streets filling with a lunchtime crowd of people, people outside our Trust Network.

We wound among smaller avenues, taking shortcuts, avoiding eyes and windows. The village part of Belle Terre has many old, historic, important buildings that have been around since before the American Revolution. The older parts—where we were walking now—were up on higher ground. Here was a High Street and an Old Main Street and a Church Street and a Hill Street that had bustled like this for hundreds of years. Their large and knotted trees offered us good shade as we came upon the historical society building from an empty backstreet.

I was enjoying myself, I realized, and my friend's bouncy steps, wide eyes and swiveling head told me that he was, too.

"This is what 'sick days' are like?" Nerdy Arty commented, breathing the warm air.

The historical society building was itself an historical landmark, as it used to be some important ship captain's house or other, before the area was named Belle Terre, before there was a United States, and when wolves still roamed the woods—possibly sharing it with Elves and Pixies, as people back then still perhaps believed.

No wonder the fairies picked this place, I thought, *this area is very folktale-ish*. But this was just another guess, another airy-fairy theory. We still did not know *why*.

Arty wiped his sweaty face and put down his overgrown backpack as I said, "Here we are!" and pointed to the historical society's wooden sign on its post just ahead.

Just where Cry was getting out of his dad's Jeep.

CHAPTER 63

Arty

"ow did you pull that off?" I asked Cry as his father's brown clunky Jeep drove away.

"My dad had to do some stuff in the village, no one else was home, so I told him I would wait for him here."

"Ingenious!" I mocked.

"Really? Why?" Big Cry said with crinkled eyebrows.

"We are just glad you came," Emma said.

We sat on a bench outside for a minute—Cry took up half, the *middle* half, so Emma and I were squished between his hips and the arm rails of the bench ends. I was anxious to get inside, but Cry had some things to tell us and wanted to sit—he was sick, and tired, and sneezing, and he also made us say hello to Peanut. As we did, politely, Cry told us about his special, emotional, caring feelings for his Pixie, and what he had been thinking and wondering—none of which is important to discuss here, nor was it important for me then, on one-quarter of a bench and behind schedule. But Emma likes listening to people—what they say, how they say it—regardless of bench fractions and how much there was still to do.

"I've been watching Peanut," he told us, "looking into her eyes, and she peeps at me and wiggles around, and I keep her warm." He said useless things like that and stuff like, "I think I would be a good, protective Spriggan, like Sprugly, since I can be big when I want," and "Sprug is also sometimes small and simple. I can be like that, too," which was all so nice for me to hear as my waist was crushed and my thighs started sweating. I popped out of it—the bench, that is—and while rubbing my hipbone asked Cry if he was done, or had a point, or had any reason for me not to go directly into the historical society in the next five seconds. He claimed he had.

"So," he started again, "it's awesome. I was reading in the car about Wights and—"

"Now it's 'awesome' again," Emma pointed out. "You were scared before, now it's 'awesome'?"

"Well, in the sun, during the daylight, it's awesome to be scared, with friends. And it's better than sitting home with Great-Grandma Dera. She's over a hundred years old."

Cry's great-grandmother was sort of legendary, and 'She's over a hundred years old' might as well be her last name, since it always followed her first name, ever since we were kids.

"Yeah, she's cool," Emma said.

"Yeah, sometimes, but not today. She was acting strange. She said, 'My Aunt Dora was taken! So, you'd better be ready, wee one.'" Cry tried to talk in an old-lady Irish brogue, and it made Peanut peep twice, then snuff her beak under her tiny wing.

I laughed but was already tired of the small talk—worse because it was small talk of hereditary insanity—when we were so close to getting the book I needed from the historical society. I urged them to get up and walk with me, and quickly.

"And it was the way she looked at me, too," Cry added. "With her eyes."

I shook my head as Emma asked, "What did she mean?"

"I don't know. Maybe she knows what's going on. She looked out the window and stared and smiled. She looked at me as if she knew about Peanut."

"Does she?" Emma jumped in just ahead of me.

"Not from me. She's mostly blind now. She hadn't left her room, either, since yesterday."

W.W. Marplot

"Maybe something found her, too?" Emma asked, reminding us of all our friends and friends of friends.

"I'll ask her," Cry said, "in the daylight. But when she came into the kitchen this morning, she was mumbling and looking out the window and then told me to take a picture of her. A motion one."

"A video," I translated.

"Yeah."

"Should we care about this?" I asked Emma, since we were at the break in the large hedge that began the walkway of the historical society.

"Well," she answered, "Great-Grandma Dera knows a lot of fairy tales—she told us all some in school, in kindergarten, way back when, remember?"

I nodded, but I was also tapping my foot loudly, eager to end this conversation.

"Well," Emma continued, stamping her foot over mine, "I saw in your notes a lot about Irish fairy legends. Maybe she knows something."

"Maybe she's nuts."

"That's not nice!"

"She is nuts," Cry agreed. He played the video for us. Emma and Cry watched; I would only listen.

A weak, tiny, tinny voice with a soft Irish lilt—Cry's impersonation had been way off—came out of the phone's speaker, clouded by background hiss and dull thuds of Cry's fingers fumbling as he recorded.

Here's what Great-Grandma Dera said.

"Nearby is the Great Tumulus, and it connects the little ones with tunnels and wells. It is the time, again, and many Mays since, my child. We are the people. My aunt was taken. Be alert! They disappear, mothers and daughters. The other people. The Sidhe, the Mounds, the doorway from the lake and the square. And soon, and soon..."

Here we go again, I thought.

"Send me that," Emma said to Cry.

"Ok. I stopped videoing then, since she was repeating herself and doing a bouncy little dance, very slow, and it was freaking me out. My dad interrupted us, and I was glad he let me go with him."

"So weird," Emma said. "What does that all mean? What's the 'she'? The Old Woman? Dera knows?"

Cry answered. It's not she, it's s-i-d-h-e," he spelled, hoping to clear it all up, "which sounds like 'she' but it's not she. The *Sidhe*, not 'she', are dirt piles, Grandma Dera taught me that, she's over one hundred years old, she, Dera, not '*Sidhe*', the dirt piles. The dirt piles are even older—"

"Thanks, Cry, we got it," I answered, "And, Emma, Irish people call fairies the 'other people,'" I added, but I didn't tell them everything I was thinking. Dera's rant reminded me of all the stuff I had been reading: *The Denham Tracts*, the lists, the stories, the strange and mysterious definitions and descriptions of all the fairy legends, and the connection to us, here, now, since Wednesday. Some of her weird words even made some sense and matched up with what we knew—doorways with portals with maps, May with May, tunnels with digging. And also…

"What's a tumulus?" Emma asked. "Maybe it's a clue."

I hoped not, and I didn't want to tell them, especially Cry, that tumulus meant a burial mound.

"Maybe," I answered. "I will find out and add it to the right lists."

Which was only half a lie because other parts made no sense—mothers and daughters?—but looking them up was just one more thing to do. And the next thing to do was go into the building in front of us, so I could do the next hundred things to do.

I reassured my friends that the Dera stuff must be a coincidence, or that she had sensed something strange going on and, from what I was reading, old Irish people from Ireland were like that—they were in tune with fairies.

It was all very interesting, and confounding and all, but it was pushing the limit of my patience level, something that I measure in hundredths of a second. Could we please just go through the historical society front door already?

But as I spoke, Cry walked to another bench and sat down before I could throw my own body in the way.

"Get up!" I urged him. "We are running late. This way." I pointed to the path between the hedge that was so close, so close.

"Ok, sorry Arty," Cry said. "I just thought what Great-Grandma Dera said could help."

I didn't answer but walked through the hedge and onto the stone steps that led to the historical society's red front door.

"Good thinking, Cry," Emma said, pulling him by the arm and off the bench.

"I wasn't thinking, I was just saying," Cry said, and Emma and I looked at him, Emma's face bright from smiling, mine dark from wondering about Cry's brain and what it did sometimes.

"Let's just go in," I demanded at last.

"Ok," Cry said, again, as he looked at the building. "Man, I feel like I was just here."

"Why's that?" Emma asked.

"I was here a few weeks ago, I guess, with Ted."

We had to stop again.

This was unexpected, to say the least: neither of them, Cry or Ted, would go on their own to historical societies, or museums, or libraries. I had forgotten about Ted as we walked down to the village and so was even more annoyed now that I'd been reminded of him.

It surprised Emma, too; she grabbed Cry's arm. "Why," she asked, "were you here with Ted?"

"I was at his house, and we had to go with his dad to pick up his mom," he replied.

What kind of answer is that? I thought but was as worried as Emma looked. I didn't know why yet, but my stomach was trying to get out of my body.

I spun Cry and reversed him back to the bench. He sat almost as gracefully as a camel would. I looked at him, eye to eye. And I asked, "WHAT?" in a way that I thought was impressive.

"We had to pick up his mother. She works here," he explained.

Ah, I thought. *Ah.*

"Ted's mother works here, at the historical society?" I asked.

"Yeah," Cry said.

"And you didn't think you should tell us that?" I asked.

"Just at night," Cry said.

"WHAT?" I asked in the same way I had fifteen seconds earlier: *impressively.* "You wanted to tell us at night? What?" And then: "What?" He knew that my last two *what*'s were completely different questions.

"No," he said, almost laughing, "she only works here at night, I meant. I think. I think she only works here at night."

Emma and I looked at each other, then looked at the building, half-expecting to see Ted. He was hard enough to get rid of without walking into his mother while she was on the job. But we had to go in, so Emma shrugged her shoulders. I talked my stomach into staying and started walking. Cry stood up, rocking from side to side with a moan and a sniffle.

Emma pushed Cry back down and grabbed my arm.

"Wait," she said.

I could not find words for my impatience, but I searched hard as Emma spoke.

"Cry, I want to ask about Ted. Any idea why he's spying on us? And why the man in brown is after him? What did Ted do?"

"I don't know. Nothing?"

"It can't be nothing—it can't be a coincidence. The man is asking about him, and Ted's following us all the time. This is important, Cry, we need to know."

I added pressure. "How much of an enemy is Ted? Any idea? This is important."

Cry looked like a big, soft pile of innocence, making me almost feel guilty, like I had rudely turned off his video game. He was having trouble adjusting to our new world, no matter how much we had told him about the Old Woman, and no matter how many Pixies lived in his backpack, it would take him a while.

I didn't have a while. I turned away from Cry, saying, "Well, we can't worry about the sneak. He's in trouble—and should be. He'll get what he deserves."

Cry finally responded. "If the man in brown guy, Mr. Alphabet, is after Ted, and he is bad, doesn't that make Ted good?"

Emma and I had not considered this, and the perfect logic of it made me mad. Emma's face was blank.

Cry mumbled to Peanut, "Nobody deserves to always get what they deserve."

Emma said, "I don't know, Cry, I'll have a hard time thinking Ted's not doing something wrong, and it could hurt all of us." But she shrugged.

"Sometimes I feel bad for him. I know he has bad dreams."

"Oh, I didn't know you guys were such buddies." I wondered why Cry was defending Ted. Was he a double agent here, or what? What world was he in now?

Emma wondered also. "Did he tell you anything about what he's doing?" she asked.

"No. Nothing else. That was it," Cry swore. So innocent.

I stopped caring. None of this changed what we were there to do. Cry's cross-examination could wait.

"Well, let's get on with it," I said. We—finally—walked up the stone path to the front door of the old building, home of the Belle Terre Historical Society, Museum, and Museum Library. Each year, school field trips bring the little grade-schoolers, those lucky wee-ones.

So, it was fun to be here, almost a whole day since my adventure at the university library when I found the codes. Little messages, left by someone, left for someone, and found by me. Clues to follow, to discover more: about fairy tales, legends, magic creatures, New Island, Eastward Manor, and what they all had to do with Belle Terre. And what they had to do with me, and my friends, and good old *Thryst the Hiding Somewhere.*

And, frankly, let me whisper between us: I think my adventure and clever detective work had been a little unfairly outdone by Emma's and Cry's accidental courage during the storm last night.

I opened the door.

W.W. Marplot

CHAPTER 64

Emma

told you I was way ahead of you," Ted was bragging to Cry, and me, each in turn, and then to Arty who was pretty frustrated and sort of twitching.

Ted had found us on the street, down the hill from the museum. The fink told us he'd gone home from school fake-sick when he saw we'd all been out fake-sick, too.

"So, now we're all so, so, so sick, I guess," he said.

Cry laughed—a strange sound—as he sat on a red iron-and-wood sidewalk bench with Arty leaning on the bench arms next to him. I stood facing Ted. The boy was definitely feeling very pleased with himself and his finky place in the world.

I needed to interrogate him—to see what he knew, and how much damage he had done, and why the man in brown was chasing him. Arty steamed and kicked at his overloaded backpack but agreed to let me do the talking.

"Why's that Mr. Alphabet guy after you?" I asked Ted, very stern and very close. "Are you in the Network? What's New Manor?"

"Maybe," Ted answered, still smiling.

"Were you in my yard today?"

"Maybe?" he answered, though the question seemed to confuse him, and he didn't like that. So, I asked a harder one.

"What found you?" I looked right in his face, challenging him for another silly answer.

"Ah—I definitely found *you*, right?" he said, but his fiendish smile was weakening.

"Where's the mountain? Well?" I pressed on with my wily interrogation.

This seemed to poke at something inside Ted's coldblooded guts, and his face changed, his smile leaving him like so many of his fake friends.

"There is no mountain. What mountain? Emma, there is no mountain, you know that. This is not a secret," he said, and his tongue may as well have been flicking and sniffing the air while he did, he was so snaky-cold. He had put on some other skin.

I looked at Arty, who was studying Ted and also looking at Cry and seeing enemies everywhere.

Sprugly moved, and it startled me—he jumpflew to Ted's shoulder, and at first Ted didn't budge but stared at the puffy, orange Spriggan.

Then, a change: Ted's face curdled, and he screamed, panicked, swung his arms, and fell to the ground.

Sprug came back to my shoulder. Peanut then flew to the ground next to Ted.

Ted swatted at her, then curled into a ball. "What is that?" he cried.

"Tell us what you know. Have you found any fairies?"

"What are you talking about?" This was Ted's usual voice.

"Why is the man after you?"

"I don't know!"

"He's asking everyone about you."

"I know! I don't know!" He peeked his head out; Peanut had flown back to Cry.

"Aren't you worried?" I asked him, eye to eye.

"I just figured I was in, you know, trouble."

"For what?"

"Who knows."

And I believed this was a sad but honest answer. Ted was always in some kind of trouble.

"Why are you following us?" I asked. As an answer, he looked at me as if he didn't understand the question, as if following and spying and sneaking were as natural as eating and texting.

"Why did you say the mountain is not a secret just now?"

He denied saying it, said he didn't remember it, and kept denying it over and over until Arty and I gave in. It was obvious Ted didn't know anything about the fairies we'd found, let alone the importance of the book he'd sneaked away from us. "You're not ahead of us, Ted, and never will be," I said. "In fact, you're way behind—but you lucked out, because it is a circle. But I'll tell you what: hand over the book, and we'll show you something you definitely want to see."

"You have to swear not to tell ANYONE," demanded Arty as he jumped on top of my words.

"No, he doesn't," I said with devious delight. "He can tell anyone anything but then live with the haircut Thryst will give him."

"Who's Thryst?" Ted asked. "That old barber dude by the railroad tracks?"

"No," I continued, "at least that guy leaves your head on."

Now, in his more natural state of defeated bafflement, Ted whined, "What are you talking about?"

I looked into his eyes. "Please just help us, Ted."

He looked at me, accepted what I gave him, the small victory, and gave in, like a wolf offering his throat.

"Ok, Emma, I'll help you," he said blankly.

"Now—give it to us. The book," Arty said. "And stop spying on us."

"I don't," he said weakly, "spy on anyone."

"Oh please," Arty spat back. "The fourth graders call it *Ted-ing*."

But Ted actually liked hearing this, the sinister alley cat that he is.

"What do you want it for?" Ted asked, getting back to the cookbook.

"No," I said, "what do *you* want it for?"

"Only because we want it," Arty answered for Ted.

"That's mean," Cry said.

There came suddenly an alarming sound that startled all of us—Cry, Arty, and I were snapped to attention because we hadn't heard this particular sound in a while, and Ted almost jumped through his skin because he hadn't heard this particular sound ever before.

The sound of a Pixie sneezing.

Though it was a faint little *achoo*, and Peanut popped out again, this time Ted was drawn to her. Looking into her eyes, he started speaking, dull and slow as if it were a dreaded speech for English class, a memorized essay about something he didn't really understand.

"I knew you guys were into something. I saw you in the library. I knew what you were reading about: fairy tales and lame stuff like that. I couldn't take any books out since my card has overdue fines on it, but my mom works there," he pointed back up the hill toward the historical society. She told me..." he stammered, not sure where to point or look.

"Who?" I asked. He looked dazed again.

"My mom. I think. And I was stuck here last night in the storm, so I looked around and found some fairy book—the one you guys now want. My mom told me to get the book. Yes. It was in my dream. I think..."

Arty and I tried to make sense of it, but pushing Ted anymore wasn't doing any good.

He removed his eyes from Peanut and muttered more weirdness until he was empty and then quiet.

Arty and I understood that this was some sort of spell, since when Ted looked at the fairies he definitely changed, and not like he was strapped into an *eye-venture* the way we had been. I thought it would be better to keep him with us, to observe him, instead of leaving him to his usual uncontrollable mischief.

"Give us the book," I said.

We waited.

Ted's face snapped to normal, a change so clear I could swear it even made a sound. "Well, I don't have the book *with* me," he said.

"Want to come to my house to get it, Emma?"

"Uh, how nice, but no thank you very much," I answered. "Just bring it to Arty's, we'll all meet there. Can you get there in an hour?"

He said he could. And that he liked me. I accepted it.

"I'll come with you," Arty said, having lost his trust in the situation, in the deal I made with Ted, and in Ted as a human being.

"Fine," Ted said. He looked at me like a bad boy who'd finally done something right and wanted a cupcake or something. Maybe he was trying to be good, maybe Cry was right. He did look a little cleaner somehow.

I gave him, "Thanks, Ted."

CHAPTER 65

Arty

I was getting mad, annoyed, and annoyingly mad at the same time. I was mad that Emma trusted Ted. I was annoyed at Ted's meddling and weird dream references and changes in mood and his "spells" that I couldn't understand yet. I was annoyingly mad that I was losing control of the situation and falling behind as the lists grew everywhere around me. The world was a loaded rainbow sticky-note.

I knew Ted would most likely screw things up in some way I couldn't predict yet but that might cause an inter-species embarrassment.

"Huh—Peanut…nice name…" He was now mumbling to amuse himself, his sarcasm flaking off him like snakeskin. His silly grin then quickly flattened when Peanut flew in a circle around him, floated an inch from his round nose, and sneezed. Peanut returned to land on Cry's shoulder.

It was my turn to laugh as Ted stood dumbfounded and looked back and forth among the three of us. Cry laughed also, always a strange sound.

Emma looked nervously around, but there wasn't anyone on the street to see four kids arguing around a bench, not at school, and playing with a Pixie with a head cold. *What's with this town?* I thought. *It's easier to keep a secret than I thought.*

I told Emma I'd go with Ted to get the cookbook he'd wormed away from us, telling her that I preferred Ted when he was in a spell. It was like having him on a leash.

"Ok, Ted," I said, "let's go get the book." We all walked.

Cry and Emma split off from Ted and me with a promise to meet at my house in an hour.

CHAPTER 66

Emma

"I want one," Ted said to me as he and Arty entered Arty's room, where Cry and I already sat. Just as we'd agreed, the two had brought the cookbook—it was thick and brown and slashed with strange drawings etched in silver.

Our fairy creature friends were with us. Cry had Peanut in a sock on a bookshelf, and Sprug was babysitting and peeping at her in some language, then coming back to me to whisper things in English, like "New Island," "One and More," "One is missing"—just hints, and hints that frankly were getting annoying. I played the game back at him, saying, "Why?" in response each time.

Thryst the Downhearted was not standing at attention, and his eyes did not burn with fire, and their gaze did not run deep. He was slumped over near a small chair, in a dark corner, twiddling his fingers on the handle of his axe, his beard swept to one side, his hood falling limp. Arty's dogs lay about the Dwarf's boots in similar repose—whimpering now and then, or exhaling loud doggie sighs.

"How do I get a fairy tale thing?" Ted was right in front of me at Arty's messy desk. The fool didn't notice Thryst. "Where do I find one?"

"I think they actually need to find *you*."

"Well, I'm right here in the open! What's their problem? Arty told me there are like ten out there now, probably more."

"Maybe you're evil," I told him. A laugh blurted from the center of Cry's big round body.

"Seriously," Ted went on, "should I go out in the woods and wait? Hold my arms out or something?"

This was pathetic—begging to be found by fairies who didn't want you. I went along with it. "Yes, Ted, do exactly that. At midnight under the full moon in a garden of poppies in an oak forest, you hold your arms straight out, and close your eyes, and spin around, and say, '*I do believe, I do believe*' over and over again."

Ted started to rehearse this in front of us, his eyes closed tight. Arty caught on to the joke and waved Thryst over, so that when Ted got dizzy and almost fell over, he opened his eyes to a depressed Dwarf and an axe, blade up.

I can't really describe Ted's reaction—but I certainly can draw it, and I will. It might make the cover of my book if I win the bet.

Thryst didn't bow but mumbled something that made ripples in our bottles of water, and then walked back to his place in the corner where the dogs sat erect for his return.

"Wow," Ted eventually said. "Is that a gnome? We have one in our garden."

"Uh," Arty replied, "I wouldn't put him near any plants you care about. He's pretty dangerous."

"And he's a Dwarf," I said. "Thryst the Magnificent. Not a Gnome—there's a *huge* difference. Maybe you should do a little reading." I tossed one of the giant fairy myth books to Ted, which he caught sloppily with two hands, pinning it to his chest, bending the pages.

Thryst snorted, and the sound made Ted jump and step backward, catching the back of his knees on Arty's bed and felling him onto his elbows.

Looking at me, he said, "Anyway—I want a dragon, I decided. Named Zamina, I decided."

Thryst shot a glance at Ted that might as well have been an arrow from a crossbow.

Dwarf Story   221

"Don't say that!" Cry advised.

I went on. "Well, you don't get to decide anyway. Our theory is that they decide to find other people that we trust."

"You guys trust me, right? Don't you? Come on, I gave Arty the cookbook."

Arty took over. "Yes, thanks, Ted, so far you're helping to undo the non-helping you already did. We're back on track, but you cost us a few hours. Do what we say now, and don't tell ANYONE, and maybe they will see that you can be trusted. Ok?"

"And then I get a drag-g-g…." the doof stammered, catching himself. "You know? A big one?"

"We'll see. If you're good," Arty said.

Arty wasted no more time on Ted and sat in silence at his desk, paging through the cookbook—"*Recipes from the Queene Faerie Habundia, and Other Youthful Cooking Legends*"—with serious focus. I was desperately curious but let him be alone with it for now.

For entertainment, I watched as Ted turned slowly to stare at Thryst, and—to put Ted back on his heels—Thryst stared back. And when Thryst stares at you, whole kingdoms come with it. It's like a landslide. I didn't know which world—or when it was, or where it was—that Ted saw in Thryst's bright eyes, but I know what I saw in Ted's pale eyes: wonder, and fear. They never blinked and though they were frozen in place, their black center changed in size, big to small, to big, and back—as if he were watching the unfolding of a new creation, a whole world, one he didn't recognize. I know the feeling.

Ted mumbled a few wow's, with his mouth open and pupils wide, and also a long "Unbelievable!" and three *Geez*es, all with the same dumb expression.

When he threw in two *but*s, it made me wonder, however.

And then a change came; an excitement bubbled in him. With a strengthening voice, Ted said, "Who is that?" and "Wow" and "Who is she?" his lips bouncing and his eyes now blinking. Thryst broke his gaze, looked at me, then turned away and back to looking like a drooping stone in the corner. But Ted remained at the border of both worlds, eyeing something far away. I was worried. I'd never seen Ted look, well, intelligent, and I'd never heard such seriousness and purpose from him before. He then uttered a very strange sentence.

"I could have helped. She wants me to. I want to help and go there." He remained in this frozen trance until Sprug flew at him, revolving about Ted's tight face and orbiting four times until Ted came back to us, to the room, to the world of Arty, Cry, and me.

Then, slowly, Ted's face melted like ice cream on fresh apple pie and he was finally completely released. Thryst remained stiff but snorted another tremor.

Arty had not moved but had taken a lot of notes. Scientists are not like, say, firemen, or action heroes.

CHAPTER 67

Ted

I didn't like that Thryst showed me things that seemed like dreams. I was confused.

But something else came into my head, and I knew what to do. For their own good. And I took some of Arty's stuff. They didn't see.

CHAPTER 68

Emma

With one eye trying to stay on Ted, I spoke with Cry. We decided we needed an update, so we set to scouring the websites of our school, the library, the village, and Belle Terre's wimpy one-page webpage that never changed, as well as the local news site. We wondered whether any adults knew about the fairy invasion yet—but apparently, they did not. No news was good news. Baffling but good.

Ted was calm and content while reading from Arty's many books with studious attention. He quickly searched pages, crisply bent the corners of those he needed, and expertly maneuvered between these texts and the Internet on his phone, doing it all as easily as if it were a favorite video game. I suppose you're never too dull to attempt new abilities. He glanced at Sprugly and Peanut now and then—but rarely at Thryst.

I kept a suspicious eye on Ted as Cry and I set about calling three of the six others who'd been *folk-friended* into the *trustwork* by *folkies*, continuing to expand and improve our new language. All were at home either playing with or ignoring their new fairy friends. Everything was peaceful: no disasters, no battles. We even had to remind Isabella about the Shellycoat in her pond. She checked on it. It was still there.

CHAPTER 69

Emma

After a long silence, I asked Arty what we should do next; it popped him out of his book piles and his focused attention.

"We need action, and we need to move fast," he said with energy. Then, with less energy, "But first, I need a few more answers. Cry, did you ever ask your father about the goats he saw? Was there one, or more?"

Cry answered, "He said he only saw one, a big one, and it was black. Freaky."

"Gwyllion," I mumbled, shivering with the memory of the storm. Arty and I nodded at each other as he went on.

"Ok. Then we have to move fast. I'm not sure where she fits in, the old Gwyllion mountain lady. There are no mountains around here, for one thing. And for another: Who did she find? You know, who did she folk-friend? Which kid?"

The question sat in the air like cigar smoke. Cry shifted in his seat. No one answered.

Arty moved on. "Ok. Anyway, we need to move fast. There are lots of folkies on the *bad* side—that were in the battle—and there are probably more *good* ones coming. To kids. And the others we saw at the university—what are they up to?" He stopped because Sprug came to whisper to me.

"He says they're well," I relayed. Arty asked what that meant— which side were they on? Did they escape? Were they warriors? Spruggishly, my Spriggan would only repeat that they were well, meaning that they were ok. I guess.

"So anyway," Arty held up his pen, "we need to act fast. Eventually, it'll all be way beyond our control. Our folkies are careful and keep themselves from being seen, and they can sense trouble. But in the legends, they *cause* trouble, they steal clothes, they bewilder children, and pretty much haunt the whole human race. And they don't always get along with each other either."

Cry yawned.

Arty went on. "Who knows what'll happen next? Another storm like that, or another day of animal weirdness, and the authorities will be involved—the cops, the government, the adults, the school, the teachers—and they'll take our new friends away, or go to war with them, or put them in movies or something. And someone else'll take the credit for finding them."

I yawned and interrupted. "So, what do we do?"

"We need to act fast."

"Sure we do," I said sarcastically since he'd already said this four times but had *done* it *zero* times. "What about the fairy cookbook?"

Arty patted the book in his lap and told us what he'd figured out so far.

"Here's the deal: We have two books that look the same, one in German and one in English. They're cookbooks. We found them by following a trail from the old fairy books to the notes I found at the Old English Library. Since someone left those old notes for us, we know we're on the right track. In these books are the answers. So, we need to act fast."

Arty paused to look at Ted, who was in his dazed state and staring out the window and humming. "And maybe," Arty went on, "we can help Ted also—whichever Ted we like better, I guess. But we need to act fast."

I wanted to bite my own nose at Arty's *sixth* use of the phrase but didn't. I said calmly, "It also means someone else knows about all this," I said, remembering the brown, crumbling clues, "and that it happened before—fairies coming here, I mean, a long time ago. And maybe it was all expected to happen again."

Arty nodded. "Either way," he said, "it's happening now, and the answers have something to do with a place called New Island and are in this book."

"So…?" Cry yawned.

"So, we need to—"

"—*act fast*," I finished for Arty. "We get that. But what do we do?"

Peanut sneezed.

"Well…um…well…read it," was Arty's many-dotted, slow, sheepish answer.

"That's your big plan? To read a cookbook?" Ted said, startling me since it was the normal Ted, loud and jarring.

"Well, yeah, for now. Then we'll have the answers."

"Ok—so…?" Cry asked again, in case we forgot.

"So…?" Arty answered, though it is really weed-whacking the English language a bit to call these questions and answers, Cry and Arty both saying "so" a few times while looking at each other. I watched the rest of this middle-school play unfold as follows.

Ted: "So, go ahead and read it."
Arty: "Ok."
Cry: "What do the rest of us do then?"
Arty: "Nothing."
Cry: "Nothing?"
Arty: "Not until I know what we should do."
Cry: "After you read the cookbook."
Arty: "Yes."
Ted: "So go AHEAD and READ IT."
Arty: "I will. You mean, out loud?"
Ted: "No, thanks."
Cry: "I meant, what do we do while you read? Just sit here?"

Arty: "I guess so."

Cry: "Ok, I guess. Seems strange, though. There's no part
in The Lord of the Rings where they sit around
while Gandalf reads."

I'd had enough, lasting even longer than my future readers will, I bet.

"OK!" I interrupted. "Arty—you read it. We'll leave you alone.
We'll go outside and take a walk, have a look around, see if there's
anything strange going on in the woods. We'll see what's up with
Isabella, Olivia, and the others. We'll be back in two hours. Ok?"

"Make it three," Arty said.

CHAPTER 70

Emma

ry, Ted, and I left Arty's house and walked. Nothing happened. Sprugly was active and very watchful, but there was no need. The squirrels seemed normal. We only saw one deer, and it acted naturally. As we made our way along the woods toward the beach, nothing happened. At the cliff's edge we enjoyed the sunny afternoon view—we could see the boats of the harbor and the buildings of Belle Terre along the coast of the bay that shone bright and blew us hugs of warm air. Nothing happened. Small birds chatted busily, but no more than usual, and we watched the high flight of seagulls sailing on crisp spring winds under blue sky. Nothing happened up there. A few boats made their way past each other slowly.

I wanted to think about the funny thing in Arty's yard.

But instead, Ted spoke, unfortunately.

"This is boring," he whined, "I want some action. My father didn't die in the war so that his son would be left out while fantasy-game characters invaded the town."

"What're you talking about?" I responded. "What war? Your father does real estate. His picture's on signs all around town. He didn't *die in the war*."

"I said he didn't," Ted replied, technically correct.

Now *I* was bored.

We walked back to the streets and out of the woods as the sun dipped behind the treetops. Nothing happened. A few cars went by, a dog barked—all normal behavior, of course. We wanted to check on our other folk-friended friends, but our cell phones had weak signals, so instead we wandered back to my house. My mom wasn't home; there was the usual note telling me to heat up some leftovers, she might be late, I should start my homework, etc., etc., yeah, yeah. Cry and I took turns calling the other *becreatured*—new word—kids, and also our parents, and there wasn't much to report. We grabbed drinks and snacks and checked the news. Not much to report. We left my house. Nothing happened.

We took some new paths, finding some old horse trails Arty and I used to wander, and that headed east, away from the bay and the action, the day dimming among tree shadows. Nothing happened. And as we walked, nothing *continued* to happen.

CHAPTER 71

Mary

This is not Arty or Emma, or Cry or Ted, nor any of their friends. And I am not of the perilous fairy tale world. Yet I am in this story with them, at the same place and time.

I walk through the same forest, in Belle Terre, though this land has many names. It would have been better for me to stay on one of the long stretches of bay beach that wrap around the harbor. In the woods, with so much Elven magic in battle, the tree spirits are loud in my ears and in my head. But I could not help them. Light Elf and Water Elf and Dark Elf and Tree Elf all joined the fight—what a noise, once together, when they move! They fight for their ancient resting place, taken from them when their lives weakened.

Before the next fight, they sing songs to their fairy ancestors and to their own legends. Though the sun is high and strong and the clouds on the horizon are threatening, dark, and fast—and even in the hot and humid, crowded forest—when the Elves sing, it is night, and bright stars sparkle in the sky, though you might have to close your eyes to see them.

They come together whenever things, beliefs, start to change, when ages end, and begin…

Underground spaces shake: Dwarves are gathering their strength; their leaders are shouting memories of past wars, the names of their greatest kings, searching for words of secret magic. They will need it all.

W.W. Marplot

Others are here that will not fight; they will find and rescue and save the ones taken. We have already seen Spriggans on the move, coming in and out, growing big and small, flying all around.

On both sides are hounds, and goats, and other animals in other forms, and some that live to themselves, or are wandering alone. They want for excitement, or a leader, or a meal. Others search for the past—and the future. Others for who they came with.

At the top of two opposing hills sit terrible forces. I feel black spells that seek through the waking woods, through walls of magic thick like fairy dust and as high as the clouds. The earth itself is alive with powers that are ancient and legendary. To my feet come shocks as the Old Woman of the Mountains triumphs over higher and higher ground and needs to make it her own.

And there her prisoners are. Some few have escaped.

And so also to the sky: the airs above will be fought for, and so, as I see now, there are dragons white and red. One's spellbinding voice calls to me, "Mary!" and I answer in my mind that I am well. The birds and other winged creatures of old folktales take flight and search the land, the sea, and the clouds—the bounds that are, and always have been, so important in their lives and legends.

It has been a long time since any of its people understood what this land is: a shared place. Dearest Dera, she is one of the few…She remembers and knows! That was nice to hear.

The fire-beasts of the air will wait until nightfall. And so will the Wights, who again are haunting the earth, and the ground shivers down into to its bones.

As I walk to the edge of the woods, to the cliff, to peek at the clouds and breathe fresher air, all the leaves in my way are bright green. Yet the sky is orange, the coming clouds dirty brown and black. Small Pixies are up high on branches, and many other fairies are going in and out of backyards carrying clothes and gear. I hope they stick to their own battle and that no children go missing. Some other fairies escape and find who they can trust. I will meet them all later.

With time and weather moving quickly, the larger creatures are stirring with the lowering sun. I see a Phynnodderee, large and ugly, lumbering up one of the bluffsides. There are hobgoblins, and trolls, and the howling yeth hounds; the sounds mix in the wind. Out of crevices come large birds, with branches in their beaks. They fly to higher ground and settle into nests like eyries—gigantic like hawks, awful like buzzards.

I feel and hear the calls of each fairy creature to each. The place is so old that only their oldest legends have the memories to contain it.

I came to help, finishing a foretold destiny. My ancestors lived among mystery and magic—but a long time ago. All I have is history, blood, the knowledge of both, and a few relics and heirlooms, small talismans and treasures. I need help from others. I need the maps. I need the books, and I need the spells.

Others are finding these things, and I need to find the others.

Yet there is still something missing…something funny…

CHAPTER 72

Emma

 knew there must be more exciting things going on, somewhere, while Arty read in his room and I strolled the forest paths with my two children, Cry and Ted. And here's what happened to we three time-killers: Nothing happened.

Bored though we were, it was still too soon to return to Arty, so as the school day ended for normal kids and dinnertime approached, we interrupted our slow ambling and sat here and there in the woods where we could at least use our phones and amuse ourselves. Ted and Cry challenged each other to climb a certain tree. I wondered aloud about boys and how they think, or don't.

Cry went first and gave the tree a big hug to start. His frame was about the same size as the rough-looking but perfectly round trunk of the oak, which stood unamused. Cry—also quite round—hugged with his arms first, then his legs—which I told him wasn't exactly the correct procedure, because, well, "Now look!" I blurted.

He hung stiffly for maybe three seconds, when the sweat started. He tried an inch-wormy dance upward, and I was able to see the differences between the way Thryst and Cry each move, and I knew I'd never get them confused. Cry scraped his way maybe a half-inch upward, like a *half-inchworm*, which I began to draw in my head. He scratched his shirt and chest badly and gave up. Peanut came to him as he sat in the dirt.

Ted then tried, with confidence, and soon with bruises. He thought he could run, hop, and with one foot forward, launch high enough to grab a low branch. His momentum swung his lower body forward, his hands caught a bough but couldn't hold on, so he flipped backward and landed on the ground, on his back, on a stick, on a rock.

There are beasts fighting in the air, there is magic, and war, the sun and moon and sky are changed, armies pass underground, and adventure lives everywhere, and here I am playing my part: which is to babysit four strange creatures while Arty reads to a Dwarf.

Then: Nothing happened.

We kept walking. Nothing happened. We moved out of the lengthening shadows of tree cover to look at the sky, but there was only a usual and nice warm spring Friday afternoon sitting on a dark blue rug above. Sprugly was quiet and didn't do much. *And you know why?* I asked myself. *Because nothing is happening,* I answered.

"Let's go to my house," I said. "I need to recharge." With electricity and food.

"Ok, good," Ted said. "I need some coffee."

I wouldn't give bad Ted any caffeine, and even good Ted was getting on my nerves—he wasn't *good*, just strange. Once we were in my house, he went directly into a spell, and no one had to look in his eyes for it to happen. He mumbled about helping, wanting to help, and we talked to him like he was a baby chimp with a diaper and everything.

Then he said, "Where's your mom?"

"I don't know," I answered honestly.

"Is this her? Is that YOU?" Cry asked, picking up a framed photo from years ago, Mom and Dad behind me, first day of preschool. I was small, smiling, in pigtails. Yuck.

"Yes."

Ted jumped from tiptoes to see the picture over Cry's shoulder.

When, finally: *something happened.*

W.W. Marplot

He ran. He yelled, "No! No, no!" And he ran. Out the back door, direct to the path and the woods we had just left.

Cry and I watched from the kitchen window, our hands dipping blindly into a tortilla chips bag. Running after Ted on a Friday night was not something either of us had on a to-do list, or a wish list, and we had no experience with the mixed feelings that came up as the sun went down.

Cry took four long swallows from his upturned water bottle, put it in his backpack, and ran.

I followed.

Ted—whichever one—made a wrong turn so I could see him ahead of us at the bottom of a slope as we neared its top. Though the light was failing, I could see him waving his arms, and once the wind hit my face, I heard his wild words.

"Take it! Take it! Old woman! Here!" he shouted to someone we couldn't see—he'd reached the top of the small hill and we were now dipping downward, but his words froze my legs and heart. He threw something—some papers, and maybe some other things—that flashed in white, and he turned quickly as he did so, to run away from some unseen other.

Cry stopped when he caught up and gazed with me. In the direction Ted was now heading—he was off the path and struggling with the underbrush—there was another figure, brown in the brown light and among the brown trees. Tall like them.

Ted didn't see him yet. I was still frozen as Cry yelled a warning to him.

Ted spotted Mr. Alphabet heading toward him now, then darted in a direction that took him away from all three of his pursuers.

I didn't know what to do. Ted seemed caught between enemies, but the thought of seeing the Gwyllion come over the hill, if that's who Ted had screamed at, frightened me so that all I could think of was to hide in a hole and wait for eyes to come and take me away.

But Cry saw me weakening and shouted again, this time to me. "Look, Emma! The man in brown isn't chasing Ted, he's heading up the hill. Let's get out of here."

I recovered and immediately directed us, cutting through some large holly bushes and over some dying logs covered in thorny vines to a new path. This would lead back to Arty's house *and* intercept Ted's path.

Enough had happened.

CHAPTER 73

Abcedarius
Zyxvuts

I didn't trust them, not one of them, as justified by their youth alone. They had stolen from me, unabashedly. They had secrets and were prying, noisy, vibrant obtruders, whining like broken violins. But I had back what they stole. And more.

Thank you, Ted. I thought. *They like you better under a spell, and so do I; it becomes you.*

I am glad I watched and followed, from library to library, their little chain of meddlers. I saw Ted throwing things—and the letter! None but me should see Mary's words. The Gwyllion should never get it. And I needed it.

Their dangerous interference almost ruined all my work, my years of following the signs.

Almost—but, thanks to Ted, I also had the notes of that central kid, named Arthur, his notes about spells. I knew it would help me tremendously, now that I saw what they were up to.

I would also get my map back. Arthur was not the only one with clues. I understood more and more.

I will see them all soon.

CHAPTER 74

Emma

his isn't good. This can't be good, I thought. And thought. I didn't know what the heck was going on, and now there were two Teds I didn't trust, or one I distrusted more than I ever mistrusted him before.

We caught up to the fink. I told Cry what I saw Ted do—yell and throw things—and Cry revealed that he saw Ted take some papers from one of Arty's folders back in the room. Nothing makes Cry *think*; everything in his world just happens while he watches.

We caught up to Ted the fink. He was walking in a circle around Arty's backyard, and with every revolution, stepping twice over the tree that Thryst had felled. I pulled him under the cover of trees and was about to give him twenty pieces of my mind when I was interrupted by a Spriggan pulling my hair.

"Where did you come from?" I asked, though that question had many levels.

My ugly friend didn't answer but only said, "Wait!" and jumpflew off ahead—where I saw, clearly this time, a man to the side of Arty's driveway dressed all in brown: pants, sweater and hat. I wasn't afraid; we were only a few yards from Arty's front door and then a few more to a massive courageous Dwarf, who bowed to me.

Mr. Alphabet was as thin as the trees he was sneaking among in the near dark of late day, his arms and legs long and wispy like branches. He tried to hide, while at the same time moving carefully up and back from the house, attempting to look into upstairs windows from the ground. Next, he moved swiftly to the driveway, his hat swiveling as he looked this way and that, but it was worn so low and tight that I couldn't see his face.

I pulled Ted down and behind thick holly boughs, and Cry followed when he saw my quick action. Then I moved closer. As the man bent close to the ground, and then actually put his ear flat down against the pavement, Sprugly sprang into action. I could see: the man was now flailing his wiry arms to shoo Sprug away, though obviously he didn't know exactly what was pestering him. He soon realized that this nuisance was threatening to undo his sneaking plans, and he gave up the fight. He ran down the driveway using only the sides of his shoes. His long brown shirtsleeves were still waving like signal flags as he left our sight and my guardian Spriggan returned to my hair, then was off again and disappeared among the treetops.

I was tempted to follow the stranger but soon heard a car start and streak away, so I knew I'd missed my chance.

When I returned to the boys, there was only one: Cry.

"Where's Ted?" I asked.

"He wandered off," Cry sniffed.

"More detail, please," I requested.

"That way." Cry pointed. There was nothing that way, back where we had come from, Arty's yard, the path through the trees.

"More please."

"He said something, then walked away."

"What did he say?"

Cry had to think for far too much time. So, I grunted my dissatisfaction with him as a person. I stood him up; he was still squatting among tall holly bushes. He now rose above them, and I looked up at his confused face.

"What did he say, Cry?" I asked sternly. I could see that he wanted to remember the exact words, so I decided to give him another three seconds before punching him in his massive side fat.

Two.

One.

And he answered as my arm cocked back to swing.

"There she is. She wants to talk to me. Yes." That's what Cry said that Ted said. Cry smiled, having gotten exactly right the words he'd heard barely a minute ago. Cry is a master predictor of the recent past.

"Who? Who was he talking about? Who is 'SHE'?"

Though I knew the answer.

"I guess the mountain lady. I didn't see anyone. But he has been talking about her a lot lately."

"The Gwyllion?" I shrieked and accidently swung my arms into Cry's side as I had planned to do anyway. "Since when? Specifically? I thought he wanted a dragon."

But I already suspected Ted's changed behavior and mesmerized words in Arty's room three hours ago and what it might mean. He wanted to help the mysterious "she." Yet he ran from her. My confusion, my fears, and my fear of my own fears were dimming the last of the sunshine.

Cry was rubbing his side fat.

"Sorry, Cry. But I'm worried."

"Me too," he said. "Where did you go, anyway?"

Surprisingly, Cry hadn't seen the man I went to follow and asked me why I'd made them hide while I speed-walked down the driveway. I told him I dropped my hat.

Cry said, "Ted's right. You're crazy, Emma. It's a good thing we're here protecting you—even though it's from nothing."

"He said that, too?" I asked, smiling and apologizing again to the big fella.

"He says it a lot."

CHAPTER 75

Emma

he three hours I'd promised to babysit were up. I pulled Cry along, and we were soon sitting in Arty's attic room as the sound of later school buses and dinnertime traffic blew through the open windows. Dusk lowered its curtains, and gloomy black clouds were sneaking sideways into the neighborhood—the same way the man in brown had. I told Arty everything that happened: about Ted's absence, about the alphabet man's presence. And that Ted took Arty's papers, and what happened in the woods, and Ted in and out dreamy weirdness.

Arty took a few minutes to readjust—he HATES when someone screws with his system of papers and piles of systems of paper piles, which were now all about us like ragged pyramids topped with sticky notes and rocks as paperweights, a nice Dwarvish touch. The dogs sat like sphinxes.

Ted had taken his spell notes, Arty said angrily, reviewing each mound one at a time.

Then, after making two piles from one that was leaning too far over, Arty reported how he'd used his time.

"The cookbook didn't say much," he said unbelievably. "I read for over an hour, almost all of it, and there was nothing in it but recipes. Some had fairy tale themes, like Immortally Sweet Elf Cakes, so I read those a few times, trying to figure out what they might mean, what the code could be, but...nothing. I couldn't figure it out."

Cry wanted to know: "Did it say how to find a Troll?"

"Not unless they go well with cinnamon. Seems like it was just a cookbook after all," Arty said, and he looked very serious.

We three humans sat in silence and considered this dead end. I felt bad for Arty. Until: *Wait*, I thought, *what's that thing cracking, and growing, on Arty's face? A baby smile hatching from an egg? Yes—it IS.*

"But…" I said and looked right through him.

He looked at me with a teenaged smile and said, "But what, Emma?" with adult fakery.

"Come on," I replied, "what else? You know something. Stop playing with us."

"Ok," Arty gave in, just like I could tell he wanted to. "I got frustrated and gave up and looked at the German version of the cookbook again. It seemed different. I don't know much German, but I noticed that the back pages—the last few, which looked like a glossary—were definitely different in the two books. One couldn't be just a translation of the other. It gave me an idea, so I looked for other parts that were different. And on the very last page it got better: there was English with no translation in the German one. The English one says, check this out…" Arty found and grabbed a sheet of his notes. "The English cookbook says:

> *The author notes that any differences arising between this trans-*
> *lation and the original German version of this content may*
> *be intentional so that the true story and spirit of the original*
> *adventures in baking can be told fully.*

"Huh?" I said.

Cry said, "Yeah, in English, please."

Arty said, "That *was* the English version, unfortunately. Obviously weird, so I thought it must be a clue. Listen: It's telling us that the differences in translation are the code to understanding the '*original adventures*'! Get it?"

"No," Cry said, his large eyes and nose reddening with some perplexed sniffling.

I started to admit that I didn't really get it either, but at that moment, Ted burst into the room. The three dogs—who'd been silent and forgotten in a corner—jumped and barked for a furious few seconds until Thryst calmly raised his hand and they plopped back down to the floor without further noise.

"Where were you?" I asked Ted. "Is everything ok?" I wondered which Ted I was asking. He didn't look like himself, which on a normal Friday would be a joyous improvement. He stared at us thoughtfully and remained standing with an almost formal stiffness, like a proper private-school boy or a small soldier.

"Everything is fine, Emma. Hello, Arty. Hi, Cry. Hi, everyone."

He talked to us with respect and courtesy.

Something was up.

"Where'd you run to? Emma wants to know," Cry said to him.

"Oh," Ted replied, "sorry about that. I just had to do something. No big deal."

Every creature in the room looked at one another, while Ted stood, his hands clasped in front of him perfectly prim and prissy. There was a smile on his face. It was out of practice and crooked.

"Are you feeling ok?" I asked him.

"Fine," he answered in a very flat and serious voice. "But I want to ask about the other kids. All the fairies they found. They need to tell the police. They need to return them. Where do they live?"

Our stares continued. The dogs took turns tilting their heads.

"And anyone they talked to," Ted went on. "You know. Anyone they trust. I want to help." This wasn't Ted, not really. This was a calm, decent boy who *looked* like Ted, perhaps like a sleepwalking version.

"How would you help?" I asked.

"Well, I'm good at following. I could make sure they were ok. Where do they all live?" Ted spoke slowly and in a dreamy monotone.

We needed to ask Ted so much—why he took Arty's papers, why he ran and threw them in the woods, and anything else he knew—but I knew that it was pointless to ask when he was bewitched like this. But it was also pointless to ask when he was his normal Tedding self.

Sprug flew to my shoulder just as Arty said to me, "I don't want him involved too much."

Sprug whispered to me, "Not good."

Cry laughed as Ted strolled into Arty's closet at full walking speed. Arty didn't object—in fact, he was tempted to shut the door, never open it again, and tomorrow buy new clothes. After a medium ruckus, Ted came out again carrying a rectangular box with a picture of a telescope on it.

He mentioned that we should to put the folkies into it and bring them back. Peanut ran. Cry laughed and sneezed. Ted brought the box to Thryst and asked him to put his foot in it.

I talked to him like a baby chimp again and explained why we shouldn't do that, not just yet, but maybe later on, since that's what tomorrows are for.

Ted dropped the box and spoke again, turning to Arty. "I can be a help, Arty. And I have other friends you don't know about."

Before Arty could say the *oo* at the end of "Like who?" Sprug sprang. His wings beat wildly, he grew in size—not too large, but tripling to medium-dog-sized, which seemed pretty big in the crowded room—and he darted from the books on Arty's desk to those spread on the floor and to others on a chair nearby. Their pages turned wildly. Arty's notes flew upward, the pages flapping and twisting within the windy blur of our Spriggan's wake. They rearranged themselves in midair and fell like rectangular feathers into Arty's hands.

A big hint, apparently.

Arty looked at the pages the books had opened to, and at his notes.

And at the pages, and at his notes, this time shaking his head.

Ted was silent; we all were. Sprug was back on my shoulder, normal size.

W.W. Marplot

"I don't get it," Arty said.

Sprugly whispered to me. "Missing still!" I heard him say, which made about as much sense as anything else. He then jumpflew to Ted's shoulder, but the boy still didn't move or react. Then Sprug said the words that changed everything.

"*Anail tá mé an Dia a bhfreasúra mar a bhabhta Uibheacha ciorcal in fiú anail,*" he said, first in Ted's right ear, then in his left, then in both again.

That voice, those words: every syllable picked a hair on my neck and made it stand straight up.

Ted snapped out of his spell, just as I had yesterday while upside down on Thryst's shoulders. *Anail,* I thought, trying to intone the way Sprug had—that was part of the incantation that moved me from world to world.

It made sense now. These sounds—still echoing in my head and crawling over my neck—were a counter-spell. Ted was in the same trance, and maybe hearing the same voice, that I had heard—the voice was "she." The one I'd promised to return to, to help, the one that made me feel good. Sprugly was trying to tell Arty to use the spell. To look in his books.

"Look for *anail,*" I told Arty. He was already digging, even as I explained about the "she" and Ted's trance.

But something was missing here.

"There is no spell, or hex, or curse, that I can find," he finally answered. "Nothing like that, and none of those words."

"Sprug told me you are missing something," I remembered to report.

"Of course! The missing book! The second book! It's the one I STILL can't find, but it's the oldest of all the books in the chain. They all point to each other, like the notes do. It must have these spells! This makes more and more sense."

"Really?" Cry asked. Ted had also returned to his normal, slick, alligator self, and he and Cry both were asking *what fairy* we were talking about.

"The Gwyllion was tempting you, Ted; she wanted your help," Arty said. "You, too, Emma."

"Yes," Sprug whispered to me. So, Ted wasn't bewitched after all—he was *beGwyllioned*. And, a few times, so was I.

CHAPTER 76

Arty

ry and Ted continued to ask questions, but I only told them what Emma already knew, saving my big discoveries until she was ready.

Yes—Ted was now back to normal, and Cry was overwhelmed at the presence of spells and counter-spells right here in my room.

One downside of Ted being back to normal was that Ted was back to normal. I wondered how much harm he'd done—stealing my notes for either the Gwyllion or the man in brown, who must now know a lot about us and what we knew.

CHAPTER 77

Emma

I was afraid but surrounded by friends—afraid that what happened to Ted would happen to me, hoping that Sprugly would protect me since I almost qualified as a kidnapped fairy now. I was also fighting some inner feelings I didn't want to share yet, with anyone. You know: There was something growing in my heart, but I didn't want to talk about that yet.

So, I let Arty go on and finish the story he'd started before like-able-Ted burst in and was cured-away.

"Let's start here!" Arty said, quickly lightening the mood and pulling out a sheet of notes, one that had landed on the floor after the Sprugnado. "Remember, I knew the two cookbooks were different, and I wondered whether the differences were the key to some message. The next differences I found were in a recipe for Gloaming Troll Pancakes, so I tested it. Check this out." He pointed to a two-columned list on the page. "These are the words that are in the German version but not in the English version: *Wilkomm, Safehaffen, Mayfair, Gudwill...*"

"So?" Cry and Ted both said. Ted's was better.

"And," Arty boldly continued, "here are words that are in the German version but not the English: *New, Island, Mountain, Woman, Child, Battle.*" Arty looked up and paused very dramatically.

We all had our mouths open; even Cry and Ted seemed to understand.

In triumph, Arty asked, "Sound familiar?"

I was definitely flabbergasted—even though I've never been that before. "Was there anything else?"

"Yes—a lot. Gretel's still doing more *crossmisuntranslating* right now," Arty answered and had to duck from Sprugly's weird wings as the fairy jumpflew to a corner carrying Peanut. The two folkies hid, just a half-second before Gretel knocked and came into the room without waiting for a reply. She didn't enter, just waved Arty to join her in the hall. Stern, serious Gretel was holding the German fairy cookbook and she had a question.

Arty left. I paced and waited, looking at the geeky stuff on the slanted ceiling of Arty's room—schedules, lists, maps, tables of information that help him through his organized days. I saw his historical society calendar that month showed an old, curious-looking picture of our neighborhood from Belle Terre's super-rich heyday. This faded brown and dirty-white photograph was a nighttime pose of some fancily-dressed women—huge gowns, hilarious hats with at least three herons-worth of feathers exploding from each, umbrellas even though the sky was clear—under pergolas of grey flowers past which showed the wide sky and shadows of the Belle Terre hills, with every edge shimmering with light from a bright moon. Too bright: it overpowered the olden camera and splattered the picture with a blur of a white halo crowning the dark, moody scene. This town was so different only a hundred years ago.

Out Arty's window, our modern sky above was clear and bright with stars between every May leaf. But through the lower branches, the horizon brooded with depressing clouds. They weren't coming toward us, but they weren't still either. Rather, they seemed to be marching in place, like troops ordering at the edge of a battlefield.

I had a funny feeling: homesick, but not for home. I needed to think. I was holding too many thoughts in my head, so it was time to sit in a chair and draw. I'll let Arty tell what we talked about next.

CHAPTER 78

Arty

"How can we make money on this?" I heard slithery-Ted ask the others as I went back into my room. Cry played with Peanut. Thryst slumped in a corner, huffed in deep breaths, and considered Ted as if wondering what the boy would look like roasting over a bright flame. Emma was in another world—the one in her sketch. No one answered Ted's foul question, no one said they were glad he was back. Sprugly the Spriggan wasn't to be seen, though his flapping wings could be heard nearby.

I was excited. Gretel had worked on more of the cookbooks and crossunmistranslated (a new word I made up for when you get new information from the differences in translation between two book versions) as much as she could and showed me the amazing results.

Everyone gave me their attention. "The better question, Ted," I said, "is what are we supposed to do? That's what we want to figure out. Are the folkies here to help us? Are we supposed to help them?"

"And *why*—that's the big question," Emma said. "If we knew that, maybe we could figure out what is going to happen, or what we're supposed to do."

Cry interrupted. "Hey, doesn't Ted need to get in on the bet?"

Despite my attempts to stop them physically, Emma allowed Ted to put his entry—his guess at the big *why*? question—down on paper, which he did with hardly any thought. Emma explained the bet and then popped the paper into a new envelope and enveloped this envelope with the other envelopes somehow—all while Cry and Ted predicted victory and I waited with my arms crossed and face red. I almost wished it was a school night.

Eventually, they settled into a half-circle around me and let me go on. Peanut, Sprugly, and *Thryst the Quiet* were even paying attention as I told the scientific facts.

The English language version of the cookbook was different in parts from the German version—it was purposely mistranslated, and eventually this code, word by word, told a story.

I expected it would all be another fairy tale, probably about the Queen of Fairies mentioned in the cookbook title, this Habundia lady who—it took me an hour to learn—was a leader of the fairies in some very old, not-exactly-web-viral stories. My mouse still hurts thinking about it.

I had spent the past fifty-six hours reading a lot of these old tales. They're kind of cool, in a two-dimensional kind of way, in a one-picture-every-fifty-pages kind of way, in an even-that-picture-is-just-a-pencil-sketch kind of way, in a most-of-this-is-in-my-own-imagination kind of way. If you like the way great-grandmama Dera talks, you would like them.

However, the cookbooks, when de-un-crossmistranslated, were not a fairy *tale*, but a fairy *history*. They told the secret story of folkie creatures living in America, and here on Long Island, and here in our neighborhood.

I told the group, "A long time ago, hundreds or thousands of years, and back when people believed in this stuff," I could hear Sprug and Thryst grumble, each in their own way, "New Island was a place where fairies would go—to rest, to escape, to be punished."

I ignored Cry's comment that it was like his room.

"They came," I said loudly, "from their homes in Europe, where the original folktales about them come from. They lived here, and…"

I stopped since the others were all jumping up with the same question:

"*Here*? What do you mean here?"

"New Island. Long Island."

"Oh," they all said, no longer thinking that the fairies all lived in my room at one time.

Sprug flew to Emma's ear and whispered.

"What did he say?" I asked her.

"He said, 'Yes. Farthest west.'"

"See? So, we were right," I said and continued the story. "They'd come here to rest, I think, but there were also fairy wars—led by, guess who, the Gwyllions. It says the Old Woman of the Mountains was the leader. She took advantage somehow and took over New Island!"

Sprugly flew back and forth from Emma two more times. Emma said to her creature, "Well then, why couldn't you just tell us all this?"

Emma reported his answer to us: "No. That's what he said, just 'no.'"

"Big help," Ted said sarcastically, and this we all agreed with.

I went on with the story. "There were many fairy battles then. All around 'War Land,' it said, wherever that is."

"There's no War Land around here," Cry said, "just schools and stores and houses."

Ted added, "And no mountains either."

"Maybe we have to imagine it. Or believe in it," Cry suggested and looked off into space watery-eyed.

"Please don't, Cry," said Ted.

I shook my head, and the heads of those around me, and continued, "But he's right, Ted—sort of. Because eventually, New Island became deserted of fairies because of the wars, and I think they were afraid to come here anymore. And also, people stopped telling the legends and believing in the creatures and believed in machines instead."

"Terrible," Cry said, taking out a tissue.

I nodded but also held up a finger to comfort him. "But at some point, the European folkies wanted to come back, back to New Island again, back here…" I started.

"When?" Emma asked.

"I'm not sure exactly. There're lots of numbers in the cookbook recipes; it's hard to figure out which ones are dates. But it seems like it was after World War II and during the sixties when people needed folktales again, to escape the real world."

"Cool," Cry said.

They all looked at me, but I had stopped.

"That's it?" everyone asked. "They wanted to come back?"

"Did they come back?" Cry asked. Peanut sneezed, and Cry smiled roundly.

"Oh, yeah. They did."

"Is that it? What about what happened last night?" Emma wanted to know.

"Well, that's all I could get from cookbook, anyway. But obviously, that's not *it*, since they *are* back."

"And they must've had help back then, and from humans," Emma added, "since someone left all these clues for us to find."

"Yes," I said, as I was getting to that. "The books say there are enchanted maps! And that these will help 'the future history,'" I said, making little fake quote marks in the air with my fingers, "and 'help the family' and 'the family's helpers,' whatever that means."

"Who is *the family*? What family?" Ted asked.

"No idea," I said. "Obviously, no one else is 'helping,'" and I made more quote marks, Cry imitating me while I did so. "I think it's us—we're the only ones that know they're here!"

"How can we help?" Emma said. "I wasn't much help last night; all I did was watch and get wet."

Ted contributed his snaky opinion. "Why should we help them? Help them do what? They're their own creatures, *they* should be helping *us*. We're the important ones, we're the humans. We have... um...evolved, and they haven't. I'm tired of begging my parents for rides, I want a dragon."

"*Some* of us have evolved, Ted," I answered, backing our wormy Ted down a bit. He's bigger than I am, but Cry is bigger than Ted, and Ted likes Emma, who's my friend, so by middle-school rules I knew Ted would back down. Plus: Thryst exhaled loudly, which always helps my case. "Some of us have evolved and have grown brains big enough to realize this is much more important than a fantasy adventure game."

"Yeah," Cry added, "thank God for evolution."

Emma laughed while shaking her head at Cry, but with admiration. Cry liked but didn't understand her look.

I finished Ted off with, "And a little while ago, you were offering to help everyone."

"No, I wasn't. Never," Ted replied.

"Yes, you did, when you were in the trance."

"What a horrible curse," Ted muttered thoughtfully.

With that settled, Sprug spoke to Emma, and then Emma to us, saying, "Arty's right, so far."

Excellent, I thought. "Excellent," I said.

At that moment, there was a rumbling, a wavy, humming vibration beneath our feet. The chairs and small things on my desk moved over to their left. I looked at Thryst as Ted jumped to his feet and said, "Did you feel that?"

Ted wasn't used to how Thryst talks. Thryst was excited, I could see. It wasn't a good-excited, though; it was a sound that told me he was getting more and more anxious.

As we all looked at Thryst, there was another tremor, but it came from outside. Another storm coming?

"The weather guy said it was going to pour, and another thunderstorm," Cry said.

"It looks that way from the clouds way off there." Emma pointed out the window and away toward the dark horizon. "They're coming this way."

"It's going to be another one of those nights," Cry said, and each of us four humans put a face to a windowpane and stared a while.

"Is that it, Arty? I want to go home," Cry asked me, Peanut on his head.

"No, but I still have a little more to do. There's more to be mis-un-reverse-translated, about *the family* and *Eastward Manor.*"

Emma said, "New Island—here—is some legendary place for them. So, where we live is a legend to them. And they are legends to us!"

"Cool!" Cry cried out in a high shrieking voice, which startled Peanut, who fell off his head and flopped onto the bed, where Sprug jumpflew to help her. Cry excited with joy is just as odd as when he whimpers; I wish it were otherwise. "The legend of a legend of a legend!" he proclaimed, in a deep, wizard-like voice.

"What is Eastward Manor?" Ted asked.

"No idea," I had to admit. "It was written on the blue book page with the clue that pointed me to the German cookbook. It's here somewhere." I found and showed Ted the browning paper that read, "Pointing. Do not bury. Discard this EL 5674.3453."

"I don't know how much more the cookbook will say, but I at least want more dates—maybe this Wednesday is mentioned in there somewhere," I said. "The only date we've figured out for sure was September 3rd, 1752, the day that…" I said, quoting from Gretel's notes, "'the family came to War Land because the Gwyllion did—'"

"There's the 'family' again," Emma interrupted. "And the man in brown yelled that in my yard—1752. I remember specifically."

"1752," Ted said. "Like a thousand years ago. Who cares?"

Thryst grunted, a small one that didn't move furniture.

"Yeah, great, Ted, pretty close." Emma jumped back in. "How did you get that date?" she asked me.

"Nine, three, and 1,752 were together in a list of ingredients," I answered.

"Pretty clever," Emma said, still staring out the window at the faraway clouds. I could see tree branches moving in the wind but no rain. Yet.

"Yeah, clever, but not very subtle—that was what Gretel came in to ask me about, decoding that date. The numbers were different in the recipes for Dragon Hoard Pudding, but unless you make it with 1,752 teaspoons of vanilla, it had to be a date."

"That's a lot of vanilla," Cry said.

Ted spoke up, "The only dragon so far, and it's in pudding. This stinks so far for me."

All the non-Teds laughed, though Thryst grunted at the end of his short snort.

"Wait," Emma interrupted, "so Gretel knows about all this?"

"No," I told her, "not about anything really happening. She just thinks it's part of the app game everyone's been playing." Cry smiled, and I went on. "Gretel's glad I'm being social."

"But you can't fool her for long, and I don't want to," Emma said.

I had to agree and said so.

"And that's another thing that we know that our brown enemy knows—1752. He is close on our trail."

I nodded as Ted continued his whining. "I don't care about a thousand years ago. What do we do *now*? Tonight?" His voice banged away at me like the treetops against the roof above—the wind was getting noisy, angry.

"It's a good question," I admitted.

Firmly, coming away from the window and the worsening weather it displayed, Emma said, "I don't want to be caught in another storm, let alone a war of returning fairies and Gwyllions. Let's all go to our homes and stay there. We should keep an eye on the fairies, and check on our trustworked friends, too. If any folkies go out into the storm, or if there's another battle, we should text each other and stay together or decide what to do."

"And bring umbrellas," Cry added.

I had no other plan, so I agreed.

As the others left, Emma pulled me aside. "Arty," she said, "you need to find that second book also, the one with the spells. Please." Then she turned and walked away. She looked sad.

CHAPTER 79

Arty

I couldn't sleep: my thoughts were too loose and the wind too loud. When I don't have a plan, when everything is not written down, when there are tasks still to be checked off their lists, or moved to new lists, or when there's a hole in the logic somewhere—I can't sleep. I can't really do anything except worry. Unfinished feelings sit in me like Gretel's huge sausage dinners. And it all shortens my breath.

And under my forced-closed eyelids were many *why*'s written like smoky skywriting, even though they shouldn't matter to a scientist. Why did the folkies they come here, this time? Why now? Why us? Why Thryst, why me?

There are too many *why*s; there always are.

I got up. I opened my eyes and propped to my elbows and saw Thryst at the foot of my bed. He was grave and stiff with his hands on his hips. But I didn't look at his face—I didn't have the energy for another ride into his volcanic eyes.

At my desk, I crumpled up some old notes and made some new ones. I started another list, this one actually a list of lists. With a timeline. I re-read Gretel's cookbook translation.

I looked at Thryst's beard because there it was again, at the side of my desk, attached to a body that was heaving leathery breaths. My little dogs were at heel, and though I kept my head down, I felt that Dwarven stare burn a few layers deep into the freckly skin on my back, which burns easily in the summer.

My own drooping eyes made a blur of the sight of endless notes and pages on my desk, so I chose to push my chair away and stare at the ceiling for a while.

I accidentally looked at Thryst because there he was again, his beard close enough to rest partially on the arm of my chair. I peeked at his face—his eye sockets were black, the curtain was down. I was glad about that and looked away quickly. I felt Thryst move away. I heard the eight small paws follow him. They stopped at my bedroom door.

I heard the door open, and then shut. I looked: Thryst was facing me again, the dogs at each side, with all six eyes glowing in the dim room and all three heads tilting and swaying in a strange way. Was it the sleep in my eyes, or were they all motioning for me to go to them?

Thryst turned, opened the door, and walked through it—he barely fit, and his axe and hammer tinged against the frame. The dogs stayed—and in three seconds, Thryst's hooded head and hairy chin alone appear back in the open space.

Ok, ok! I gave in. I got up and followed, since this was what he wanted, acting like some clever TV dog. The real dogs followed.

Thryst led me downstairs and though rooms, walking silently through the shadowed halls of my dark house. My feet creaked the floorboards, but the massive Dwarf seemed to skim along, light as a dust ball. We headed to the basement crawlspace and were soon hopping up through its small door that sits about four feet off the ground. Thryst managed this in a leapfrog hop, his boots first, springing right through the entrance hole. My own effort, in the dark, resembled more a spider on too much cough medicine; all my limbs were stretched and pushing in different directions in order to shimmy and lift myself up and through.

Inside, I had to crawl—it was just easier that way. From the cement slab floor to the wooden-framed roof measures about three-and-a-half feet, and this space runs under the main floor of the house, which is a long way. Since it's a cluttered maze with storage boxes, crates, and other flotsam, there are many tunnels and dead ends. When I was younger, I thought this all was a fun hangout, a land of caves where the walls and rooms were made up of piles of forgotten stuff from my parent and grandparents and great-grandparents (probably). The farther we went, the older the memories and weirder the junk.

Thryst stopped. We were now, I think, under the front door of the house and heading, I think, toward my parents' master bedroom, and the boxed items around us were from, I think, my grandparents' day. The air was stale and cold.

They only light came from a pale-yellow bulb back at the entrance, and we were now wrapped in the angles of the many shadows left by our winding path's walls.

But I did see Thryst's eyes, and that is always light enough. He had one hand in a pocket, shuffling some gems there or rocks or who knows what—but the clicking and the nervous restlessness of the Dwarf made me afraid. I looked away, but he held his gaze and drew mine back to him. *He wants me to see something*, I thought, *to experience something with him. But why here? Is he lost?* I wished I could get him a phone, with a map, or GPS.

My brain was tired; I was weakening.

Ok, ok! I give in. I will look. I will look into his eyes.

CHAPTER 80

Arty

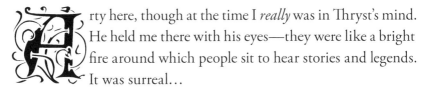rty here, though at the time I *really* was in Thryst's mind. He held me there with his eyes—they were like a bright fire around which people sit to hear stories and legends. It was surreal...

The place seems like the normal world, but more. The land looks like Belle Terre, but more.

It's a dark night, and all around is stiff and still. Atop a steep hill, with a village twinkling below, I see shapes of people heading toward a building, a small house, but soon they descend, passing through open, angled doors that lead down into a cellar. The shapes are broad and short; they are Dwarves and dressed for battle, as Thryst is. I don't see The Magnificent, but I know he's with me, as if in this world, somewhere outside my own basement where we sit, we're the same person, and he's seeing through my eyes, just as I'm staring into his.

The stairs lead us beneath and then directly toward another descent—this time down a bulging wooden ladder that plunges through a circular hole. There are many steps before we land in a wide space lit with torches. Their flames reflect everywhere—off the glistening mud of the floor, off shields and the metal of axes and armor. The air is thick and musty; there are maps on the walls where wood beams cross and support a ceiling that creaks and bows under the weight of the others assembling above.

I see that there are two tunnels leading away—they are ground level, just high enough for Dwarves to walk through, as some do, into the glow of small fires that line the passage walls. In a third direction there's another hole, with its own hole and ladder whose steps disappear into blackness.

Most of the Dwarves here are large and stout and ready, just as Thryst always appears. Several leaders are debating something loudly in their coarse language, and at times dirt rains down in answer to a slammed hand or a shouted, guttural command.

The energy grows. Axes and spears ring out like wind chimes after each shout and war cry.

Many other Dwarves have circled around, near to a map that looks like a War Game version of the village of Belle Terre, as two large and one very old Dwarf—he's dressed all in silver—yell at Thryst, at us.

Silence falls. We walk away. Reaching the top of the ladder, we hear shouting and outrage below as the debate continues, inflamed by our absence, it seems.

Outside again—the stars above dead, and the trees of the hilltop unmoving—Thryst is upset and nervous, his beard hanging limp and his eyes and cheeks puffed with worry. I can sense his frustration, and he stares at the sky, rigid for a moment before grunting some ancient curse.

Across the valley—past the village below—is an opposing hill, the other that borders the bay of Belle Terre, though it looks as if it belongs to a different time or alternate world. From there, lights flare, bright white and yellow—not normal firelight, nor even the bluish hue of manmade electric light, but magical blasts like summoned lightning, illuminated beams that are at someone's command. Power sits atop that mountain.

Thryst begins to run down the hill. His way is a zigzag; he sniffs the air for direction, and at times stops to look out across the land, or within it: behind trees, under boulders, into small dips in the surface of the earth.

He's searching for something.

We pass others—not only Dwarves but small fairies I know to be Light Elves. Thryst confronts them, face to face, and searches their expressions for information.

He's searching for someone.

Many Dwarves on their way up the hill stop to beg to Thryst to return with them.

"We need your strength. Yours. Your family's. Your forefathers'. You are not alone. You are not a lone Dwarf," I understand them to say, though the words at the same time are deeply foreign. I read this on many Dwarvish faces, faces so similar to Thryst's that I doubt I could tell them apart in the daylight, let alone under this moonless night.

"We will need light," others say. Because we have entered total darkness. Thryst has moved underground.

We are in a bare tunnel, it appears freshly and hastily dug, and I feel root-ends and wet, fresh dirt brush my body as I pass. Thryst can barely maneuver his shoulders in the narrow way, but he somehow keeps up a good pace, hunched over and driving with his powerful thighs. The smell is of salt and seawater; at times my feet sink into a cold, wet sand.

This way then joins a larger one—an older and more completed underground road. There is light enough to see oncoming turns ahead, and many crossroads—though the source of the light isn't clear. Thryst is sure of the direction and starts to run.

Soon our tunnel road starts to rise, and a steep climb angles us forward. My legs are numb, but my heart is excited and I'm able to keep up. With each step, the light reveals increasingly impressive stonework. These tunnels are old and important. Each corner and offshoot are decorated with ancient, silver symbols, and the air becomes dry and fresh; sometimes at a side passage I feel a breeze of fresh air that's no longer salty but smells of fresh wet leaves. And the way underfoot is now paved with brick.

The way levels, the rise completed, and Thryst zooms onward through a wide space that's a major intersection of at least ten other tunnels, his choice never in doubt.

W.W. Marplot

I skid to a stop—he's gone straight up! I see now that there's an opening above, and he's leapt up a dozen stone ladder steps built into the wall and is now above me. Soon I'm pulled up myself and pop out of a hole to find myself on wet grass that's lit, but not by any moon. It's an ugly, blue, artificial light that bathes us, and Thryst scurries into some bushes.

We are, inexplicably, in a front yard in Belle Terre, my neighborhood; I recognize the surrounding trees at the main road just a few yards away. This is the normal world now, and there's no sign of Dwarves or dragons or Elves, only a family watching TV—their large front windows shine at us, and we can see them all clearly.

And, at the other end of the house, a second-story light shows dimly, while a young girl is pacing in her bedroom. Thryst brings me up a drainpipe to look in the window.

I recognize the girl. It's Isabella, one of the friend-of-a-friend network who were found by folkies.

I know I'm just a passenger in this eye-dream-fantasy, but I'm still surprised.

There's no sign of the Shellycoat Water Elf, but Isabella is acting strangely. Stranger than you might think; strange even compared to the all-time weirdest Wednesday, Thursday, and now Friday night of all time.

Why are we here?

But the vision continues. I see and hear poor Isabella talking out loud to herself, and sometimes to friends on the phone, and complaining she doesn't feel good. And she doesn't look good, either: she has many marks on her skin. Blisters dot her face, arms, legs, and shoulders. Some are dotted with a thick, yellowy cream; others shine raw and red and look irritating, if not really painful.

She's talking about catching her Water Elf, and she also wants to give it to an old lady she has met.

Her friends are calming her down. But when alone, and not on the phone, she sits and mumbles and isn't convinced of what to do. She knows the Shellycoat is real. No one else believes—instead, they ask when she'll be back in school; they tell her to rest and stop posting online.

She's under a spell.

I don't know the counter-spell.

Why did Thryst bring me here, from the crawlspace, through his mind, to the town, to some other world, but not help me?

What is he looking for? Who?

Not Isabella. We leave.

After we return to the tunnels, we retrace our steps, then turn down a new path, and pop out again: at another house, this one in Belle Terre, another with many lights on, and with another isolated almost-teen, another trusted-friend-of-a-friend in their room.

It's Olivia, my own friend who helped me run last year's Research Club. I spoke to her in math class Thursday—she asked me why I kept turning around, and if I'd started the social studies project yet. At the time, I couldn't tell her I was trying to make sure my Dwarf wasn't shaving any of the kids. Of course, I didn't know then that talking to her would send a signal to kidnapped fairies everywhere that Olivia Patrick was looking for a roommate. Or that it would lead to so much trouble.

Her Silky's small, womanly face is peeking through a round hole of a large, colorfully painted toybox hidden among a disarray of clothes in a closet. As Thryst and I watch, the closet door closes and Olivia sits on her bed, hugging her knees and rocking back and forth in silence.

Until her stepmother comes in and yells at her.

And then her father, who yells some more.

Olivia starts to cry and then approaches her folkie—a small female figure that squeaks and throws a doll-sized, feathery hat out the hole. Olivia turns to the window, as if she sees Thryst and me, and says, "I don't know what to do. I love her. But she said to do it…"

Another spell from the Old Woman of the Mountains.

I don't know the counter-spell.

The rest of my trip within Thryst's eyes passes with visits to the other folkie-finding friends-of-friends. Alex seems ok, but his house is in an uproar, with parents upset and arguing, police searching inside and outside, and neighborhood dogs barking fiercely. I overhear talk of "monsters" and of the policemen scoffing and saying that they were probably garden snakes made bigger and scarier by the imagination of a young boy. I believe the monster version.

Sophia's household is similar—but Animal Rescue workers are with the police, and the monsters are crocodiles, and much harder to explain: even Sophia couldn't mistake a cricket for a crocodile.

Ethan and Jacob are both upset, looking sick and blotchy and poxy, and sitting deep in thought, even in another world of thought, the way I travel with Thryst the Seeker. But Thryst keeps searching, pulling me on. For him, these are more dead ends.

For me, they aren't.

Thryst doesn't stay to help any of these kids, our friends. Instead he has to keep looking, and we return to the underground stoneroads. Heading back.

On our way, we're again met with many turns and intersecting tunnels and paths. This time, the Dwarf isn't sure of the way. This time, each new opening is followed, at least partially, by my guide, Thryst the Seeker, still searching: but he only increases his pace and panic at each reversal as, each time, he finds nothing.

We're back to the sand and seawater, back under the beach, I guess.

I'm terribly tired, we both are, in this world. Just as I think Thryst will go mad with his failure and frustration, he stops, and stands, and sees ahead a new way that he must follow. He seems sure of it and coughs a small word of excitement. The pass is well-lit, though the tunnel air reflects a ghoulish, greenish shade. I'm nauseous from weariness, and the dirty feel of the tight space that only allows us breaths of unclean, impure air. I gag as if it were poison.

Thryst attempts to run ahead, but even he now stumbles. And then they're on us—enemies come out of the green glow and fill the road ahead. They come on.

It's an army of creatures that I recognize from the books.

Wights: They are sleek and slim and float like ghosts along the walls. They wear robes or capes, and they screech horribly; it sounds like laughter.

Goblins: They are large and clumsy, dressed in rags. Their skin looks like grey death, and the stench of rotting meat covers all.

Spunkies, Buggaboos, Tor-Ogres: Smaller, devilish imps tramp along in stride, smaller but equally wicked.

There are others, barely seen except when being pushed or pulled violently, and they're slight, and scared, and surrounded—they're captives. Their fairy light is extinguished and overwhelmed by the sickening green illumination. A Sprite, a Buggaboo, a Luridan, a Gunna….

I want to shrink to hide behind my Dwarf. My skin feels frozen and rippled with fear, but I realize the sensation is only in my eyes. All sight blurs but doesn't close.

To my shock, Thryst doesn't turn back, or stand to fight, but tucks away his axe and tries to push onward and ahead, into the throng, to get past them. They catch him and throw him back, also unwilling to fight. I can't think of a reason. Thryst tries again to break through—this time they attempt to hold him and drag him down and away, but he kicks and punches, and the spasms of his power are enough to free himself. He's grown angry and wild, and his screams strike his enemies as forcefully as his muscles.

His axe, finally, rings a clear tone, and a clean light comes to shine. The enemies back off a step.

I know to turn and run, and I do…

I came out of the spell of Thryst's fiery eyes, while remembering the spell that our fairy friends were under. I needed to help. I needed to do something.

CHAPTER 81

Arty

rty here, still. Here meaning *sitting exhausted and cross-legged in my basement crawlspace across from Thryst the Frantic.* He nodded to me that I was allowed to leave.

I went to bed, and in seconds was in a fitful sleep dealing with prickly dreams. In the last one, I followed the sounds of harsh clanking, like tolling from a huge and heavy iron church bell. Its rhythm led me to giant doors where rattled a hanging sign that read, "Eastward Manor." I tried to find magic words in a small red book, spells to make the banging bell stop, but I couldn't even hear my own voice, and the noise went on.

White light flashed and lit the world with each strike. The light made me want to not wake up. The sound made me want to wake up.

I woke up. The first few seconds of leftover dream reverie had turned the bonging church bell into a smaller, tapping sound—just like the one I'd heard yesterday morning, the familiar clinking of metal on stone. I snapped from one dreamworld to another—this one, where I had found a Dwarf and was in a fantasy adventure.

Trying to trace the tapping, I opened a window. The sound became clearer; it was from the front driveway.

I yawned into the fresh morning air. It hadn't rained. The sun was out and blasting bright rays through the new leaves above. I yawned again as two thoughts fought for space in my tired brain. One was the tapping...*Oh no, not again! On Saturday! It's going to wake every-*

one! My brain began to sweat as my arms and legs argued over the quickest way to get dressed.

Then came the other thought that had waited patiently in line: *Why's it so bright out? Why's it so late! It's 11 am already!*

I had one leg in a sweatshirt and one arm in my jeans as a third thought came: *Wait, no one called me last night. Did NOTHING happen with the other fairy creatures? What about the vision from Thryst's eyes, the Trust Network friends and their struggles? The strays at the university?*

I reached for my phone with my free foot. No calls. Only a single text from Emma that her mother would drop her off at my house at 11, and with Ted and Cry.

Any minute!

Louder than before, the clacking noises rode a cool breeze in through my window. I gymnastically corrected my clothing combination, grabbed the map and the blue book, and ran to find the tapping and the tapper.

The house was empty, but there was a note—my family were all at their usual Saturday morning sports rituals—and a buttered bagel that reminded me how hungry I was.

Outside was *Thryst the Tapper.* In the driveway, and under it, his hammer and axe and arms had been hard at work. Between two of the large, white-painted decorative stones that lined our driveway was a pyramid of dirt seven feet high and ten around that showed a rainbow of soil from dark brown at bottom to the wetter golden stuff on top sprinkled with hundreds of surprised worms. All of it had come from the hole nearby, certainly a tunnel entrance, from which odd grunts and flying dirt still came.

The story in Thryst's eyes from last night in the basement came back to me. Thryst was still searching.

Poor Dwarf, I thought, *but it's going to be hard to hide this!* I then realized how little it mattered. Soon everything would be known, and to everyone. Battles were raging, kids were caught in spells. I needed to act! I knew what to do—like Thryst and his searching. I just didn't know *how*—like Thryst and his not-finding. I needed to find the counter-spells, the second book, the missing one. Or get Sprug to help. I needed to join this adventure. I couldn't help Thryst, but I could do *something*.

Maybe.

I called to my Dwarf, but he didn't surface. My three dogs, however, did come, covered in mud and panting like living engines. Apparently, they were apprentice diggers in service to *Thryst the Master*. They reentered the hole.

I stepped backward until I leaned on the nearest, largest white rock—and felt a sharp pain as something cut into my ankles. I jumped away and looked back, noticing for the first time that the rock had been sculpted. It wasn't simply a round stone anymore, but a three-foot-high alligator head whose sharp lower fangs had just bit into my legs.

Now I saw: All the driveway stones, and many of the trees nearby, were cut and carved. They were popping with symbols and writing and many beautiful shapes—statues of beasts and birds and snakes. Around the tunnel entrance—the one with dog tails wagging out of it—were stone columns with arches made of tree branches. Smaller rocks and shrubs were all perfect spheres and cubes. It looked very cool and medieval, a mythical Dwarf garden, their own legends written in the living rock.

Cry will like this, I thought, though I admit I was amazed and as struck with wonder as any fantasy fan.

But my family! They won't like this! I remembered my dad's unrepeatable screams after my brothers tore up the lawn riding like bronco-busters on their motorized quad-bike—though I had a feeling that, just as Thryst went unseen when he wanted, that this too, somehow, would not bring death or punishment or battle from my real world.

I sat on the white alligator's level head to wait for Emma.

Flat on the ground near the hole, sitting deep in the green grass was a slab of dark rock like a tombstone. It was covered in runes, and with simple pictures chiseled deep into the slick rock and in clean strokes. Three of these hieroglyphics, the largest and deepest, were a mattock, a throne, and a weird drinking mug. With my mind on magic spells, I wondered if the strange marks were actually charms, and how I'd know the "missing" counter-spells and incantations or witchy voodoo hexes if I could see them, if I could read them, if I could ever find the second book, the one titled with only symbols.

I watched as Thryst emerged into the sunlight and began writing again, his small hammer in his right hand, his mighty arm moving around and around, carving more symbols into the slab: a harp, a horn, a hammer.

When he finished with those, Thryst added pictures around the runes. Two looked like Dwarves that were almost identical to each other, though one had a staff instead of a weapon, while the other had a shorter hood similar to Thryst's. Between the two Dwarves stood trees, and cartoonish ripples of water. It was a meaningless scene to me.

Thryst sighed just ahead of a strong breeze, as if his breath were taken and driven along by the skies.

I wish I could help him find what he seeks.

That wish mixed with the free time I had, sitting on an alligator and thinking. I had a new idea, probably an awful one, definitely a dangerous one, but at least it gave me something to do, a list of one thing that I could accomplish today, with Emma. And maybe it would stop the ringing in my head; the huge doorbell was still tolling.

I used the blue book and the map to find Eastward Manor.

It had the red symbol on it. The man-in-brown's map was there.

My dangerous idea just got dangerouser.

I said aloud that we should get inside, since Emma's mother would be coming soon, and the Dwarf dragged his axe and beard and hood along the ground on the way back into the house.

As we reached the front door, a car pulled up. Emma got out—alone. Her mother had her head down and fiddled with her phone a few minutes but then left without noticing the Dwarf Tunnel Garden. Her mom never stays, she just drops Emma off—which is good, as we would have the house to ourselves—but: "Where are Cry and Ted?" I asked.

"They're both at Cry's house. Ted went there last night and slept over. I texted you all this," she said.

"I just woke up and came right outside. Look what Thryst did!" I opened my arms wide to the wild statues and bright dirt pile.

"Wow," Emma admired the Dwarven craftwork while she explained. "Ted said his room was too small, that a dragon would never be able to find him there. So, he went to Cry's house to wait for his creature to come."

That was fine with me. I like Cry, but him being overwhelmed with wonder 24/7 wasn't a help, and we needed to act. And, like parents say: the less time with Ted, the better. Let Cry do some Ted-sitting, and they could cancel each other out.

"Emma," I said, after a few seconds of silence, "I need to do something."

"You want to read more?"

"No!" This was exactly the problem. "I don't. I can't figure out Thryst, and I didn't figure out Ted, and there's so much going on and I always feel one step behind. But there is something I can do now. I want to find the man in brown and get my notes back and see what his part is."

"But he might be on the side of the Gwyllion."

"Actually, I think he is. They were in the woods together. And I found him on the map. He's at Eastward Manor. I think they took over the manor. The bad guys are trying to take New Island over from the fairies."

"Then let's NOT find him," Emma said. "I've had enough battle and adventure to last me 'til my Sweet Sixteen."

This was exactly the problem. "Well, I need to do this."

"Why? Why him?"

"He has my notes." I said it as bravely as I could, and Emma still almost laughed.

"Great reason to get killed or turned into an orc zombie," she said.

"It's my little part of the war."

"Oh please. Stop."

I had to convince her. "We have Thryst with us, and Sprug, and it's daytime, and I can find him with the map. I'm going to do this."

"So, we're going to Eastward Manor? Maybe run into an army, or millions of Gwyllions?"

It was a very, very good question. I checked the map, and showed Emma, and it told us that we didn't need to go that way. The man was in the woods, near to the stop where Ted threw my papers, but moving. Closer.

"Great," Emma said. "We just have to wait, and maybe he'll come here."

"No. Let's go," I said. "We have to go to him, or it doesn't count."

"You're nuts, and you should save your bravery for rescuing a princess or something, or for your first prom date."

But: I walked, and she followed.

I led us through the woods, and toward the beach, first to see what we could see, and to talk about what, exactly, to do when we found Mr. Alphabet the thief.

"You're procrastinating," Emma said.

We brought *Thryst the Downtrodden*. She hoped it also would cheer him up.

"What if Thryst and the Sprugster leave us when we need them?" Emma asked. "They've been popping in and out."

"They won't," I said but convinced nobody.

Emma commented on the lack of a storm last night, real or fantasy, and today's bright sunshine and warm breezes. There were also no animals in sight, and the change was odd. The creepy calm of the woods replaced the weirdness of things like squirrels hugging bluebirds. Between wind gusts it was too hot, too quiet; you could almost hear the grass and vines grow.

"Is this the calm before the storm?" she wondered. "Or after?"

CHAPTER 82

Arty

"Or both?" I puffed, my sweat now forming itchy drops on my face and neck. "And where is the Old Woman of the Mountains?" I wondered in my turn, thinking of the Gwyllion, and thinking of the many spells. "I'm worried about the other kids and their fairies. I think the Gwyllion is after them. She's not on the map at the moment, at least not the page we have, though I can control it a little to cover other areas, using other symbols from the books. Her thing comes and goes. I'm not sure really what that means."

Emma asked quietly, "If you find that second book with the spells—what will you do with it?"

Another superb and excellent question.

I had no answer. And Sprug wasn't talking, just ugly. So, I shrugged my shoulders, looked up at the sun, and we walked.

The little Spriggan then detoured us, jumpflying briskly—he and Thryst had their own things to do as usual—until I finally had to sit and rest. Sunlight spotted the floor of the woods, its streaks scattered, uneven and blurred, like giant eyes squinting through eyelashes of many young leaves. When the wind gusted, these forest eyes blinked rapidly—or perhaps that's how Emma might draw it, capturing the magic that had taken over our neighborhood, Belle Terre. I was glad she was with me.

But sitting and resting are not Dwarfish habits, certainly not of a Dwarf on an obsessive secret mission. Thryst climbed a nearby tree, a huge oak, in his usual manner with axe and hand.

"I never get tired of watching this," Emma remarked. Sprug followed Thryst upward, and in only a moment, they were back down and led us off our path and in a line straight to the cliff edge.

I checked the map for the red symbol, the man in brown.

"Why does he get a rune, and we don't?" Emma asked.

"He doesn't—that map rune just points to itself, to the main mother map. So maybe our map shows up on his, too. How nice," I answered with bold cowardice.

The glassy map piece showed that he was closer now, though stopped. In fact, if we hadn't followed the fairies to this spot, we would've crossed his path. I gulped. Bravely.

I looked for my Dwarf, who was on his way back to earth. Directly above him lay a powdery blue sky and the strong yellow noon sun.

Otherwise and all around, stretching halfway down the sky, were dark clouds. They had amassed in every direction and now formed a ring around us, as if to surround the neighborhood, which was still glowing in bright sunshine. But past Belle Terre, and everywhere else, even out over all the distant water of the Sound, was a cover of dark and dirty clouds. It was like we were in the eye of a hurricane and trapped by its violence. The clouds looked to be fighting over each other—they tumbled and swirled yet remained in a ring, as if an invisible circular border protected us. Emma, Thryst, Sprugly, and I.

It still scared the crud out of me. You can never be sure how much crud you have in you until it is all scared out of you. During this calculation, I heard two rumbles: one was Thryst grunting louder and louder, but it mixed with the other, more distant sound, a massive growling and shattering clap of thunder from the sieging, surging sky. I saw no lightning.

"What do we do?" Emma asked.

"Run!" I said. I wasn't proud of the idea, or of this as a general plan, but it was good enough for Thryst, whose colorful boots were already far ahead of us and back into the woods.

W.W. Marplot

As Emma and I followed—which was slow going, since we had to jump roots and vines and thorny bushes until we rejoined the main path—I yelled to her, forcing my voice to outdo a growl of thunder that seemed to come from directly under our feet.

"We don't want to get caught in another battle, like you and Cry did."

"I agree!" she said.

"But are they going to it anyway?" I asked, meaning Sprug and Thryst.

"Probably," Emma answered over another blast from the storm clouds. "It seems like Sprugly's job. But Peanut and the others are safe."

"Are *we* safe?" I hollered. We were now running directly toward the man in brown.

There was a sudden silence from the earth and sky so that my own words startled me, and Thryst stopped to check on us.

"Isn't that why we came out here? To find the man?" Emma asked, darn it.

"I just thought of something I want to read first."

"No," she yelled from her jog, darn her.

As we ran, I peeked at the map page from my pocket. It glowed in a prism of colors; a jumble of symbols joined at its center.

"Why now? What does it mean?" Emma raised her voice above a sudden wind.

"I don't know. This is happening too fast!" I panted, almost breathless from running and yelling.

Emma looked back to answer once more, but just as she turned, I was jolted stiff and stopped in my tracks by the sight of a man ahead of her. It was a wild sight: not because of the man himself, but because he was trying to deal with Sprug the Spriggan, and not doing well at it.

Emma stopped, skidding up a bit of dirt, and we approached the scene slowly together. Salty sweat caught up to me, running into my eyes. There was no more wind, the air was stifling, and I felt tired and small among so many big things I couldn't control.

Ahead I watched the man in brown flail his long arms wildly, making me glad that *Thryst the Heavily Armed* was right behind us. Our little Spriggan had doubled in size, quadrupled in ugliness, and was zipping around in a blur. I could feel Dwarf-breath blowing, though Thryst didn't need to join the fight.

Yet there was something extremely odd happening. Now that I'd caught my breath, wiped the sweat away, and watched more closely this matchup of fairy-versus-man, I heard that the man was speaking—*to Sprug*! He was trying to reason with him! He spoke almost calmly, and I even thought I heard the man use the word *Spriggan*! Even as he talked, though, his arms and body were twisting, flailing, and ducking feverishly to defend himself as best he could.

Emma looked at me with little hills of confusion on her forehead and eyebrows.

Personally, I'm all for talking things through in a difficult situation. But I think I'd act differently if I was a tall, thin man attacked in the woods by a watermelon-sized fairy creature who kept slapping and biting my head and neck. And note that I do actually have some experience in this.

This is what I thought I heard:

"I am not here for them. Welcome back! You can stay here! I have been west of west and east of west…" from a deep, long, thin, brown voice. And, "1752!"

Emma and I simply stared until Sprug calmed and flew back to Emma's ear, smaller in size and whispering with satisfaction into the wind.

Huffing, the notorious Mr. Alphabet brushed off his shoulders and upper arms as Emma leaned toward me and relayed Sprug's message: "Sprug says its ok. He thinks."

"What do *you* think?" I asked Emma, just as the man began speaking to us, and he was not very polite.

"I guess it's a good thing that this wasn't a *fenrir* attacking, with all the help you gave me." I remembered his nasty voice from the school hallway when he'd offered candy.

He leered at us.

My mind zoomed ahead of itself with possibilities: *Sprug trusts him? Why? He knows about Spriggans, and fenrirs, which are huge fairy wolves. Are some of those nearby? He has maps. He's after us, after Ted, and doesn't even seem surprised or scared. He's not in our Trust Network; does he have a folkie of his own? Where is his ally, the Old Woman of the Mountains?*

Before I could form any of this into pronounceable words, brave old Emma was already talking back.

"You're lucky it wasn't worse, sneaking up on kids in the woods." She stepped aside and let the man get a good view of our Mighty Dwarf. Thryst stood firm with his steel blazing gold from the sun, his eyes bright, his breath coming in boulder-rolling bursts, his sweat and hair trembling and all of him ready for action. Dwarf glared at Man, deeper and graver than Man could at Kid. *But can this guy actually see Thryst? Is that good, or bad?*

Then, as if things couldn't get any less predictable, the man laughed! And came closer! To Thryst! And said…yes! He actually said, bending down to Thryst's face, "Magnificent!"

As I wondered, and *Thryst the Might Have Actually Been Blushing at This Point* wondered, and Emma wondered, the tall man looked from the leafy trail to the tip of Thryst's bent hood with continuing exclamations of his own wonder.

Who is this guy? I said to myself, and the words must have also come out of my eyes and cheekbones because Emma answered me.

"No idea."

"No," the man said, standing now upright and tall but keeping an admiring gaze upon Thryst. Although the powerful warrior-Dwarf's grunts sounded like an army helicopter crashing, Thryst appeared uncomfortable and awkward with the attention, so honestly, some of his visual sting was gone.

To Emma and me, the man remained snotty. "No. You haven't any idea; that is true. And obviously, you don't know much, but to your small credit at least you are not false. I have a lot of questions for you, notwithstanding. Do you even realize what is going on here?"

"Well…" I started to mutter.

"THAT WASN'T one of the questions," the man snapped back, capitalizing the first two words.

"Hey, listen…" Emma tried to jump in.

"No, YOU LISTEN," the man said, capitalizing the last two words this time, and maybe even using a bigger font as well. "I just saw, I think, a Highland Quoit Spriggan…"

I didn't know Sprug had a last name, I thought as he spoke.

"…and here's a Dwarf. So far south! How many others do you know of, and what are your plans? Who else knows about this? So far, you are the only ones I have caught. Plus, your two other extremely dull, dangerously meddlesome friends."

"That's everyone," I said and soon felt as dull as he thought I was.

"Ok—tell me everything you know," he said, asked, commanded. As I considered an answer, I could feel Emma's temperature rising.

"Hey, listen," she started again. This time the man in brown didn't interrupt. This surprised her, so she then said, "Uhhh, ummmm."

Sighing his impatience, the man observed Emma, but not for her sake. He looked around her neck and shoulders, I figured it was for signs of Sprugly. Thryst was still still. Emma spoke. "Yeah, well, why should we tell you anything, ESPECIALLY if we don't know much?" This was kind of an odd question, I thought, but I understood her point.

The man calmed, and long, thin, brown bristles of moustache straightened with the muscles on his face: he smiled. He began to speak, and his voice was now quite soothing and smooth. He stood straight and thin within his clothes—which were all plain and brown to match his hair and moustache and cropped beard. Everything about him was clean and neat and straight despite his having just fended off a Spriggan in the heat of the woods.

"Ok. Ok. Ok." He spoke slowly, with almost a kind look. "For one thing, do you know that Spriggans protect other fairies?"

"Yes," we both answered.

"And you know that Dwarves are, shall we say, fairly warlike also?"

"We noticed, yeah."

"Ok. Ok, ok. And did you know that Spriggans, once they accept your gifts, will also accept you into their realm?"

"No," we answered, looking at each other like baffled kindergarteners learning long division.

"And did you know that Dwarves and Spriggans and most other beings like this—that are to us legendary—have special senses—that are to us magical—and they can understand us completely, though we might not understand them at all?"

"Yes," we said.

"And they are good at climbing trees," I added worthlessly.

"Oh...OK," the man said, caught by surprise. His head tilted just slightly. "Ok." He straightened. Then do you really think that—with this little army you have—that if I meant you harm, that I would still have all my arms and legs attached?"

Good point. I had to ask, "Why can you can see them?"

"Ah, good. Now you are finally with me in my realm, the realm of sensible people. That is a good question. And, even better, the fact that you are asking me good questions shows some worthiness. Not a lot, but some. At last." He looked back at Thryst, staring rudely. "Two worthy things you have done. The rest was useless, childish, and dangerous."

"Which two?" Emma asked, continuing to prove his point.

"Talk to me. And think sensibly," he answered but did not take his wondering sight from Thryst.

"Don't look into his eyes," I said to the man. "We don't have time."

CHAPTER 83

Emma

"Faeries, come take me out of this dull world,
For I would ride with you upon the wind,
Run on the top of the disheveled tide,
And dance upon the mountains like a flame."

—WILLIAM BUTLER YEATS

This is Emma. I'm letting the Man in Brown give a chapter quote so you can see how snooty he is.

Our desperate hurry to outrun the ring of clouds and the oncoming storm was replaced with fascination for this strange man who had scared us—*chased* us!—so many times. Arty's courageous adventure-seeking was replaced with a mix of scientific curiosity and little-boy fear.

Sprugly's sitting place in my hair was replaced with regular jumpflights among nearby trees to check the winds with his ears and nose.

He seemed content. The air remained hot, but the sky was quiet. The man was interested in Thryst. The proof was his willingness to kneel in the dirt after tiring of bending to Dwarf-height. Thryst grew bored, returned to his normal self, and *stonestood* in place. This was the scene as I repeated Arty's question.

"So, tell us—how come the fairies can see you? So far, they haven't seen any other adults."

"How do you know?" the man asked.

"We are keeping track," Arty answered.

"Of the ones our friends have," I added.

"Have!" The man looked surprised at our answers. "How many fairies, and where are they?"

"Well, there were a bunch in the storm," I said, "and a bunch at the university. Where you chased us."

"Where you stole my map."

Ah, *touché*. But I had an answer. "No, Peanut did." And he did not get to answer back, since Sprug flew very near to his face, protectively flapping his freaky wings. The man in brown backed a few steps, his arms raised defensively, but his eyes peeking out in fascination whenever Sprugly got close.

The storm made a rumble off in the distance, and Arty and I whispered to each other that this standoff, the man's secrets versus our secrets, was not helping anybody, and we need to get to shelter. We decided to make the first move, to tell him what we knew, and trust him. And, as he said, if he were an enemy, he wouldn't still be in one tall piece but two-Dwarf-height pieces, at least.

Arty shared this updated plan with Mr. Alphabet, and the almost-enemy crooked his head to the right, while a thin smile sort of tilted the other way.

"Well, I am surprised, and impressed, I must say." And he began with his questions.

"Ok then. How many other fairies?" the man bent down just enough to be me-height.

"Besides the storm and the university, that we couldn't count," I answered, "we know of seven other fairy creatures, besides these two."

"Seven!" Mr. Alphabet exclaimed, surprised again at everything we said, standing so suddenly straight to full height that he almost made a twanging noise, and almost tipped over. He wasn't very nimble, and his knees cracked like old twigs. *No—like pretzel rods*, I thought and realized I was getting hungry.

"And yet," he continued, softly this time, and more to himself, "and yet, *only* seven…" He arched a bit backwards, placing both hands to his lower back.

"Yeah, seven," I went on, "but there might be more by now. Last we checked—a little while ago—there were no more, not with our friends anyway, though we sort of expect one more to find us any minute." I was thinking of Ted waiting for his dragon.

"*Find you!*" the man repeated. "Very good."

"Yeah, uh, thanks." I went on, "We've kept to ourselves since we realized that more folkies—"

"*Folkies!*" the man quoted me again, with no indication of a reason, only like he enjoyed providing echo. So, I continued.

"We realized that they were finding—"

"*Finding…*" he said.

"—anyone we talked to, that they could see we trusted—"

"*Trusted…*"

"—them."

Arty laughed as I went on.

"So far, it's only kids. We've been all over town, and the folkies follow us around, the three of us: Arty has Thryst the Dwarf—" I pointed to cue the echo, and it came:

"*Thryst!*"

"I have Sprug the Spriggan—"

"*Sprug!*"

"—and our other friend Cry—"

"*Cry,*" he said, out of habit, but then, "Cry?"

"Yeah, that's our friend's name. I wish it wasn't. But anyway: Peanut found him." I let this sink in. The man was staring over our heads and off into space, into the woods, then up to the blue, perfect sky. "Peanut, the Pixie," I said again and waited.

"Say it!" Arty prompted.

"Peanut the Pixie," the man said from out of some distant daydream. Then, back at attention, "A Pixie! Very good."

"Yeah, she's really cute, just a baby, we think."

"*Baby,*" the man said, a smile wide across his face.

"Six more appeared, then they stopped coming to our friends, as far as we know. But there was a whole night with the Old Woman of the Mountains."

No reaction from Mr. Alphabet.

Why? I had to know now. "Do you know who I am talking about?" I asked.

"Unfortunately, yes. The Gwyillion."

"Are you on her side, or ours?" I pointed to all four of us.

"What do you think, young lady?"

"I saw you in the woods with her."

"No, you didn't," he said, calm as the eye of a storm.

As a matter of fact, I didn't. He was right. I only saw him and Ted, not the Old Woman, not that time.

"Go on with your tale," he said. "You're forgetting someone."

Ted. I answered the man in brown, "The only kid we have talked to so far, who has no fairy—which is fine with us—is this kid Ted. He spied on us, like you, so we had to let him in on it."

Saying this now made me realize how stupid, and risky, it sounded. Once again, speaking to this towering adult made me feel like I was caught all sticky with peanut butter. "But it's been a few days, and nothing, no fairies, have found Ted yet."

"Really? You don't think so?" He smirked. "How many days?"

"Well, he has been spying on us since…" I looked at Arty for help with the facts.

"Wednesday," Arty huffed.

"So," I finished, "that's three days, but we only let him in on it since yesterday morning. With the others, fairies found them within a few hours."

"A whole day," the man said, stroking his thin beard in a very particular way and with two fingers.

"Why did you follow Ted?" Arty asked him.

"We'll get to that," he answered, looking off to the distance, toward the storm.

"Why did you follow us?" I asked him.

"We'll get to that," he answered.

I told the man about the spells, and Ted's strange behavior before and after.

He thought for a moment. "Unwise of Ted. But I have watched him. He should be safe now. He, and you, were lucky. He is back on the correct side, though it was back and forth. They were like dreams to him, but I fear the Old Woman's work." Then, looking again to the storm, and the sky, he continued quietly, almost to himself. "Surprising. It seems too easy, only a *Creideamh Sí*? I wonder if anyone else…" he trailed off, and I was tempted to ask about my own spell, but quickly he faced us again, saying, "Did anything else happen to him? Tell me everything," the man ordered, as direct as he was brown.

"We've done a lot of our own research," Arty answered.

"Yes, you have. And you have caused me pain and cost me time. It could have led to disaster, but I think I understand now. Maybe I understand now…maybe. An interesting distraction. Perhaps."

"Do you, um, have any, of the, fairy tale creatures?" Arty asked awkwardly, but I was glad he did.

The man came out of his trance of self-maybe-understanding, looked sternly at Arty, and then actually smiled. He answered in our own lingo. "No, none of the folkies have *found* me. Not yet. Though I have looked for them, and for a long time. You are lucky…"

"Or special," I said.

"We will see."

"How are you searching for them? By spying on us?" Arty asked, wiping his face of bright sweat.

I added, "Yeah—the school, my house, Arty's house, the university—all you, right?"

"We'll get to that." The man scoffed again, the smile gone, his mouth as flat and thin as his beard. "Or maybe you should pay for the trouble you caused me—wasted time explaining myself to security nincompoops at the school, chasing truant miscreants through the rain and pinewoods…"

I didn't like where this was going.

"But," he went on, "maybe we can work together. There are pieces to this. Like a puzzle. Each is special—and maybe you are—but none more than the rest."

"In that case, you need us," I said.

"Maybe. If your *research*," he mocked, "is better than just recipes. Hmm?" He raised a too-thin eyebrow.

Thankfully, Thryst changed positions at that moment, and his axe sung a brief, clear note that made the trees quiver in fear for their limbs. Maybe this was to remind the man of who was in charge—it certainly wasn't Arty or I.

I looked at Arty, who looked as mopey as Thryst had been all day. I think he'd started seeing this as his big chance to be bold and brave, and it fizzled. He should just be happy that what we thought was an enemy magic wizard had turned out to be—well, a snooty non-enemy. And maybe Arty and this guy could compare nerd-notes and someday be friends.

Then again, there might still be plenty of chances for everyone to be brave, since just being in the woods with the storm surrounding us took some guts. I commented on it as a gust of wind blew the hair across my face. Arty then checked the magical map and told us the storm was just rotating, it hadn't moved. We were in the center. And we hadn't moved either.

When he looked up from the glassy glow of the page, Mr. Alphabet was staring at him with a seriously tilted head.

Arty—sheepishly—handed the map page back to its original owner.

"Sorry," Arty and I both said.

"*Mmm hmm.*" The man accepted it, smiled at it, and left it in one of his long and slender palms, while opening his other long and slender palm.

Arty placed within it the letter from the mysterious Mary.

"Thank you," the man said, while adjusting papers in the satchel high on his hip and bringing out other papers that he handed to Arty—the return of my friend's spell-notes. "Not bad work, Arty."

"Who is Mary?" Arty asked quietly in reply.

"We will get to that," the man said, for the fifth time. "For her sake, and from her hints, I think I will trust you. For the present."

CHAPTER 84

Emma

Thunder struck, not only adding drama but vibrating urgency into our conversation.

"Well, can you hurry and tell us what you know?" we asked simply, and politely, without any weapons.

"As you will!" He seemed happy to and looked around, seemingly searching for something on the ground.

As he did, I said, "Well, first, I told you our names. What's yours?"

"Zyxvuts," he said.

"Oh please," Arty accidentally said out loud. "You made that up."

"Perhaps," the man said distractedly as he was still looking around, and now taking steps in various directions to widen his search along the path. "But no, I didn't make it up. Though maybe someone did. That's my last name. My first is Abcedarius. And, yes: I am sure someone made *that* up."

I made a *yeesh* type of face to Arty, who made one back. His was better and more heartfelt. And he mouthed to me without sound: *Mr. Alphabet.* I nodded.

"Ah, here. Come!" Zyxvuts had finished searching and invited us off the path to a large fallen tree log, where he then sat at the larger end. "This will answer more questions. I will show you my piece of the puzzle."

Next to the log was its former trunk, now a large rounded stump jagged with broken sinews of bark and raw, veiny wood. It was blackened but shiny and still seemed fresh and alive.

"It looks like this tree was a victim of the storm battle. Two nights ago," Zyx said as he noisily and with obvious pain raised himself again, just enough to pull something from his bookshelf-colored satchel. He unfolded the thing—an odd display, like a magician making something preposterously big come out of an impossibly small space—then he sat again, moaning. His large, bony legs with knees pointing to the sky, his chest bent toward his thighs, his whole skeletal package pinned to the curves and bumps of the fallen tree trunk—all made him look miserable. He pulled the contents from the satchel. One by one and carefully, he removed and untied flattened sheaves of magical map, each like the one I'd sort of stolen. He placed them on the stump in the bright light of what was, thanks to the recent weather, a brand-new clearing.

Arty forgot his haste, and we forgot the brewing, spinning, nearby storm and leaned in closer as the direct sunlight showed that many of the pages were actually collections of even thinner material, each of these as thin and fragile as tissues, a white ghostly paper upon which lines and shapes were drawn in very fine, golden lines. Zyx was careful to arrange these square pages directly on top of each other, with their edges precisely aligned. His long, bony fingers were perfectly suited for this.

When almost done, he stretched and held them out, so that Arty and I could clearly see the last two small tissue pages. The sun blazed on their golden marks. Zyx looked stiffly and seriously at us, then at the sky, at the sun, at the leaves, and at Thryst and then Sprugly, who had approached. Thryst especially seemed interested, even excited, as he always was when Arty used a map page on our adventures—no doubt such a thing would help Thryst on his own adventures, whatever they were. I understood.

The man straightened his long back, and held out his arms fully— first sideways, then to front, then in circles over the paper pile on the stump below him. The last two pages were placed on top. Finally, he said in an oddly shrill and echoing voice, "*Hendyadis* and *Hendyadis!*"

His hands tilted downwards, following his gaze. We did likewise, watching the sun on the cubic pile of skins, and waiting through a few quiet moments for a definite and specific *whatever* to happen.

W.W. Marplot

Which didn't.

Our Dwarf grunted, and our Spriggan laughed. Then Zyxvuts slumped comically, saying, "Just kidding, there is no incantation needed." He suddenly shot a bumpy, mustached smile at Arty. "Only its own magic! You had only a small piece. Look at the whole!"

He passed his hands over the page pile, shading them from the sun, and I could see that their individual drawings aligned, like pieces of a 3D puzzle, and formed a picture. Cool. Then, for just a second...*Maybe,* I thought. *Maybe.* Yes! The image started to move, the lines of the drawings shifted, and, briefly, there was motion, or the illusion of motion, like a black and gold hologram.

Thryst exclaimed many words that seemed to come from underground and rattle like zombie corpses; his excitement shot out like dragon fire, both his beard and hood stiffening into points.

But, just as quickly, the illusion was gone: a burst of hot wind came, or a few of them, blowing fiercely in different directions, first this way, then that, then another. Our eyes shut against the small sandstorm it raised, even as the thinner pages scattered high, low, and up and away, and down and around. Sadly.

We had stupidly underestimated the storm, forgotten our enemies, ignored the situation, and stopped our hurry, hypnotized by this new magic and our puzzle pieces. I wondered if there was a voice, even laughter, on that gust.

Helpless, Mr. Abcedarius yelled the punishable-word we were all thinking as he tried to react. The trails of the papers blew off in so many directions that differing parts of his body tried to follow them at once, and the result was not pretty, nor comfortable, nor describable. Only his mouth seemed capable of consistent coordinated motion, and its stream of bad words created its own hot breeze.

Though the wind blew only a few seconds, the scene of lighter-than-leaves pages filling the clearing, like giant, upside-down snowflakes, took a few seconds longer. And just as Arty and I acted to help gather them, I felt another swirl of air, close and personal, a whirlwind that began at my shoulder and went like a small tornado outward and around, and even more quickly than the pages could scatter they were now collected—Sprugly at his lightning-quick, jump-flying best. I sat back down as Sprugly returned to my hair and whispered, "Ok." There on the stump-desk were the ghostly pages, once again in a perfect stack. I smiled, and Arty smiled.

But our tall, thin friend was still frowning from eyebrows to beard. Soon I could see why: the page pile on the stump looked different, there was no definite image, and no 3D movie picture forming within. *Had I imagined it before?*

Mr. Zyxvuts Abcedarius spoke. "That's nice," he said, his voice still smooth, "but it will take me a month to get them in the right order again. These are maps, or, more accurately, all are parts of the *same* map, a three-dimensional topographical representation of these woods. This was *my* research, my piece of the puzzle, and it took years to find them. Many long years to gather them. And more years to connect them properly. Piece by piece, hint by hint, a puzzle within the larger puzzle..." He ended in a soft chant.

I think I knew what he meant. I thought of our own hints, the ones that led Arty to the books that gave us the fairy history of New Island. Arty winked at me to show his common understanding. Thryst was pacing in heavy footfalls; his excitement over the magic map was now kindled to a boot-stamping frustration.

"Of course!" Arty and I said to each other. We were thinking the same thing: a map like this would help the Dwarf tremendously. Magically! Legendarily! What a shame. "Can it be fixed?" I asked Zyx.

He didn't answer me, not straight-out anyway. Instead he muttered to himself, accompanied by the harsh creaks of his long bones as he fidgeted on the log; otherwise all was silent under the strong sun. He glanced at the sky, saying, "There are marks on the map that you can only see in the moonlight."

Thryst grunted at this, his boots stamping loudly in the windless silence of the woods.

W.W. Marplot

Arty said, "Cool—Cry would like that, magical moon runes."

"Yes," Zyx said, "legends come from somewhere, and these were real."

Thryst grunted again, mashing the butt of his axe into the earth.

I spoke up. "Why didn't you number the pages, or something?"

"I suppose I am quite stupid," Zyx answered, too easily, because, as he went on to say, "I tried to write on them, but it was impossible; this is not spiral notebook paper, you know."

I began again, "Then why didn't—"

"I make copies?" Zyx finished for me. "For one thing," he said, "I only recently obtained all the pages. For another, they do not exactly fit into your everyday color copier. For a third, they are quite detailed and, to copy by hand—for me at least—would have been almost impossible. For a fifth, I don't have any moon-rune ink lying around."

Thryst grunted again and shifted his weight and his axe. He looked about to burst like a volcano filled with dragons.

Zyx went on, staring forlornly at the pages, "And lastly, sixthly, and bestly: Nor do I have any magic. When put in the right order, these pages create—"

It was my turn to interrupt. "A 3D movie," I said.

"Precisely," Zyx answered. "As, I suppose, you started to see."

"A movie of what? I only saw the opening credits," I said.

"It shows the movement of fairy creatures, in this area, over the years, and into the distant past. A history, and a map. Very helpful, it might be."

Thryst swung his axe in frustration. It whistled as it traveled straight through the sleek trunk of a young, Zyxvuts-sized oak tree. We all made to scatter, but the tree remained standing, its new top plopped back perfectly onto its new bottom.

In thoughtful awe—and with sympathy for our Dwarf—we looked again at the thin, gold-scrawled pages, brightly lit in the sun, their edges showed glints of silver and green.

Zyx went on softly. "Very helpful. It shows itself—its pieces, in red, so they can be gathered. They show land, and paths, and also towers. And caves.

"And tunnels…" Zyx ended.

This was too much for one very dangerous and capable warrior Dwarf. He looked to the sky—not only the peaceful, blue brightness above, but also at the surrounding army of camped clouds—and screamed and moaned his own spell and malediction in a potent, growling, mountainous voice. His neck was thick with muscle, the veins gnarled and bulging black with their fairy blood.

"*Bull na Amenta! Níl mé doite, Níl me chaitear. Is mise an Oidhre, an chumhacht priomhuil gluaisne agus de chuid eile!*"

We heard. I think the storm heard.

Then *Thryst the Living Legend* started in motion.

I can't tell you and could never draw precisely what I saw or how he worked, but, as when using his axe to climb trees or when confronted with enemies, his body moved like a perfectly-made machine operating through gracefully interconnected, smooth motions. For this task he must also have used much Dwarf experience: being underground, building and imagining in three dimensions, divining new creations with the help of magic and spells. For what I saw within a few minutes was that Thryst was able to stack the pages in their correct order once again. I wondered at the new map pile as if it were a thousand-squared Rubik's Cube, and at Thryst as its solver.

The Dwarf said, "*Hmmmph. Arka Fessa-fisi.*"

Arty and I applauded.

Zyx was so happy he looked as if he wanted to do what Cry would have done.

CHAPTER 85

Arty

I looked at the tree-stump desk and the pile of magic paper—and then saw the image Emma was talking about. Instead of a pile of pages, I saw a model of a town. The sides of the pages were no longer visible, but instead was a view into the three-dimensional picture. And, if I moved like a hologram, the image shifted, and I saw the town from a different angle. There were labels and names and writing like on any map. It also showed, through lines of light that changed as you moved, the structure of the land, the buildings, and what was underneath—so that there were what looked like caves and tunnels. It was confusing, and there were many points and colors and shapes and other lights and other places that I couldn't understand, and as the sun gleamed, it seemed to react and change and move. It was overwhelming but beautiful in a scientific way—and really cool.

There was a lot of information, all within a small cube that had started as a pile of single pages—so it was map, model, *and* hologram. A *mapmodelgram* with sun and moon runes—when the sun twinkled on it, just as Zyxvuts had told us, new markings appeared in brilliant gold. A *solunarmapmodelgram*. I was getting good at making up words and noted this one down in my notepad.

Thryst was studying it grimly, lying on his back and looking from underneath, from bottom upwards. Abcedarius, in a relieved but serious tone, told us a story of a family who used to own vast (his word) lands in England and left there a few hundred years ago, coming here, to Belle Terre. Legend—and accusation—was that they lived among fairy creatures, were deeply involved in their lives, had some secret, odd, and dangerously close relation to the Faery Realms, and knew many secrets.

So, this is the "family" we read about. I nodded to Emma.

And that there was strife (his word) among the fairies at that time. *We already knew that.* Emma nodded to me.

According to Zyx, the family preserved its knowledge and secrets and also prophesied (tall, brown word) that the battles would continue again someday. Then one of their descendants would be born with the special abilities needed to help.

Emma and I tried to read each other's minds, but it was mostly questions marks and cross-outs. We crinkled sweaty foreheads at each other.

"And," the man went on, "just as ancient Dzogchen monks left portentous treasures in Tibetan hillsides for discovery when predestination calls…"

Emma and I exchanged blank looks. Was he inventing words, too?

"…the fairy-friendly family left clues behind to help future generations."

Aha! Emma and I thought, *This is where we come in.* The books! The notes! The translations!

"As the fairy world diminished, and the interaction with humans grew less, the decades passed and generations of the family, as families do, went separate ways, moved back to England, and forgot—perhaps purposely and out of embarrassment," the man explained, "—or *mostly* forgot, their history and destiny."

Zyxvuts looked at Emma and me. He explained that since he was a kid, he had followed—clue after clue, step by step—signs that led him along.

*Like us…*Emma and I smiled as our thoughts met in midair.

"Yes, like you. I suppose," Zyx said, rudely adding his mind to our meld; I supposed we looked a little too smug. "I think I understand."

Zyx's path, though, hadn't been through books but to map pages: each pointed to the next, he explained, adding, "*If* you could interpret the signs." And he did his research, a lot of it before the Internet—he looked at us like we were spoiled. This was the way he met his wife, actually, a distant cousin of the English family.

"Is she..." Emma started.

"No, she is not the one." Zyxvuts shook his head. She wasn't the "gifted" child that the family predicted would help in the fairy wars when that day came.

"Trudy has no special powers, but she's very smart and an excellent cook," Zyxvuts said.

"The Trudy from the Mary letter!" Emma added.

"Then who is Mary?" I asked.

"Mary IS the one."

"Oh." Emma and I both exhaled, starting to see the vase turn into two faces.

Thryst grunted and removed himself from the map. He smelled the air and then proceeded to climb a tree. We three humans watched this in wonder; it never got old, and for Abcedarius it was new.

The storm was still rotating, only.

Zyx went on. He and his wife Trudy together found and gathered all the pages and finally, just last week, completed the map and watched in amazement as it moved and told its own story of lands and times with pictures and signs.

He waved his wispy fingers over and around the map, his life's work. "One piece at a time..." he said softly.

This was his puzzle piece, this living, glowing map that Thryst, back on the ground, was again poking with a thick, hairy finger. But Zyxvuts hadn't known about the books I'd found, and the notes, until he'd spied and followed. I felt good about that.

The rest of the story might only be known by the *fairy-family* and their direct heirs—about the battles, about the fairy invasion, about the past and future, and why all this was happening here in our town.

"How can we find them?" I asked, meaning the family. "Do you think the map can show us?"

"My wife did not know any of this until she met me, so if any of the original family kept these secrets and any magic as heirlooms, no one she grew up with knows anything about it. But we think they will show up here. Don't you?" Abcedarius smiled, a fat and true one.

Emma let him put a guess in the envelope of guesses.

I asked Zyx about how the map moved, and why, and what controlled it. He thought that while it almost definitely could relate (his word) the past, it also "shows small, curious paths, unlike the rest, and shifting, and fuzzy, but beyond the current time."

"The future?" I looked at him as a scientist would look at someone in a yellow hat describing what kind of cheese the moon is made of.

"Yes, beyond the current time would be the future. But I support your skepticism," he answered. "Though there are, for sure, some paths, some shifting faint paths, that project beyond the current time. But that is something I need more of: time."

I nodded and also wondered, to myself, whether the map could give directions to magic-counter-spell bookstores.

Thryst stood suddenly, like a boulder avalanching upward. "*Aosi!*" he exclaimed in the same way Cry said, "Awesome!" The Dwarf stroked his beard and seemed out of breath and as agitated as ever. He then reached deep into a front pocket beneath his beard and pulled out something, though he kept the something in a clenched fist. He moved closer to the mapmodelgram, and the map danced! It twisted, it shook, it did the Wave, it did the Hokey Pokey almost, and it certainly did the Worm—in fact, it looked like colored gummy worms were slithering through the center.

"Wow," Abcedarius whispered.

Emma and I agreed. I couldn't get a good look at what was in Thryst's hands, but I knew he had some magic there—like the mini-crystal balls that he used sometimes, maybe. And he definitely wanted to combine it with the wizardry of the pages dancing in front of us.

"Can Thryst borrow it?" I asked, meaning the map. "He's looking for something, we don't know what. How does it work?"

Thryst put his hand back in his pocket, and the cube took a breather. Zyxvuts pointed here and there at it, and he had to shield it when the sun tickled it with bright rays so its contours would stay still. He pointed to areas on the map that showed parts of the village—the library, the school, the hospital. He told us that there were tunnels—and safe places marked using words from other languages, like Old English, Irish, Gaelic, and others—and escape routes.

"Wow," Emma whispered.

Then he motioned his branch-like arms and twig-like fingers over the mapmodelgram, letting light through his fingers. As he did, a large crowd of dots and colors combined and sparkled at one area, the area that looked like the fields by the power lines, where the storm battle had been.

Emma and I gazed in thought.

"Yes," Zyx said, "I know about the trouble in the woods, though you didn't mention it in your tidy adventure story to me. That event was *there* and meant to be *then*, and more is supposed to happen *here* and *now*—unless we do something, as you can see."

We could.

"I have been waiting a long time for this." Zyx stretched his limbs out far like a giant starfish, as if a whole life of tiredness had formed into one giant ache.

Emma stumbled her way into a question. "Why, um, could I not, um, see the whole battle, though I, kind of, sort of, knew it was going on?"

"I don't know for sure, but I think that you can only see them when they want you to," Zyx offered.

"That's true with Thryst," I said. "Nobody saw him when I brought him to school." I shouldn't have admitted this, I guess, because Zyxvuts gave me a look that was a more intense version of smacking himself in the head at my lack of common fairy sense.

He continued to Emma, "You are only partly in their world. I think when the worlds overlap, you can know or experience more."

Of course, we can also look in their eyes, I thought but did not speak.

"The ones we can see," Zyx said while pointing at Thryst, who was sniffing the air again, and in the direction of Sprug, who he guessed was on Emma's shoulder somewhere, "might have a different reason for them to see you. But maybe not the battles, or eviler ones like the Gwyllion. I am just guessing."

"Thryst doesn't seem too interested in the battles. He's here for something else," I said. "And Sprug is here to save and protect other fairies."

I had other questions, but the man in brown was focused on Thryst, who had started pacing. The map gave a weather update—the storm was moving and tightening in on the circle where we all stood. And worse—there was an orange G rune at its opposite edge.

"We'd better get out of here," I said.

After a long crackling of thunder, Abcedarius said, "Yes. And yes, Thryst can borrow it, and you too, Arty."

"Why do I need it?"

"Well, I have a lot more to tell you."

"Do you trust us now?" Emma asked the man.

Zyx smiled. "It is more than that. We are following the same clues. I think we were meant to work together. Do you trust *me* now?"

"Yes," Emma said, "anyone who chases Ted can't be all evil."

Abcedarius's eyes shined brown, from high above us, and he laughed. "I only did that," he said, "since I saw him at the places on the map that I was starting to believe were associated with acts of the Gwyllion and her servants. He connected me to you of, course, but I was also worried about what looked like a spell—his bad dreams, his daydreams. Following that saucy young man was not my favorite task in all this."

"He's always been an enemy, before we knew what real enemies were," Emma said, "but we thought you were, too, and now you are a friend. Right?"

"Yes, which is a nice, unforeseen praxis—so let's hope no more friends become enemies."

W.W. Marplot

Emma quieted, as if his words said more to her than they did to me. A thrum of thunder took the place of an answer.

"What else do you need to tell us?" I added hurriedly. The three of us gazed upward in agreement that we had stayed much too long.

"Just one more thing…" Abcedarius began, finger again on the map and to a glowing purple dot. Every few seconds, it enlarged and became a strange symbol, like a few letters on top of each other. Then back to a dot. "This was not on the map when my wife and I first put it all together. It popped up Wednesday."

I waited for explanation.

"Wednesday morning, early," came the hint.

"Oh!" I now recognized the shapes and lines on that part of the cube: They looked like my street and my house. "This is when and where I found Thryst!"

"Yes. Now I know that," Zyxvuts said.

"What is the purple dot?" Emma asked.

"I don't know. More than once, I tried to investigate but was chased away." He pointed at the glowing little raisin again. "I had the map but could not figure out these symbols or what this new purple dot might mean. Funny little thing."

At those words, Emma shocked me by suddenly leaping to her feet, and then jumping up and down while she yelled my name. "Arty! Arty! ARTY!"

"What?" I asked.

"The funny thing! In your yard!"

"I don't want to talk about that yet," I stated from mouth-memory.

"Well, maybe you'd better." And she pointed at the purple dot, which glowed and shrunk exactly where that darn funny thing was growing.

Thunder crashed and echoed all around us.

CHAPTER 86

Arty

I was jogging along with Abcedarius Zyxvuts, Emma, and Thryst. Sprugly was flying high above.

Our haste: I had the thing in my yard to investigate, and Thryst now had a magic map to help him keep looking for whatever he was looking for. Emma wanted to check on the Trust Network friends because my stories of the spells had her worried. Sprug would want to get ready for the battle, as Emma said, and pick out some larger clothes or something from her closet.

And: we all agreed that the surrounding circle-storm would soon attack.

Following Abcedarius's big brown strides, we were soon out of the woods and beside the main Belle Terre road. Thunder boomed again, and the sky was darker. The tired, thin sun was well past noon and heading toward the walls and towers of the black, bursting clouds. I saw no lightning.

Emma and I watched our friend in his awful brown sweater stare at the ominous sky and speak quiet words to himself. "Belle Terre! All three names of your names are true today," he said. I think.

"What, Mr. Zyxvuts?" Emma asked.

"Nothing. Now I have to leave you," he said with a smile to Emma and me, and with a nod, and slight bow, to Thryst, who nodded back. "Keep going! We are on the same side, and you might be helping. I was not sure before, but I do, now, understand. But I need to get home to my wife."

"Where do you live?"

"Nearby. But I have to tell you more first, especially if you are taking the map." Which we were—Thryst hadn't stopped studying it and was being very selfish. Asking for it back would be a mistake; his grunts alone would slay a medium-sized troll and shrivel a Wight to a napkin.

Zyxvuts went on. "On the map, there are other spots marked, and it seems to show the history of fairy migrations, and wars. One of the spots is at Arty's house..."

"Where the funny thing is," Emma interjected.

"Yes, but also where Thryst first arrived—it is clearly marked."

"Ok, but we knew that," Emma added. She was clearly in a hurry.

"Yes—so use those symbols to find where other fairies are...and stay away."

"Why?" Emma asked without thinking; we both knew the answer.

"The ones who found your friends must have escaped," Abcedarius said for all of us.

"From the Gwyllion," I stated.

Emma shrunk quietly.

Thryst interrupted this time—not with words but with a quick swap: his axe went into his belt, and he pulled out the map pages and quickly had them assembled. This allowed Abcedarius to point out what he meant.

"At these spots," he said as he carefully indicated certain symbols on the map—those that looked like the Funny Thing Spot, like many fancy letters all jumbled together. "I think there are more fairies who have not escaped and are in trouble."

From the Gwyllion, the Old Woman of the Mountains. Emma grew pale.

"Where exactly?" I asked, thinking of my poor friends and their fairies and the bad spells that even Emma and Ted already had cast on them.

"It is hard to be too exact; I have had insufficient time to really understand things homotopically or even topologically."

Emma hates when I talk like this, so I wasn't surprised to see her turn her attention away from Zyx, anxiously scanning the darkening sky. The sun was being captured and brought behind enemy lines.

"And," Zyx continued, twisting his fingers in the air as he spoke, "it shows the land as it was hundreds of years ago, and many roads are the same, but the man-made changes are many. And it is magic, you know, and I am not."

But there was something more. A glowing spot caught my attention. It had the same symbol as the one in my yard.

Abcedarius went on. "The only other thing I can tell you is that the colors, and the brightness of the illumination in certain light, also show the time: what was past and what is happening now. Perhaps even the future. I needed more time. But maybe you can figure it out."

He showed us examples: the map, using the colors from last rays of the defeated sun, showed a rainbow of dots that indicated the locations, and order, of the appearance of the friends-of-friends' fairy finders. The Trust Network, in order.

I thought for a moment. I said, "Well, maybe that explains why we can see some but not others. We're seeing the kidnapped ones, they're finding us, coming more to our world…?" I realized that I was just guessing. I hate to guess.

Emma spoke, finally. "But what about Sprugly and Thryst?"

"They are Rescuers, perhaps," Zyx said.

The spot that caught my attention was still glowing. "What is that one?" I asked. "It's like the one in my yard, sort of."

Abcedarius responded. "That is Eastward Manor. My home."

"Huh?" Emma popped, her ponytail bouncing with her surprise. "You live there?"

"You missed that rune," he said, "but it was on the map all the time." He wished us luck and walked away.

CHAPTER 87

Emma

I'm going to start this part of the story, but Arty has to finish it for reasons you'll see but that I didn't see at the time. Sorry about this.

Arty and I were in a hurry; the storm was choking the afternoon sky, and after leaving Abcedarius Zyxvuts, just a man in brown after all, we had a lot to do.

We could barely keep up with Thryst for the rest of the walk-run back to Arty's house. We did get two breaks though, when Thryst axe-climbed two large trees, balancing the three-dimensional map as he did, using it to direct his gaze in every direction, grunting with frustration at the darkening weather and with anger at the light-stealing clouds, which were now piled high like thunderheads, leaving our neighborhood at the bottom of a well of imposing weather.

During the first of these climbs, Arty and I planned. We hadn't heard from the friends-of-friends in a while—Olivia, Isabella, Jacob, and the rest—so we decided that would be a good thing for me to do next: contact them all, go to their houses if necessary.

We knew so much now! We knew more about the fairy war, and who "the family" from Arty's cookbook was, and we'd even found the real Eastward Manor. We knew that these fairies—the Silky, the Shellycoat, the Light Elf, and the rest—had escaped from the kidnapping Old Woman of the Mountains, the fiendish Gwyllion.

Arty wanted to get to the funny thing in his yard—which he liked to talk about now. We didn't know what it was, only that it was important on the map. He hoped Thryst would be there to protect him when he dug it up, or laughed at it, or watered it, or whatever he needed to do. The mystery was overwhelming, and our imaginations ran up through the hole in the sky, and deep into the ground, and scared us silent. Soon we were running again, trying to keep up with a newly motivated Dwarf.

At Thryst's second climb, Arty asked me a question.

"Did you hear what Abcedarius said to himself, when he was looking at the sky? He said something about Belle Terre."

"Yes," I answered. "He said, 'All three names are true today.'"

"I wonder what that means," Arty said and joined me in watching Thryst high above. But the twilight shadows—there was nothing but the merest grey glow in the sky, like extinguished ashes—hid all but the Dwarf's silhouette from us.

"I was thinking about it," I answered, resting against the wide tree that Thryst had scaled as easily as a cat up a couch, "and—well, you know what Belle Terre means, right?" I knew he did, and he answered.

"Of course—Beautiful Land."

"In French it does, and they told us in school that this part of Belle Terre was named that when they started building the mansions here, a hundred years ago."

"That's one name," Arty observed. "Zyxvuts said there were three."

"I know," I said, "so I was thinking about Latin. You math geeks know some Greek, *alpha* and *beta* and all that, but we authors know Latin because lots of other languages came from it. Like French. *Terre* means *land* in French because it meant *land* in Latin, where it comes from."

I could see Arty was as bored as he usually was in English class or with anything without formulas or chemicals. His face wandered around, but I got in front of it. "But," I said, "*Bel* in Latin means *war*."

He put two and two together and did not get a remainder. "So, Belle Terre means…War Land?"

"Very good," I said. "Yes, we live in a fairy legend war zone." I pointed at the cloud army as evidence.

Arty burst out, "It's cooler than that, Emma! Remember…"

And I watched curiously as he struggled with his backpack, soon pulling out a small flashlight and his notes.

"The cookbook," he read from his notebook, "talked about fairy battles in War Land, and that the family came to War Land because the Gwyllion did."

This had all happened before—the Gwyllion at war, here on Long Island—and it was happening again. And we were in the middle of it, literally: we stood directly below the last star still visible in the warring sky. I looked to the tree; I couldn't see Thryst, but I could see twinkling from his solunarmapmodelgram or whatever Arty tried to call it. The leaves of the forest canopy shone a pretty green and red, like Christmas trees.

Arty broke our awed silence. "But that's only two names: *Beautiful Land* and *War Land*. What's the third one? What does it mean in Chinese?"

"No idea," I laughed. "Why don't you look it up in the fairy books? Did you bring them?"

"Of course—well, two of them. But I tried looking up Belle Terre already—there was nothing."

"Look again, try to spell it different, like it was translated again or something, and try to…" I attempted to say, but Arty interrupted by tossing me the lit flashlight—it created a dance of spinning shadows around us while in midair—then handing me the larger of the fairy books. "Fine, I'll do it," I said with attitude.

I flipped open the pages of the book, a long, wordy history of fairy stories and their strange creatures that had no chapter numbers, no clear order, no table of contents, and no pictures.

But there was an index! I flipped to it and looked for *Village* first, just because I happened to land in the V's. Nothing.

I went to the B's for Belle Terre. Then the B-E's, then the B-E-L's, then the O-M-G's because what I found was this: *Beltaerne, 465.*

And Page 465 said, in a box in the middle of the page:

Beltaerne, Gaelic, time and a place celebrating fairy life and white, or west, portal opening, to Aos Si, midway betwixt equinox and solstice. Alternately a Habundian Faery Royalty Coronation.

Which made no sense except that it made perfect sense.

"Arty," I gasped, "look at this," and handed him the book with his flashlight as a bookmark. "Read what's in the box!"

"OMG," he said and quickly opened a second book, summarizing what he found with a string of excited exclamations. "Beltaerne! Habundia! Portal! Aos Si!"

I said to him, "We live in a fairy war land portal. That explains a lot of the 'why's, huh." I looked up at Thryst as if for the first time, letting the wonder blow over me like the strong wind that had just whistled around the trees. The Dwarf's shadow above reminded me to ask, "Habundia is that fairy queen, right? In the cookbook title? But what is *Aos Si*? It sounds familiar."

"Yep—Thryst has said it a few times—he yelled it before, remember? I thought it was Dwarfish for *awesome*—guess not! I just looked it up: The *Aos Si* are underground fairies from Irish mythology. *People of the Mounds*. Wow."

"So, it's more like Dwarfish for *Heavens to Betsy* then, or something."

Arty looked up at me with a knuckled face, then back at his book. "Listen to this," he said, studying the book. "Beltaerne is a place, here I guess, the portal. But it's also a time, and it's still celebrated. Guess when it is?"

"It said halfway between something—an equinox—and what?" I asked.

"Equinox and solstice. Spring and summer." He slammed the book shut after putting the flashlight in his mouth and said, "Vay fush!"

"Swallow the flashlight before speaking, please," I said like Arty's mom would.

"Sorry," he replied. "May first! Beltaerne is May first."

I made the quick calculation. "Wednesday, three days ago."

"The day it all started, with Thryst. And the funny thing in the yard."

Wow.

"I need to get back and check that thing out," Arty said, switching from foot to foot and looking up toward Thryst anxiously. The Dwarf had been in the treetops longer than usual.

"Like Zyxvuts said," I said, "our town has a lot of names, and they're all crashing at once—on beautiful-fairy-war-portal-Wednesday." My mind wandered with thoughts of the Gwyllion, the battle, our friends, the Gwyllion, the spells, the clouds, the kidnapping, the escaped folkies, the kidnapper: the Gwyllion.

The Old Woman of the Mountains. She could see all.

The words shaded the light in my mind, and I felt heavy and sleepy. My eyes. Her eyes.

"Can I borrow those books, Arty? I asked him.

"Yes—why? And what's taking Thryst so long? I want him with me when I go in my yard."

"Can I have them now?"

"Oh, now? Well, I wanted to read up more on the Queen Fairy, Habundia, she must have something to—"

"Yes, now."

"Ok, yeah," Arty said, I think…

Next thing I remember was walking along the beach late that night, in the dark, alone.

CHAPTER 88

Arty

This is Arty. I have to tell the next parts.

Once Thryst came down from the tree, I excitedly made him follow me to my house, though I knew he wanted to keep going in his search, climb more trees, and explore more tunnels. I needed him first. I explained with the map, pointing to the Spot of the Funny Thing in My Yard, then did my dog/yeth hound imitation again—"*Arooo!*", etc.—and also gave him the inter-species hand signals, kneeled, begged, groveled, and said, "Pleeeeasssssseeeeee????"

He followed. Emma dragged behind us with my flashlight and one of my fairy books open, stumbling more than once and grunting like a female Dwarf in jeans. At my empty house, she went directly to my room—"To nap," she said. This was good because I needed somehow to distract my family when they returned. I didn't want to have to explain why I was digging, or was being strangled by an evil tree root, or talking to a Dwarf and his glowing magic hologram, or opening war land fairy portals in the yard.

I had told Emma the cover story, just in case: Although everyone knew that I am one of seven males in America under forty-years-old *not* playing the latest viral mobile-app game scavenger-hunt fantasy thing, the one that Cry has promised his parents to limit to five hours a day and to not take to bed or in the bathroom, that was our excuse just in case someone asked.

Finally, there I was, standing over the funny thing in my yard, which I need to talk about now.

With the map collapsed, an anxious, uninterested *Thryst the Reluctant Bodyguard* stood behind me, tapping a red boot with thick impatience. The wind pushed at the trees off in the distance, and the few near to my house banged against windows. The neighborhood—my family included—were preparing for a wild storm. They had no idea.

I stared down at the thing, getting a good look for the first time since I approached Thryst with my dogs and phone on Wednesday, May 1st—which seemed like six-and-a-half years ago. It caught my eye because it—in the midst of green, straight lawn grass—popped out like a fat elbow of a tree root, or a giant dinosaur bone, since it glared white as a sun-bleached skeleton. I knew that, large as it was, and twisted with many sub-roots, this big loop, coming out of the ground and back, was just a small piece that continued under the earth, under my yard. It was easy to trip over when distracted by your first Dwarf experience but hard to miss, even in this dark storm funnel.

What made it "funny" the first time I'd seen it, besides its existence, was that it was purple—the white bends of root or bone covered a brightness, and now I could see a blue-shifted rainbow between spaces, various shades like those in the sky over the course of a day, from the weak blue-grey of morning, to high-sky blue, to the violet of exciting sunsets, and to the deepest azure colors of mighty seas. Here, the purples were the brightest.

It was a root. As I gazed at all the pretty purples, Thryst, to hurry things up, could not help himself but to come and chop the funny thing very rudely. I snorted at him, and his beard rippled at me in response.

The root, now splintered and split, held something. I was afraid but reached before Thryst could decapitate it. It held a box, and despite being freshly popped from the ground, and captive by thick-grown tree roots that must have been hundreds of years old, it shined as if new, of a material that seemed soft like green wood but shone dully with the hardness of a gemstone—mostly, again, purplish. The base of the box was smooth and rectangular; I could balance it in my one palm though it was shoebox-sized. The sides and top were etched and richly extravagant, its curved cover decorated like an arch in a church, where small circles and varying patterns were lined with gold and silver. On one side there was a latch—this of a dark metal—connecting domed top to flat bottom so that it appeared it would open on an unseen hinge.

In the night, with the wind blowing a dark foreboding, and the trees restless and disturbed, and the skies ready to battle, the thing in my hand seemed to me like a casket.

I was afraid to open it. I looked at Thryst for support and strength. His eyes gleamed. He came and took the purple coffin from me and read the symbols on its side, lines that meant nothing to me. He nodded, saying, *"Adamnan nain unthen tarba,"* as if he were drinking a glass of rocks. He shook his axe in a harmless way, then handed the box back.

So, I opened it, pulling at the small latch slowly.

There was no dead Elf body, or skeleton, or any dry, beating heart. Or ghost, or poison smoke, or even any bad smell.

Inside were pieces of a very thin, black material, pages of something like tissue paper, light but opaque and strong enough to write on. Rising from the back of each were shining scripts and shapes. There were fourteen of them, each the size of the box, a foot long and a few inches wide. They smelled sweet but looked old: the flashlight showed torn edges, ancient markings of varying sizes, and some pages were decaying and grey. I noticed that in some places, the edges of the paper interrupted the writing, cut through it, as if the sheets were just parts of a whole, pieces of yet another puzzle.

A bright, moving light startled me. It shined into the trees at the back of my yard, then its double-beam scanned across and toward me. It was my family's giant SUV returning home, the headlights panning with the car along the driveway to park in front of the house.

I stopped moving to the point that I tried to replace breathing with only *thoughts* of breathing. I put into practice everything I knew about Buddhist meditation and achieving perfect, calm stillness, which didn't take long since I knew nothing about it. The troupe—parents, brothers, sisters, Gretel—argued loudly over doughnuts—a power-outage tradition for some reason—carrying shopping bags into the house until our nanny spoke stern orders in Germanglish. Then order and quiet. Candles were lit. No one but me and Thryst was outside. I resumed normal existence.

The wind and I both exhaled, mine weak but the other a forceful, sudden gust so that I shut the casket defensively, reflexively—but even so, a single page escaped and blew up toward the treetops, sucked helplessly into the night sky. *Not again,* I thought. I looked at Thryst, who shook his head but didn't move, only waited.

The paper wafted down after a few seconds. I followed it with my flashlight's beam, guiding it like a butterfly into a net. Catching it in hand, I saw something that made my heart beat with a happy hope: the symbols it showed—in silver and gold, again like the box—I knew. I'd spent hours scouring the Internet for them; they were burned into my memory.

These pages must be the second, missing spell-book.

Which meant it was also: *The Book that Should Not Be Used, The Book that Can't Be Named, The Book of Unspeakable Words and Unabiding Acts.* Those were the warnings, from long ago.

And the newer one, from whoever led me here: *Dead legend and should not be unburied.*

Too late.

Like a human Spriggan, I could help my friends now.

CHAPTER 89

Arty

rty here. You won't hear from Emma, because I hadn't. And I'm in a too much of a hurry to wonder about it. When I sneaked into my house from the yard, the purple box in my backpack, I called her name. Thryst disappeared, since my family, with Gretel shouting orders, was gathering to leave to get dinner and supplies in case we lost power during the storm, which had become the talk of the town, everyone preparing. The local news channel was predicting floods of rain and increasingly wild winds, and flooding, and thunder and lightning, and probably loss of power.

Booooorrrrrriiiiinnnnnggggg, I thought. They didn't know there was also a 90% chance of fairy battles and scattered evil spells.

No one seemed to have cared much about that wild ring of clouds over the harbor or armies of creatures gathering or the miles of uncovered tunnels. Adding to what I've said before: *What does it take to get this town to notice War Land Portal Time?*

The family gone, having told me that Emma left a few minutes ago, I dragged my tired legs up the stairs. My room was a non-magical mess, as was my mind: all my lists and notes were disorganized, my own fault, which gave me a lightning headache with no thunder.

I tried to ignore it and get to work. I even shut off my phone as it charged. I had a new red-sticky "Do Now" list with one big item on it: "Translate this Sucker and *Figure out the Spells and Save Everyone.*" Three items, fine.

I retrieved the shiny box, the little purple rainbow coffin, from my backpack. It played with the desk lamplight, filling the room with the blue hues of parallel spectrum bars that sliced diagonally and from floor to ceiling—a purple-shifted, straight rainbow.

Spreading the thin sheets across my bed—after shoving books to the floor—made it easy to assemble the fourteen pieces into order by connecting their edges, rejoining symbols that had split across pages.

I used my new skill—the ability to crossmisuntranslate—matching the symbols to those in the Queen Faerie cookbooks and seeing what fit like we had done before. But I didn't need Gretel; any new German words I needed were easily translated online.

The minutes—120 of them—went by. My family came home, hollered some good nights, and still I worked on.

I typed the translations into my computer. Finally finished and bleary-eyed, I double-checked some of the harder words and, satisfied and incapable of continuing anyway, printed the results.

I put my new pages on the bed and moved the ancient ones back to their violet-screaming casket to keep them safe. Massaging my fingers, I bent over the new information like a mad wizard, wondering what my creation, all my word alchemy, meant. Here, destined for me to find, at the end of the trail of clues and the last piece of my puzzle, was a book that had been passed down somehow, from somewhere, from someone, who knew about these legends and the fate that war would come again—here in War Land, and during this time, the Beltaerne.

The text of English words in front of me on normal, everyday printer paper was very strange and made no sense. None of it. Arranged in groups were passages of a few sentences each.

Like this: *Snakes get up, for you have eaten a mouse, which is detested, and you have chewed the bones of a putrid cat.*

Wonderful, I thought. The words looked like things Ted would say during dinner conversation. I had failed. My destiny was to fail. I wasn't a human Spriggan. *"The book that can't be used"*—by me, at least.

What am I missing? I thought and yawned. Failing makes me tired, but I looked through my notes. The words that Sprugly used, the ones he said in Ted's ear in this very room for example, the spell that he said was missing from my books, were not in English, though I never had time to look them up. *What language are they?*

I let the Internet answer.

Irish.

How stupid of me.

Swallowing my yawns like the bones of a putrid cat, I translated my symbolic English German crossmisuntranslation codes into Irish. How obvious.

I guess in fairy-world it's ok if things make no sense as long as it's in Irish, I said to myself, sort of like the way things sound fancier in French, or more important in Latin.

When done, I printed all of it, again, and put it all on the bed, again.

I began to read them, chanting each section out loud, softly.

The wind blew from a narrowly-open window and whistled sharply after every translated symbol and sentence, and louder and louder, like angry sighs.

I was enchanted myself, reading foreign, meaningless words to an empty room, but I pressed on—until one jumped off the page as if it had frogs' legs.

Anail chuid focal ar na fir na gluine a thabhairt do dhuine a mbain-fear anail.

I recognized this right away—the words that stuck in Emma's head like an annoying song, and that I had written down in my notes.

I had decoded the book of spells.

This all formed the book I'd been looking for. The *how* and *why* of it being in my backyard, growing in the tree roots, had to wait for someone smarter to solve.

For now, I knew the *what:* these pages should have the fairyland magic word-potions I needed to undue the spells cast by the Old Woman and her allies and help my friends.

The entries made sense now: they listed maladies, their symptoms, and their magic counter-spells. I had just spoken the one that Sprugly had used to release Emma from the Gwyllion's eyes and "malediction" as Zyx would have said it. To double-check, I also found the very similarly phrased one that the Spriggan used on Ted.

I read on, with new understanding. There was mention of blisters, toothaches, boatmen, hawks, hearts, and tears, with miracle cures made up of a few words to be spoken. Some were more serious: crocodiles, body parts, the netherworld, "faces of death." Each had a counter-spell: incantations that, although in English, were not the way our dentist or local crocodile-catcher talked. I liked them better in Irish anyway.

I turned on my phone and called Emma, but it went right to voice-mail. Of course—she hadn't had a chance to recharge her phone yet.

Then the wind blew, and my eyes shut as I swooned with buckling knees. I was wrung from thinking-work, my legs sore from running in the woods, my wrists and fingers achy from writing. My whole being was exhausted from the hours and the adventure that was always a few feet ahead of me, and miles bigger.

But my new plan was clear. The dark of my closed lids helped me understand the simplicity of what I had to do. My quest, my role, was in front of me: Use the counter-spells to help the friends who had found fairies, and anyone else affected. They were struggling, and the next battle might involve human kids if the Gwyllion had her way.

I was the only one who could do it, and I had to start now.

The trouble was keeping my eyes open. When I did, they burned with the bright blue on the walls; the hypnotic striping seemed to move, in waves, like waves, like a troubled ocean, and I was adrift. A warm wind shouted at me through the window, I felt dizzy and fell onto the bed. I just needed a minute…

CHAPTER 90

Emma

orry: I don't remember much from any of these parts of
the story; next thing I knew I was at the beach, walking
alone, calling to Thryst up above on the beach bluff. I
remember that clearly, but the rest is fuzzy, as if the
storm clouds had entered my mind. I will tell what I can; it is not
very scientific, and not very artsy either.

As Arty and Thryst searched his backyard, I read the books and
notes Arty had in his room. Maybe I fell asleep? I kind of remember
dreamy visions of a nice old lady with a beautiful castle in the mountains, and she had many children, one big loving family.

I remember wanting to walk home, where I knew my house would
be empty. I went back through the woods and down to the beach.
I felt pulled that way, the long way, as if I was in one of the eye-ad-
ventures that we have had, Arty with Thryst, and mine with Sprugly.
But whose eyes were they? I was alone. I pulled a bruised apple from
my backpack; it would be dinner. I remember that making me sad.

When I looked to the sky, I saw more clearly. I watched it perform
a weather ballet, or probably a war dance, and worthy of the old Greek
gods. The cloud ring was gone, replaced by forms like armies stretching
out across a field. Large white clouds, small black clouds. Large black
clouds, small white ones. In lines and perfectly arranged one minute,
and then, with some intelligent—or at least magic—wind guiding
them, they curled around to form new geometrical shapes. Mixing,

W.W. Marplot

and separating again. A voice—not inside me but heard as if it were between my soul and the sky—asked whether the sky was beautiful.

A sun-heated wind picked up on the beach and blanketed me, reminding me of a book I read where "a warming wind blew everyone some good," as it said. I hope for that; the voice is encouraging me, as if it had eyes that look into me saying, "Yes, of course, it is like that, it is good…" *I don't want to see another battle*, I answer with an effort of thought. But it doesn't seem to matter what I want, or what Arty wants, or Cry—we seem very small, considering the big sky, the huge sprits, the long years of legends.

"No, you are important. You are a good girl…" I am told by the voice that seems to come from the sand under my feet, then hisses with the waves, then whispers through the trees, and rolls from the hills—and all the time as if it also has eyes that meet my eyes.

My mind wandered and wondered as I walked along the sand.

The voice listens as I think aloud about my own life, and the bay to my right shows me its vast, empty world; no gulls, no ducks, no boats, no lights, just repeating waves. The warm wind sounds angrily in my ears. I think of my dad. I hardly ever see him; last year he moved away—close but still away. The hilltop trees to my left stand tall but dark and remote.

My thoughts go on into the emptiness. When someone says, "I love you," don't leave them, or you will be alone. And so will they. Like I am now. Like everyone ends up, since everyone dies alone. You die alone, but you are born with your mom.

I realized I was talking out loud, and that this was a conversation with the voice—it came from all around, from the very dark itself, from the very earth, and somehow, I knew it looked at me.

Some thunder from over the bay struck me as if it was lightning instead—I jolted back to waking, real life and was suddenly afraid yet wondered why I hadn't been before, how it was possible to feel happy, and protected, despite the troubles all around and running in and out of my mind.

But now the trees were loudly thrashing their arms against each other, losing a fight with the wind. The waves from the bay, normally barely a few inches high, were rising in force and pounding the beach. The sky showed a field of enemies. I walked faster, I needed to get home. Alone…but alone is better than in another Folkie Battle.

I heard thunder again. No—not *again*. This was not thunder; it definitely came from underground, from under the cliff to my left.

I hurried; I fell. Groping for my dropped bag, I felt a wet nastiness in my right hand. During my walking dream, I had finished my apple and now aimed its core at circles of light sand that rose and fell a few yards off…

…and I soon wished I hadn't: the circles weren't just sand formations but the first of a bunch of a movie-ish but no-doubt real or actual (?) tracks of large footprints in the sand. Very large footprints, in the sand. Very large, oddly-shaped footprints. *Like an animal's? What animal? And how big is this animal if its feet are five feet long?* The wet pools looped away from where I stood, back along the beach, and up into the side of the cliff, and back down.

I got to my feet and tried to hurry. The fresh apple in my stomach didn't help, nor did my legs, but the fear assisted tremendously. I ran.

The dreadful, distant, real thunder then crashed over the dark bay, followed by the rumbling hill-thunder once again under the cliffs. Looking there, I saw Thryst up in the hillside near what looked like a cave or a hole. Despite the dark, his stout Dwarf shape and pointed hood gave him away. I felt a brightening relief. I was anxiously glad to have his thick-armed company. I called to him, then again louder, and not only did my own voice scare me, but my shout sounded at the same time as another rumble, underground. The Dwarf looked up, had heard me, but did not come. Why? *Thryst the Lonely*, I thought. He looked odd, and bowed, and…crying? *What's he looking for?*

Maybe I was mistaken—maybe *I* was lonely, and crying, and looking, and I had pushed it onto Thryst, who had his own adventures to be in.

The small Dwarf-shape went into the hill, but I couldn't follow because the voice drew me onward, to stay on the beach, and toward home. I heard growling, and the caws of black crows, growls all around, animal screams, but I was back in a dream and only remember hearing encouraging words, and that I did not need Thryst, or Sprugly. With yet more rumbling from above and below and from left and right, birds scattered. Now the world seemed alive and crowded.

Then I was home, my mind replaying images from my "eye-adventure" with the mysterious voice: a battle in the skies and underground, folkie against folkie, fairy legends on the move and in action. A fight for the right to heaven, or to escape, or to not. But I wasn't alone and was being shown what *I* should do, to make *my* world what *I* wanted. It was all very big, and it pressed down on my heart and on my mind, as if this storm were now deep underwater, far from the light of day and the air of air. I closed my mind's eye, using my mind's eyelid, and the other eyes disappeared also, those of the voice.

But words kept coming, and I did what they said.

CHAPTER 91

Arty

awoke when heat like a furnace blast rushed over me, scattered all my papers, and shook the curtains on my windows and the posters on my wall. It then left, sucked back outside. The papers took flight on windy wings, and I ran to shut the window. Outside the sky showed a few last brave stars directly above—the rest were cut off by the encircling clouds. Their ring was closing in. The trees seemed angry about it.

The spells! The thought and the story rushed over me just as the warm wind had. I had found the spells I needed, counter-spells to undo the bad confusion that the Gwyllion, and perhaps her army, had put on the kids, our friends. *How many? And who else?* I didn't know these things, but I knew what to do. The thoughts flushed out of my mind and my body went into motion.

Thryst! I need his help.

I realized as I carefully arranged my spell-translations into my pack that my ears were picking up a signal, that sharp tapping sound I had gotten so used to that it rode the waves of my thoughts without disturbing them. It was my Dwarf, digging or carving away with his axe, his hammer, his huge arms. Sometimes it was like the beat of a song, sometimes like a transmitting code, sometimes like a heartbeat or ticking clock, sometimes just mindless and sad.

The sound was coming from the basement.

The last paper I shoved into my bag was my own map, one I'd marked all our movements on during our adventures around Belle Terre. In red was Thryst's trail—where I found him, where he followed, where he didn't, where he appeared and disappeared—no pattern. It looked like red paint dripped from a paintbrush held high above.

I leaped most of the way down to the basement and into our crawlspace to visit him and the dogs. I bent over a bit to avoid the beams of the short ceiling. As a kid, I used to be able to walk upright in here. I was getting older and taller.

The tapping led me around the same corners where I'd found *Thryst the Mopey* last time. Before me yawned an oval tunnel that fit the following descriptions:

1. was never there before

2. was one Dwarf high and about two Dwarves wide

3. angled downward and went off straight, into black...

4. ...except for a tiny speck of light way, way in the distance, weak as a distant summer star

5. echoed the sounds of tapping and scraping and grunting

"Thryst!" I called but had to go find him myself. I walked a long way through the tunnel—it's hard to judge how far, even under your own neighborhood, when walking hurriedly in the mostly-dark. The path leveled after a minute but then took many turns before the end, where a flickering light showed a Dwarf-led wolfpack. My dogs were digging with their paws near where Thryst was sweating and shining in the mixed light of Abcedarius's magical mapmodelgram and the reddish torchlight. And sure enough, there was the torch, blazing and smelly, with one end stuck into the dirt wall, the other thick with a twisting fire.

I walked up—the dogs wagged their tails seeing me, but quickly returned to work—and I watched as Thryst moved the greasy fingers of one hand over the edges of the cube. I wondered whether he was using it as a map, or to watch a movie clip of the past, or to peek into the future, and how any of it would help him. I thought of my own map, and the random red drips that showed Thryst's wanderings.

"What are you searching for?" I asked.

"*Thryst*," he grunted after pausing his hand for a moment, his beard twitching to one side astride his jaw muscles.

"I give up," I said to the dogs. "It's like talking to a deaf Japanese three-year-old from around a corner."

Anyway, I had my own business now.

"Thryst, I need you to come with me. Look." I removed the casket that now also held my translations of the book of spells. I showed Thryst the pages, carefully holding the thin, black ones up with my own. He looked. "I can help fight the Gwyllion with this. I think it came to me for that reason, it was growing in my yard."

The Dwarf said, "*Thryst*." Then he said, "*Thantan*."

It was my turn to grunt.

He then collapsed the mapmodelgram and barked some command at the dogs that I wished I learned when they were puppies, since they all sat at attention, ears up, six marble eyes shining red as small setting suns with their keen and direct gaze. Then all four beasts walked away.

"Where are you going? You have to come with me! We need to fight."

I had to repeat it.

And then run to catch up with them and repeat it again.

"Fine," I shouted, "I'll go by myself. Where are we?"

What I really wanted to know was: If I went straight up and above ground from here, where *would* I be? At Olivia's house? Or Jacob's? Or old Mrs. Kenning's bathroom?

I looked above, then realized how stupid I was—I had no paws to dig with. My only tools were pens and paper and a phone, and I didn't want to test the loyalty of my dogs and embarrass myself by commanding them. And I definitely didn't want to poke up through the earth to find the bottom of the school's cesspool. Tunneling upwards could definitely mean death by dry, dirty drowning. So, frustrated and animated, I began to walk back the way I came, using my phone as a headlight.

Thryst stopped me and saved me some time. He jammed his powerful hands into his pockets and looked into my eyes.

CHAPTER 92

Arty

m, yeah. Thryst definitely took me on a shortcut, all around town, traveling at the speed of dreamy Dwarf magic, as before. And, once again, Thryst wandered for his own secret reasons.

Belle Terre was the same but different. There was a charge in the air, like electricity, buzzing with heavy power. Something else was present, energies from some other world. And all living things were choosing sides.

Except humans. Most of them wondered at the storm and hid inside, explaining away their sense of dread and fear to thickening clouds and attacks of an angry, dispiriting wind.

Their children, though, were more aware, and some were involved. They were under magic fairy spells.

I was a follower in this dreamscape, as before, though I tried to steer us toward those I needed to help—Jacob had seemed the worst off, sick and shaking and muttering. Now I knew the counter-spell to cure them; I had specifically underlined each needed cure in the translation.

But Thryst owned this mind trip, the magic mastery was all his, so he led, and I had to follow.

Elves came to us when we were cutting through woods. They walked in a formation; their leader spoke to Thryst in his language—their high voices smoothed the harsh Dwarf-words like a clean, hot knife spreading clumpy, cold butter—and it fascinated me, but Thryst shook his hood and asked his own questions, which, going unanswered, meant it was time to keep searching.

The sky was almost completely shrouded in an oily black, the clouds made noises like muted thunder, and every few minutes a spark of blue lit everything menacingly, in streaks that looked like giant, rotting bones. The hot wind gusts came more often and in swirls.

There was noise in the treetops, and I saw a sight I'd never forget, or forget *last* among all these things that I would ever forget: birds, in groups of hundreds or more, forming shapes, scattering, and reforming into new shapes. The shapes were of larger birds, like eagles or osprey or others more exotic and grander. Giant birds made up of many smaller birds—the cardinals and blue jays and robins of the neighborhood.

Then I saw why: they were being menaced—screamed at, lunged at, attacked—by winged creatures that seemed to strike whenever the covered lightning did. There was fire at their wingtips, and their giant, curved claws shined dully as if made of iron.

Even this Thryst ignored, and when a small grey finch flapped in frenzy near Thryst's shoulder and piped into his ears some desperate notes of bird terror, the Dwarf warrior just pulled his hood down and walked on.

On: to where I saw Emma. She does not remember it. Thryst combed the sandy shore of the bay, checking especially the cliffs where trees had fallen over from the erosion of rising land. Where roots were exposed, Thryst searched. Not for funny things, not for books: but for tunnels. I knew that now. We found one and followed it almost straight up. We ran ahead and up with our hands as much as with our feet, and quickly; we seemed to float upward, under the bluff.

But higher.

When we came out, directly above us was the only patch of remaining sky, and soon it was gone. The army of storm clouds had finally closed their circle, and the rumble of their meeting was deafening. I was in a land above the land, covering two worlds, and the menacing cover of the overcast sky lowered and shortened our world, squeezing us as if we were under a vast crawlspace ceiling, and I bent over. I panted, my lungs pumping air that was grey and unclean. The rain roared, but it seemed beneath us, and all about, as if we were in the midst of a waterfall.

I was afraid suddenly—and that's when I saw Emma.

She was far off, on top of a hill that was one of many. Each higher and higher, oddly curved at their peaks as if the land itself was warped with malice. They rose in the distance until the last was a mountain, and seemed to be the source of the misery, and I wanted to run away—but I called to Emma. She didn't reply. I could see that she was talking to creatures, black, ugly ones that croaked with a nasty laughter. In iron cages atop the other hills were folkies of many kinds—one in each cell, each different, all captive prisoners.

Emma didn't answer me. Instead, a skin-rattling scream filled the air with terror beyond anything I had felt even on this dark night of fear. And I knew. Through the dread, I sensed the center of the curses and spells, and knew that the Gwyllion was here, the Old Woman on her Mountain in the sky. I dropped to the ground, but Thryst quickly picked me up. I worried for Emma, and I wanted—while I had Thryst with me—to look at the spells to rescue her from these beasts. But he carried me back, down through the storm and into tunnels, and we escaped. He wouldn't help the Elves, and he wouldn't help the birds, and he wouldn't help Emma either.

I was on my own.

W.W. Marplot

CHAPTER 93

Arty

was on my own. As Thryst released me from his eyes, he and my—his?—dogs walked away. I trotted back through the tunnel to my basement, then outside to the lightless, powerless, wet streets.

I had no idea how to find Emma—she was on a mountain somewhere that wasn't on human maps, and I knew I couldn't oppose the Gwyllion by myself. Her scream alone knocked me down. I could go to Eastward Manor and ask Abcedarius for help, or ask Ted and Cry, or Gretel—but what could they do? I knew only what I could do, and I had to use the spell book and the counter-spells I had prepared to help the Trust Network friends.

My bike, which I hadn't ridden in two years, was tangled in the back of our garage with some rusty tools and rakes and snow sleds that had come to know each other well. My effort was wasted: It had two flat tires, and hopping on it, my knees hit my elbows anyway—I had grown in two years, I guess. And this little thing you could ride through the crawlspace.

My oldest brothers' bikes were too big; on them I couldn't reach the ground, and my books and backpack made me unsteady. *I need a giant, speedy, fairy tortoise,* came a thought, then came another: *I am so tired I can't think.* The night was moving on, the battle forming, the clouds were now overlapping and burst warm gushes of giant raindrops that smacked the driveway and came sideways into the garage just to try and discourage me. It did. I never felt more help-less, overmatched, powerless, or wretched. And, even in just a few days, I had gotten used to being part of a powerful team of folktale legends, their friends, and my friends. My new loneliness circled, then squeezed, then crushed my mind the way the cloud battalions had done to the blue day.

Lightning struck. *Why not?* But when it did, a red flash struck back—from the bright metallic paint and red reflectors on our ATV four-wheeler quad-bike, whose cover had blown off in the wind. My older brothers' lawn-trashing pride and joy—mostly joy—that I had ridden once on the beach with about as much skill as a slinky riding a mechanical bull. It threw me into the sand after I hit a log, and I could swear that it laughed even before my brothers did.

But there it was, shining like a giant ruby motoring machine, not a giant speedy fairy tortoise but still a gift from fate, showing itself as a sign, a solution, a signal that I should *not give up.*

It would help with the hills, and the fallen trees…and it has a light, I thought. *That's the spirit!*

I snapped on the red helmet, pulled the visor down, and like a spaceman heard the echo of my own breathing loud in my ears. I felt protected and strong. I hopped on the quad's long red seat and started the engine, prepared to zip along the slick streets and their downed trees to the rescue of my folk-friended, spellbound, dou-bly-enchanted friends.

Ouch. A few moments later, I was rubbing my shoulder and looking through my backpack for something to stuff in my quad-helmet to make it fit my small, wet head tightly enough to move left when my head turned left—the way I did and it didn't at the bottom of my driveway—where I panicked and bailed out without a parachute.

Some sticky notes will have to do, I thought and used a half-inch worth of them—not any orange ones but mostly pink, since there might be no tomorrow anyway—to *more-pad* the helmet cushion in three spots.

Now I was snug as a Pixie in a glove.

Now I could zip along the slick streets and their downed trees to the rescue of my folkie-finding, spellbound, doubly-enchanted friends.

First to Isabella, who I knew had blisters and sores so that I was prepared with the counter-spell, an easy one for my first ever attempt at wizardry.

I parked the loud quad and ran to stand directly below Isabella's second-story window, not attempting the drainpipe this time. The incantation I had saved on my phone for her was this:

A cill le leaba, mias le feoil, cupan le fíon bheith gan trí huaire diabhal shaol na saol go deo.

Though: It hit me that I knew the words but not the music. I don't speak Irish, can't impersonate great-great-grand-grand Dera, don't do any fake accents, and I had been kicked out of the role of Happy Sunflower Number Two in a kindergarten play once because of my poor acting skill even compared to the fifteen other Sunflowers, two of whom always smelled like peanut butter. But the punishment for screwing this up could be worse—the wrong word at the wrong time might put me on a magic carpet or turn Belle Terre into a frog or Ted into a prince or who knew what.

I steadied my shaking hands and tried to sound like Thryst—confident, bold, and ready.

I began. I intoned the invoking incantation. "*A cill le leaba, mias le feoil, cupan le fíon bheith gan...*"

I worried about the pronunciation, but as I spoke, it felt as if each word pushed the next one out, as if a force was behind them, and a spirit was guiding me to make the right sounds.

"*...trí huaire diabhal shaol na saol go deo,*" I finished with my eyes closed.

"Please," I added.

It worked!

Isabella came to her window and called to me. We had a short, hushed talk: she understood what was happening, had heard my words, and her blisters were already feeling better. We both laughed with relief and the release of a breathless joy. At that exact moment, her Shellycoat began a Water-Elven song outside, nearby—of course!—from the fake fish pond.

I felt a thrill like an electric current run through me and shock this world over which I had spell-casting powers. Isabella was happy to return to playing that viral app fantasy game that Cry also played. Imagine that? Why? The real world is so much more fantastic, *And normal kids are missing it*, I thought. *I am a wizard's staff, and they are all thumbs.*

Anyway: it worked, and I was energized with new powers. I felt I was riding into battle, a noisy quad as my horse, a phone my weapon, my eyes a source of magic voltage. Five more friends-of-friends to go, and thanks to *Thryst the Tour Guide*'s eye-ride, I knew of every enemy curse, had the counter-spells ready, and knew where to go to fight malicious Gwyllion forces with my own scientifically-researched magic, though I didn't know what I was talking about.

From Isabella's I went to Alex, and it was the same scene: watching for snakes, I rode near to the house and demanded, "*Fhail ar bun, do ta tu ag ithe an luch, a fuath ra, agus tu chew na cnamha a cat ag lobhadh*," which in English is the "putrid cat" one that is my personal favorite. I made a better attempt at an accent, part Irish-lord-brogue and part wet-science-geek.

It worked! Alex and his Hobgoblin snapped out of it—and continued playing their app game, together, looking for fictional beings on Alex's phone map, the same game as Isabella, Cry, and a billion others had used up many weekends playing. This generation obviously prefers video game worlds with their explosions and lawless chaos to the real world with its boring schools and motor vehicle rules and Giant Ghost Spriggans. I shook my helmeted head like a cranky grandpa.

I motored to the other fairy-trusted friends. I was getting better at riding, and better at Irish, and not too bad at wizardry—which is just science-ahead-of-its-time after all.

Ethan was easy, with his upset stomach and achy body parts. I commanded, and the fairy world obeyed.

For Sophia, I mouthed the crocodile counter-spell—a long one—from a distance and repeated it while riding around her house from outside their backyard fence.

Chludu An speir na realtai, chludu draiocht a lonnaiochtai,
agus chludu mo bheal an draiocht ata ann.

I admit I was nervous this time, and the words came more as a polite request not to eat Sophia's family. A monster croc was not something I wanted to see, or hear, or feel, despite my spell-master spirit powers. Crocodiles can get physical, and I did not have an axe-app on my phone.

Just as I started to think I might have to get closer—it worked! Then I saw Sophia's fairy, a small Elf, in a garden, springing about on light feet and waving to me excitedly. I took this as a happy sign that all was well, but I had no time to stay and listen to its stories.

Well, maybe just one: the Elf got my attention when I heard its flute-like voice pipe something that sounded like "Emma." I drove closer, shut off the quad's stuttering engine, removed my space helmet, and listened. Emma had been there earlier, the little guy told me, and she had said some weird things to Sophia that made no sense to this Elf of another world. And, before returning to the rain and woods, Emma left behind a small beast—Sophia's Elf described something that sounded like a Troll but small, only a foot high—that acted as master to the crocodile demons. That is, until my counter-spell dashed them all.

"Emma did that?" I think I said, though no one heard or answered. *Emma did that.*

The Elf danced away, tooting a new song. I put my helmet on to be trapped with my thoughts: my childhood friend was now on the same team as evil mini-Trolls and nasty monsters that were haunting schoolchildren and—was she helping to distribute them? Fairy delivery? The memory of Emma on the mountain came to me, hit me in the gut: she had been laughing.

Emma was helping the Gwyllion.

Sophia's mom must have sensed something: According to the fairy, she sent Emma away, saying she should go home, it was late, no one should be out in the storm, and where was Emma's mother, etc.? And that Emma should know better.

I agree, I thought, though I also knew the whole story better than anyone else. The Gwyllion was powerful, and I was not, and Emma was pulled to the wrong side. Fairy eyes were everywhere. I should go rescue Emma.

Rescue her? Or battle her?

Oh, wow.

Emma was *helping* the Gwyllion, I remembered.

And there were still Jacob and Olivia and maybe others, in trouble, and it seemed that I was the only one who knew and could help them. And this job seemed to fit my small courage. But the mountain, the Old Woman, her army, her powers, her weather? I needed more wizard practice before I tried that. *I will never try that*, I realized. *I have to try that,* I also realized.

And as a scientist, I knew to stop that endless illogical brain loop and get moving—and that meant having to decide where to move to.

My mind and heart were torn into four pieces. I wanted, needed, to follow Emma. Although she had little Trolls with her, and a low-flying thing that looked either like a fat bat or a small, ugly, baby dragon, I was not afraid and had to save her.

Yet I knew of the damage Emma was doing to our friends-of-friends right now, and I was combating it, pretty well, so far.

So, I decided and hurried: to fight this battle first, to save Jacob and his Light Elf. *Sprugly the Spriggan would be proud of me,* I thought. Of course, I had spent three days wandering aimlessly with our folkie characters and doing nothing, and now when we needed a team effort—to combat thick crocodiles, to help distressed Elves—I was on my own.

I spurred my trusty quad back to the roads, even jumping off a small brick wall on Sophia's terraced property—on purpose—though the jolt moved my helmet over my face so that I then jumped another brick wall—on accident. But I stayed in the saddle. I also learned how to skid around turns without wanting to throw up.

My fat tires spun when reaching Jacob's rain-soaked driveway and up its long climb to his four-car garage. From there, the main yard was blocked by a locked fence, interrupted only by an eight-foot high stone retaining wall that I had to fall off twice before finding a diagonal that allowed me to rock-climb it—under dark night and with rain-soaked, grimy hands—before I could find a way closer to his large house.

Once there, I saw Emma! Leaving! Going down a path through a now-visible gate in the fence and then back down the steep drive-way, thirty yards from me. I was on her trail! I had just missed her at Sophia's and now at Jacob's.

I followed, back down the rock wall, which was much faster this time since I only had to fall once, and on the quad. Emma was gone, but I used the gate to enter the front yard. Steering to a gazebo, I leaned under to shelter my phone from the unending enemy rain and find my next words of sorcery. I spoke them. Then I ran to Jacob's front door to check on him, leaving my quad running on the squished grass just off his family's grand front porch.

Because of Emma's visit, however, Jacob's parents answered quickly, surprising me when the double doors opened at the same time, with the same speed, one by Mom, one by Dad, and me surprising them with my drenched clothes and astro-helmet, visor-down. They each grimaced, recognized me as I removed the helmet, then asked why I was mowing lawns at this time of night with a mega-storm coming—the quad was unseen but loudly sputtering and coughing metallically nearby. Kindly but honestly came their request to get lost, mentioning that kids were crazy and that insanity was contagious: Jacob had been sick and confused since yesterday. It worried his parents, since their only son hadn't even touched his mobile app scavenger hunt game in two days, even though it had been an obsession, and Cry and Ted had even called to get Jacob to log back on. His parents smiled and boomed the double wooden doors shut like huge castle gates.

Contagious Jacob gave me an idea. Mounting my ruby red ride, I posted the Jacob counter-spell online, just in case. I also posted one to cover bats, and one for Trolls, in case Emma was delivering more of them. And then all the spells for everything I had seen—I copied them all into one long Irish sentence.

Jacob's virus, and Cry's viral gaming, gave me another idea. I knew that these friends-of-friends must have spoken to others since the "interlude," especially given the storm and the weekend. So, I logged into that stupid mobile app scavenger game that everyone but me and one of my dogs played and listed the long, lone sentence of mega-spells, offering tons of game-points and fame and fortune to anyone who read them, said them, sent them, posted them, or repeated them to any of a list of totally fictional, made-up, fantasy, legendary, fairy-tale creatures who happened to also be truly running around the real world tonight. Social networking for the 16th century.

I straddled the quad again; when I plopped down, water wrung from the spongy seat, and it wheezed a miserable hiss. I patted my machine to show my appreciation and revved away, off to Olivia Patrick's house, the last of the friends-of-friends and a few miles away. Back to Belle Terre, that War-Fairy-Land-Portal-Heaven. I sped and splashed across lawns and squashed already muddy ground, hoping to stay on Emma's trail: hers and her new, awful, trickster friends.

Nearly to Olivia's, ahead I saw them: in the air! Emma's form against the dark sky: she was performing Sprug-like jumpflying acrobatics but in awkward spurts where she spun uncontrollably or jerked ahead with neck-bending starts and stops, her hair in her face and sticking there with the rain. *I am better at driving than she is at flying*, I thought—and in this small way good triumphed over evil, though we were both still learning.

Her bat-friend waited for her at each restart. I did not see the other little monsters; perhaps they were following along on the ground. I hoped to catch them and run them over.

To be ready, I risked checking my phone while quadding, which is as dangerous as they say. The ground ahead changed every second. There were dips and turns, dark holes, fallen branches and trees, and here and there odd pairings of animals: for example, a large deer stooping its antlers to push and hurry along a small, nervous beaver, and cutting across the new path I was blazing in this last frontier of War Land woods. But I wanted to be ready with the correct spells—I was ready with one for Olivia but was looking for what to use against bats or flying things. With wizard wisdom and fortune-teller foresight, I had emailed all the translations to myself, just in case. And this was definitely *in case*; there was never a bigger case and no thirteen-year-old was ever more in it.

Done. I steered to my fellow Research Clubber's ground-floor bedroom; I did not want to risk being turned away at the front door.

Emma must have or obviously or apparently thought the same thing—against Olivia's lit windows I could see her nasty company assembling.

I gained speed, seeing that I had a chance to surprise them. Emma was stuck in the low branches of a nearby tree. Her landing had been a rough one; the wind was howling, and small leaves were smacking her in the face as she dangled.

I drove my quad directly at the nasty, black creatures—with the low groans of the wind and the screams of the bending trees, they did not hear my attack, and aiming my front tires at a small, shadowy shape that was popping up and down animatedly while pointing at Emma, I made a final, roaring acceleration and prepared for impact.

Just as the thing was caught in my single headlight, it tried to jump and was caught between the front grill of the quad and the brick wall of Olivia's house.

I had a great view of this, since I was flying over the quad handlebars, banging off the thick, plastic windshield, and thudding sideways into the same wall just above the little Troll-like demon. I fell to the front tires and landed in the mud.

CHAPTER 94

Arty

I was dazed. I heard Emma speaking—*Did she say, "Arty, go home"?*—as she passed to the bedroom window a few yards from the crash.

I sat with my back against the house, more clearly hearing Emma's voice: "Keep him there," while in the air in front of me appeared the flying thing; I still could not decide whether it was more *a pudgy, stupid bat* or *a small, deformed dragon.*

At my outstretched feet stood another little Troll, smoke coming out of its nose and billowing wildly with the wind.

I pulled off my helmet and tried to remember the spells I had memorized just before my own accidental jumpflying, which was even worse than Emma's. The words did not work, my head was not clear, I was woozy and panicked, my voice uncertain.

Emma repeated her command: "Keep him there!"

Her voice, saying an enemy's words, brought me out of my fog. I shouted in a clear voice whose sudden power must have come from the Faery Realm:

Is mise ga oithe an chumhacht priomhuil
gluaisne cheangal cre!!

Only after speaking them did these sounds ring familiar—Thryst had shouted something like it when fixing Abcedarius's map after its pages scattered and rearranged. A dim, happy memory.

The flying thing in front of me froze in midair, its hooked wings stiffened, it fell to my lap, and I looked hopefully at Emma.

The spell did not work as well on my friend as it had on her bat-ish companion, who I flung to the side by its abominable clawed feet, while wishing I could reach my hand sanitizer. Emma only smiled, spun around, put her palms to Olivia's window, slid it open with a squeak, and climbed inside.

I tried to rise, but after ten inches noticed some bad news and crashed back down. The spell that grounded the bat-thing had done nothing to the Troll-thing; it grabbed my legs and pulled until I lay flat. I felt its small body grip and climb up my leg. I kicked to get away but only slipped backwards a few feet in the wet grass. Sitting up, I tried another word of spell from the top of my memory, but nothing happened. It was now on my stomach, heavy as a bowling ball but six inches high. Its stone body moved slowly but with awful weight and strength—its tight, hard muscles and large head and hands popped with black veins, the skin scarred in many places like cracked cement. It then held up a small weapon that reflected the light from Olivia's room, a black blade. The few holes in its head—its foul mouth and eyes—opened and made an awful, cracking sound: a warlike troll scream.

Time for one more spell, I thought, but my body acted quicker and smarter and suddenly swung the helmet in my hand, catching the diminutive Troll inside like a block of stone butterfly in a hard, red net. The troll was heavy and trapped for a second, but my swing was shortened and ended when it hit the brick wall of the house. The nasty little beast popped out, fell to the ground, but I trapped it again, now under a red domed cage. I pushed the helmet into the soft, wet ground until there was no space for it to escape, stepped on it to be sure, and quickly rolled a front tire of the quad over it was

W.W. Marplot

well. It held: the creature banged like a trapped wasp inside, cursed small-curses, and spat—but the sounds and his effort died against the shiny red helmet walls.

I then laughed as I heard the sound of tearing paper—it was ripping up the Post-it notes, my plans and lists, that I had placed inside to better fit my head. It had nothing else it could do.

I knew from movies that I should rub it in somehow, have the courage to say something cool to my enemy combatant—but I never took notes on this, and they were now ripped up anyway.

"You started it!" I managed, which I hope will be rewritten someday by whoever wins the bet.

Now: To the window!

I opened it and climbed inside, exactly as Emma had, provided she too dunked herself awkwardly onto the floor, shoulder-first, then butt, then face. Try THAT sometime.

My head now hurt—a lot. And holding it, I saw Emma yelling at Olivia, who seemed to not notice either of my crashes into her house.

With an effort to speak loudly, though each word seemed to break another vein within my new bruises, I said, "Emma! Stop! Why are you—"

But she was stronger in voice and attitude. "Shut up, Arty."

I did. I watched in order to try and answer my question myself. And—*Which counter-spell might help? What has happened to my oldest friend Emma?*

She went on screaming, her wet hair hanging and overall looking like a witch who had lost her pointy hat. Emma looked down on Olivia's smallness and meekness, while Emma herself seemed to have grown, her voice menacing, her face tight, her body stiff and focused on this friend-of-her-friend's.

Then I then saw the Silky, a little fairy woman, looking out from the colorful toy box, looking like a worried mom. For these folkies that were hiding, and had escaped the Gwyllion, Emma now had switched sides and was the enemy.

"Ok," Olivia whimpered, "stop, Emma, you will wake up my dad."

Emma looked at each of us with a sly smirk from a face still wet with rain and dirty sweat. "No, I won't. I know for sure. Now: do what I tell you."

More whimpering, from kid and fairy both. "But my mom said no, not to ever…"

The words enraged Emma; her body twisted into one big fist, and she screamed to the ceiling. "No! DO NOT listen to HER! THAT is what this is ABOUT!" And she screamed again, though not in words, not English words anyway: it was more a call from one wild part of herself to another.

A small rain of tears wetted Olivia's cheeks, her face a puffy, dark cloud.

Emma calmed but continued in a strange voice, like a small, clever animal; her whole aspect had changed. "You don't need anyone," she purred. "I don't. I know how it is for you. Come with me. Listen to me."

Olivia was listening and starting to believe.

I tried to grasp unfamiliar things: Emma was not Emma, and the fairy battleground had moved to a new place. She changed again and stood seething, breathing heavily in and out of her nose like a bull readying to charge. Rain blew in from the window on a strong, foul wind, as if Emma had called for it.

I shut the window and stared that way to sneak a look at the spells on my phone.

I found one and spoke it.

Me oscail cosan sa speir agus ar domhan ta me an inion dea de mo athair!

With that, the window slid open again, letting in thick rain and a heavy Dwarf. Thryst!

Emma stood still, and she looked like Emma; the droopy brunette curtains moved back from her face, and it was Emma's face.

Bolder, I stood and asked, "Why Emma? What is going on?"

She looked at the open window and sniffed the air. Freshened with it, she looked at me for a long time.

"My mom," she said, "I think that she...she..."

But the spiteful wind came again, a gust that spoiled worse than the other freshened: Emma's expression turned witchy again, and bewitched, and a scream, like Emma's howl to the ceiling but coming down instead from the sky of black armies, made Thryst draw his axe, and its tone blended with the whistle from the whips of stormy air. Olivia and her Silky cowered; I did, too. I felt a presence, coming, the evil from the Mountain, the Woman, the Gwyllion.

Thryst did not swing or curse or fight or run; he instead took his turn to speak words to the battling air and sky.

"*Thantan namka! Thantan namka ung finachta ta thann!!*" His voice brought the earth to the fight. Each syllable burned into my brain, such was its power.

A scream, and horns of metallic thunder and a shock of bluish lightning, answered.

But I had my eyes on the battle within Emma. Her face wavered, in between bad and good, but after a few seconds of doubt, her eyes twinkled blue, charged with the electric sky. Thryst's words affected her the way Olivia's answers had earlier—exasperation, anger—and her new mistress, the great and horrible Gwyllion, answered for her from above.

And answered *to* her—and so Emma was recaptured and re-charmed. A spell came on the wind—their power surrounded and scared me, and I did not dare to move as Emma walked past, to the window, and out. This Gwyllion-spell enveloped Thryst—I could see him struggling with its meaning and, though he was not under anyone else's power, he mumbled helplessly to himself. He and I could only watch as Emma searched my scattered backpack items, the far-flung wreckage from the quad crash, and picked up the box that glittered with purple rainbows, its sparks rising with the current of the sky. Then Emma was gone—upward, and within another flash from the sky. Mocking thunder echoed its laughter everywhere.

Emma had taken the casket that held the counter-spells and symbols, the fourteen pieces. She was following orders, I hoped. She must be, I hoped. For once I could not tell what she was thinking.

Though blinded for a few seconds, or minutes, soon I was anxious to continue the chase, thinking to get on Emma's trail again if I could figure out what friends had spoken to which others, and get some help from Zyxvuts. And Sprugly certainly would want to know, and Cry and Ted—especially Ted, who would want a shot at rescuing Emma if he knew. My head hurt, but I scribbled over the ache with new plans and ideas.

"Come on, Thryst!" I said.

He would not move. He would not listen. He stood still as stone, staring into his own beard.

I spoke the spell—*Tá mé uasal spiorad feistithe O gach biotáillí agat a ullmhú cosán dom!*—that I had come to speak, and Olivia and her fairy visibly changed like they were plucked from a nightmare to find themselves in bed with their parents on a snow day. As they laughed, Thryst darted away—out the window with a vengeful cry.

I watched: Thryst shoved over my quad angrily, feverish with rage. The little Troll popped out of his helmet prison and was quickly cut in two—vertically down his middle—by the waiting warrior Dwarf. A stream of greenish blood shot straight upwards, but the two body halves crumbled to dusty pebbles before even hitting the ground. A Dwarf boot came down heavily onto the pile. Then Thryst cried aloud again and ran off.

I saw that my trusty battle horse had two flat tires.

And my cell phone was dead.

The rain fell harder and drowned me in mud and foreboding. My mind and vision went black. I started to walk home; I almost had to feel my way. My hopes were gone.

W.W. Marplot

Why were our fairies not helping: were they helpless? Why were they all taken in the first place, and how did they escape? They—we—were losing. The world was going dark, even Thryst was defeated, it seemed. I was helpless and small; I had even lost Emma. Above was a living, natural horror show: the black clouds had won the sky, and evil things were in it. The earth moaned as bolts of blue knocked out power, struck down trees, and started fires. All animals were hiding and confused. I was blind because the world had lost light and color.

I walked, weary and hurt, my mind lost and my thoughts circling helplessly. I only wanted to see day again, to see a normal bright sky again: a smiling one of blue, yellow and white, or a yawning one, late and grey and angled with orange edges.

CHAPTER 95

Cry

ry here, not my real name. I was with Ted but won't let him tell about it; Emma and Arty said not to about a million times.

We were at my house, which is next to the fields that used to be farms or something but now are being cleared for apartments and stores. My father can tell you all about that if you want. It's all he talks about. I don't see the big deal.

My room looks out into the fields, so much dirt and brown grass. From here Ted and I were watching the action: ground action and sky action. Because, obviously, some big things were going on; I could see it in Peanut's eyes, when he let us look. Ted and I took turns. We added it to a war game we were playing, which has a lot of dragons. So cool. Just so awesome…

But anyway, I had two bigger things going on while Ted was in and out of the bathroom hiding.

One: he was hiding because: Ted found a fairy! It tried to kill him though. It was really nasty, so we put it in a hamster cage, but it could get out unless Peanut the Pixie and I guarded it. Sprug was here; he would leave and come back—we figured he was checking on Peanut, who was just hanging out with us just like a normal Saturday night of fantasy games.

Sprug whispered to us that "Little Nasty"—what we call Ted's folkie—for some reason thought Ted was trying to steal a fairy wife.

Which is one of the worst things you can do, Sprug said. I thought maybe it was because Ted was playing with Peanut. Peanut likes him. Ted still wants to find a dragon.

Two: I had two big things happen, and the second is we met Abcedarius Zyxvuts, and his wife Trudy, and her cousin Mary. They came to my house through the fields. Mary all the way from England, and she brought her accent. And she knew what was going on. She was the one who wrote those letters, before we knew what was going on. She told us then. So, we watched the sky and the field. Another battle was coming, and the Gwyllion had kidnapped folkies from all over and brought them here, to New Island, to Belle Terre, War Land, and the holiday that opens their portal to heaven. So sad. So awesome.

Trudy was nice.

Zyxvuts reminded me of the social studies teacher that I don't want to get next year. He told us about the magic map model movie thing, but we didn't get to see it, since he said he gave it to Thryst and Arty to help them. Ted looked mad at that.

Great-Grandma Dera woke from a nap and came into the room when everyone was there, slowly like she always does, like the light takes longer to find her wrinkly eyes. She asked Mary if her last name was Hynes (it isn't), and she looked out the window for a while, said that "someone had opened the door" and would I be ok, that Wights were only to fear "near the brook of the raths and lisses." So, she is still the same. She's over a hundred years old.

She winked at Ted, told him that "May is the month of dragons!" Ted liked her a lot after that.

She winked at Trudy and told Mr. Zyxvuts to "Beware! May first spouses might be enchanted women of the underworld! *Aos si*!" Then she left, tired from winking and talking. I told everyone that she is over a hundred years old.

Ted was still mad that Arty had the magical map. "What a waste!" He told everyone, "We could have used it to find a dragon. It is the month of dragons. They are probably everywhere. Arty will just take notes and measure it or something."

"I am sorry, Ted," Zyxvuts answered him, smiling from out of a brown moustache way up high. His voice reminded me of the cello I tortured with my bow in orchestra before being asked to switch to stage crew. "You have your hands full with the folkies you have but are doing well. Some of the other kids are not as lucky, and some of the other fairy creatures are in trouble, but not the two of you. Well done."

They told us about the spells; Mary spoke in perfect English. She must get an "A" in English every year. "How potent the conjurations are! As are fairy eyes," she said. "Abcedarius was right to warn you not to look. It takes a special spirit to not be carried away, far away. Or to be pulled inward, which can be worse." I felt guilty for looking in Peanut's eyes, though Ted and I never left the room.

Me and Ted told them—with New Island accents—about Ted's strange daydreams and about Sprugly.

"Yes," Mary said, "that must have been very frightening Ted, but you were very brave, all things considered."

Ted smiled big and red, and Little Nasty growled. Ted asked tall Zyxvuts, "Can I get the map next? Are there dragons on it? Big ones?"

Zyxvuts started to say, "No, I didn't see any—"

But Mary said, "Yes! There are."

Ted pumped his fist like he does when his video game character cuts off someone's head. Then he put his open hand up to Zyxvuts, you know, for a high five.

And the old man gave him a high five then looked like he wanted to take it back.

"Arty and Thryst both had need of the map," Mary said. "Abcedarius justly lent it to them. Fate stepped in, and that has helped, as I see now, to move the last pieces of a century-old puzzle into place. But we are not finished yet."

This part all confused me, so it is better to have Mary explain it.

Then we were invited to Eastward Manor. Then they left. That was it.

Ted had the binoculars, and he wouldn't come out of the bathroom until I trapped Little Nasty again.

CHAPTER 96

Mary

Many years ago, a girl who lived near Nether-witton, returning home from milking with a pail upon her head, saw many fairies playing in the fields, but which were invisible to her companions, though pointed out to them by her. On reaching home and telling what she had seen, the circumstance of her power of vision being greater than that of her companions was discussed in the family, and the cause at length discovered in the grass pad she wore on her head to help carry the pail. This was found to be of four-leaved clover—persons having about them a bunch, or even a single blade, of four-leaved clover being supposed to possess the power of seeing fairies, even though the Elves should wish to be invisible...

—The Denham Tracts, Volume II

Pleased to make your acquaintance; I am Mary. As the forces gather, I am going to tell you about them and other things that I know.

Fairies are as old as life, though their legendary, magical form came into being in companionship to humans— together, but sometimes as rivals, sometimes friends, sometimes as enemies, sometimes as each other's myths, dreams, or shadowy fears. As the spirit within living things grew—as waking separated from dream, as emotions covered instincts, as awareness of other worldly beings woke them further still—fairies increased in number and kind, their own world rising in parallel that of mankind.

And their memories, though buried within legends, reach back to the beginning of beginnings.

Many thousands of years ago, humans began to recognize life within the eyes of other creatures. The fairies were there, too, in the south of the dawning world. Those who awakened came north, then some east, and some west, following either the new or the old sun, depending on where they felt the heartbeat of their new world as it reached noon. Fairies grew and adapted with this noontime of humankind, splitting and following along every path.

Legends and myths blended together, and the waking worlds of fairies and men came close together; the old stories show this. But fairies kept their most ancient beliefs alive like morning stars despite the bright new days—they knew there remained a haven in the farthest west. Though it was now apart and long ago the lands had changed, New Island was real, part of the Faery Realm that included places of spirits and dreams.

A thousand years ago, the legendary creatures thrived in Europe and involved themselves in human lives, and they grew powerful enough that even now they live in the folktales behind every human story of magical, other beings. These folkies thought they could find the true New Island, through a gateway that they named Eastward Manor.

Five hundred years ago, it was found in the New World of humans. But evil things came to it, and its heart was renamed Mount Misery. There was War in War Land. The Gwyllion came, the Old Woman now had her Mountain—and in the Faery Realm it was much higher and darker.

The Wise Elf spoke: When a human child comes, the special one, last of the legendary line, Eastward Manor could be made pure again. So, fairies sought children, for good and for bad—many folktales tell what happened.

Who am I? I am from a very interesting family, one that has lived in more than one world for more than three centuries. Of those that have received this gift, I am the last. We can sense fairies; we are legends to them. My parents told me I am the one that the wise, old Elf predicted: I could help the fairies take back Eastward Manor, their heaven and their place of peace and rest since ancient times. The Farthest West. The Land above Two Oceans. The Land Once with Us. Parting Cliffs. It has many names, both a myth and a lost paradise, their oldest and newest home.

I am here now.

Over time, fairy lives faded, and Eastward Manor was cut off from their lives. But I am here now.

My family kept the land for a long time but eventually left for England and our own ancestral home. But my ancestors left clues! Magic, for some to find and for others to use. The glowing map, the book of spells in its purple coffin: I thought they were lost!

They are found, and they are the remaining pieces; I need that magic. But time is running out.

And fairy friends suffer. Arty has lost both hope and the book, Emma and other children are in trouble, and their warrior Dwarf, even with Mr. Zyxvut's mystical map, cannot find what he seeks.

So, another battle will curse the land tonight. The last storm battle was a test, a trial—we caught the Gwyllion off guard and the rescuers helped. This time she is ready, and tonight will decide the future.

CHAPTER 97

Arty

I kept walking and was almost there. Not to home—where I thought I was going—but up this fancy, circular driveway and past an iron sign on an iron post that said, "Eastward Manor," the place I have wandered to in both body and brain.

Abcedarius Zyxvuts and his wife Trudy greeted me at the door of their large, Tudor-style mansion. Many of these historic old homes near the beach cliffs were built a hundred years ago when rich people used Belle Terre for vacation and spent summers in these cottages—each three times the size of my house—all centered around one big country club that burned down before all the other, more normal homes were built.

Walking up, clothes and backpack drooping and drenched with rain, my face and hands chilled in the gale, I gazed at the outlined shadows of six chimneys and too many gabled roofs to count, their points looking like haunted mountain peaks cutting the black sky. Entering, I felt transported backward in time when railroads and oil were what made people rich, and science and technology were replacing beliefs in anything else. From the entry foyer I looked over an internal landscape of rooms, halls, arched doorways, wooden walls and ceilings, large paintings, and a wide, open staircase curving down toward me like the tongue of some giant, defeated beast. Brass, wood, paint, and colored glass were everywhere.

In the "library," where high walls of books and stretches of massive oak desks filled a space where I could spend a whole summer as easily as my family wastes a day at the beach, I found Ted and Cry and was introduced to Mary, a teenaged girl dressed like an English lady, her hair in golden, curly tresses, her face rosy. She was the lass in every happy fairy tale. I was given two towels and a seat in front of a fireplace the size of a hockey net.

They told me Mary's story, *THE* story, of all and everything, and I told them about my night of riding around dark and stormy Belle Terre neighborhoods fighting big magic with little magic. I felt like a failure who tried his best—because I had lost Emma. The others made me feel a little better about that. After telling it, I did not want to talk anymore and slumped into a broad, high, billowy, many-buttoned chair that seemed confused that I did not want to smoke a pipe or contemplate Shakespeare.

The others talked, sitting on sofas and on the floor, each far apart. I listened, I rested, and I looked around the vast room, lit only by the fire and a few candles in corner eaves.

After answering Abcedarius's questions about the funny mini-coffin from my yard, Mary added—in a soothing voice that seemed to fit the surroundings, matching the furniture, the dark, rich curtains, the grandfather clock larger than any grandfather I ever saw—"The casket goes to whom it can serve, according to legend. I have heard of it before but not of the counter-spells, and of it being in pieces. I don't know about that. But the box has a long history."

"But Arty said Emma took it," Cry said.

"To give to the Gwyllion, if I understand his story correctly," Abcedarius said. "So that is discouraging. It will serve the Gwyllion."

As the others fell quiet, Mary continued talking. She was the type of girl whom people liked to pay attention to, to listen to. I noticed that even Ted was behaving. Others—non-human and important for the War in War Land—came and went.

I also saw now, for the first time, the thin body and long, wavy blonde hair of a strange folkie—a Gunna like the one I'd seen held captive and marching with the Wights underground. It was sitting in a dark space where the firelight was blocked by a large table on which brown-edged maps were spread. The Gunna was singing quietly to itself, inaudibly unless one looked at it carefully and matched slight whispers to the movements of its eyes and mouth, as I strained to do.

Mary said, "He was rescued. By the same Spriggan that you know well."

"So, it's the same one, the Gunna, that was the prisoner of the Wights?" I asked.

"Yes. The Old Woman of the Mountains kidnapped only one of each spirit type, of any who resisted her."

I tried to remember what I knew about Gunnas but then thought it easier just to watch the real one. I faded away from the conversation as Mary and the others discussed what should happen next, and how the next battle could be won. The words put me to sleep.

I awoke to Mary's voice, jolted by the mention of my name.

"We now know that with the right casting of words and ancient symbols," she said, "those that Arty was able to find, following the clues left by our departed allies, I can awake the right and veridical spell-power to oppose the Old Woman of the Mountains and help the fairy forces. Faithful help from the past, but is it too late? My family could not be here, at the right place, at the right time. Only I. And now, to align the small powers that we have gathered, piece by piece, thanks to Arty, and Trudy, and you, Abcedarius, and everyone here."

I thought of Emma. She helped and was not here. She was with the evil fairies.

Mary looked at me warmly, but I did not know what to say.

Trudy tried to help. "Mary does not need the book of spells or the purple casket any longer. Arty, it was brilliant that you sent the incantations themselves out to everyone, all of them. We now have them all."

"I didn't know what I was doing; I was only thinking of my friends who were in trouble."

"But we sent those same messages to Mary," Ted said, "so she has been working on it tonight and meeting with all the leaders—Elves, Dwarves, and whatever. It was my idea."

Abcedarius said in his tall, smooth, lecturing way, "Well, you wanted to make money on it, but yes, Ted, you did a good thing also. It is a team effort. You are definitely a key member of the advertising team."

I felt half-lost in the conversation; *What are they asking me?* Trudy again read the question on my crumpling, firelit brow, and said helpfully, "Do you have the cookbook? It had the original symbols that went with the spells. Mary needs that against the Gwyllion."

They were in my backpack, drying near a second, smaller fireplace. I did not get up.

Ted burst out and up, saying, "I found the cookbook first, Zyxvuts, I only lent it to Arty," ran to my bag, and soon the book he had borrowed from the Historical Society was back in his hands. He handed it to Mary like a dog returning a slobbered-on stick.

What does this have to do with Emma? I thought dreamily.

My mind and eyes roamed. In a corner near the rounded, front-facing, checkered glass window was another fairy creature, a horned, scaly thing on a leash tied to a hook in the wall that also supported a full suit of medieval armor. The thing growled through yellow fangs.

Ted spoke to it. "Shut up. I hate you, too."

Mary held the fairy cookbook in reverence between the upward palm of one hand and the downward fingertips of another. "Many paths are meeting, feet are following mapped steps, foretold promises are being fulfilled; generations of fairies, good and bad, are today aligned in destiny. And fated people, some long dead, have helped even from the mists of the past. I feel now that the all our magic is together, like the fingers of a fist. The armies have the help they need, and many have been saved and rescued, even for a second time."

Mary left the room. Erect and with long paces, as if the book were balanced on her head, she continued to come and go mysteriously into the story as I was living it. Following her down a hallway were a dozen or so small Elves and a few flying creatures that were colorful, more handsome versions of Sprugly the Spriggan.

Trudy spoke to me again, mistaking the source of my foggy doubt. "You did your part, Arty, and did it well. The counter-spells are where they are needed, and you connected the pieces of the puzzle. My husband's map, the books, the fairies that found your friends: the story is filled in, and now there is a chance."

"Where is Mary going?" I asked. My mind, dry and warm now, was trying to fill in a hole. A wide one.

"She needs to meet with the fairy captains, the leaders in this battle. Also there are 'The Rescuers'"—Trudy said these words with special flair and a flourish of her hands—"who came to save their friends, those that the Gwyllion kidnapped.

"She tried to conquer the fairies' land of escape, Eastward Manor, and Beltaerne," Zyxvuts added as he joined hands with his wife. "To save it came Dwarves, and Elves and Spriggans and spirits and creatures that would fill all your books, and then some."

I did not smile. There was still a hole—Emma. And just then, I was reminded of another hole—Thryst—who had just walked in the room.

Will I ever know what he is searching for?

His beard was torn; it hung in triangular chunks like stalactites, caked with grit, matching a face that was tired from unending chase. Leather garb, his packs, and weapons were wet with war and rain and sweat, his red and green boots hidden beneath a crust of dirt. He bowed to Abcedarius and placed the mapmodelgram pages, unformed and two-dimensional, on a desk between them. Lately the Dwarf was always in one of two modes: either fiery and fierce and frustrated, or down and depressed and disheartened. He stood looking into the bright flames of the hearth as if deciding which to be next.

"*Arooooo?*" I asked, wondering about my three-family yeth hounds and where they were.

"*Kahzlin,*" he answered evenly, squeezing brown rain from his frayed beard, which told me my dogs were ok.

Mary re-entered the room as he spoke, her long dress hula-hooping about her. "That means 'home,'" she said.

I didn't wonder how a teenaged girl had learned Dwarvish but instead shook my head thinking of the time and trouble that would have saved me on Wednesday.

"Can you ask him what he is looking for?" I looked at Mary; her pretty face was present and lively just as her speech and clothes were old-fashioned and reserved.

"Dwarves do not speak of their own lives to others."

"I noticed…" My face dropped into my towel. "But he tells me with his eyes sometimes," I said into it.

Mary heard. "You are fortunate then! He might even dub you a 'Dwarf-friend.' There aren't many of those so far south, you know."

I felt her smile on the back of my head.

"I don't know what your Dwarf prince seeks, Arty," Mary went on, "but his people need him."

"He's a prince?" I looked up wide-eyed from the towel.

"No." Mary looked at me quizzically. "You gave him that name, Thryst, I believe. Out of endearment, hadn't you? Because *Thrystomos*, in their language, means an heir to a king. But he isn't. He is a great and noble warrior, to be sure, and an important leader of his clan. But not royalty."

"Oh." I explained, "He said 'Thryst' when I asked him his name. But we were both just guessing then…" I felt quite stupid giving Mary these stupid answers; she knew Dwarfish and Elvish and probably spoke Advanced Ancient Spriggan, too, while I had drawn stupid dogs in the stupid dirt. But I continued anyway, telling her, "I added 'The Magnificent' also." Stupid.

"Well, that he is!" Mary smiled.

I asked. "Can't we help him somehow? If we do, maybe he can then help the other Dwarves, right? And he should be in the battle."

Mary answered, her eyes staring directly into mine. "Each of us— even I, even he—can only play one part in the play, the one written for us, and walk only one path at a time, the one under one's feet. I can only help those that are leading the action, and on the main road. Thryst, as you call him, is on his own, separate way."

I left Mary's eyes and thought to myself that it was the same with Emma. I was sad knowing that my path and hers were so far apart.

There was a bigger war going on, and no one could help the two people I most cared about: Emma and Thryst. Sprugly protected fairies only, as I'd seen. Mary, Trudy, and Abcedarius were making plans at a large table; they considered my part valiant but finished. Others—of all different races and species—met in the next room, a large banquet hall, around a large dining room table as if it were a Thanksgiving with maps and relics and weapons instead of food.

I sat, the fireplace heat now stinging me into a sweat.

Soon Cry needed an emotional rest and left the big meeting when Ted was kicked out. They had asked Ted if he was a man of his word, and he said, "Sometimes."

I wanted to find Emma, and it seemed that Thryst didn't care about anyone else's plans either. He gazed into the hearth, the fire of his eyes rivaling the licking flames, his body as still as legendary stone. Parts of his boots showed again their traffic-light colors.

Cry's large shape came and tried to sit on a very low, Pixie-sized footstool, and it was like he was landing a parachute. He teetered between the fireside Dwarf and me, casting a shadow that dimmed half the room. Ted went off and teased the folkie on the leash, the one they call 'Lil Nasty,' until Thryst—with that cute, life-threatening, monosyllabic grunt of his—told Ted to sit down and shut up and to keep sitting down and shutting up for as long as Thryst and he were in the same room, thank you.

Cry and I spoke as he shifted on the stool in a struggle to find his upper-body's exact center and talk at the same time; we both knew that his effort would really only put off the fall.

"So, let's go find her!" Cry said with wide eyes and high cheeks after I shared my thoughts.

"But I have no idea where to look. Last time, I took the Thryst Eye Train. And Emma is somewhere between our world and fairy world, according to Mary, and I believe it. I could never get there myself."

Cry sniffed. "So, just use Thryst again. Can I come? I don't want to come."

I smiled because I knew Cry and knew what he meant—adventures are tempting but dangerous. And I shook my head as we both looked at the Dwarf's faraway, adventure-less eyes—he was not an option this time.

Then, as if it was the simplest thing in the world and so, of course, had to come from this simple source, Cry said, "So, use the map." And he fell off the stool, fulfilling his small destiny. He plopped just six inches to the ground, but it rattled the chandelier into a jangly chuckle.

Although I said, "What do you mean?" it had already come to me how ingenuous it was. Emma had the royal purple box, and that box was on the magic map.

Thryst had heard, and simultaneously he and I walked to the table where the mapmodelgram still sat. He built it into its living 3D form, while Ted smirked various insults at Cry as the big guy rolled a bit before getting to his feet. They joined Thryst and me.

Sweet as fairy cakes, we found on the map colors of a sky sun-setting after a storm, all in curved patterns and leading our eyes to a corner of the cube: the grey glow changed to grey-blue and then to purples mixed with orange—and there was the sparkling spot, like a dragon's eye charming us: the location of the casket. Thryst pointed his finger at it, then along some lines that showed how to get there. His gestures recalled to me the ever-higher dream-hills rising like werewolf fangs above the rain, the caged folkies, the birds, and the devilish shrieks of the Gwyllion. The memory bit me like a snake, sudden and venomous.

My stalwart Dwarf stepped closer and placed in my hand a small stone. It shone for a second, miraculously white rays escaped between thickly-carved markings of green, red, and gold, but Thryst quickly closed my fist around it. The others did not see.

My skin bubbled with a thrill that went from my toes to head and back, my body grew and my mind expanded, then relaxed. I had something to do, the last step in all my plans. I understood and trusted the path along secret, buried ways that Thryst had showed me and whatever magic he had just given me. I had to go where East-ward Manor met the open sky above the beach then down the cliff, to the tunnels below, and follow. I got ready to leave, conquering my scientific doubt and trusting in some inexplicable, un-provable spirit in some deep, Dwarfish cavern within me.

Thryst left while I packed, leaving me the map. He was silent and sternmore, and I thought about our first meetings, the clash of our worlds that were now joined and yet still separate. Thryst was not even his name.

His stone was in my pocket; I did not inspect it in front of the others. I patted Cry on his broad shoulder to say thanks; he yawned and sniffed. Ted then patted my shoulder for some reason. As I walked to the front door, I heard him ask Cry, "How cool am I, on a scale of eight to ten? It must be in there somewhere."

There are advantages to being Ted, like staying in a warm, bright mansion during a fairy battle with nothing else on your mind but a getting a good view.

I instead had to step outside. It was blacker than night, and even the night would be passing soon—it was 3:30 in the morn-ing, and power and cell signals were dead. I was not tired or sore anymore, I was not thirsty, my pack seemed light. It was part of me, I was a camel, and it was my hump; I gritted my teeth. My only burden was the sky—it pushed down darkness into a pile on my bumped back.

I walked across soft lawn to the boundary of the Eastward Manor estate, where it overlooked the bay, the world's edge. Here the shadowy lip of the earth met the troubled sky and the dark sea called from beneath—it sent up mists that were invisible until lightning struck, which then reflected in miserable, blurry puffs like giant ghostly beings rising to haunt a graveyard. Waves, abnormally large, crashed in between gusts of noisy, madly swirling wind, as if jealous of the thunder that roared to assert its majesty over all.

The turf ended abruptly, my feet half over the blank edge. I took a quick look with my flashlight downward—after a few feet of exposed tree roots, the drop was angled and sandy enough to scurry down as I had done so many times. With Emma.

I descended.

I remembered the map, and the path, and the location of the tunnels that Thryst had told me, with his finger, to find.

Grandma Dera knew: Mount Misery, Belle Terre, was a tumulus, a big one, and was connected underground with other dark places. Thryst knew, too, all along.

I walked along the bay—it roared; the sky roared louder. The only other sounds were of fire engines or police sirens that seemed small, like children's toys that only mimic the real world, which was at war with real life and death.

I came to place where the tunnel should be. There was nothing but sand and dead beach flotsam where the coastline met the angle of the towering bluff and the bushes that grew there, and of course the doomed trees holding to the eroding earth as their world crashed downward.

This is where I followed Thryst last time, to the dreamscape of fairy hills and to Emma. There was no entrance to that world here, from this world.

Were the tunnels not real?

I looked to the sky; as I did, lightning struck, the light escaped between the cloud armies' arms, and the shapes reminded me of something.

Something white and wonderful: Thryst's stone. I removed it from my pocket. Its pure shine escaped, first spraying across the land near to me and underfoot, then narrowing to focus like a laser to a place in the sand.

I looked there. The ground rose, sand slid away as a mound grew. It returned the Dwarf-stone's rays in a prismed rainbow that wowed my eyes as if they were seeing color for the first time, as if these shades still needed names. It was beautiful.

The mound grew, and then caved in, its rainbow extinguished, as a passage emerged—a hole, an opening in this magic funnel—until it was large enough to see into, and to enter.

I did, returning the stone to my pocket.

The way went upward, as before, but at intersecting tunnels I checked the mapmodelgram, and each time my path was laid out before me: The Dwarf-stone shone its light outward to the glowing cube, touching it with a slender beacon, marking where I—and it—were; its white light split into red, green, and gold where it struck the map.

"Coming, Emma!" I said to the tunnel walls.

At the last turn, the stone and map showed that the purple rainbow of the casket was near to my own emblem of colors: green and gold and red and purest white.

I smelled fresher air and saw a vague glow escaping from what must be the end of the tunnel. The air sought me, and sounds came, as if calling me.

I ran the rest of the way with no concern or weariness.

What a mistake.

CHAPTER 98

Arty

his is Arty; I was trapped.

I ran up the final paces of the tunnel; it was not steep but painfully bright with glare, and my last steps leveled me into an open, white world. The ground was hard, it was of flat stone, the air was cool and fresh, the smell of a May meadow. But I could not see yet, my eyes glazed, blinded in a negative white that I tried to blink away.

Then iron bars slid, metal clasped, doors slammed, gates shut, and as my eyes blinked, I found myself in a cage, like those I'd seen here before—near to the fairy dream mountain in the sky, which is where I was, at its foot.

The sky was white—plain, empty, clear, it hovered as a staggering, unreal, inexplicable well of white. Looking there was a frightening version of being blind. I did not look there.

Raised near to me, in a flawless pyramid, was the last height of the last of the rows of higher and higher, jagged, curved hilltops. This triangle—straight, perfect angles as if drawn by schoolchildren—sat atop a few others that descended below me on the opposite side, all of straight, smooth grey stone. The connected hills below were covered in rich green, and here and there were speckled with bright flowers, despite their ugly shapes.

Although this was a mountain, and the distances were great, I could see everything clearly, as if my eyes had special lenses, or this world itself was shaped and rounded to fit all its features, magically, into a smaller space. Clouds floated all around, above and below, but when they parted. the horizon itself seemed close, and small, as if it were a ring that I could put on my finger.

But I had certainly landed right in it: into a jail in fairy world. I was trapped by black iron bars as thick as Cry's arms, and the tunnel entrance was closed. It had a door of stone made of the very rock of the mountainside and clasped with a silver steel lock.

I looked at the map. My red-green-gold was near to the purple rainbow—the box that I thought Emma had. It never occurred to me that someone else had it—like the Old Woman of the—*this*—Mountain, and I was leading myself directly to our great enemy.

Suddenly, I was struck and fell to the hard ground. The sounds and colors on the air that had called me from the tunnel were now all around—they were the words and spells of the Gwyllion, and they grew louder as I cowered, my face to the stone.

I heard words, and thoughts came to my mind that confused me because, unlike anything else in my world, they made sense. I looked up but was snowblinded by the pure light and fairy airs.

Just as suddenly as I had been knocked to the ground, the spell stopped, and I saw clearly my surroundings. Dirty, ugly creatures fenced my cage, but the larger force was gone, and the words with it. All around—the mountainsides, the hills, the sky, the distant waters—were in motion: thousands of living things were flying, or marching, or crawling, all toward a large flat plain beneath me, jutting from the mountain. It looked familiar: I had seen it in Thryst's eyes, all those years ago, on Wednesday, my first eyeventure.

The battle would be there.

But I didn't see any Dwarves. I was as alone as is possible.

There was a crack like lightning, and I was stung with a sharp pain in my right leg. I cried out, and my thigh bled through a rip in my jeans. Tears came to my eyes, and anger rose up into my throat, choking me. There was another crack—above my head. It was a whip.

Its many black tails fell to the ground and retreated to the ugly, Orc-like monster who held it.

The other creatures outside my cell were taunting me. I backed away, thinking that I had a lot of data but no weapons. Through all my adventures it never occurred to me to be armed.

I thought of Cry and Ted and their fantasy and video games as I moved into a far corner to avoid my attackers.

I tried to be brave; I thought of Emma and why I was here. The largest of the creatures—I did not want to look at them but saw that this fairy was about three feet tall, had a large, reddish head, ugly grey thick hair, and otherwise was gangly and rotten like an unwanted vegetable lying in a field—was spitting words at me. I tried to understand them, to picture them in English letters, to search for them in my memory of counter-spells to perhaps fight back. I cowered in the corner as bravely as I could—not crying and calling for my mom was as far as I got. My hands trembled, and a thrown stone knocked the phone out of my hand, another hit my lower lip, and I screamed back at them.

My scream was not heard—a larger, more potent voice had shrieked at the same time and it still echoed beneath and throughout the world. More armies of folkie bad guys moved then, coming out of holes in the mountains, and rising from the depths below. And my taunting captors also left me.

Then I saw Emma.

And I heard Mary. Not heard, *felt*. No, not felt, *sensed*. I knew she was near, or coming, or had her own spells that were doing battle in this valley—her will, and other spirits that were clean and clear like melting snow in rays of the sun—were opposing the will of the specters of the mountain. I sensed Sprugly the Spriggan; it felt familiar and good. The air was thick with the strength of Dwarf armies, the mystical motions of Elves, the magic of wizards and witches, and others who were part of legends and lands and had friends to rescue, and a future to save.

Just as I was here to save Emma. Would she let me? Was there a spell for best friends turned bad?

She was with other children our age, coming up one of the green hills, almost directly below, a hundred yards away. I vaguely recognized some of the kids from school. Ahead and behind them walked and flew more of the type of nasty things that had stood outside my cage.

Was Emma now a leader, promoted by the Old Woman? Were these other kids her troops, or captives? This was worse than the two Teds, since those weren't all that different.

I yelled to her. The wind picked up my voice and carried it to her. She looked up but did not respond.

I yelled to her to stop. *To go back home. To be careful. To beware. To escape.*

She marched on.

To help me?

She marched on.

To capture me?

I read spells from my phone and started reciting—screaming—every word of everything I had, until my voice rasped with weariness and was weakened with tears.

Sore, my lower lip blubbered; my leg throbbed from the whip's slash, it bled cold into my jeans. I grabbed the iron bars and, on tiptoes, watched as Emma's troupe traveled along a ridge directly below me; their path headed directly to the battle plain.

"Emma?" I yelled once more. It died against the wind. "Emma!!" It disappeared among other screams coming from above, and in response to those, the evil fairy armies all cried aloud at once. They were following orders.

"Emma…" I said as I slid down to my knees on the stone. Clouds settled around me.

"Emma, I am sorry…" I said weakly, hoping a benevolent wind would deliver it. There was none.

Emma and I—and so many others—were in the battle, because of me. We shouldn't have been. It had all gone wrong. I regretted the whole thing.

I give up. I said to the mist. I don't think I had ever spoken these words before, but I thought of the changes in Emma that I saw in Olivia's room, and I was sadder than this fairy mountain was high.

Then, for no other reason but to fuel my regret, my soul lightened then lit, aflame, and my mind echoed with remembered words so that my voice cried out, "*Thantan namka! Thantan namka ung fonsha ta thann!!*" I don't know why; I suppose it was all I had left, like throwing up your own stomach acid. Gross. I was now empty of words.

The mountain shook. I stood, gazed about, but then looked down to the path. Emma was looking up at me. She had stopped. The other kids stopped behind her, but now the enemy creatures were pushing her along. Lightning struck, near to them, and the group went into a frenzy.

Voices came, came on the wind—a sweet-smelling wind that cleared my senses. They spoke words similar to mine, the ones I had recalled from Thryst's incantation in Olivia's room when the Gwyllion came. The ones buried inside me. They came back in a stronger voice on that wind.

Aha!

My memory was charged like the electricity now bolting all around the battle plain—where war had begun. The mixed spells in my ears assembled in my mind, there was something familiar…

I searched my phone and found…

I did not hesitate and screamed in a voice backed by mountain echoes, magical winds, and all worlds of goodness:

> *Ta me ar cheann an omos rinneadh a bheith ann!*
> *Sula raibh si, ar rugadh do, defhas me suas agus sean,*
> *agus bhi se thar na i ghloir a bhi liom!*

With the fire of battle below, the land and sky trembling as curses collided and fairy heaven erupted, my words were a small thing—but they floated like a feather among the smoke, noise, and cloudy glow and hit the mark. As my cage bars rattled, crumpled, and bent, I held on and watched as Emma broke away, back along the path, fighting past the folkies that surrounded her. The other kids followed. The creatures were confused and did not know whether to stop the kids or to follow orders and join the war ahead of them.

What is she doing?

She looked up at me and then staggered: The world shook all around, the mountain weakened. A dislodged angle of stone finished off the cage—I snuck between bent bars just in time and was free…

…for about three seconds before everything went black.

CHAPTER 99

Emma!

Yes, it is normal Emma, who understands what was going. I didn't then.

At the Mountain, on the pass beneath Arty, I was with other kids who had followed me as I followed the Old Woman of the Mountain, helping her schemes and believing her promises.

Arty's last counter-spell saved me. The Thryst-words he remembered were also powerful; they punched the Gwyllion in her rotten core. But she was very strong and grew with each fairy she hypnotized with visions of their own heaven, even though they were lies. I could not see Arty now—he had been knocked flat by falling rocks from the mountaintop; my heart broke for him. I had to get to him, though I could see no path upward. My friends and I backed into an opening in the pass that cut into the mountainside—we needed to hide from the avalanching world above. We were safe, but many of the fairy creatures around me were being struck and killed, knocked down and off the cliff that bordered the pass.

Then the Troll came. It was a like a walking boulder, at home among sliding stones that seemed at his command. The opening was too small for him to get at us, but he let loose some hex that caused our space to shrink from the inside: the mountain was squeezing us. The noise was awful, as if the whole mass of rock was reshaping itself, millions of years of seismic shift concentrated into a few awful seconds.

I noticed, for the first time, that I was carrying something, under my shirt and pressed tight with my forearm; I took it out and shielded my eyes from the banded bluish gleam coming from this box. I had no idea what it was, but it seemed to anger the Troll, so I threw it at the beast. He kicked it away from him, and its light was gone.

I yelled for Arty; I don't know why. We all did, the others joining my pathetic screams.

We were answered by more rumbling. I stood closest to the opening, to the mountain Troll, and it eyed me with an evil that froze everything but my eyes. I looked around wildly; there was nothing I could do except run at the Troll and try to fight it.

I pictured it stomping on me with its huge foot, like being trapped under a hill, and then it picking me up, crushing me in its grip, and simply tossing me over the cliff edge and into the valley below. But I could not think of anything else to do. Sunrise—which would stun the Troll to stone as even I knew—would not be here in time, even if it could reach this high.

I closed my eyes to release myself from its cold, paralyzing stare and ran out of the colliding crack.

I ran and hit...nothing. I fell forward because I had expected impact against the Troll's tonnage or to be stepped on as I'd imagined.

I opened my eyes to a sudden jolting noise, loud and awful like a car crash, and the ground split all around me.

Looking up, I saw a massive ankle—greenish flesh and its giant, rounded bone-end. Above that a bent knee in torn pants, then a crusty elbow the size of a beanbag chair, then far above, at the mountain plateau of Arty's cage, a hairy chin within, impossibly, a colorful scarf.

This Giant had stepped on the stone Troll, renting the mountain pass into cracks and crags. The Troll struggled to free itself with wild power and an awful, throaty roar—but he could not do anything but knock a few of the other enemy fairies into the abyss.

Then the Giant picked up the Troll, crushing it in a tight, bulging fist, and simply tossed it over the cliff edge and into the valley below. Neat.

That same hand lowered, palm open, then the other hand joined to cup me and my friends. We were lifted to the plateau above.

As we rose, I saw a strange sight below, and I squinted to be sure…Could it be? Thryst! His Dwarf-shape was moving skillfully over the pocked ground, and he made his way along the path but away from the battle plain where we had been headed. His arm shone purple; he had picked up the box I had thrown at the Troll, and he ran with it through the mist, the light now a fuzzy dot moving away and soon disappearing down a new fissure in the broken mountain's side. I yelled the Dwarf's magnificent name, but, just like when I was walking the beach alone in my daze, strangely he did not answer.

At the flat space, we stepped off the Giant's hands. Then the massive body shrunk and newly sprouted short, fat wings began to buzz at its sides. Its chunky legs now straddled the cliff edge and climbed up and continued to change appearance and diminish in size. Once it was four feet tall, the ugly thing jumpflew away, back to the battle plain, in my scarf.

"Thanks again, Sprug!" I yelled.

This roused Arty. I cried when I saw him: his leg was stained brown and wet with blood, his lips were bruised and swollen, he was scraped and scratched through his torn shirt. Sitting up, he rubbed the back of his head and whimpered.

"Emma," he whispered.

"I am here, Arty. Are you OK?" Each syllable came through sad gasps. I was sobbing.

"Can we go home?" he asked.

How? I wondered to myself as I nodded. I had no idea where we were, or how I got here, or how he got here. I looked around, seeing the battle plain and the raging and ravaging of the fairy war. There were voices chanting in the winds, much magic, but also armies and smoke and weapons that were very real.

Arty pointed at the stone tunnel gate with the silver lock. There was no keyhole. I pulled at it, I had everyone bang on it with the largest stones we could lift, but it only sparked.

I returned to Arty; he was recovering. I picked up a stone near him, then dropped it in horror—it was red with blood. Arty grabbed his lower lip in a recoiling reflex with pain remembered and still real.

But then his eyes lit up with a fire like the furnaces of the Dwarves. He smiled—though it was stretched with suffering—while reaching into his pocket. He pulled out a stone of his own.

Rising to his feet, he hunched and stumbled to the tunnel door. The stone he held gleamed brightly, its pure glow was white as wool and much more commanding than the ghoulish mists and grey stone of the mountain, and when it neared the lock, a beam of gold transformed the silver of the lock to red and green—and it clicked open.

Black smoke mushroomed up from the battle, the air grew dark, the mountain continued to slide and change. We helped Arty into the tunnel and followed him single file.

The *stoneroad* paths had shifted, and Arty used the magic map-modelgram at times. Of all the fears of the past few days, for me this was the worst: being underground as the earth moved and its roots shifted, petrified of being buried alive, stumbling ahead in the loathsome dark with the sounds of crashing and crushing all around, falling over and tasting dirt and breathing in thicker and thicker air in a claustrophobic nightmare, while having no idea when the road would end, or who would be mastering the world above when it did.

I noticed on the map's lighted pages that we were the gold/green/red spot—Arty had explained that Thryst's stone and the symbol showed Eastward Manor. I also saw that the purple rainbow, the casket, had its own signal—but we were leaving it farther and farther behind.

I told Arty that Thryst had picked it up, and how I had watched the Dwarf head away from the battle. Arty nodded and told how Thryst was going his own way and would help no one else. This made me sad.

I followed quietly. The tunnel arched to keep its course. Everyone remained silent. All wonder peaked. As with the ground, the sea, and the sky, inside each of us were forces tangled in indescribable struggle.

The end was near.

CHAPTER 100

Mary

Some can picture the battle in their mind's eye, or in others' eyes, or by using magic to help them see. For the rest, I can tell them what I know.

The Old Woman of the Mountains, a Gwyllion of great and strange powers, made herself stronger by taking one of each kind of fairy: to start a new kingdom in heaven, to steal the ancient place of rest, and to make new creatures and rule over all them and their world. And then, perhaps, ours.

More folktale legends joined the war, and on both sides. Some came to rescue their friends from the foul Gwyllion and her armies of Wights, Trolls, and dark spirits.

All who fight have their own special energies and enchanted abilities; some humans believe in them, most do not. But that does not always matter.

Now the battle rages, using nature, and the earth, and the sky.

In and out of the fight, many struggle to find their way back to Eastward Manor, knowing it as the path home. Some captives that can escape the Old Woman seek and find children and hide. This is a strange occurrence, the strangest of the whole story, for me. The fairies' connection to these young people, all friends, can only be guessed, and is personal, so should not be guessed.

All the rest, of the living fairy creatures, struggle in the War. The dead only the earth can help.

To conquer the Gwyllion, I will use the spells, and counter-spells, and the ancient symbols that secretly kept the story alive for hundreds of years, waiting for this part of the tale. They complete a mystical alchemy of words and magic. I am here, I was born to be here, to help the armies of folkies, as Arty and Emma and the adopted human children call them: the Spriggans and the Dwarves and the Elves, with any birds and trees who have taken sides.

It was those human children that the Gwyllion did not count on. When Arty sent the counters-spell out to his friends of friends, as he says, the words were read, and spoken out loud, and contemplated. And passed to others, to friends, and to friends of friends, along and along. That is turning the tide—help unlooked for!

And Ted doesn't know it yet, but our side has a dragon. My dragon.

CHAPTER 101

Emma

Still underground, Arty was in bad shape, exhausted. We tried to carry him when the going was easy, but at every dead end, or intersection, or when the path threatened to cave in on us, we needed him, and the map, and the stone.

Until all at once, every heart lifted; a light air was around us, a sweet breeze on the air, a soft breath on the breeze, a pure voice on the breath, and a quiet song on the voice.

We came out of the tunnel and onto the beach where the water gleamed calmly and the surf continued the hushed song. Above was a clean, argent moon showing a sideways, crescent smile.

The war had been won.

Arty could not climb the bluff, so we walked along the sand. At a turn, once the shadow of the cliffs bent away, I saw, faint but clear, the yellow of dawn in the east. Each of the friends turned for home when the right way came to them.

So did Arty and I.

My home was not the same—it was better. I climbed into bed with my mom, and she hugged me like in the old days, sleeping and hugging at the same time as only a mom can do.

CHAPTER 102

Emma

he next morning, I woke up late. There was note from my mom: she did not want to wake me, but there was a nice breakfast, half at the table and half in the fridge, and a nice promise to go shopping later today—not what tomorrow is for!—and then get dinner, just us girls.

OK!

No mention of the Faery Realm apocalypse, so that was good. Even evil Gwyllions and black-hearted Troll armies were good at hiding from adults.

Magic was weird.

But: I checked messages, and Cry and Ted were meeting at Arty's house at noon—in twenty minutes! Everyone was up and waiting for me. It was sunny and warm. It was Sunday! Everyone was waiting for me. The war was over!

I hustled. I called and texted but did not hear back from Arty.

Not surprising...but was he OK? In the hospital? In fairy prison?

I put the local news on TV, which showed only excited versions of the traffic and weather—and weather damage—reports. I expected video footage of "The Fairy War—Live!—From The Dreamy Mountain Top"...but there was nothing like that.

There were, however, plenty of clues if you knew how to look and were an expert adventurer like me. The busy police and fire department reported much strange vandalism: holes dug, windows broken, an abandoned quad vehicle, lawns ripped up with tire tracks, footprints of strange animals imprinted all around the town and village. Odd, unidentified screams and howls, and large birds crashing through trees…

Then I knew for sure that Wednesday-Through-Saturday was not a dream.

I shut off the TV, dressed, brushed some things, relieved some others, and left.

Outside: was a giant sprugmess, like the whole neighborhood had spent a night with a Spriggan and a hurricane. Trees and telephone poles and road signs and mailboxes looked like they had been dropped from the sky—though some seemed to rather have switched places and uses. People were looking here and there with a mixture of relief, fright, and amazement and pointing at things you don't see every day, for example an upside-down tree, or a hole where there was no hole yesterday. Quite a Sunday. Though: I checked and noticed that the U.S. Army wasn't maneuvering; in fact, they weren't even here. And no one was carrying away Pixies in a box or picking up mini-Troll corpses with a stick.

My mood shifted with a shudder. A shadow fell over me that not even the brilliant overhead sun could turn away. But I promised not to think about those things, and the bad things I did, and the worse things I almost did, until I could apologize to my old and new friends and see that everyone was OK. And meet Mary.

Just then I felt a tug of the hair near my right ear, and Sprugly whispered, laughed, in my ear—the shadow passed.

I really missed him. "Where have you been? Don't do that to me! I was worried sick," I said, just as moms do, and he answered:

"The war is over," in another raspy whisper, adding happily, "You did good!"

I could never get tired of him telling me that. With a chill up my spine, I half-ran to Arty's.

From the bottom of his driveway, through the sun-blasted glare, I could see Ted's standing shape and Cry's larger shape with him—next to each other they looked like a lower-case p. I was tired and had to drag myself up the hill, having time to notice sadly that the beautiful Dwarfen stonework was covered up and gone, and no statues remained.

Cry and Ted came down to me, the bigger one struggling to control his speed, and the smaller of them laughing about it. *Boys*, I thought, *will be boys.* I was proud that they did not change even after adventures and spells. Cry was only more Cry, and Ted just more Teddish.

Arty wasn't home, Gretel had told them; he had gone out an hour or so before. Gretel also told the boys that she *vanted to talkink with Emma*—but we all agreed that this was not a good idea—and with this news I hurried away, out of sight of my friend's house.

"I wonder where he is?" I worried aloud as I followed the boys—we decided to go to Eastward Manor.

"He is probably fine," Cry offered, and I accepted. "Everything seems OK and over now."

"We could find him if we had the map thing," Ted said. "Arty needs to stop hogging it."

But I wondered about Thryst…Things wouldn't be "OK and over" for Arty until Thryst said so.

After twenty more minutes of Ted and Cry walk-talk—mostly about their latest ideas for conquest and moneymaking in a new mobile app game they were going to create—they pointed ahead for me, to the sign for Eastward Manor, a place I had never been.

"It's awesome," Cry said with glassy eyes and satisfaction, as if that was a detailed description.

We walked uphill along a shortcut side-path until I saw a large, shiny pile of fresh-smelling dirt that covered part of the circular driveway of Zyxvuts' big, beautiful, timeless house—and there were engraved stone signs near the mound, like those that had been at the head of Thryst's tunnel at Arty's. And, like there, the dirt angled into a hole, and exposed roots led into a black tunnel.

Cool. A Sidhe-mound and connecting road.

The man in brown called our names from the doorway.

CHAPTER 103

Ted

"Everyone around me is so lucky."

—Ted

 took over as leader since Arty wasn't there, and since him and I were the co-leaders of the whole adventure, I had to take over. They were lucky I was there—just like my chapter quote says.

Cry followed Emma and me. We wandered around Eastward Manor to check out all the different folkie things that were there. In every room of the mansion, and even outside hidden in trees and bushes and holes, there were fairies moving around and doing weird things. They liked to steal things and hide them, they liked to dress in strange clothes, they liked to sneak up on you, they liked to sing stupid songs. Some just sat. Most were useless, some were cool, none were a dragon.

My dreams were way better. They weren't *all* spells.

We didn't see Thryst, but Peanut and Sprugly would fly by every now and then and drop dirty tissues on us.

"She is feeling better," Cry said.

"Who cares?" I said with strength.

Emma wanted to meet Mary, so I made it happen. We all waited for her in the big kitchen. We were at a big square wooden counter, and over our heads were kitchen things hanging—pots and pans and more pots. Small, green, Elvish beings were up there climbing around and making a lot of noise. I stayed close to save Emma in case a pot fell. And then a pot fell. I blocked it so it hit Cry in the face. We had a lot of fun.

Mary came in. She spent a minute talking to us as a long hello. Cry said I was blushing, but he should not talk, since he started blubbering and had to pull out his stupid tissue case.

Mary's long, straight, blonde hair was hanging down long all around her; the bangs in front, they curled like the small waves on the bay beach, almost connecting to her eyelashes. She wore a few ribbons here or there, and she stood tall and like a royal princess. Her long, complicated dress did not seem weird or out of place.

I noticed that Emma was now wiping down her jeans and straightening her shirt and pulling at her own hair. Ha! Girls: they all want attention.

So now, after the battles and everything were over and things could get back to normal—better, but normal—Cry and I had things we wanted to do, and we talked about that.

I said, "You ever see those animal shows? I like that one where millions of ants gang up and kill bigger animals. They eat the eyes out of squirrels and raccoons to start, they hang on when the animals tries to run, but it crashes into things, so they keep ganging up. Good for them! Right?"

But no one got my point. I didn't care.

Emma gave me a mean look, but Abcedarius interrupted it. "Ted, you should know that Mary has a dragon."

"I love her," Cry said.

"Why would you reward him and tell him that?" Emma asked Zyxvuts.

"I have my reasons, Emma," he answered.

So, ha. And I could use a dragon in my future plans. I was thinking that I might let Mary help me. I would follow her later and ask her.

Cry said to me, "Mary is special, too, like she lives in both worlds. She makes us feel special, too, right?"

I nodded and asked Zyxvuts about where she lived. "Around here?"

"She is special, right?" he started to answer—

CHAPTER 104

Emma

OK, that's enough, I will take over the writing duties from here, before Cry writes a love song and Ted and Zyxvuts sing backup.

While the boys were drooling over Mary, who is kinda pretty, I guess, in an old-fashioned way, I asked her to explain some things that I needed catching up on.

Mary was happy to, she said, and spoke to us as she stood tall and regal, as if reciting from one of her own letters, with her hands palm-to-palm and the lace from her sleeves drooping in front of her.

"After many battles," she began, "the war is won: the War for the Beltaerne gateway, within the Beautiful Land. The Gwyllion's plans, continued from many years ago, to abduct many individual spirits, then rule and populate the fairy haven here, in their farthest west, and spoil the May Day equinox with her own corrupt necromancies, has been won. And the Old Woman of the Mountains, in her most devilish manifestation, has gone."

Cry applauded softly for as long as it took him to realize that no one else was.

Mary laughed, thanked him, and went on. "This place can revitalize to what it was, and return to whom it belongs, to the special creatures, their place of restoration restored!

"As in the age-old story, the Gwyllion's own devices were used against her—not only the spells and symbols, long known to human helpers, and my own family, and not only the Sidhe-mounds and tunnels—but also her tactic of kidnapping of souls. That only led us to each other. She shortly missed with Ted, almost had him, and others, and it turned to our good and helped our helpers, like Trudy and Abcedarius. Each helped each, every type realized, and every role was played, and all helped all."

Except for me, I thought, and I hoped it was unfair to think so, but I didn't want to ask. Ted actually helped Abcedarius, and Ted's spell was reversed before he did any real harm. Mine wasn't, and I did. I helped the Gwyllion, until Arty helped me, and who knows how bad it would have been for me, and the fairies, if he hadn't.

My face must have showed a printout of my thoughts, since I looked up to see Mary reading me.

"Everything happened for its reason, and sometimes it takes a long time for the full story to be realized," she said before looking again at the others gathered. "But for now," she went on, "the prison on the top of the Great Tumulus was cast down. The ways are free again. The worlds between us all, the roads and the understanding, the places of space and mind to be shared, can all be rebuilt. Whether they will or not is up to those who carry on."

Mary left the room, lastly saying that there was still a lot to do for today.

I left my self-pitying funk behind because I noticed that none of the "a lot to do" had anything to do with Arty. No one knew where he was or was worried.

And Thryst—*where was he?*

"Who knows?" Ted answered. "For a warrior Dwarf, the guy really moves around a lot."

"Even goes to school, where I met him!" Cry said.

"He was probably looking for Mrs. Burns, the librarian," Ted said as I tried to shush them both. "She is short and mean and has a beard."

I threw a pen at Ted's head, retrieved it, then threw it at his stomach. However, the Mrs. Burns crack reminded me of something Arty had told me—that, in fact, Thryst had almost approached one of the teachers. That thought bothered me and crawled ickily out from the dirt in my mind, but I didn't know why, so I quickly kicked rocks back over the thought and stood on it.

Zyxvuts said he did not know where our Dwarf was either, but they had been very busy with "what will happen next" and there were so many fairies to take care of—as anyone could see who walked around the place.

He was dressed this morning in all new, same brown. "And this is my wife Trudy," he said as they led me to a tufted chair nearest the large fireplace in the antique living room, where a small fire popped; its flames seemed shy but happy.

Mrs. Zyxvuts was nothing like old Abcedarius—she was nice and friendly and pretty and smiled at us. No offense to her husband, but I would rather talk to her; she cheered me up.

I asked about their house, and she explained.

"My relatives were spooked by the place over the years. Things happened that they could not explain: noises in the moonlight, stolen articles, voices among the trees. But we knew, Abcedarius and I, we knew enough, though not everything. We knew that nearby was a great Tumulus—we always laughed at how people could live on "Mount Misery" and not wonder about it! And we knew that this house sat near a fairy mound, a Sidhe-mound, of the *Aos Sí*: that was a matter of confirming some local legends and some old maps that showed geological connections, like one near Arty's house. Though it was mostly guesswork until the map came to my husband, piece by piece."

I smiled at the mention of Arty's house, the beginning of so much of our adventure, and Zyxvuts smiled lovingly at his wife, proud of his own part.

"We did *not* know," Trudy continued, "that Mary lived, and, it goes without saying, we didn't know that Eastward Manor—the land—was a fairy portal and the center of so much trouble. We followed the clues given to us, but…"

"But," Abcedarius jumped in, "I was hoping to see a dragon, not a Gwyllion."

Ha! *Boys: they all want dragons.*

Trudy said I should rest; they told me to wait for Arty here, that he would come eventually. "As everyone does!" she said, opening her arms to the bay window, where people—like me—who knew where to look would see magic everywhere. I took out my sketchpad and started to draw. The house was amazing; the scene—fairies dancing, songs coming from the treetops, the living magic show circus—was fantastical.

After an hour, watching humans and non-humans flit around me, I grew worried. No one was asking about Arty, or Thryst; they were all busy with "what to do next," which they winked and hinted about, but no one said specifically what was being planned. Unless you counted Ted's gag-reflex dream to recapture Mary's dragon for her—it and the Gwyllion had vanished together in the battle, I was told. I did not understand this but put it out of my head for two reasons: *one,* because anything that came from Ted was not welcome in my head; and *two,* there was too much of the Old Woman of the Mountains in my head already.

As for Cry, he was very impressed and proud of being the expert on sword-and-sorcery fantasy games, books, movies, and now, reality. He had an idea for the first reality TV show based purely on fantasy. I drew a big, cheeky frown on my pad and showed it to him.

I was soon to learn that Cry's starring cast was disappearing fast…

CHAPTER 105

Emma

But wait!

"Where have you been?" I ran outside through East-ward Manor's dignified front door after seeing Arty climb out of the Dwarf-hole, covered in bronze dirt.

"In this tunnel," he answered.

"I see that. Why? Are you OK? Where have you been all day?"

"In this tunnel," he said.

My friend looked...*older*? Beaten? Lost? Hurt? Changed? Stiff? Older?

He spoke again after sucking two lungs full of fresh air. "I am OK—just tired. I woke up with my cuts healed but not the bruises or the headache. I got up and went looking for Thryst. Is he here?"

"No one has seen him. I sat in that room," I said, pointing toward the bay window, now blasting reflected afternoon sunlight at us, "and kept asking about you, and Thryst, but everyone is pretty busy."

"I know. And I know the feeling..."

"A lot of fairies are here, but the war is over, and—"

Arty interrupted. "I know. But this is not over for me. I have the solunarmapmodelgram—it shows everything. I saw what happened. But I still can't figure out Thryst."

Arty and I found a brick patio nearby, with chairs made of curvy, black iron that were surprisingly comfortable. He warmed his face with the sun and told me about the morning he spent in the tunnels.

The one he came out of interconnected with his house, near where the Sidhe-mound was in his yard, and it also had ends at other places around Belle Terre and the village. Important places, as the maps showed with special symbols and blended colors. The passages were old, but Thryst knew where to dig down to get to them—like Arty's basement and front yard, and here at Eastward Manor.

"They connect fairy mounds, Sidhe-mounds," I said, happy to contribute.

Arty smiled. "The *Aos si*, right? So many obvious clues that I missed! We heard that phrase a lot!"

Then he continued his tale. Since my black spell, and until now, Arty had tracked Thryst's movements, their history on the time-capturing map—above and below ground, he went, and all over, and his course made no sense. The warrior Dwarf had not rescued any fairies, had not been in the last battle, did not seem to help anyone or do anything for long, except search.

The war was over, yet he still searched.

Arty knew about the mountain fight—he'd watched it on rewind in a hologram on the map. Depending on the light, and how he used his fingers, he could play it like a virtual reality game. He saw Mary's moves, all around this world and the other.

He saw the Gwyllion—as an old lady, but huge, a witch, her voice making sounds of many women talking at once.

"I know all about her," I said sadly.

Arty apologized, looking at me. "Sorry."

He changed the subject, his face returning to the rays of the sun. "I saw back when Abcedarius was putting the map together, piece by piece. And the hologram on the map showed the map, and showed the holograms on the map, which showed itself again, and itself—like parallel mirrors, into infinity. I saw Mary using it to plan the battle, I watched her use the spells, and I saw both armies. I saw folkies disappearing, I saw the other kids that were captured, caught in evil spells, with you."

"Folkies disappearing? Dead?" I asked.

"I don't know—just gone."

"They said that the—Old Woman—disappeared with Mary's dragon. I don't get that."

"Yes, it ended like that, pretty much," he went on. "I saw us, in the past, doing everything—finding the books, running from Ted, the first battle. I could go back further, but I just kept looking for Thryst. He is here now, somewhere, sitting still, like he is giving up." Arty's head sank, his face in shadow.

"I'm sorry you can't help him. Let's go talk to him."

"I've tried. I can't. I couldn't. I can't."

"Well, we have plenty of time now!" I moved closer to smile right at him. "We can figure it out."

"No," he said. A wild look came over his eyes, and sad panic tightened his throat, so that his words came out muffled. "Thryst disappears, too! According to the map. It shows 'small paths, shifting, and fuzzy, but beyond the current time' or however Abcedarius said it. That is how I knew you were here. It shows the future. I saw enough of it. The map never lies," he paused, thankfully. The tears then came.

Then Arty stiffened and simply stared. Then almost smiled.

I wondered at his trance. *It is not a spell*, which I am kind of an expert in. *What combination of confused, or sad, or exhausted, or crazy is he?* I thought.

"His triangle disappears..." Arty mumbled.

Crazy, 90%, I thought.

I did not know how to reply so just followed him into the house. He limped a little and was hunched as if still in the caves and weighed down with Dwarf tools.

Inside, Arty showed Trudy and Abcedarius how to control the map to look into the past, and to where the past ends. And past the past...

"On the map, and in life, the past is certain. But the future we are shown is not perfect—it depends on the light and the heart of the viewer," Mary said.

Arty answered nothing.

To continue they needed sunrays, so they sat for a time in the solarium, a large greenhouse attached to the westernmost part of the house that was an ocean of light and heat. I went back to the fireplace to think.

Soon Arty rejoined me. He slumped in one of the bumpy chairs, moved his eyes slowly everywhere, but did not speak.

CHAPTER 106

Many Pairings

his is Emma, and as I write this, I am in the kind of mood that deserves a chapter title. Somber. Sad, like the ends of stories always are for me, no matter how happy they are supposed to be.

The others, one by one, found their way back to us. Arty and I were still at the large fireplace as afternoon peeked in from the big windows, the sunlight making their shapes reach across and brighten the room.

"What happens now?" Ted asked to the silent room, though he only looked at Mary.

"Your 'folkies' will go back to their world, as they will, and as they wish," Mary answered.

"That's it?" I complained.

Ted continued, orbiting Mary—his sun—his speech excited, his words pulling toward her. "I mean, can I keep one? And not that Nasty one, I mean, can I see the dragon, and maybe…I don't know. I guess they should go home, but…I think I want…I guess…it would be great if…" His talk, like a frightened goose, could not decide whether to run or fly and got stuck in between.

"I know, Ted," laughed Mary, "but let's see what happens."

Ted, shining like a poet in Paris, forced a smile on Mary, with all the grace of a cafeteria spitball.

"Will they go back to England? Or some other world?" asked Cry, shining also but more like a baby polar bear at noon.

OK: just assume the boys were *smiling-shining* whenever Mary paid attention to them—my last invented word of the adventure.

Mary explained that, yes, they would go back to their homes, both in our world, and theirs.

Ted asked, "All of them?"

"YES," Arty answered with enough sternmore force to clamp Ted's mouth shut.

Over the next few hours, so many fairies came and went that I stopped trying to keep track. My fairy—good old Sprugly—was here. He was one of the Rescuers and paid special attention to those that had been kidnapped by you-know-who.

Arty awaited the end—his belief that his Dwarf, *Thryst the Mysterious*, would soon be gone, and all mystery and adventure with him.

For one example: Mary, with Olivia's Silky in her hands, led the way to a small foyer at the back door where Little Nasty was, hissing at Ted as we came in. The Silky leapt toward Nasty, and, well, there is no other way to explain it other than to say that they vanished. There was no smoke, no mist, nothing spun, nothing rhymed, nothing changed colors, there was no lighting and no thunder, no music, and no speeches. As a matter of fact, it seemed to happen while the two fairies were in the middle of speaking. They first made a few chirping noises to each other and then started to speak when they were—*poof*—just gone. There was nothing to draw.

"Rescuer Brings Kidnappee Back Home" would be the title of a blank canvas.

CHAPTER 107

Arty

As I looked all around from my chair, I should have had a thousand things going through my disorganized mind, I should have been going nuts trying to keep up and to track it all. But instead it was simple: I waited for the end and had no thoughts after that. No plan. I didn't care about the future; I had no use for a magical map.

And there, at Eastward Manor, it was *The End*. Abcedarius, Trudy, Mary, and everyone observed hundreds of fairies haunting dozens of rooms, and wandering the outside spaces of their portal, only to then gather and leave it. Usually in pairs.

"Like socks," Cry said and then explained that socks also were paired and sometimes disappeared. Ted and Emma stopped him from giving any more of this comparison.

I sat alone and sad, and uninterested. Unlike Emma, who was all over the place.

CHAPTER 108

Emma

Ⲩou can call this chapter "Emma Figures Things Out."

Poor Arty. Although the fairy masquerade ball was sad and fascinating—a folk dance where each chooses a partner, then disappears from the world to the music of our *ooohs* and *aaaahs*—I returned sometimes to watch my forlorn friend instead. Sprugly the Spriggan—small, his job done—sat on my shoulder after placing Peanut in a large white vase on a nearby table. Her squeaks echoed until replaced by the small, clicking whistles of Pixie snores.

I wandered the house. Wherever Mary was, usually Cry and Ted followed. Seeing me, they unanimously asked if Mary could judge the bet: to pick, out of everyone's guesses, whose was closest to telling "why" this all had happened. I agreed and dug for the envelope of guesses in my bag but couldn't find it. I realized that I must have dropped it last night on the beach, after falling with my apple, seeing Thryst while going in and out of my daze. So much to remember, so much to forget.

"Do you know where Thryst is, Mary?" I asked. "Arty thinks he was supposed to be here somewhere."

Leaning in, she whispered to me, Sprug-like, "Yes. He just arrived, I am told. He is in the cupola gallery."

Something in Mary's manner always made you trust that things were part of some plan that was going well. "Oh. OK," I whispered. "Can I ask something else?"

She nodded.

"What is a cupola gallery?"

Mary smiled. "The easier question is 'where.' Take those stairs all the way up." She pointed to the corner of the room where we stood, a large dining hall, where spiral steps with a green iron railing went through the high ceiling.

Sprugly flew high ahead of me, and I climbed—through four floors—until I was in a broad hall that ran the width—front to back—of the house. The hall was striking because its walls were paintings: floor-to-ceiling artwork in thick, protruding wooden frames, each piece a different size—some canvases as small as a postcard, some works larger than life. They showed people from long ago, and longer, all dressed in olden garb but from many different periods.

This was the "gallery" part, I figured.

The paintings were aglow in afternoon light that burst from everywhere, since the ceiling here was like Arty's room: it was the roof of the house. Framed in angles of glass whose center rose in a beautifully bright, gently curved dome, all edges glistened with rainbows, many small ones that winked and smiled at me as I passed. So strong was the light of this magical day that a rosy-white hue touched everything; rays crossed the air and lit the pictures into life.

Sprugly jumpflew to the height of the dome, enjoying himself. Shielding my eyes from the glare, I let the outside view take my gaze and breath away. The land stretched away far and wide in a bright green spring that was making up for time lost to the war.

This must be the "cupola" part.

There was only one place for Thryst to hide; at the opposite end of the hall was a closed door. I called his name.

The door opened, and a dirty hood half-covered the dark, grim Dwarfen face that showed itself. Thryst poked his head out, then three dog heads appeared just beneath his.

"Hi Thryst," I tried, slowly, to begin a conversation. "What happened last night? I waved to you at the beach..."

Sprug whispered, though it echoed loud off the glass above, "No. He was with Arty."

Thryst seemed as confused as I was and said, "*Zak ug uatha agzagah gah*," or some such. It sounded like it might be a question; the tone was weak, and nothing shook as he spoke. Almost human it sounded, and vulnerable—not as sure as rocks and not as steady as a waterfall.

He went on, "*Thantan. Thryst. Thantan?*" He had never asked me anything before. There was sadness in his eyes that even a blind person could sense; it filled the air between us. His thick beard trembled. I shook my head to show my loss for words, and from that Thryst could tell I had no answer for him. "*Thryst*," he said again, without a rumble, and he closed the door.

I returned downstairs to the fire. Sprug flew ahead of me and to Arty's shoulder and ear. Arty brightened briefly, then slunk back into his chair, his eyes to the crackling blaze.

I told Arty where Thryst was, and he answered, "I know. But he wants to be alone."

Mary joined us and asked Arty, "The words you used, the spell that rescued Emma, where did you find such? It was not in the *Book of Symbols*."

Arty answered slowly. "I heard all that from Thryst. It almost worked in Olivia's room, and it was all I could think of, I guess. It upset the Gwyllion but didn't help Emma. Before I went back to find her, I looked up those words in the books, but they made no sense. The only thing close was some old 'mothering spell,' so I used that. And it worked."

Ted and Cry walked over in time for Ted to say, "A mothering spell! That would come in handy for faking notes for school. That stupid nurse…"

Mary ignored this, turned from Arty to face me: a silent prompting.

"It makes sense," I said. "The Gwyllion's hex on me, starting in the storm battle, was…like that." I did not want to say more.

"Thryst's words are interesting," Mary said. "*Thrystomos* means 'prince.'"

"What does *Thantan* mean?" I asked, recalling my own memories of the Dwarf's words, and those of a few minutes ago. Arty remained silent.

"Mother," Mary answered.

"So, Thryst was trying to help Emma, too. A Dwarf-mothering anti-counter-spell?" Cry wondered. "Why didn't Sprugly? Everything is too weird and complicated. Games should be simple."

Mary walked away still looking at me, again prompting, as if she wanted me to finish something for her. I returned to my thoughts; I felt as if there was an idea lost in the neighborhood of my brain, a small idea, a stranger in town, and it could not find its way to me.

The boys continued talking. Abcedarius Zyxvuts came and sat at the largest desk; he had brought the mapmodelgram pages and was assembling it.

"I feel bad for Thryst," Cry said, a tissue pack coming from his bulky front pants pocket. "He is not celebrating. He isn't done. But he stayed home from the battle. I wonder why?"

"I should ask him," Ted answered. "He will tell me, we are buddies."

"I saw him on the mountain. When I was trapped. He was below. Near Emma," Arty said quietly, and slowly, eyes toward the fire and nowhere else.

"No," Cry said between sniffles. "He was here, at Eastward Manor, all night, while you were gone."

"Trudy told me that," Ted said, as if bragging. "Wake up, Arty."

My thoughts tried to find that idea; it was still lost and knocking on the wrong doors on the dark streets of my brain.

Thryst was here last night?

And Thryst was with Arty when I dazed along the beach. *You die alone*—that old thought of mine while walking home in and out of the Gwyllion's control.

Thryst was alone.

The casket goes to whom it can serve, Mary had told the others while I was missing.

Thantan, Thrystomos. Mother, prince.
Rescuers, and Battlers, and Kidnappees. And Spells.

These thoughts were falling like breadcrumbs to lead the lost idea home, to me. I waited impatiently for its arrival. I wish I could have borrowed Arty's scientific brain—but it was busy doing nothing.

Cry and Ted walked to the desk where Zyxvuts sat with the mapmodelgram. It was fully formed but only sleepily reflected the dim light of the fire in dull points and lines.

I watched the boys run their fingers around it and through it and play with the effects of light from a candle that Ted now held.

"If I were a dragon, where would I be? Come to me! Come to me!" Ted intoned, his hands curling and fingers twisting in a pretend wizard's incantation.

Zyxvuts shook his head, and Cry was laughing. "This would really help with our fantasy games. Can we borrow it, Mr. Zyxvuts?"

"You don't know how to use it, Cry," Ted snapped.

Cry stood up for himself. "Hey, I am the one who told Arty how he could find Emma. The purple thing on the map."

"That was real life," Ted said. "Games are harder."

But I had jolted up with Cry's words—the long-awaited idea had burst through the front door of my mind and wanted to party.

"Arty?" I shouted.

"Arty?" I shouted again.

Then asked, "Zyx—does Thryst have the casket? The box with the fourteen spell book pieces?"

"No…*hmmmm*," the man hummed in his cello-ish voice. "Good question, Emma! Mary does not know where it is either. I had forgotten all about it."

Arty had turned away from the fire and sat at attention. "Last I saw it, you had it, Emma."

The idea had just popped open a bottle of champagne.

"I don't have it," I announced to the room. "But I know who does." My mind was bubbly.

Zyxvuts found the purple rainbow signal on the map. "It is here!" he said, pointing a long, curled finger. "But with whom?"

"Here? Where?" Cry asked.

"Here, here!" Zyxvuts pointed a second finger straight down, meaning that the purple casket was somewhere in the house.

They all looked at me in confusion.

My smile told them that I, finally, understood.

"Go get Thryst," I said. "His search is over."

And I clinked fancy crystal glasses with the idea, which was happy to be in the right home.

CHAPTER 109

Emma

found a Dwarf, thanks to something funny that was growing in Arty's yard. But I don't want to write about that yet. What is more important is that my Dwarf needed to meet Arty's Dwarf *Thryst the Thryst*. Right away.

Mary returned, and she and Zyxvuts helped me use the map—the casket was blinking a blue prism arch that pointed *under* Eastward Manor, not within it. Zyxvuts then led us far below ground where, now we understood, many ancient tunnels came together, as did the past, present and future, as did war and peace, as did legend and reality: the reality of my friends and me on a Sunday.

We went down: down dark, iron stairs past the main basement to a deeper level that opened and ran the whole length and width of the house—almost as one single room. And yet it must have been even big bigger, according to the mapmodelgram that we controlled with lit candles and an orange flashlight Cry had pulled from a bottomless front pocket.

Mary and Abcedarius led through passages and around corners and eventually to another area that was much older, as they explained, and within that to even more ancient rooms—each belonging to older and older foundations of this house—and any other structures built on this site over the centuries, over the history of Eastward Manor, in fact.

With each, the ceiling came a little lower, and the walls were darker, closer, and the air thick as Dwarf tears until we were, of course, at the head of a tunnel.

"I have never seen this before!" Abcedarius said to Trudy first, who shook her head in astonished agreement, then to Mary and the rest of us.

There was fresh dirt all around, and steps leading down to a wide space. From there the path continued very far—the map and lights both showed this. I wondered if we were at sea-level now, and whether this led to the caves at the beach on the bay. There were small circles of light sparking from either side as we gazed ahead. I could hear an echo of water rushing—like an underground river.

"Wild," Cry said, which summed it up well enough.

"Looks familiar," said Arty. "What is this?"

Then, just ahead, caught in the orange of Cry's roaming flashlight, was a Dwarf. We had become fairy experts by now, and I knew the classic Dwarf form, just like *Thryst the Genuine*'s. This was not a warrior—the colors and clothes were lighter—but there wasn't much time for wonder, because things happened fast.

I squeezed past the crowd and back to Thryst, who was following last of all, his hood down. I peeked under it, into his face. "Go?" I said to him. "*Thantan!*" I pointed ahead into the orange glow and the yellow Dwarf silhouette.

CHAPTER 110

Arty

Thryst was face to face with the new Dwarf, who looked hard at him in the dim light that died against the dirt walls. I wasn't sure for a second whether this was friend or foe. I could feel the tension for the second that it took for their eyes to blaze at each other. I knew the force that must be at work; their magic filled the tunnel. Then Thryst turned his head down and fell to his knees. I had never seen him show any weakness before. Sadness, but not this.

What was going on? It seemed like Emma knew, and Mary: they smiled at each other as everyone else only stared.

The new Dwarf spoke—a voice similar to Thryst's, and strong, though more like lava than an avalanche, more like a bass guitar than a drum. The sound mesmerized the others, but what struck me was what this new Dwarf chose to say.

"*Thryst*," the voice said; it was a female voice, still Dwarfish, but with a difference in tone like the difference between stone and earth. The voice was sternmore and deepdownded, but somehow lush, and understanding, alive, and loving. "*Thryst*." Yes, no doubt about it. The voice said "Thryst" to Thryst.

Thryst stayed on his knees and did the oddest thing yet. Here I watched the strangest and most wondrous scene in this whole story: my Dwarf put his arms around the waist of the new Dwarf and hugged.

He looked at Emma, then Mary, then Zyx, then me, with tears in his eyes, yet also gratitude—it was as pure in meaning as anything anyone could say with words. He was thanking us, I had no doubt.

And just then, Thryst and this Dwarf disappeared, together. The black of the receding tunnel met my watery eyes, and I walked away.

CHAPTER 111

Goodbyes and Ends 1

mma here. Once out of the tunnels and the basements, and facing a broad, bold sunset that could out-orange any artificial light, Arty stood stiff with emotion and tall with his own thoughts. I told him what Sprug had told me: that their world was our world. That, like Sprug himself, it was also larger than we thought. These were words of wisdom that had given me the hope that we could all meet again. I did not know, of course, whether we would.

CHAPTER 112

Goodbyes and Ends 2

ed here. Long goodbyes are lame, and short ones aren't worth it. They were such wimps: Emma and Cry crying, they could barely talk, saying goodbye to smelly, ugly, and useless creatures. Sprug whispered something to Emma, and Emma turned and walked away, looking out the big window and staring out over the water and under the sky. She would need me to make her feel better. Then Sprug and Peanut left together. They were there, then they were gone. Nothing special.

So, that was the end of the story. I am happy to end it. Then Arty started blubbering, too…

CHAPTER 113

Goodbyes and Ends 3

 am fine—this is Arty. Ted is right; we are at the end.

CHAPTER 114

Two Last Things

A rty again. Mary had two more things to tell us.

Emma's Dwarf had left behind an envelope that had been found down on the beach, straight down from the Eastward Manor cliff edge. It was, of course, our list of guesses, our bet as to why this all was happening or, now, why it *had happened.*

Emma explained. "It wasn't Thryst I saw last night—it was her! She must have picked up the envelope I dropped. And she was also there on the Mountain and picked up the purple casket that I threw."

"Who is she?" Cry asked Mary.

Mary did not name names and admitted to us all, "What a dunce I have been!" But then she guessed what she said she should have figured out long ago. "That if *Thrystomos* means prince, it also means son of a king, so we should have known that *Thryst* in the Dwarf language means 'son.'"

Cry cried out loud with joy. "I won the bet!" he said.

CHAPTER 115

The End

The End.

W.W. Marplot

Acknowledgements

G.G.D. Marplot

As hinted in the dedication, my great-grandfather feels a kinship and indebtedness to those who tell their stories, the contributors to myths and legends and fairy tales of all types, all connected in time, the "long chain" as he calls it. I inherit the same debts. In the effort of publishing his manuscripts, I have also been humbled by the assistance and advice received and needed. A story isn't a story until someone receives its telling. Holding this book is possible only because of the creative efforts and expertise of many other contributors, and they have been appreciated personally and specifically over the years of work that are producing the Marplot books for presentation to the reading world.

To thank them by category:

> *The Editors*, for guiding my head as it delved the soul of the manuscripts.

> *The Producers*, for mastering the thousand steps that bring it from head to hand.

> *The Readers*, for offering their minds.

> *The Visionaries*, for alignment of spirit.

> *And Friends and Family*, for patience, support, encouragement, and love.

> *Lastly: To those learning to know me anew* through my process of personal change and growth over the long preparation of this *Dwarf Story*.

W.W. Marplot

Thanks and kudos to young Ms. Marplot, my twice-beloved amanuensis and great-granddaughter, and spiritual daughter of Scheherazade and Grimm, Aesop and Lady Gregory! How exciting to release more stories to the world, ones that I could never have achieved. That wonderful young girl and pen pal is now a woman, co-creator, and fellow contributor. New excitements are a rare thing in my world; I celebrate this in happiness.

Let FICTION come, upon her vagrant wings
Wafting ten thousand colours thro' the air,
And, by the glances of her magic eye,
Combining each in endless, fairy forms,
Her wild creation.

—Akenside,
The Pleasures of Imagination, 1744

Made in the USA
Middletown, DE
18 March 2022

62679809R00250